LOVING JOSH

The baby's rosebud lips had parted, and her tiny chest rose and fell with each sigh of breath. Across the room, Zak leaned his head on Josh's shoulder, and his eyes drifted closed. The tenderness in Josh's face as he glanced down at the little boy tugged at Rachel's heartstrings.

She wished she could freeze this moment in time to warm her during the long, lonely days and nights. Nights when she dreamed of Josh's arms around her and jolted awake in a chilly, empty bed. Days while she quilted and daydreamed of a different future. A future encapsulated by this moment.

Josh broke the spell by setting Zak on the bed. Rachel, eager not to let Josh see where her thoughts had floated, stopped rocking and started to rise, but she'd settled too deeply into the worn seat.

"Wait." Josh hurried across the room. "Let me help you." He reached down for the baby.

As he slipped his arms under Marianna, he brushed Rachel's arms, sending shockwaves through her. If her fantasy were true and they were married, she'd reach up, wrap her arms around his neck, and draw him toward her. Then their lips would touch.

Rachel lowered her lashes so he couldn't see the longing in her eyes and soul . . .

Books by Rachel J. Good

HIS UNEXPECTED AMISH TWINS

HIS PRETEND AMISH BRIDE

HIS ACCIDENTAL AMISH FAMILY

AN UNEXPECTED AMISH PROPOSAL

AN UNEXPECTED AMISH COURTSHIP

AN UNEXPECTED AMISH CHRISTMAS

AN AMISH MARRIAGE OF CONVENIENCE

HER PRETEND AMISH BOYFRIEND

DATING AN AMISH FLIRT

Published by Kensington Publishing Corp.

DATING
an
AMISH FLIRT

RACHEL J. GOOD

ZEBRA BOOKS
Kensington Publishing Corp.
www.kensingtonbooks.com

ZEBRA BOOKS are published by

Kensington Publishing Corp.
900 Third Avenue
New York, NY 10022

All Kensington titles, imprints, and distributed lines are available at special quantity discounts for bulk purchases for sales promotion, premiums, fund-raising, and educational or institutional use.

Special book excerpts or customized printings can also be created to fit specific needs. For details, write or phone the office of the Kensington Sales Manager: Kensington Publishing Corp., 900 Third Avenue, New York, NY 10022. Attn. Sales Department. Phone: 1-800-221-2647.

Zebra and the Z logo Reg. U.S. Pat. & TM Off.

First Printing: May 2024
ISBN-13: 978-1-4201-5646-1
ISBN-13: 978-1-4201-5647-8 (eBook)

10 9 8 7 6 5 4 3 2 1

Printed in the United States of America

PROLOGUE

Josh Yoder raced after his older brothers, but his nine-year-old legs couldn't keep up with their teenaged strides. By the time he reached the bushes they'd sprinted behind, they'd vanished.

He plopped onto a huge flat rock, propped his elbows on his knees, and screwed up his face to fight the tears threatening to fall. He was much too old to bawl like a baby.

A girl with hair the color of sunshine mixed with strawberries popped out from behind the bushes. His eyes blurry with moisture, he didn't recognize her at first.

"What's wrong?" she asked.

Her sweet voice, clear as a bell, clued Josh in to her identity. Rachel Glick. The new girl at school. She sounded as if she really cared, so he spilled out his frustration. "My brothers won't let me play with them. They always run away."

"That's mean." The feisty girl who sat two rows over from him in the *schulhaus* flounced over and sat on the rock beside him.

"*Jah*, they are." He scrubbed his eyes with his fists.

"You crying?" she asked in a gentle voice.

Josh turned his head away from her. "*Neh.*" He spat out the word in his gruffest voice, trying to sound indifferent. Maybe even strong and brave.

"*Jah*, you are." She set a gentle hand on his arm. "But it's all right. I won't tell anyone."

Then and there, she earned his undying gratitude.

"How come your brothers don't play with you?" She didn't seem critical, only curious.

Choking down the thickness in his throat, Josh shrugged before answering. "They say I'm too little. They're thirteen, fourteen, and fifteen."

Rachel's face creased into an adorable frown. "That's not nice. My brother's fourteen, and he'd play with us."

Us? She'd included Josh like they were already friends.

"Want to ask him?" She bounced up and beckoned for him to come. "I know where they are."

Chattering the whole way, she led him to the tire swing at the creek, where her brother greeted her with a huge smile.

"Want to take a turn, Rachel?" He turned to Josh. "And who's your friend there?"

Josh barely caught her introduction, because his three brothers stood in line, waiting for their turns. They all glared at him.

Their scowls grew even darker when Rachel's brother called out, "Hey, everyone, let's give these two a turn. We've all had several."

Josh gulped. Swing over the creek? With his brothers watching?

But Rachel took his hand and strode to the front of the line. She flashed her brother a smile. "*Danke*, Tom."

Gratitude glowed from her as she waved at the line of boys who'd stepped aside for her. "*Danke*, everyone."

"Want to go first?" she asked Josh.

He shook his head. Actually, he wasn't sure he wanted to go at all. "I—I'll go after you."

But as she clambered onto the tire swing, he regretted it. He should have taken the lead and done the scary thing first.

Rachel didn't seem frightened. Her face lit with excitement. When the nearest group of boys pulled the swing back and let go, she squealed.

Josh sucked in his breath as she flew up and out into the air. What if she fell? Did she know how to swim? Suppose she cracked her head on one of the rocks down there?

He grew lightheaded, but he didn't release his pent-up breath with a loud *whoosh* until she landed safely. Then his chest constricted. Now he'd have to do the same thing.

Rachel's triumphant grin sparked his bravery. If she'd done it, so could he. He clamped his teeth together to stop their jittering and strode toward the huge tractor tire.

He squeezed his eyes shut when the swing left the ground. His stomach plummeted along with his courage as he ricocheted into the sky. All he could do was hang on for dear life and pray.

Dizzy and winded, he thanked God over and over when the swing reached the bank and hands reached out to grab the tire and steady it so he could climb off.

His *danke* came out breathless. But he'd done it. And he'd proved to his brothers he wasn't a coward.

Rachel rushed over. "Wasn't that fun?"

Not really, but now that he stood on solid ground, safe and secure, he shared her enthusiasm. "*Jah!*"

"Want to go again?"

He shook his head. "Let's do something else."

"What do you want to do?"

Josh loved to catch tadpoles and salamanders. He even kept a tank in his bedroom to watch tadpoles turn into frogs before he released them. He shared that with her. "You probably wouldn't like that."

To his surprise, she clapped her hands. "I've never done it before. Can you teach me?"

And that became the start of Josh's closest friendship ever. He taught Rachel about his favorite things, and she taught him to be fearless and daring.

A year later, tragedy struck. Rachel's *daed* died. Some of her liveliness leaked out. She became more hesitant to try new things, and she wanted to stay close to home because her *mamm*'s health had declined until she needed a cane.

Tom went to work full time, so Josh and Rachel didn't hang around the older boys as often. But on days when Rachel needed to stay with her *mamm* and didn't want company, Josh spent time with Tom's friends. He tried to take care of Rachel to be sure she and her *mamm* had everything they needed.

But as Rachel stayed home more often, Josh invited other friends from school to keep him company when he hung around with the older boys. As Josh's popularity increased, Rachel's waned. She preferred to sit under a tree during recess rather than join in the baseball games. For the next two years, he still walked her home after school, but she kicked leaves or pebbles and didn't talk much. And she always thanked him for being her friend, even when she didn't feel like playing.

Josh didn't mind that she stayed silent. She'd been his friend when no one else had. And he'd be hers forever.

CHAPTER 1

Eight years later . . .

Josh sprinted through the Hartzlers' back door and down the basement, where the rest of the *youngie* had gathered for games and singing. He'd asked his girlfriend, Anna Mary, to go on ahead because he didn't want to make her late too. He hoped he wouldn't get a letter reprimanding him for being late, but his border terrier had gone into labor, and he'd stayed with her until she'd given birth to six puppies.

He slid into place across the table from Anna Mary and held up six fingers. She beamed.

Caroline Hartzler's forehead creased. Never one to stay quiet, she announced, "You're too late to play this round, Josh. We already divided into teams."

"He can be on my team," Anna Mary offered, "or take my turn."

"It's all right. I can wait." Josh settled back in his seat and checked out the others at the table. "It'll give me time to catch my breath."

All the usual *youngie* were there, including Rachel

Glick. His pulse stuttered a little, but he hurried past her. The sight of her was both pleasurable and painful. Her beauty would set any man's heart racing, but every time he was around her, it brought up old memories and a mountain of guilt.

Better to concentrate on Anna Mary. Besides, God wanted them to focus on the inner person, not the outward appearance. And Anna Mary provided an example to others by her faith.

Josh tamped down the comparisons bubbling up about Rachel. She wasn't as outspoken about her beliefs as many of the others, but she'd always had a deep, earnest desire to do God's will, even during the most trying times in her life.

He shook himself mentally. Why did his mind keep wandering to Rachel when he should be paying attention to Anna Mary?

The miracle of the puppies' births had made him sentimental. When they were younger, Rachel had adored baby animals. He'd never forget the wonder on her face when he showed her his first litter of puppies. She'd squealed with joy when he let her choose one to take home. Then she threw her arms around him and hugged him. He may have been only nine, but he'd fallen in love with her that day. Every time his dog whelped, he remembered their shared past.

A past that had ended abruptly. And he could never go back. If only he could erase those events, but he had no way of changing what had happened.

"Are you all right?" Anna Mary set a copy of the *Ausbund* in front of him.

Josh started. He'd been so lost in thought, he hadn't

realized the game had ended. He dragged himself from his regrets and reminded himself of the new puppies. That brightened his spirits, and he smiled up at her.

"Are the puppies doing well?" she asked.

"*Jah.*"

"I'm glad." She moved down the table, helping Caroline set out the rest of the hymnals.

Anna Mary caught his eyes several times during the songs. That and keeping his eyes glued to the words in front of him prevented him from being distracted by Rachel.

When they broke for refreshments, Anna Mary made a beeline for Josh. He never had to chase her. She always found him first. It should be flattering, but for some odd reason, it left him feeling flat. He would have enjoyed more of a challenge.

A challenge like the one Rachel Glick posed for most of the males there tonight, just as she did at every other singing. Like a flower attracting bees, Rachel only had to smile softly and hesitantly, and a crowd of boys buzzed around her, all vying for her attention. Yet, she never bestowed her favor on anyone in particular.

As he and Anna Mary took their plates and moved away from the dessert table, she leaned over and whispered, "Look at her flirting with all the guys."

Pretending Rachel hadn't caught his eye earlier, Josh followed the tilt of Anna Mary's head toward the pretty, petite strawberry blonde, so sweet and fragile, surrounded by a circle of admirers.

Although he struggled to break his gaze, he quickly turned to Anna Mary. "You'd never do that."

"Absolutely not. And the worst part is she doesn't want to date any of them."

Grateful he didn't have to worry about his girlfriend being the center of so much male attention, Josh nodded.

"I'm so glad you never chased her. You wouldn't, would you?" Jealousy tinged her question.

"Of course not." Josh could answer that honestly. He couldn't even meet Rachel's eyes. And no matter how alluring she appeared, his stomach churned whenever he got around her.

He didn't want to think about that. "We should get back to our seats. The singing will start soon."

His excuse to get away from Anna Mary didn't make sense. The group fluttering around Rachel hadn't eaten yet. But luckily, Anna Mary's best friend, Caroline Hartzler, grabbed Anna Mary's arm and dragged her back to their seats while chattering about something in an overly loud voice.

Caroline seemed to be talking to Anna Mary about working at the Green Valley Farmer's Market, but Josh tuned Caroline out and headed to his place on the opposite side of the table. Someone else had taken Josh's place. He hadn't intended to sit where he faced Rachel, but he'd accidentally picked the seat across from the last girl he wanted to look at, a girl he'd vowed never to have anything to do with, a girl who brought up all his old guilt. He'd abandoned her and her friendship years ago. Since then, he'd put her firmly out of his mind.

To make sure, Josh had chosen to date someone the exact opposite of his childhood companion and first love . . . if a nine-year-old could fall in love. He'd traded honeyed curls glinting with red highlights for straight black hair that never sprang loose from a bob. Sea-green eyes with long lashes had been replaced by no-nonsense brown ones. He erased memories of a delicate build and dainty hands with a sturdy frame capable of hard farm work. Josh preferred a wife who was practical rather than whimsical, one who had her feet firmly planted in reality, not one who drifted off into flights of fancy.

Why, then, did he sigh with relief whenever Rachel turned down an offer to ride home in someone else's buggy after a singing? And why did his nightly dreams haunt him with images of strolling through fields of wildflowers, hand in hand with a fragile beauty whose sun-kissed curls floated behind her on the breeze?

Wherever Josh went in the room, Rachel's senses followed him. He'd brushed by her when he'd hurried into the room tonight, and her pulse had flickered warning signals ever since.

Surrounded by a circle of eager male faces during the break, Rachel tried to respond to the conversation around her without bestowing too much attention on anyone. She'd turned down at least a dozen invitations to ride home after singings this past year, and she'd broken many hearts. Even staying aloof hadn't stopped the requests for her company.

But the more males who gathered around her, the more the other girls acted standoffish. They didn't seem to understand she had no interest in any of the boys except one. And he was already taken.

But she couldn't confide in anyone because the girls all kept their distance from her. It hurt not to have friends. But Rachel's greatest heartbreak—outside of her *daed*'s and brother's deaths—was the loss of Josh's friendship.

Her heart throbbed with a deep ache each time he

walked past without acknowledging her. What had she done to drive him away? She'd plunged into sorrow following her brother's death, but Josh had understood her silence when Daed died. He'd stayed close then and supported her. Even at Tom's funeral, Josh had offered only polite condolences and then ignored her.

After that, she had no free time for anyone. Mamm ended up bedridden, and Rachel needed to take care of her. Her friendships shrank to none as she couldn't attend any of the youth events, except singings. Women in the church took turns caring for Mamm so Rachel could attend church every other Sunday. Even so, Rachel remained isolated.

Well, as isolated as she could be while surrounded by a bevy of boys. Unfortunately, even that made her heart ache. Most of Tom's friends had married, and Rachel had never really gotten to know the boys her age. The breaks during singings only reminded her of how much she missed Josh.

After the singing ended, Martin Allgeyer hurried up to her. A few weeks ago, she'd turned down his offer to drive her home. Rachel hoped he didn't plan to ask again. She hated saying *neh* and seeing faces fall.

He surprised her. "You going to the volleyball game on Saturday?"

She swallowed hard. If only she could. When she was younger, she'd loved playing baseball and volleyball. Since Mamm had become bedridden, Rachel didn't want to impose on others, so she never asked anyone to watch her mother for the fun get-togethers. Women from the *g'may* already took turns staying with Mamm on church Sundays.

"Rachel?" Martin interrupted her musing. "You going to the game or not?"

"I can't, Martin, but thanks for asking."

Josh passed behind Martin as she answered, and a sharp pain shot through her as nostalgia washed over her. Her brother, Tom, often set up a volleyball net in the backyard, and she and Josh sometimes played with his friends or even practiced alone, just the two of them. More than anything, she wished she could go back to those days again.

The longing on Rachel's face when Martin said the word *volleyball* cut through Josh. And he recognized that faraway look in her eyes and the little smile that played on her lips. She always did that whenever she was recalling happy memories of her *daed* or brother.

Josh wished he could ask what she was thinking about. Was she remembering the fun they'd had playing volleyball with Tom?

Tom's name brought up the past Josh wanted to forget, but he yearned for the days before that. Back when he and Rachel did everything together. He slammed a door shut on those times and turned to find Anna Mary. He needed to focus on his future rather than the past.

But Josh's sense of fairness wouldn't let him forget Rachel's yearning. He hadn't realized she might want to come. She avoided socializing, except when she was forced into it. Like now, when she couldn't get away from those boys who circled her. But she always looked uncomfortable. Josh had assumed she stayed home from youth group activities because she'd rather not be there. Maybe that wasn't true. What if she didn't show up because she disliked asking for help with her *mamm*? That would be just like Rachel.

Now that he'd figured it out, he had to do something. Maybe Mamm would be willing to sit with Rachel's *mamm* during volleyball games. His mother had always loved Rachel, and Mamm had been sad when Rachel stopped coming to visit. She'd often said Rachel was the daughter their family never had. For sure and certain, she'd be happy to help.

The only problem for Josh would be seeing Rachel more than one day a week. And having to deal with his guilt.

CHAPTER 2

A knock on the door on Monday afternoon startled Rachel from her quilting. She'd hoped to finish this quillow and get started on the next one before the Green Valley Farmer's Market opened tomorrow. She'd already completed the quilt that folded into the pillow and only needed to quilt the small design on the square pillow top.

Reluctantly, she tucked her needle into the fabric so she wouldn't lose it and headed for the door.

"Miriam?" She opened the door and stepped back so Josh's *mamm* could enter. "How are you? Are you here to visit Mamm?" Her mother had just gone down for another nap, but Rachel could wake her for this unexpected visitor.

"Actually, dear, I've come to talk to you, but I'll look in on your *mamm* if she's awake."

Me? What would Miriam need to discuss with me? Rachel's heart clenched. *Had something happened to Josh?*

Rachel had been standing there with the door open, but she hadn't actually invited Miriam inside. "*Kumme* in. Mamm's asleep, but we can talk in the living room so we don't disturb her."

Miriam followed Rachel into the living room. Rachel

gathered up the quilt part of the quillow, which she'd left spread out on the couch.

"That's beautiful, dear." Miriam picked up the quilt end and admired it. "What I wouldn't give to be able to make such tiny, straight stitches. My *mamm* despaired of me ever making a quilt fit to use. She used to say I'd never make a proper wife."

"But you're such a good wife and a wonderful cook. And you raised four fine boys." Heat splashed onto Rachel's cheeks as one in particular came to mind. She hoped Miriam would think Rachel's flushed face came from the compliment on her sewing.

Josh's mother laughed. "If I stayed around you for long, I'd be asking God for forgiveness for pride." Her eyes twinkled. "It's a good thing my Ephraim didn't care about my quilting skills."

Miriam bustled over to a nearby chair. "Feel free to keep sewing. I know you need to get your quillows to the market tomorrow. It wonders me that you've been able to support your *mamm* since you turned fourteen."

Talk about *hochmut*. If Miriam stayed much longer, they'd both end up puffed with pride. Rachel giggled inside at the thought.

"It's so nice to see your smile." Miriam beamed. "I won't take much of your time. Although I do miss our long-ago chats. It was nice to have a girl around with a houseful of boys."

She gazed at Rachel with such fondness, Rachel's chest ached. She'd forgotten how much love a *mamm*'s smile could hold. It had been so long since her own *mamm* had been able to give anyone a genuine smile. Most days, all she could manage were clenched-teeth grimaces that matched her pain-filled eyes.

Miriam settled back in the chair. Rachel put down her sewing to concentrate on her guest, but Miriam waved to the quillow as if encouraging her to continue. Rachel picked up her needle and bent her head over her work. That was easier than meeting Miriam's searching gaze. Could Josh's *mamm* sense Rachel longed to ask about him?

Perhaps his mother had read Rachel's thoughts, because Miriam went straight to the topic of her son. "Josh talked to me about you yesterday."

Rachel's head shot up, and she pricked her finger with the needle. She quickly raised the finger to her lips to prevent a blood smear on the fabric.

"He wondered if you minded missing out on the youth activities. And I told him, 'Of course, she does.' I don't know why it never occurred to any of us to sit with your *mamm* so you could go."

A burning sensation began in Rachel's chest and spread through her. Josh cared enough to want to include her. It didn't change the fact that he was courting, but at least, he'd thought about her as a friend.

"Anyway, I came to apologize for not doing this sooner. I'll be over this Saturday so you can play in the volleyball game. And from now on, I'll come whenever the *youngie* have events."

"You don't have to do that." Rachel couldn't expect Miriam to care for Mamm every time. "I-I, um, often have to work anyway."

"Well, we can figure that out. But I'll be here an hour or so before the game on Saturday, so you have time to talk with your friends before you start playing." Miriam stood. "You don't have to see me out. I'll peek in on your *mamm* before I go."

"But—but . . ."

Miriam held up a hand. "I won't take *neh* for an answer. It's time you had a chance to join your friends and have fun. You work much too hard. Besides, I miss talking to Betty. It'll be a joy to spend time with her."

Before Rachel could protest any further, Miriam walked down the hallway to Mamm's room, eased the door open, and peeked inside. Seeing Mamm was still asleep, Miriam shut the door quietly and left.

As much as she disliked letting others carry her burdens, Rachel was thrilled to be able to play volleyball. But she hadn't played in years. Would she be any help to the team?

She pushed that worry aside and concentrated on the most important part of Miriam's conversation. All this had been Josh's idea. Did he still care for her—as a friend, of course?

"I'm ready to go, Josh," his *mamm* called upstairs almost two hours before the Saturday volleyball game began.

"Why do you want to leave so early?" he projected his voice so she could hear him.

"Rachel might like to spend time talking to her friends before the game."

Josh shook his head as he descended the stairs. That might be true if she had any friends. The thought made him sad. He'd been a terrible friend.

But if Rachel left this soon, she'd arrive at a deserted field. That wouldn't make her feel accepted or a part of things. Although, if the boys knew she'd be there, they'd show up early too.

"Nobody will be at the field." Did Mamm tell Rachel

the wrong time? "Does she know what time the game starts?"

"*Jah*, she does. I promised to be there an hour or so ahead of time. I don't want her to worry I won't show up. Rachel's eyes lit up when I mentioned volleyball, so I expect she'll be eager to go."

A warm glow filled Josh. He was so glad he'd suggested Mamm should stay with Betty. Rachel deserved to have fun. It couldn't be easy to take care of her *mamm* all day, every day.

He often wondered if the barn fire had caused Betty Glick's rapid decline in her health. Before Tom's funeral, she'd been getting around with a cane. Within a few weeks, she'd gone downhill fast. Soon, she couldn't get out of bed.

When Mamm yelled for him again, Josh bounded down the stairs. He entered the kitchen, where she was pulling food from the refrigerator. After he'd hitched up the horse, Mamm came out with a casserole dish she held on her lap and asked him to load the tote bag filled with several other casseroles and a pie.

They rode in silence until Mamm said, "You know, Josh, since we'll already be at the Glicks', you could offer to take Rachel to the game."

"Mamm!" That wouldn't be appropriate. "I'm courting Anna Mary." He had no doubt Anna Mary wouldn't appreciate him doing that, even if he only did it to be neighborly.

"But Anna Mary's at work, and she'll be coming with Caroline."

How did Mamm know that? She wasn't usually into all the gossiping the community did.

Mamm continued, "You'll be coming back after the game to pick me up. Why not drop Rachel off at the same time?"

"It wouldn't be right. Besides, Anna Mary will be riding home with me."

"I see." His *mamm* made a slight face. If Josh hadn't glanced at her right at that moment, he never would have noticed. What was that about? Did she not like Anna Mary? Mamm hadn't said anything negative about his girlfriend. But now that he thought about it, his mother had never said anything positive either.

It also was odd Mamm had asked him to drop her off instead of taking her own buggy. Had she been planning to throw him and Rachel together? And send them to the field more than an hour early? Not only that, but was Mamm trying to cut his evening short with Anna Mary by having Rachel come along? Even if Rachel drove herself, Mamm would know when the games had ended, so she'd expect Josh to pick her up shortly after. That would prevent him and Anna Mary from taking the long way home.

From Mamm's sigh, she'd been hoping he'd take Rachel. Mamm had never understood why he and Rachel had stopped spending time together. But to interfere with his life like this was so out of character for her. And he'd never known his mother to be underhanded or manipulative.

Her mouth pinched in disappointment. "I just thought Rachel could use some company when she gets to the field for the first time."

His heart went out to Rachel. He disliked the way the other girls left her out. To lessen his guilt, he reminded himself Rachel was rarely alone. "I'm sure she'll be fine. She's usually in the center of a crowd."

"Josh!"

His *mamm*'s sharp rebuke startled him. She was so even-tempered, she rarely got upset.

"You know as well as I do, Rachel doesn't like being surrounded by all those boys. I thought maybe"—her voice quavered—"you could protect her from them. You used to take care of her when you were younger."

Why did Mamm have to remind him of that? Josh pushed those old memories to the back of his mind, but he couldn't erase present-day ones. He knew Rachel better than anyone in their *g'may*, except for her mother, so he could tell it distressed Rachel to be the center of the boys' attention. He often berated himself for ignoring her trapped expression.

"That's the main reason I hoped you'd take her there early."

"I see." Although he didn't understand what he could do to stop her admirers. If he were her boyfriend, they'd stop flocking around her like vultures.

Josh brought himself up short. What in the world put that idea in his head? He already had a girlfriend. Everyone at church knew that, so he'd be no deterrent to the other boys. Still, something inside him yearned to find a way to help her.

All week, Rachel's excitement had warred with her dread. At church, they filed in to the benches in order, so girls her age sat on either side of her. And if the girls ignored her or gossiped about her after the service, Rachel busied herself in the kitchen to hide her loneliness.

Singings forced her to be the center of unwanted attention. Technically, she was never alone there, although she felt like it. Meanwhile, the girls steered clear of her and whispered about her behind her back.

But at a volleyball game, she'd be on her own. She had no friends, nobody she could depend on, nobody to talk to, except her band of admirers. Would any of them be there? Or would she stand out, look like a loner? A loser?

Rachel had almost decided not to go when Josh drove into her driveway. *Josh? What was he doing here?*

A casserole in hand, Miriam hopped from the buggy and hurried up the driveway. Josh had only come to drop his *mamm* off. Rachel's spirits plummeted.

When Miriam neared the front door, she turned and called to Josh, "Could you bring the tote bag from the back seat?"

Josh was too far away for Rachel to read his expression. Did he frown? Make a face? Resent having to come into her house?

He got out, reached for something in the back, and strode toward his *mamm* with a bag in his hand. Miriam waited until he caught up with her. Then they headed to the front door, and Josh knocked.

Although Rachel had moved away from the window as they approached the front door, his knock was unmistakable—firm, determined, masculine. His *mamm*'s the other day had been more of a tap. If a knock could stir Rachel this much, what would happen when they stood face to face?

All she wanted to do was run and hide. Good manners forced her to open the door and invite them in. She barely managed a welcoming smile by keeping her eyes focused on Miriam. "Let me take that casserole."

As Rachel reached for the dish, she sneaked a quick glance at Josh. His smile appeared pasted on, and his eyes revealed reluctance. To carry in the bag? Or to be around her?

Miriam refused to let go of the casserole. "I'll just take this out to the kitchen." She sailed off, leaving Rachel and Josh in the doorway together.

Josh shuffled his feet, revealing his nervousness. "I, um, I should probably take this out too . . . if that's all right?"

Rachel's cheeks burned at her choked "of course." She prayed he wouldn't guess her clogged throat was connected to him.

He brushed past her, setting her aflame. She stood paralyzed at the door, unsure whether to close it or to leave it open to allow Josh to make a quick escape.

Before she could decide, he returned from the kitchen. "I'll see you later." He rushed out the door, then stopped on the doorstep. Without turning around, he added, "I'm glad you're coming. You always were a good player."

Rachel wondered if he was happy she'd be there because he needed someone who played well. He might be sorry if he'd been hoping for an outstanding player. She hadn't touched a volleyball for the past five years, so her skills were rusty.

"I might not be very good. I haven't played in a long time."

Still keeping his back to her, he said, "I'm sure you'll pick it up quickly." He rubbed the back of his neck. "I, um, should get going."

Rachel's heart sank. Her hope that they'd have a friendly conversation vanished. She shouldn't have made so much out of a few sentences of polite chit-chat. Josh had probably dropped his *mamm* off early to give him extra time with Anna Mary.

Miriam popped up behind Rachel. "You know, I suggested to Josh that you could ride with him, since he has to head back here to pick me up."

Rachel gasped. "*Ach*, I couldn't do that. Isn't Anna Mary with him? I'm sure she wouldn't want company." Especially not me. Anna Mary was one of the more judgmental girls in their buddy bunch. At least toward Rachel. She didn't seem that way with others.

"Anna Mary's coming from the market with Caroline," Miriam assured her.

Miriam wanted Rachel to travel alone with Josh? Her heart pounded . . . with anxiety. And, if she were honest, anticipation. But she couldn't ride with someone else's boyfriend.

"*Neh*, Miriam. *Danke* for your thoughtful suggestion, but I'll go on my own."

Josh expelled a long breath. "I'll see you both later." He sprinted to the buggy.

"I can always count on you to do the honorable thing." Miriam reached out and pulled Rachel into a quick hug. But Josh's *mamm* sounded sad.

Part of Rachel—the part that dreamed of going back to her childhood relationship with Josh—echoed Miriam's disappointment. But the sensible part of her breathed a sigh of relief. What would she and Josh have talked about? They'd either sit in silence or have an awkward conversation.

"Well," Miriam said, "why don't you head to the field? I have everything ready here." She started down the hall to Mamm's room, but not before Rachel glimpsed a hopeful smile.

Does Miriam want me to get there early so Josh and I can spend time together? It certainly seemed that way. Rachel had never known any parents who interfered in their children's choices of dates. And Rachel hadn't expected Miriam, who seemed like such a relaxed, caring, and encouraging *mamm*, to push Josh into a different relationship when he already had a girlfriend. It seemed so out of character.

What objections did Miriam have to the girl Josh was courting? Anna Mary had a reputation as an upright, godly young woman, who was known for her honesty, deep faith, and good deeds. The whole situation didn't make sense—unless Rachel had misread Miriam's intentions. *Maybe it's only wishful thinking on my part.*

But if Rachel wanted to make the game on time, she needed to leave now. Miriam coming so early had been a blessing. It gave Rachel enough time to walk the six miles to the field. Her buggy had a flat tire. The metal rim had partially detached two weeks ago, and she'd repaired it with duct tape. That had gotten her home from the store, but the fix hadn't lasted long. Since then, she'd been walking everywhere—to church, the market, and the grocery store. She had no money for repairs.

If she had friends, she could have hitched a ride with someone. But she didn't. And she didn't want to lead any boys on by requesting a ride. She preferred getting there on her own rather than depending on someone else's kindness.

To be sure she arrived on time, Rachel alternated between walking and jogging. The sun beat down on her head, and after several miles of worrying about arriving red-faced and sweaty, other doubts kicked in. She fretted about sitting on the sidelines with nobody to talk to. Nor did she relish the idea of being the center of the boys' attention. She debated skipping the game. But if she didn't show up, Josh would mention it to his *mamm*.

Rachel sighed and plodded on. When she neared the field, she cut into the trees. The canopy of leaves overhead shaded her and cooled her heated cheeks. Moving down the hill toward the field, she concealed herself behind a huge oak and observed everyone without being seen.

She waited until they'd started the game to slip out and sit on the bench with the replacement players. Most of the boys who normally bothered her faced the net, their backs to her. With everyone concentrating on the ball, nobody except the person she sat beside noticed her. Not even Josh had seen her arrive.

Rachel relaxed into the invisibility . . . until an opposing player glanced her way and did a double take. He raised his eyebrows and gave her a cheeky smile. A smile that warned her he'd make a beeline for her after the game.

CHAPTER 3

Whew! Josh wiped his forehead with the back of his arm as he moved back to server and waited for subs to replace the other positions. He and Caroline Hartzler were the only two who stayed in for the whole game. They couldn't afford to lose Caroline, their top player. The game had been fast and furious so far, and their team always fought hard when they went up against these opponents.

Anna Mary drooped as she headed toward the bench. She never lasted long. Josh hoped someone with stronger skills would take her place. It might give the team an edge. He turned to study the subs and spotted Rachel, hunched into herself as if hoping nobody would notice her.

"Rachel," he called, "you can take Martin's place."

His spirits lifted at the joy on her face. But when most heads swiveled in her direction and several boys' eyes lit up, she cringed and shrank back. Two of the *youngie* who'd been planning to take a break, including Martin, elbowed each other to snag a place beside Rachel. Josh regretted that he'd made her the focus of everyone's attention.

Anna Mary scowled. Her eyes narrowed and her lips thinned as Rachel took her place in the right front.

Uh-oh, he'd made a huge mistake.

He'd put her opposite Abe, the second-best player on the other team. Caroline stood across from Tim, their outstanding spiker. And Josh wanted Rachel in front of him so he could assist if she was out of practice. But he hadn't considered the rotation. Rachel would end up beside him on their next serve.

But he didn't have long to think about Anna Mary's hurt feelings. The other team yelled for him to hurry up and serve. Josh flexed his arm muscles and readied the ball, but across the net, that Tim, who always taunted Caroline, smiled at Rachel. A slimy smile that turned Josh's stomach. How dare that creep stare at her like that?

"Come on," someone yelled. "You too scared to serve?"

Josh jerked his gaze from Rachel and did his pre-serve warmup. Anger at Tim fueled Josh's muscles, and he slammed a powerful serve toward their worst player, whose weak hit barely lifted the ball's downward flight.

Another teammate got under it, but only managed an easy lob over the net straight to Rachel. She jumped to meet it and smashed it down on the other side of the net. Right beside a startled Tim, who'd been busy gazing at her.

"Tim," Abe shouted as he dove for the ball. He managed to hit it, but his high arcing return headed straight to Caroline. She spiked it for the point.

Tim growled as Josh congratulated Caroline and then Rachel, who glowed. Although she'd been worried earlier about her skills, she'd demonstrated she still had them. He hoped she'd keep coming to their games. She'd be a great addition to the team.

He mentally celebrated until Anna Mary shifted on the bench, and Josh read the hurt on her face as everyone cheered. As Caroline tossed him the ball for his next serve, Josh decided he'd better invite Anna Mary back into the game as soon as they subbed again. But judging by Anna Mary's annoyed expression when Rachel became the next server, Josh would pay for that thoughtless mistake.

When they subbed out, Anna Mary liked to play beside Caroline, who covered for Anna Mary's misses or fluffs. The two of them actually made a good team. Once Anna Mary had her back to him, Josh gave Rachel an encouraging smile and a whispered "good job" before she headed to the bench.

She soaked up the praise like a wilting plant drinking in water. She must be so starved for genuine appreciation. Maybe all the attention from her adoring would-be suitors didn't mean much to her.

Tim stared after Rachel with longing. For the first time ever, Josh thanked God Tim never left the game to sit on the bench. His team couldn't win without him.

The game stayed competitive, and each team racked up points. Usually, every time his team got one point ahead, Tim's side eked out another point to tie the score. But now they'd managed to move ahead by one.

Someone on Tim's side yelled, "Game point."

As usual, Caroline rallied their team. "Don't let them get this point. We can take them."

The other team served, but when the ball flew over the net, Anna Mary batted at it but missed. Josh rushed up behind her to pop it into the air. As the ball floated down, Caroline slammed it to the ground right behind Tim.

He whirled around but not fast enough to intercept it. The ball bounced at his feet. With a disgusted groan, he kicked the ball up into his hands and pitched it over his head to the other side of the net without turning around.

Caroline caught it and grinned at Tim when he turned around. Josh wished she wouldn't provoke Tim, whose blazing eyes and ferocious scowl warned of his rising fury.

After that, the ball whizzed back and forth over the net several times. Abe jumped up and spiked. Caroline dove for the shot. She tipped the ball into the air a few inches. Josh dove forward and managed to lob a high-arcing shot over the net.

But the save threw Caroline off-balance. She splatted facedown into a muddy spot. Josh tried to stop his forward movement after the saving the ball. But he'd leaned too far forward. He tripped over her and landed on the ground too.

Anna Mary screamed and ran to them.

Tim was laughing so hard, he muffed the easy return. Abe scrambled to hit it, but the ball caught the top of the net and dropped at his feet.

"Abe!" Sharp anger edged Tim's voice.

The tall boy shrugged. "Don't blame me. You messed up first."

Gritting his teeth, Tim kicked the ball under the net right where Caroline was struggling to her feet. The volleyball splashed into the small puddle, splattering more mud over her face and arms.

Ooo, that Tim! Josh clenched his teeth. That was such a lowdown way to treat anyone, especially a girl. *Jah*, they sometimes made vicious shots to win, but nobody deliberately slammed a ball into an opponent.

As Caroline scrambled to get up, Anna Mary rushed over to help her and Josh. But he didn't need assistance. He pushed himself to his feet and whirled to face Tim.

Struggling to rein in his temper, Josh glared at Tim. "I can't believe you did that."

"Did . . . what?" Tim's words shot out between snorts of laughter. "You two . . . did it . . . to yourselves."

"You didn't have to kick the ball at Caroline. That was just mean."

"It was . . . an accident." Tim snickered.

Nearby, with no concern for her own clothing, Anna Mary helped a dripping Caroline out of the mud puddle. To Josh's surprise, once Caroline had steadied herself, Anna Mary grabbed her friend's elbow, dragged her out of earshot of the other players, and barraged her with questions.

Tim stopped his mocking laughter long enough to call something insulting to Caroline.

"Leave her alone." Josh used a threatening tone he hoped would deter Tim.

Tim only laughed. "What are you going to do about it? And what does your girlfriend think about you defending another girl?"

"She's glad I'm standing up for someone who's been mistreated." Shaking his head, Josh stalked off.

While Rachel had been absorbed in playing volleyball, she'd become part of the team. They'd helped and supported each other for a common goal. Now that the game had ended, she'd returned to her loneliness and isolation. She drew back into her shell, and her self-protective instinct went on high alert.

She didn't want anyone to realize she'd walked. Her teammates might feel obliged to offer her a ride. And she didn't trust that Tim, who'd been making eyes at her during the whole game. She still couldn't believe what he'd done to Caroline. Splashing mud all over her at the end of the game had been nasty.

Caroline did get loud and boisterous. Sometimes she even bragged about her shots. But she didn't deserve being treated like that.

Behind her, Josh was confronting Tim. To her right, Anna Mary was scolding Caroline. That seemed a bit harsh after what Caroline had just been through. Rachel wanted to step into the girls' argument the way Josh had done with Tim, but she'd never be that brave.

Instead, she scurried over to a line a few of her teammates had formed. As much as she disliked slapping hands with strangers after a game, she'd never be rude. The others were waiting for everyone to join the line. But if Rachel went through now, before Tim joined the line, she wouldn't have to touch his hands. Eyes downcast, she started through the line, startling the other players.

At the end, one boy from that team stopped her. Nausea filled her. Why did she have to endure this?

"Good game."

At his friendly voice and genuine words, she lifted her head. "*Danke.*"

She gave the tall boy called Abe a tentative smile. His eyes shone with admiration, but not the lovesick kind. Just honest appreciation for her volleyball skills.

"You had some great serves," she told him. After all, he'd made many of their team's points.

His heartfelt *danke* and kind smile relaxed Rachel. Why couldn't all boys be like this? Or even better, like Josh? But nobody would ever match Josh.

Abe complimented her on two great shots, leaving her with a warm glow. For the first time in a long time, she didn't feel left out.

Martin headed her way. Rachel murmured a quick goodbye to Abe, pretended she didn't see Martin, and rushed toward the blue portable toilets at the top of the hill. When Martin's shoulders drooped, guilt filled her. She didn't like hurting people's feelings, but why couldn't he and the others take a hint?

Instead of entering a toilet, Rachel veered behind one, checked to be sure nobody was watching, and entered the trees. She wanted to start home now to escape the crowds, but she'd have to wait. She didn't want anyone to offer her a ride home.

If only the parking lot would clear soon. Today, though, Caroline and Anna Mary were arguing while Josh and Tim were still having words.

Rachel sighed and picked her way downhill through the trees, moving slowly and hiding behind the large oaks, praying no one noticed her. When she reached the trees close to the field, she couldn't resist peeking out at Josh.

He strode across the grass in her direction.

She ducked back behind the trunk, hoping he hadn't seen her.

Steaming after his confrontation with Tim, Josh stomped toward his team's line to congratulate the other team. It bothered him whenever someone bullied others. His three older brothers had picked on him for years until he'd made friends with Rachel. Her brother, Tom, had been an example to Josh, showing him how to treat others with kindness, especially those who were younger, smaller, or weaker.

He'd love to vent some of his frustration, and Anna

Mary usually listened. Right now, though, she was so busy scolding Caroline, she ignored him.

He sighed. He didn't mind his girlfriend helping Caroline. She needed it, particularly after Tim's nastiness. But sometimes it seemed to Josh that Anna Mary would rather spend time with her best friend than with him. Both girls might be a while, so he got on line and slapped hands with everyone on the other team and congratulated his teammates for a great game.

Anna Mary and Caroline hadn't even started through the line yet. And Caroline usually took forever talking with everyone, so Josh chatted with several friends. Most people were eager to get home or had to go work, so everyone cleared out pretty quickly.

Caroline and Anna Mary still seemed to be arguing. Josh didn't want to interrupt, so he started for the parking lot. He could wait for her in the buggy.

A flash of blue in the nearby woods caught his eye. Someone had darted behind a tree when he'd glanced that way. The hem of her dress stuck out from behind the trunk. Why would anyone be hiding? Had someone been bothering her? Maybe that annoying Tim?

If so, Josh would protect her. He headed over, stepping carefully to avoid cracking twigs or crunching dried leaves. He didn't want to frighten her more.

Before he rounded the tree, he asked softly, "Are you all right?"

The girl squeaked in alarm.

Josh peeked around the trunk. Rachel.

Her green eyes wide, she froze like a startled deer.

His heart constricted. He hadn't meant to scare her. "I won't hurt you." But that wasn't true. Years ago, he'd done something unforgivable and hurt her deeply.

* * *

Rachel couldn't meet his eyes. Josh would never hurt her physically. But as for not hurting her, he was wrong. Very wrong. He'd hurt her more than he'd ever know.

When he'd stopped speaking to her in eighth grade, she never understood why. Until then, they'd been best friends. More than best friends. Even though she'd only been thirteen, Rachel had expected to marry him someday.

But after her brother died and she needed Josh the most, he suddenly avoided her. The friend, who'd been there every step of the way after Daed's death, had disappeared. She'd dealt with her grief alone. Mamm had spiraled downhill both emotionally and physically, so Rachel had to be strong for her mother. That left Rachel with no one to lean on, no one to confide in, no one to listen, no one to assuage her sorrow.

Tom's friends—all except Josh—stopped by to make sure she and Mamm were all right. They helped with Tom's chores, and their mothers brought food. The church ladies came to keep Mamm company, but Rachel hadn't made friends with the girls at school. She'd spent all her time with the boys, especially her brother and Josh.

Now, she had neither one of them.

As he used to do, Josh stood still, waiting for her to process her thoughts and to speak. His accepting silence had always encouraged her to spill her problems, her worries, her heartaches. But she could never share her present heartache.

She cast about for something to say. "That was nice of you to defend Caroline." Rachel's throat tightened, and her eyes stung. Once Josh had done that for her.

Except in her case, she'd mostly been teased by girls who were jealous of her friendships with all the boys.

Things hadn't gotten much better as they got older. At singings, boys clustered around her, and the girls glared at her from a distance.

Josh's fists clenched. "I couldn't believe anyone could be that cruel. To deliberately kick a ball at someone? Especially a girl who's on the ground trying to get up? Who does that?"

"It was awful. Poor Caroline. And I'm sorry you ended up falling too." She laid a hand on his arm. Sparks shot through her. She shouldn't have done that, but for some reason, she couldn't bring herself to lift her fingers. And Josh didn't shake her off.

"You played a great game," she said to ease the tension building between them. "We wouldn't have won without your spikes."

"*Danke*." He chuckled. "And you were worried about your skills being rusty? I'm sure most people would like to play that well for their first try in years."

"You think so?" Rachel struggled to suppress a smile of pride, but she didn't quite succeed. The compliment filled her with such buoyancy, her spirit floated upward like a balloon.

A sudden pinprick deflated her and brought her crashing back to reality. For a few minutes, she'd forgotten Josh had a girlfriend. A girlfriend who was stalking straight toward them.

CHAPTER 4

As Anna Mary headed toward him, irritation evident in her stride, Josh shot her a smile tinged with guilt. Although he and Rachel had only been talking, he could picture this scene through Anna Mary's eyes. Him hiding with Rachel in the trees. Her hand on his arm.

He should have moved away, but that light, delicate touch had stirred memories of the past. He'd drifted back to their childhood friendship, their closeness. Although their meeting had started out innocent, Josh couldn't believe he'd forgotten all about Anna Mary while he'd talked to Rachel.

Caroline, her face and apron caked with mud, followed Anna Mary. Shock and judgment radiated from both of them.

Rachel shifted uneasily. Usually, she waited for others to speak first, but she tried to do damage control. "I was just telling Josh what a great job he did in the game. Those two spikes were awesome. If it weren't for him, we'd never have won."

Anna Mary, her lips pinched into a thin line, studied Rachel for a moment. "What about Caroline? She set up both of those shots for him. Maybe you can thank her."

Anna Mary's words held a sarcastic bite. She waved a hand in Caroline's direction.

Josh blinked. Never had he seen Anna Mary act so cruel.

"And if you don't mind"—Anna Mary elbowed her way closer to him—"I'd like some time with Josh. Alone."

Her sharp tone didn't faze Rachel. "Of course. I'm sure you couldn't wait to rush over here to let him know what a great player he is." With a sweet smile, she waved and slipped away into the trees.

Caroline, evidently sensing a coming explosion, backed in the opposite direction and headed for the parking lot.

"What did she really want?" Anna Mary demanded.

Josh shrugged. "To tell me *good game*." Not wanting Rachel to endure more of Anna Mary's anger, he steered his girlfriend out of the woods.

Away from the scene of the crime? his conscience taunted.

He should be honest and confess he'd been the one who'd approached Rachel, rather than the other way around. But with how upset Anna Mary appeared, it wouldn't be wise to stoke the flames.

His heart hurt for Rachel as she melted into the trees. He longed to apologize, to defend her from Anna Mary's barbs. But first, he had to calm his girlfriend. Once he did, he'd confront Anna Mary about her attacks on Rachel.

Anna Mary's eyes narrowed. "Why didn't she tell you *good job* on the volleyball court?"

"I don't know. Maybe because I was arguing with Tim and you were arguing with Caroline."

"I was not."

Josh had to calm her down. "Sorry. It sounded like you weren't happy with Caroline. Maybe I misheard. You know what they say about eavesdroppers." He smiled, trying to offer a peaceful solution to their conflict.

"Are you accusing me of eavesdropping?" With an indignant lift of her chin, Anna Mary scowled at him.

"Of course not."

How had she gotten that from what he said? *Ach*, did she think he was accusing her of listening in on him and Rachel? Instead of soothing Anna Mary, he'd only made things worse.

He fumbled for a reply. "I meant me. About hearing you and Caroline, um, talking." *Talking* wasn't the right word to describe Anna Mary's exchange with her best friend, but he hoped it might lower the temperature of his girlfriend's emotions.

Anna Mary's eyes flooded with tears. "I can't believe you're accusing me of fighting with Caroline. You're trying to distract me. And trying to change the subject from you and Rachel."

Josh steadied his voice and said each word clearly and distinctly: "You don't have to worry. There's nothing between me and Rachel." As soon as that sentence left his lips, a deep well of pain overflowed inside him. Speaking with Rachel earlier had reestablished the closeness of their childhood bond, but they could never go back to what they'd once had.

The suspicious look in Anna Mary's eyes made it clear she didn't believe him. "I thought I could trust you. You told me last Sunday you'd never be one of those admirers flitting around Rachel. But the minute I'm not with you, what did you do?"

Barely pausing for breath, Anna Mary continued her tirade. "You're worse than the others. At least, they don't pretend not to be interested and then sneak off when nobody's looking."

Josh tried to protest, but she cut him off.

"You'd rather be with Rachel than me." With a loud cry, Anna Mary whirled around and dashed away.

Instead of following her, Josh stalked off for the second time that day. He headed into the woods, but in the opposite direction from Rachel. He needed time alone to get his emotions under control. And he had to get right with God.

Anna Mary had hurt his pride by insisting she couldn't trust him, but was that the real reason he'd walked away instead of going after her? If he were honest, he had to admit her accusation had hit too close to the truth.

Rachel's eyes burned. Being so close to Josh had stirred her childhood dreams. And when he'd dropped his guard, she'd been thrilled. If she hadn't woven fantasies during those few minutes, she wouldn't be aching inside now.

She'd forgotten all about his girlfriend. But Rachel's daydreams had shattered the second Anna Mary appeared. Now, Rachel ached with regret. Some for herself, but more for Josh. She hadn't meant to cause trouble in his relationship.

But he'd come seeking her. That had set her pulse pattering. She shouldn't have read anything into it. Josh would have come after anyone who looked lonely and left out. He resembled her brother that way. They both cared about people who were hurting.

Look at the way Josh had jumped to Caroline's defense. He'd done the same with Rachel—tried to help her. His first question had been *Are you all right?* He hadn't known

who was hidden behind the tree. He'd come to rescue a
person in trouble.

That hadn't struck her when she'd gazed into his caring
eyes. She'd misinterpreted his concern. And she'd responded inappropriately. Setting a hand on his arm . . .
Rachel shivered at the memory of his warm skin under
her hand. She struggled to gain control of her runaway
emotions.

Viewing the scene through Anna Mary's eyes shamed
Rachel. Hidden among the trees, she'd been staring up at
Josh and touching him, starry-eyed. How incriminating
that must have appeared to his girlfriend!

Rachel's face flamed. People called her a flirt behind
her back. She'd caught the whispers. A few even said it
loudly enough so Rachel could hear. If the girls in her
buddy bunch had disliked her before, how would they
react when Anna Mary told them this story?

When Rachel reached the top of the hill behind the
portable toilets, she checked the parking lot below. Only
two buggies remained. Josh's and Tim's. She'd seen Tim
drive in before the game. He hadn't come from the direction of her house. And when Josh took Anna Mary home,
they'd take the long way. Rachel decided it would be safe
for her to walk home now.

Still, she stayed in the woods for the first half mile.
Then the trees thinned out and fields spread before her.
Rachel picked up her pace. She needed to make it home
before Josh, so his *mamm* wouldn't guess Rachel hadn't
driven to the game.

She'd gone another mile when hooves clip-clopped
behind her. *Ach!* Josh's buggy. Rachel searched for a place
to conceal herself. But only knee-high plants lined the
cornfields this time of year. Perhaps he'd drive by without

recognizing her. Or maybe he'd be wary of offering her a ride after Anna Mary's fury. Besides, Anna Mary probably wouldn't be in a charitable enough mood to share Josh's buggy with someone who'd been making eyes at her boyfriend. Not that Rachel would have accepted a ride from them anyway.

After a bit of grumbling about Anna Mary's attitude toward Rachel and all the misunderstandings afterward, Josh had buckled down to deal with the truth. The Bible warned about beholding the mote in someone else's eye rather than considering the beam in your own. Isn't that what he'd been doing?

Anna Mary had accused him of distracting her. And here he stood, using her actions as an excuse to avoid facing his own failings. He hadn't behaved honorably with Anna Mary or Rachel.

I'm sorry, Lord. Please forgive me. And keep me from temptation. Help me to focus all my attention on my future wife.

Calm descended on his spirit along with the pressing need to make things right with Anna Mary. Josh exited the woods to search for her and apologize. He also needed to ask Rachel for forgiveness, but it might be better not to get tangled up in that for a while. At least not until he'd made things right with Anna Mary.

Nearby, Tim and Abe batted the ball back and forth over the net. Tim seemed to be practicing his spike.

He grinned as Josh emerged from the trees. "Having girl trouble?"

Josh's hackles went up at the snarky tone, but he let

God's peace flow over him. "I'm looking for Anna Mary. Have you seen her?"

"Is she the brunette? Or"—Tim waggled his eyebrows— "that delicious strawberry blonde? I don't blame you for cheating with her. I'd do the same if I had to choose between the two."

"You don't have a girlfriend to cheat on," Abe pointed out.

Redness crept into Tim's cheeks. Then he tossed his head back. "Which leaves me free to go after blondie."

The idea of Tim dating Rachel sickened Josh. Only the knowledge that she had better taste lowered his blood pressure.

"Anna Mary's a brunette." He kept his tone even.

Abe spoke up. "I saw her over in the parking lot not too long ago."

Josh followed Abe's hand wave in that direction. No Anna Mary.

Tim sneered. "She probably went home with someone else. That's what most girls do when they catch their boyfriends cheating on them."

Abe pinned Tim with a piercing gaze that made him squirm. Had Tim lost a girlfriend—or multiple girlfriends— because of that?

The urge to feel superior leaked out of Josh. He had no right to judge Tim. Josh had been caught in that situation himself. Sometimes an innocent meeting could be totally misconstrued.

Josh nodded to Abe. "*Danke.* I'll try the parking lot." He needed to find Anna Mary and get things sorted out. Maybe she was sitting in the buggy, waiting for him.

But when he got close enough to see inside, an empty

passenger seat greeted him. His heart sank. She must have been so angry with him she'd asked Caroline to drive her home.

He circled the lot and the edge of the woods. No sign of Anna Mary. Dejected, he climbed into the buggy and headed for Rachel's house.

After he'd gone about a mile, he spied an Amish girl in a green dress walking alongside the road. Even from this distance, Josh recognized Rachel. She still had the same bouncy gait she'd had when they were young. Back then, it fit so well with her lively personality. Even now that she'd lost that bubbliness, she'd kept her gait. He couldn't help wondering if her high spirits could be recovered. He slammed the door shut on his desire to be the one who helped her. Unless he could do it from a distance.

He clicked to encourage his horse to trot faster and pulled up beside her. She didn't even glance his way. She just kept going.

Rejected by Anna Mary. Ignored by Rachel. He deserved it. But he couldn't let her walk all that way.

"Rachel, I can take you home," he called out the open window. "I'm going there already."

She shook her head. "No, *danke*."

Josh eased his horse forward to keep pace with her. "Mamm will be upset if I arrive first. And she can't go home until you get there."

Rachel stopped suddenly. "*Ach!* Your *mamm*. I forgot all about her waiting for me."

"Mamm doesn't mind. I'm just worried she'll be angry with me." He grinned, but Rachel didn't look at him.

"I don't want to cause you any more trouble today." She hurried around the buggy to the passenger side.

The worried look on her face tore at him. He regretted his teasing. She used to laugh at his humor. "I'm only kidding. You know my *mamm* wouldn't get upset. She's the calmest person I know." *Except for you,* he wanted to add, but he didn't.

Rachel's lips curved up. "*Jah*, she is."

"Maybe if she hadn't been so patient, I'd have grown up to be a better person."

"That's for sure and certain." The old Rachel—his childhood friend with the impish glint in her eyes and playful smile—reappeared. Then she sobered. "I shouldn't have said that. You turned out fine."

Josh's chest constricted. He longed to bring out that fun side of her again, but he had no right. To keep himself from straying into that temptation, he changed the subject. "Why didn't you drive to the game?"

After some hesitation, she admitted, "My buggy has a flat tire."

"Why didn't you let me know? You could have gone to the game with me."

"Anna Mary wouldn't have liked that."

"That's not—" He stopped before he told a lie. Once, Josh had believed Anna Mary was unfailingly generous and charitable. Today, he'd seen a different side of her. Since then, he had to admit Rachel was right.

If only he could erase Anna Mary's unkindness. "I'm sorry. I wish it had never happened. I should never have . . ."

"*Ach*, Josh, don't blame yourself. You didn't do anything wrong."

Her soft melodious voice strummed chords deep inside his soul. And when she peeked up at him through her lashes, sparkling with a trace of tears, he softened into putty that she could shape into whatever she wished.

Now he understood how all his friends got caught in her snare, like flies wrapped in a spider's sticky web. Who could resist her feminine wiles? Everyone flew blindly—and willingly—into her trap, not realizing they'd never escape.

Rachel didn't do it deliberately. She didn't even seem to be aware of her power to turn men inside out and upside down, making them lose sight of rational thought. That's what made her allure so dangerous.

The vulnerable look in her eyes compelled them to feel sorry for her, to want to help her, to rush to care for her, to—

Josh dragged his mind away from this danger zone by reminding himself of Anna Mary. Memories of his girl-friend sloshed over him like a bucket of ice water, bringing him back to earth with a thud. Wet and irritated in his imagination, Josh blocked out his disturbing thoughts. He had no right to think those things. Not when he was courting another.

"Are you all right?" Anxiety crinkled Rachel's face.

Guilt washed over him, adding to the heap he'd already stuffed down inside. Rachel hadn't done anything wrong. She wasn't responsible for his wayward thoughts.

Before he could answer, she hung her head. "I'm sorry. I shouldn't have taken a ride with you. Anna Mary will be upset when she finds out."

"It's not your fault. I'm happy to take you home. Be-sides, no one would fault me for giving someone a ride when their buggy has a flat. Not even Anna Mary." Espe-cially not Anna Mary, who always tried to do the right thing.

Rachel kept her gaze on her lap as she twisted her hands together. "That's true. She can be a very caring person."

At Rachel's wounded tone, Josh shot a glance her way. The hurt in her words showed in her expression. He'd seen how the girls in their buddy bunch passed by her without speaking, and he'd heard them talking behind her back.

In fact, she usually stood alone until the boys flocked around her. Some girls stared at her with envy, others with anger, if their boyfriends joined the group. From being the most popular scholar in the *schulhaus*, she was now left out of everything the girls in the buddy bunch did together.

Josh cleared his throat. "I guess Anna Mary and the others aren't very friendly to you, are they? It must be hard not being a part of the group."

"That's some of it." She turned her head away to look out the buggy window. From the slump of her shoulders, something had cut her deeply.

Josh wanted to reach out to her, to make up for all she'd endured. "I'm sorry."

She darted a quick glance his way. "It's not your fault."

But the weight of guilt rested heavily on his shoulders.

Rachel sucked in a breath. She'd just lied. Then again, it wasn't a total fib. She didn't blame Josh for her pain. He'd never know how much she'd ached inside when he started dating Anna Mary—and still did.

But the sadness hadn't started then. It began years ago, after her brother's death in a fire, when Josh had walked out of her life and never looked back. When he'd avoided being around her. When he'd looked at anyone or anything rather than meet her eyes.

As they pulled into her driveway, Rachel sighed both

in relief and disappointment. Riding in Josh's buggy and sitting so close to him, knowing he loved someone else, brought up all her old feelings for him—from best friend to childhood crush to teenage hero—and all her old heartache. They'd been so close until he'd turned away after her brother's death.

Losing Tom had been devastating. She'd longed to depend on Josh the way she had after Daed died. Although Josh had tears in his eyes at the funeral, he'd never looked straight at her. Not then. Nor any time after that.

After the funeral service, he'd kept his head down, and she'd longed to ask him *You crying?* like she had when they first met. He'd looked up to Tom as the caring older brother he'd never had. But her own grief proved too great. She couldn't get the words out past the tightness gripping her throat.

Overwhelmed with sorrow, she'd gone into her shell and stopped going to Josh's house to ask him to go fishing or take walks into town. She had no desire to do any of the things she used to enjoy.

Instead of reaching out, he and his brothers steered clear of her. And never once had Josh come to visit her. At school, he didn't even glance her way.

She'd finished out her eighth-grade year, lonely and isolated. And nothing had changed since. She still watched from afar as others had fun together and left her out.

Josh wished he could say something to ease Rachel's loneliness. She'd just drawn inward, the way she had after her *daed* died. She'd often gone silent and gotten lost in thoughts or daydreams, but when she'd come back to the real world, she'd shared them with him. Now, though, he no longer had her trust. At that realization, it was as if a hand reached into his chest and wrung his heart. The crushing pain and loss made him groan.

"What's wrong?" Rachel stared at him with fear-filled eyes. "Are you all right?"

He hadn't meant to frighten her. Her *daed* had died of a heart attack.

"I'm okay. It's just that—" He couldn't tell her what had caused his reaction. But he needed to reassure her he wasn't dying. "I, um, suddenly realized how much I regret"—he stopped himself before he spilled the truth—"well, certain things."

Her brows drew together. She didn't believe his explanation.

Josh lowered his eyes. And all the agony of the breakdown between them, and his part in it, choked off his words—and his breath.

CHAPTER 5

Rachel often experienced that heartrending regret. So many things left unsaid and undone. With Daed. With Tom. And, most of all, with Josh.

That hurt most of all because she still saw him. But she couldn't mend their relationship. It took two people to do that. And Josh showed no desire to participate.

She cut off her musing. Instead of pitying herself, she should focus on Josh. Because of her, he had problems with his girlfriend. "I'm sorry."

"For what?" Josh jerked his faraway gaze to the inside of the buggy and concentrated on her for a few seconds before returning to the road.

"Was Anna Mary really angry?"

"Anna Mary?" he repeated, as if he had no idea who she meant.

Unsure whether she should drop the subject or encourage him to talk, Rachel opted to plunge ahead. "She didn't ride home with you."

Josh shook his head as if to dislodge unwanted memories, and Rachel's heart went out to him.

He didn't speak for a while, and she decided to drop the subject. Maybe he wanted to forget their disagreement.

Then he broke the silence. "About Anna Mary. *Jah*, she's upset. I don't blame her. I did something foolish."

Rachel swallowed back her hurt.

Josh's brow furrowed into troubled lines. "I deserved her anger, but I'm sorry about the way she treated you."

I deserved it. I'm the one who caused the trouble. Rachel wished she'd kept her hands to herself.

"When I tried to make things right, Anna Mary took it all wrong. I made a hash of it." He sighed.

Rachel struggled to picture Josh making a mess of his apology, but she couldn't. He'd always been the most popular person in the *g'may* because he was so good at smoothing over problems—his and others.

"And I'm not proud of this, but I walked off. I should have stayed and made things right. When I got back, she was gone. I guess Caroline drove her home."

"*Ach*, Josh, that's too bad. If you give her a little time, I'm sure she'll realize her mistake. She knows you're trustworthy."

Josh shook his head. "I don't know if she believes that anymore." His sigh seemed pulled from the depth of his being. "Even though I don't deserve it, once I apologize, Anna Mary will forgive me. Then she'll let me explain."

"That's good." But was it? For Anna Mary and Josh, perhaps. But not for Rachel.

Josh couldn't decide if it was good or not. Somehow, this first break with Anna Mary had revealed cracks between them that might be hard to mend. Asking for forgiveness could glue things back together, but like a bowl that had shattered, would it make their relationship more fragile?

He'd seen his parents fight or have misunderstandings, but they never let the sun go down on their wrath. Apologies always brought them closer. Maybe he and Anna Mary would discover his parents' secret for healing breaches.

"Josh?"

Rachel's quiet voice interrupted his worries. He glanced over, and she waved to the other side of the road. He'd almost driven past her house. Tugging the horse to the left, he steered into her driveway.

His *mamm* came to the window and smiled as she caught sight of Rachel in the passenger seat. *Ach!* Now Mamm would get the wrong idea. He hoped she wouldn't say anything to embarrass either of them. Or mention it to her friends. He'd never work things out with Anna Mary if Mamm talked about Rachel riding home with him. Not after what had happened at the volleyball field.

Mamm met them at the door, looked from one to the other, and beamed. "How nice."

Rachel smiled back. "*Danke* for staying with Mamm."

"My pleasure. I'm fixing a snack for Betty. She just woke from a nap, so we're going to have a little chat."

"You're not ready to go?" Josh itched to get away. If he stayed around Rachel much longer, he'd be drawn into that web of hers.

"Why don't you come in and talk to Rachel while Betty and I finish our tea and shoofly pie?"

Exactly what Josh hoped to avoid.

His *mamm* pattered down the hall, leaving him and Rachel alone.

He had to do something other than sit face to face with Rachel. Having her beside him in the buggy had been difficult enough. That gave him an idea. "Why don't I take a look at your flat to see if I can make it secure enough for you to take it in for repairs?"

"That's all right. I wasn't planning to get it fixed right away."

From the way Rachel avoided his eyes, he guessed she couldn't afford the repairs. He'd ask a friend to handle the metal work and take care of the bill. But he could wrap it for now. "With your *mamm* ill, you might need to drive her in an emergency."

When Rachel still hesitated, he started toward the back door, which led to the barn where she parked her buggy. The two of them had walked this path so often when they were younger, he knew it by heart. To take his mind from those memories, he concentrated on planning the repairs. "Where's your duct tape?"

"In the junk drawer."

Josh walked to the correct drawer, rummaged through balls of twine, masking tape, screwdrivers, pliers, and other assorted tools.

"You still remember?"

Her whispered question sent heat swirling through him. Tongue-tied, he could only nod. He'd never forgotten. He found the roll of duct tape and quirked an eyebrow. "Orange?"

Rachel laughed. "What can I say? I like bright colors."

Another sign of the lively little girl she'd been. Once again, Josh wished to bring out that side of her. But he had no business even thinking that.

He gripped the tape, picked out a pair of scissors, and strode to the door. "I'll see what I can do."

"*Danke* for doing this. I've been worried about getting Mamm to the doctor if she needed to go."

He hadn't expected her to follow him. How would he ever keep his attention on the job?

As they entered the barn, he focused on the buggy rather than Rachel, but he didn't look where he was stepping. He banged his foot against a pail, sloshing water onto his pant leg, his shoe, and the barn floor.

"*Ach*, I'm so sorry. I forgot to empty that today." Rachel grabbed the bucket handle, hurried from the barn, and dumped the water. When she returned, she set the pail in the middle of the floor again.

That confused Josh. Everything else in the barn hung neatly on pegs or sat on shelves. "Wouldn't it be better to put this in the corner?" He hoped he didn't sound critical.

Rachel's cheeks pinkened to a lovely shade of rose. "We need it there."

He almost asked why, but stopped himself. They'd had a storm last night. He craned his neck to study the rafters and roof. Bits of blue sky peeked through a hole above the bucket.

"I can fix that for you." They had leftover materials from various jobs their family construction company had completed. Daed liked to use leftovers to help others who couldn't afford repairs.

"*Neh*, we'll get it done." Rachel didn't meet his gaze. She'd also done that when he'd suggested getting the buggy wheel fixed.

If she and her *mamm* had financial troubles, the church could help. Back when they were best friends, he would have blurted out the question on his mind: *Do you need money?* But now, he and Rachel had become strangers.

Despite her *neh*, he intended to stop by with a few tools and supplies to patch the roof. A wooden extension ladder leaned against the back wall of the barn, so the job wouldn't take long. Right now, he had a different job to do.

Skirting the empty bucket, Josh headed over and knelt by the wheel with the wrapped rim. Rachel must have put on this tape. She'd spaced it too far apart and left it much too loose. He could only imagine what a rough ride she'd had getting home.

In case she had to do it again, he explained how to hold the metal band tightly in place and wrap it well. She leaned close to watch, and he struggled to control his zinging nerves. If he didn't concentrate, he'd mess this up more than she had.

When he finished, he stood and brushed off his trousers. "That should hold for a short distance." Automatically, he reached down to give her a hand up, and she took it.

That had been a mistake. A huge mistake.

He let go the second she stood. Then he turned his back so she wouldn't see the longing in his eyes. They'd left the barn door open, and there, framed in the kitchen window, his *mamm* stood, a smile playing across her lips. Had she seen them holding hands? He hoped not.

"I—I'll put these away." After picking up the tape and scissors, he hightailed it out of the barn.

Her soft *danke* followed him, chipping away at the ice he'd packed around his heart.

For a short while, all of Rachel's dreams had come true. When she'd squatted beside him and he'd taught her how to press hard on the broken metal rim to keep it in place, his muscles had rippled under his shirt. She'd sucked in a breath.

Earlier, after they'd rotated in the volleyball game, Josh ended up directly in front of her. She had trouble concentrating on the game. He'd filled out since they'd last played together. Of course, she'd already noticed that at church, but when he jumped or stretched or dove for the ball, his damp shirt clung to his broad shoulders and strong back.

But here, only inches separated them. He even brushed against her shoulder twice as he tugged to tighten the tape before wrapping it around the wheel again. She hadn't meant to get so close. She just wanted to be sure she understood how to tape the wheel properly. They wouldn't be getting it repaired anytime soon, so she might have to fix it more than once.

And when Josh had offered her his hand to help her up, her whole arm tingled. She'd completely forgotten about everything, including his girlfriend.

Now, shame heated her cheeks. What had she been thinking?

As she started toward the house, a movement in the kitchen window caught her eye. Josh's *mamm*? Had she seen them? Rachel's face burned even hotter. What must Miriam think?

Rachel wanted to stay out here and not face either of them, but she couldn't do that. She forced herself to walk into the kitchen.

Josh had stored the tape and scissors. And Miriam's *cat-lapping-cream* smile left Rachel wondering for the second time that day. She got the distinct impression Josh's *mamm* had seen them, and it delighted her.

Before Rachel could assess Miriam's eyes to confirm the message in her smile, Josh's *mamm* headed to the refrigerator.

"Is it all right if Betty and I have some of your strawberry lemonade? It looks delicious."

"Of course. I'll pour it and bring it back to Mamm."

"*Neh, neh.* You and Josh stay here. I'll do it. In fact, he might like some too." Miriam set four empty glasses on the counter. Then she hastily poured two cups and rushed from the kitchen.

Rachel couldn't be impolite. "Would you like some lemonade?"

"That'd be great."

She didn't want to sit in their small living room, so she suggested, "Why don't we sit on the porch? The trees shade it this time of day."

"I know." Josh took the glass she handed him and headed there. "Remember when we used to play Uno out here?" He sat in one of the rockers.

"*Jah.* And I always beat you." She couldn't resist smiling.

"I let you win."

"You did not." Rachel laughed. They'd had this argument after every game.

Josh laughed, too, and their old comradery returned. As they sipped their strawberry lemonade, they reminisced about favorite toys, games, and activities.

"Remember that time I dared you to go out on the rocks in the creek to catch a frog and—"

"I slipped and fell in?" She finished his sentence for him the way she used to do.

"*Jah*, and you went all the way under water."

She'd panicked when the water closed over her head, because she couldn't swim. Josh had rescued her. She'd never forget how his arms had encircled her, lifting her, supporting her. And the blessed relief of gulping in air. She'd felt so secure in his arms as he pulled her to shore.

"*Danke* for saving me. I always felt safe with you."

Horses' hooves clomped past the house. Rachel cringed. She hoped nobody who knew them would see them laughing and talking on the porch. If there'd been more time, she'd have ducked into the house. She didn't want rumors to get back to Anna Mary, who might misunderstand this casual conversation between old friends.

Even if it meant so much more to Rachel, Josh didn't have the tangled feelings and childhood love coloring those flashbacks. He had a girlfriend and the opportunity to make newer and different memories. She couldn't stand in the way of his relationship.

The last thing Josh needed right now was more gossip tying him to her. People already blamed her for breaking up several relationships, even though she'd never encouraged or dated anyone. Many girls didn't want to date boys who spent time staring at her or talking to her.

Although Rachel sipped her lemonade and pretended to ignore the buggy slowing down as it went by, she remained very aware of it and checked out the occupants.

"Tim?" The name hissed out between her clenched teeth. He lived in the other direction, so what was he doing out here on her country road? Had he come looking for her? The thought sickened her.

Josh jerked upright from his relaxed position and almost spilled his lemonade. Was Tim stalking Rachel? Why else would he be driving past? He didn't live anywhere near here, and this country road only went to a handful of farms.

Ach! Tim had accused Josh of cheating on Anna Mary with Rachel, and here he was, sitting on Rachel's porch, looking like they were dating or something.

Who else was in the buggy? Josh glimpsed Abe in the passenger seat and a brunette in the back. Of course, Anna Mary would never be out riding with Tim, but seeing a girl with her hair color jagged at Josh's conscience.

If it had been Anna Mary, would you have been happy for her to see you here?

He jumped to his feet as soon as the buggy passed. "I have to go. I'll see if Mamm's ready."

"I'm sorry, Josh. Do you think they'll tell anyone?"

Rachel looked so guilty, he wanted to reassure her. "I don't know. He might not."

But if Josh knew Tim, he'd use that information some way to torment Josh. And in the process, Rachel and Anna Mary might get hurt.

He and Rachel had been having their first friendly talk in years. He'd even relaxed and forgotten about the past and her brother's death. Rachel hadn't done anything wrong, but she'd get all the blame. And if Anna Mary believed the gossip . . .

How had this day gone so wrong?

CHAPTER 6

With the next day being an off-Sunday, Josh headed to Anna Mary's as usual. He had to apologize and make things right. He hoped that, after he explained what had really happened in the woods, she'd realize she'd misunderstood and forgive him. Then they could put all this behind them.

He walked in expecting to smooth things over, so he was unprepared for Anna Mary's fury and accusations. She'd found out about him spending time at Rachel's house. How did she know about that? Josh couldn't ask that question, because she'd take it the wrong way. All he could do was let her vent and try to be understanding.

When she ran out of steam and stopped to heave in a tear-clogged breath, Josh tried to brush away the visit to Rachel's house as a chore he been forced to do. And it had certainly started out that way.

"I had to go there. Mamm offered to stay with Betty so Rachel could go to volleyball."

"You were at Rachel's *before* and *after* volleyball?" Anna Mary's voice rose almost to a shriek.

Josh tried to calm her. "I only dropped Mamm off before the game."

"And you didn't see Rachel at all?"

"Not really. I carried Mamm's tote bag into the kitchen. I might have exchanged a few words about the game with Rachel. Nothing important." He took a deep breath. "You don't have anything to worry about. Mamm was right there."

But if Anna Mary had heard Mamm's comments, she'd be doubly upset. And if she could have peeked into Josh's heart and mind while he'd been around Rachel, she'd be triply upset.

"Your *mamm* wasn't with you two after the game, was she?" Bitterness laced Anna Mary's tone.

"*Neh.*" Josh hung his head.

"Want to tell me about that?"

Not really. He'd prefer to keep most of it to himself, especially his reactions to Rachel. How much did Anna Mary know? And who'd told her? It had to be Tim. If so, he'd told her about the porch, but who knows how he'd embellished the story.

Anna Mary didn't know what had happened before the porch, but Josh decided to be honest about that. "When I got to Rachel's, Mamm and Betty were chatting, so I taped Rachel's wheel because she had a flat."

For a moment, sympathy edged out Anna Mary's anger. "I hope she wasn't too far from home."

"I don't know." Josh hoped to appeal to Anna Mary's softer, charitable side. "She walked to the volleyball game in the heat."

"She should have asked someone for a ride."

"I doubt she'd want to impose." Or she worried people would turn her down. Nobody would do that, but with the way the girls treated her . . .

"That's silly. Anyone would have driven her."

Including Josh, if he'd known she had a flat. But it might be best not to mention that now. Not when Anna Mary seemed to be rational and ready to listen. Should he try to explain about the woods?

He drew in a deep breath and opened his mouth, but Anna Mary beat him to it.

"Just because I'm sorry she had a flat, doesn't mean you don't have more explaining to do." Her irritated tone signaled she hadn't reached the forgiveness stage. "You fixed her wheel. And then what?"

"I put away the tools, and Mamm was in the kitchen pouring lemonade for herself and Betty. She told Rachel to pour us both one too while we waited for our *mamms* to finish their snack. Rachel seemed reluctant, but she did it."

"Reluctant? Really?" Each word came out choppy and furious. "Then why were the two of you smiling and laughing and—"

He had to interrupt her before she spewed any of Tim's lies. "I don't know what Tim told you, but . . ."

"Tim?" Her voice rose to an indignant screech. "Tim? Why would I need him to tell me?"

Josh furrowed his brow. Who else had seen them?

Anna Mary went very still and stared at him. "You watched the buggy go by and didn't even recognize me? I thought you didn't wave because you were so caught up with Rachel."

"You were in Tim's buggy? It's not easy to see into the back seat, but I saw your color hair and—" He stumbled to a stop. Why hadn't he looked closely at the face? "I didn't think you'd be riding in Tim's buggy, so . . ." So he'd ignored her?

He couldn't tell her that. Josh shifted uncomfortably. "If I'd known it was you, I'd—"

Anna Mary sliced into his explanation. "You'd what? You'd have flirted with Rachel inside the house instead of on the porch?"

"We weren't flirting." At least Rachel hadn't been. Had his thoughts crossed the line? Heat burned up his chest and across his face.

"Really?" Anna Mary's voice turned to ice. Her teeth clenched as she stared at him, waiting for an admission of guilt.

Josh ducked his head. "I'm sorry it looked that way. We were only laughing about the time Rachel fell into the creek." He added hastily, "Back when we were nine years old."

"Must have been hilarious," Anna Mary muttered. The hurt in her eyes cut into him.

He'd never confided in Anna Mary about his childhood feelings for Rachel. He pushed those memories out of his mind whenever they taunted him, because the ending had been so painful. Maybe that was a blessing.

"But why were you riding with Tim?" Anna Mary might accuse him of changing the subject, but her being with someone who'd kicked a ball at her best friend made no sense.

"Like you don't know," she snapped.

The venom in her words indicated Josh had been to blame. That made him even more confused. "*Neh*, I don't."

The anger on her face melted into sadness. "You drove off and left me at the field. Abe saw me walking home crying, and they went out of their way to make sure I got home."

"What? You were still at the field? I looked all over for you. I thought you were still angry with me, so you'd gone home with Caroline."

"I told you I'd go home with you. I wouldn't have left without saying anything. No matter how upset I was."

"I know you wouldn't. I'm sorry. For everything. Will you forgive me?"

Anna Mary turned away, but not before he glimpsed tears trickling down her cheeks. Her shoulders shook, and she didn't answer.

"Maybe you need some time?" he asked gently.

"*Jah,*" she choked out.

"I'll go now. Maybe we can talk again later in the week." When she didn't respond, he let himself out. Guilt filled him at all the ways he'd hurt Anna Mary.

He resolved to pay more attention to her and put Rachel out of his mind completely.

A knock on the door early Monday morning startled Rachel. Who'd be here at this time of morning? None of Mamm's friends would stop by until later in the day, because they knew Rachel needed time to get her mother fed and dressed.

An older man with a long white beard stood on the porch. "*Gude mariye.* I'm here to fix your buggy wheel."

How did he know about her flat?

Rachel fumbled for an explanation. "*Danke,* but I, um, wasn't planning to get it fixed just yet."

"You don't want it repaired?"

She couldn't lie and say *neh.* Lowering her eyes, she forced herself to admit, "I need to save up for the bill."

The man's face brightened. "I see. Well, you needn't worry about the cost. I've already been paid. Shall I go out to the barn, then?"

"But who gave you the money?"

"I can't say."

She had a good idea who'd paid. Not even Mamm knew about the flat.

Rachel didn't want to accept charity, but the man headed for the barn. He had his payment and intended to do the job. Now she had to find a way to repay Josh.

That turned out to be the first of two blessings that day.

In the late afternoon, Josh showed up with supplies for fixing the barn roof. When Rachel protested, he held up a hand.

"These materials cost us nothing. Most homeowners expect us to clean up and dispose of the leftovers, but we save them for jobs like this."

"But your time."

"I'm happy to do things for others. You are too. That's part of being in the Amish community."

Before she could say anything more, he headed for the barn and brought out the extension ladder. Still feeling obligated, Rachel went inside and started a batch of sugar cookies. They used to be Josh's favorite. She hoped they still were.

While the cookies baked, she stood by the window, admiring him as he worked. He must have sensed her watching, because he turned and stared down at the kitchen window. Rachel ducked out of sight. Had he seen her?

As much as she wanted to take another peek, she restrained herself and checked on the cookies. After she'd slid the first batches onto the cooling racks, she put in the second cookie sheets. Then she carried a plate of cookies and a glass of milk to Mamm.

"Isn't it too warm to be baking cookies on such a hot day?" Mamm asked. "And what is all the banging outside? It woke me from my nap."

"Josh Yoder is fixing a hole in our barn roof."

"Ah." Mamm looked down at the plate. "Josh's favorite, eh?" A half-smile relaxed some tense lines in her face.

Even Mamm remembered.

Rachel couldn't meet her mother's gaze. "*Jah*, I wanted to thank him."

"I'm so glad you and Josh are back to being friends. Betty and I both hoped . . ."

Rachel interrupted. "I have to take out the next batch of cookies." She rushed from the room before Mamm could finish. They all hoped Rachel and Josh would have a future together. Well, all except Josh.

Tears stung her eyes as she removed the next batch from the oven and packaged up the cooled cookies for him.

Outside, the banging stopped. A short while later, the top extension of the ladder racketed down. Josh had finished. Before he could rush away, she opened the back door and beckoned to him.

When he hesitated, she held out the cookies. "For you. As a thank you."

Josh closed his eyes and sniffed the air. "Umm . . . sugar cookies?"

"I have some cooling if you'd like warm ones."

"How can I say *neh* to that?" He followed her into the

kitchen. "You didn't have to do this. You don't need to pay me back for the roof."

"*Jah*, I owe you for that and the buggy wheel."

"The buggy wheel?"

"Don't pretend you don't know. You're the only one who knew I had a flat."

Josh hadn't intended for her to guess he'd been behind the repair, but he'd forgotten her isolation. She didn't have friends visiting.

"I'll pay that bill as soon as I can."

"You don't owe me anything. Please don't fret about it."

As if she hadn't heard him, her brow drew into worried lines. She nibbled at her lower lip, drawing his attention to her bow-shaped mouth.

He jerked his gaze away.

Although he'd prayed about avoiding temptation, he kept putting himself into situations he shouldn't. Why hadn't he thought about the consequences of entering the kitchen with Rachel? They practically bumped into each other in the confined space. And the tantalizing aroma of butter and vanilla swirling around them brought up memories of happier times.

Rachel brushed past him to get to the counter. "Want some milk?" she asked as she slid cookies onto two plates.

"I can get it." Josh went straight to the cupboard that held glasses. How many times had he helped Rachel fix snacks? He always poured the drinks while she filled their plates.

Suddenly, Rachel giggled. A sound of pure joy. Once again, Josh yearned to bring out that side of her.

"Remember that time we tried to bake cookies?" She set heaped plates at their familiar places.

How could he forget? Every memory of her was precious.

They'd made cookies and other treats together, but he knew exactly which time she meant. It had been only a few weeks after they'd met.

Josh couldn't help laughing. "*Jah*, I wanted to help."

Rachel couldn't reach the flour container in the cupboard, so Josh had climbed onto the counter and lifted the ceramic jar from the shelf. It slipped from his hands, smashed against the edge of the counter, and shattered into millions of shards on the counter and floor.

Clouds of flour engulfed them, coating every surface.

"All that white floating down." Rachel had her eyes closed as joy flitted across her face.

Josh would never forget the wonder on her upturned face. She'd ignored the broken crockery, lifted her hands heavenward, and giggled like she had a few moments ago. *It's snowing! It's snowing!* she'd exclaimed as she danced around.

And Josh, who'd been mortified and fearful of getting in trouble, had been mesmerized by the sweet little girl below him who'd turned a disaster into high-spirited fun.

"I was terrified," Josh admitted. "I'd just broken the flour canister."

Rachel's eyes popped open. "You were? You never told me that."

"*Neh*, I didn't. I thought you'd be mad at me and that we'd get in big trouble. But you distracted me. I couldn't believe you were enjoying it."

She beamed. "You'd created a snowstorm in summer. It was so beautiful."

"*Jah*, it was." If you looked at it through a nine-year-old's eyes. She'd convinced him to slide down off the counter and throw handfuls of snow, until they were both covered head to toe and they'd iced every surface of the kitchen in white. Josh had never laughed so hard in his life.

"Poor Tom. He was supposed to be watching us while Daed and Mamm were gone." Rachel's eyes reflected her love and admiration for her brother.

Josh's gut twisted. He'd been responsible for that light dying, to be replaced by pools of sadness.

But Rachel pulled him back to the past. "Remember his face? His eyes and mouth both opened so wide. He couldn't believe it."

Even now, Josh's body tensed as it had when Tom studied them and shook his head. And his mind drifted back to that day.

Josh squeezed his eyes shut, waiting for the blows his brothers would have inflicted.

But Tom laughed. Actually laughed. "Rachel, Rachel, what am I going to do with you?"

At those words, Josh opened his eyes and threw himself in front of her. "Don't hurt her. I'm the one who made the mess. It's all my fault."

Both Tom and Rachel stared at Josh.

"Punish me, not Rachel," he begged.

Tom cast a stern look at his sister, and Josh's stomach clenched. He had to protect her, but he didn't know how. "I'm going to punish both of you."

Josh bit back a whimper. His mind raced, trying to come up with a way to save Rachel. He stayed in front of her to take the worst of it. Maybe Tom would be too tired to hurt her afterwards.

Then Tom spoke, and Josh couldn't believe his ears. "I hate to tell you, but your punishment is to clean up every bit of this mess."

"Are you all right?" Rachel's soft question startled Josh back to the present.

"I thought your brother was going to beat us both." Even now, Josh's stomach still held that tight ball of fear. "I wanted to protect you but didn't know how."

Light dawned in Rachel's eyes. "That's why you jumped in front of me? I always wondered about that." Her face soft and dreamy, she gazed off into a distance. "You offered to take my punishment."

"I assumed Tom would be like my brothers. They would have pounded me with their fists. I didn't want you to get hurt."

"*Ach*, Josh. I didn't know. Why didn't you tell me about your brothers? We shared everything with each other."

"I didn't want anyone to know." He'd hidden that shame the way he did his future guilt. And he'd built a huge wall between them.

If he stayed here any longer in Rachel's accepting presence, he'd spill that secret too. And all the love he'd bottled up would come pouring out.

Visions of Anna Mary flagged him to a stop. He'd moved on from Rachel and had asked Anna Mary to date. His future belonged with her.

Josh scraped his chair back. "I should go."

"But you haven't finished your cookies."

Anna Mary's presence hovered over him. "They're delicious, but—"

"I see." As if Rachel sensed Anna Mary in the room, too, she stood and bagged the rest of the cookies. "Here." She thrust them at him. "I'm sorry. I shouldn't have invited you in. *Danke* for fixing the barn roof."

He nodded, took the bag, and turned his back, afraid he might give away more than he intended. "Goodbye," he said, before the screen door banged behind him.

CHAPTER 7

As Josh rushed away, coldness crept through Rachel. Rather than saying *sehn dich schpeeder*, the Amish farewell promising to see her later, he'd used the *Englisch* word *goodbye*, a word that ended everything. *Goodbye* had a chilling finality. He'd splintered her heart like he'd once shattered the canister into shards.

"Rachel?" Mamm called faintly. "Send Josh back here."

Had Mamm not heard the door slam? The loud *thwack* had destroyed Rachel's joy. For a short time, she'd been basking in warmth and shared memories. But those had all been frozen out by Anna Mary.

Rachel swallowed hard to force the words from her tear-clogged throat. "Josh is gone."

Gone for good, she whispered to herself.

He'd galloped out of here so fast, as if he couldn't wait to get away. The boy who had once promised to be her best friend forever had moved on to someone else.

Why couldn't she accept that fact? Why did she keep torturing herself with fantasies that couldn't come true?

Rachel shook herself. She had to make supper for Mamm. Luckily, they still had the casseroles from Josh's *mamm*. Rachel wasn't sure she could put together a meal without missing essential ingredients.

She slid a chicken-and-rice dish into the still-warm oven and choked back the waves of sorrow washing over her. She'd had so much fun making the cookies to surprise Josh, and they'd had a wonderful conversation.

After turning on the oven again, she moved to the spot where they kept the flour canister. Mamm had replaced the broken one with another pottery container. This one had a rooster head on top that she claimed reminded her not to strut around full of *hochmut*. Every time Rachel and Josh had cooked in the kitchen after that, they'd both glanced up at the proud bird and laughed their heads off.

Back then, if Rachel wanted to send Josh into gales of laughter anytime, anywhere, she only had to crow *cock-a-doodle-doo*. That had been their shared joke for years.

After cleaning up that blizzard of flour, both of them had become careful cooks. Until Tom had joined them to help, they'd been making a sticky mess by using wet cloths. He suggested brushing the counters and sweeping up the dry powder rather than turning everything into a gooey dough. Then he'd pitched in, and they'd managed to get everything back in order before their parents returned. Tom even took the blame for the fiasco, insisting he should have been keeping a closer eye on both of them.

Tom had been the best brother ever. Like she could with Josh, Rachel could talk to Tom about everything. He always listened and offered sage advice. A twinge of loneliness shot through her. What would Tom advise her to do about unrequited love?

Tom's voice came to her as clearly as if he stood beside her. *Casting all your care upon Him, for He careth for you.* How many times had he repeated that Bible verse to her when she fretted about things? Things that seemed so small and minor compared to her concerns now. But 1 Peter 5:7 still held the key to peace.

Rachel had brought her sorrow after Tom's death, her burdens over Mamm's illness, and her worries about money shortages to the Lord. But not since she'd begged as a young teen for God to mend her friendship with Josh had she prayed about her grown-up attraction to him.

Lord, I don't know what to ask about Josh. I've never gotten over my childhood love for him, but he's tied to someone else now. I need Your help to straighten out my feelings. Please give me the strength to do the right thing.

Despite not knowing what that might be, a sense of peace descended over her. She needed to trust God to untangle her emotions and direct her path.

For the first time in a long while, Rachel could think about Josh with a sense that all was well. She didn't need God's warning to stay away from him. She shouldn't have interfered in his relationship with Anna Mary by inviting him into the kitchen. She no longer had the right to tug on those old bonds of friendship.

Josh clicked to his horse to speed away from Rachel's house, but he couldn't flee his thoughts and feelings. Even though he'd left her behind, Rachel's bell-like laughter floated around him, stirring a longing to return to those carefree times. Back when they were young and innocent. Back when no tragedy had marred their friendship.

But that could never be. And the faster he erased those desires, the more his relationship with Anna Mary would improve. He'd been holding back a lot about himself and his past, things he should share with the woman he'd spend the rest of his life with. Maybe opening up to Anna Mary the way he'd always done with Rachel would bring him closer to his girlfriend.

Now he understood why God suggested not letting the sun go down on your anger. Being at odds with someone made it easier to get entangled with someone else. To avoid the temptation Rachel posed, Josh had to make things right with Anna Mary as soon as possible. She'd asked for time. Would yesterday and today be enough?

Daed had scheduled a job near the Green Valley Farmer's Market this week. Maybe Josh could stop in and ask Anna Mary to have lunch with him. They could discuss everything and get back on a better footing.

Despite going to sleep that night resolved to improve his relationship with Anna Mary, Josh woke, as usual, holding hands with Rachel. Only this time, they weren't children strolling through fields of wildflowers. He shook off the sleep fog that clung to him along with the nostalgia. The dream must have been caused by eating sugar cookies and chatting with Rachel yesterday.

Today would be a *gut* day for a fresh start. Josh completed his chores and his breakfast, then he talked to his father while they hitched up the team.

"Daed, I need to stop by the market to ask Anna Mary a quick question. I'd like her to go out to lunch with me."

His father's forehead wrinkled. "Can it wait until after work? We have much to do today. It's a new customer, so I want to be sure to give him our very best."

"It won't take long, and I'll work extra at the end of the day to make up the time. Besides, we're not that far from the market."

With a put-upon sigh, his *daed* gave in. "Drop me at the construction site first. And make it short."

By the time Josh got to the market, a crowd had lined up at Hartzler's Chicken Barbecue, where Anna Mary worked. If he waited on that line, Daed would get annoyed. All Josh needed to know was what time Anna Mary would take her lunch break today.

Neh, that wasn't all. He needed to know if she wanted to talk to him.

While he wrestled over whether it would be impolite to move to the far side of the counter and wave to get Anna Mary's attention, two boys jumped the line and elbowed people out of their way to get to the front.

One set an elbow on the counter and flirted with Caroline. The other stared longingly at Anna Mary, who returned his look with a sweet smile. Josh swallowed hard. She seemed pretty happy to see this guy.

Josh's gaze strayed to the boy holding her attention. To his shock, it was Abe from volleyball. Beside him, Tim must be making outrageous remarks to Caroline, who glowered at him.

Abe and Tim? They'd driven Anna Mary home after the game. Had there been more to that ride than just a simple lift?

Josh turned away. He couldn't speak to Anna Mary now. Not when she was tied up talking to someone else. He'd do what Daed suggested and wait until after work. But they might have more to discuss than Josh's transgressions.

He shoved on the door to the parking lot, almost knocking over an elderly lady. She teetered on her cane, and Josh reached out to steady her.

"*Danke*, young man." She peered at him through her thick glasses. "You're Josh Yoder, right?"

He smiled politely. "I am."

Her lips stretched into a pleased grin. "I thought so."

How did this *Englischer* know who he was?

As if she'd read his mind, she said, "You—and your brothers and Daed—worked on several of my projects." She named three of them.

Light dawned. He'd heard so much about the elderly lady who built houses for the poor and homeless. She also owned the Farmer's Market. "You're Mrs. Vandenberg?"

"You've heard of me?" she asked in surprise, as if her name wasn't common knowledge throughout the area.

"*Jah*, I have." He wanted to thank her for all the help she'd given the community, but he got the impression she didn't like to be thanked.

"Oh, dear, I hope what you heard was good." She chuckled. "You don't have to tell me. I don't like putting people on the spot. Well, except in matters of the heart."

Huh? She left Josh thoroughly confused. What did the heart have to do with it?

A knowing look crossed her face. "I can tell by your expression you're befuddled."

He nodded.

"Don't worry. Everything will become much clearer soon."

Gut, because, at the moment, his mind was muddled with this woman's cryptic statements as well as the thoughts of Anna Mary and Rachel swirling through his head.

As if thinking about her made her appear, Rachel, her arms piled with quilts and pillows, reached the door he and Mrs. Vandenberg were blocking.

Mrs. Vandenberg turned. "Ah, there you are, Rachel, we were waiting for you."

Had Rachel asked Mrs. Vandenberg to hold him here?

Did Rachel have something to ask him? Maybe not. She seemed as *ferhoodled* as he was.

She blinked a few times. "Josh? What are you doing here?" Then she answered her own question. "Oh, seeing Anna Mary. I heard she works at the market now."

"Not exactly," he said. "I mean, I came to see her, but she's talking to Abe." Maybe *talking to* wasn't the right description.

"Abe?" Rachel's eyes widened. "From volleyball?" When he nodded, she shot him a sympathetic look.

Mrs. Vandenberg's smile broadened. "God works in mysterious ways."

"*Jah*, He does," Rachel agreed, but her puzzled frown showed she wasn't sure why the elderly lady had made that comment.

Sometimes when people got older, they rambled off on tangents. Maybe that's what was happening. Yet Mrs. Vandenberg's eyes, bright and alert, contradicted Josh's theory.

She pinned him with a knowing gaze. "You might not understand me now, but you will."

Unsure how to respond to that, he remained quiet.

"You know, Josh, perhaps you could help Rachel carry some of her goods. It would be a shame if those beautiful quillows tumbled off the top onto the dirty parking lot."

The pillows seemed to be balanced well on top of Rachel's quilt, but Josh reached for them. Rachel backed up a few steps.

"You don't have to do that," she said. "I know you need to get to work."

Mrs. Vandenberg wagged a finger at Rachel. "You need to learn to accept assistance when it's offered. Insisting on doing everything yourself can be a form of pride."

Her eyes misty, Rachel lowered her head.

Before Josh could jump to her defense, Mrs. Vandenberg added, "Practice the art of gratitude. All most people expect when they do things for you is thanks. Or, in your case, *danke*. Isn't that right, Josh?"

She'd put him on the spot. He didn't want to put Rachel in the wrong, but he did want to prevent her from paying him back. "I guess so," he muttered. "I definitely don't want to be paid back for the wheel or the barn roof."

Mrs. Vandenberg addressed him. "Which reminds me . . . that roofing job your dad's starting out in Gordonville on Wednesday is for a house I'm fixing up. I had him order extra shingles. They should match Rachel's house roof."

He stared at her in shock. How did she know the color of Rachel's roof and that it needed repairs? He'd noted the problems when he'd climbed onto the barn roof, but he hadn't said anything to Rachel, because he didn't want her to worry about paying for fixing it. He'd planned to return when he had enough leftover shingles to do the whole job. Now it seemed Mrs. Vandenberg intended to provide all of them.

Josh couldn't resist asking, "How do you know about Rachel's roof?"

"God gives me nudges from time to time." She turned to Rachel. "I'm sure Josh has a list of other projects to do around your house. Remember my advice."

He wasn't about to question her again. But she was right. He did have a mental list: the pasture fence, the wooden well cover, the timbers holding the barn roof, the sagging back porch roof . . .

Mrs. Vandenberg interrupted him. "Order any materials you don't have and send me the bill."

"I can take care of it," Josh informed her.

"*Neh.*" The word exploded from Rachel's lips.

Josh and Mrs. Vandenberg stared at her.

"I can't let either of you pay for my household repairs. I'll do it myself as I can afford it."

"Rachel, dear, did you listen to what I said? Don't let your pride deny others the joy of helping." A hint of steeliness underlaid Mrs. Vandenberg's gentle words.

Josh suspected she'd never take *neh* for an answer.

Rachel shifted uncomfortably. "I don't want to put people out."

"Giving benefits the giver as much as the receiver, isn't that so, Josh?"

"*Jah.*" He'd enjoyed helping Rachel.

"And a smile and a thank-you satisfies many a man's heart. I'm sure that was payment enough for Josh." Mrs. Vandenberg looked to him for confirmation.

A tangle of feelings welled inside him at the thought of Rachel's smile directed at him, and his face burned. He tried to lighten the moment. "And some sugar cookies."

Rachel laughed. The light, airy sound took his breath away.

"Remember when you were children?" Mrs. Vandenberg looked from him to Rachel. "You helped each other all the time with no thought of who owed what. You need to go back to those feelings."

Rachel's eyes grew shiny with nostalgia.

A sharp pain shot through Josh, and he stared at the asphalt under his feet. He couldn't meet Rachel's eyes. No way could he go back.

Mrs. Vandenberg reached out and set a hand on his arm. "Guilt from the past casts long shadows over the present. When you shine the light of God's forgiveness into the dark places, your path will be made clear."

Could this elderly woman see into his soul? All the guilt and shame he'd hidden over the years made Josh squirm. He had to get away. First, she'd lectured Rachel about accepting gifts; now, she'd turned the spotlight on him.

To his relief, she glanced at her watch. "I have another important errand, but I'd be delighted to see you help Rachel, Josh."

"Of course." He took the quillows from on top and, to quiet his racing pulse after being so close to her, he studied the lovely, intricate designs. "These are beautiful. All your coloring and drawing when you were little really paid off."

She kept her gaze on the ground.

"The perfect time for a thank-you, dear," Mrs. Vandenberg prodded. "Accept help and compliments with grace. Then pass them on to others."

Rachel, her cheeks pink, flicked a quick sideways glance at Josh. "*Danke.*"

"You're very welcome."

"For everything," she whispered.

"And, Josh," Mrs. Vandenberg said as she turned to go, "sometimes we hang onto the old when God wants us to move ahead to the new." Her cane tapped out a jaunty rhythm as she headed off in the opposite direction.

What in the world was she talking about? Let go of the old . . . Did she mean Rachel? But he'd done that. He'd moved on to Anna Mary.

Her voice floated after them. "Be sure you don't misinterpret what I said, or you'll only add to your troubles."

Now she'd thoroughly confused him. Not for the first time. With the weighty way she pronounced her messages, they came across as mini-sermons. Wisdom shone through each piece of advice. But did he have the knowledge to understand and apply it?

He and Rachel walked in silence as he pondered Mrs. Vandenberg's words. Then he laughed uneasily. "She sure makes you think, doesn't she?"

"That's for sure." Rachel glanced sideways at him. "I know I'm too proud to accept help. But it hurts to have people do things for you when you can't return the favor."

"But you do," Josh said, eager to make her see it through his eyes. "Mrs. Vandenberg's right. Every time you smile, you pay them back." Josh would sacrifice anything to have her sweet smile directed his way.

"Hello, Josh," someone called, and then added in a scathing tone, "and Rachel."

His breakfast curdled in his stomach. Cathy Zehr. The *g'may*'s most notorious gossip. And Anna Mary's next-door neighbor.

"What are *you* doing here?" Cathy ignored Rachel and directed her question to Josh.

"I came to see Anna Mary."

Cathy's eyebrows rose. "Really?" She glanced pointedly at Rachel.

To his surprise, Rachel spoke up in a kind tone. "Mrs. Vandenberg worried I might drop the quillows, so she told Josh to carry them. It wasn't necessary, but Josh did it because he's always so helpful to everyone."

While Cathy's mouth opened and shut as if searching for the best putdown, Rachel sailed past her. "If you'll excuse us, I don't want to keep Josh from seeing Anna Mary."

Rachel tilted her head toward Suzanne Schrock's craft stand, filled with faceless dolls, grapevine wreaths, wooden toys, baskets, and birdhouses, as well as a gorgeous array of quilts. Quilts Rachel must have made.

"Josh, if you could just hand Suzanne those pillows, I know you can't wait to see Anna Mary. I'm sorry Mrs. Vandenberg pushed you into carrying them," Rachel announced in a voice that carried to where Cathy stood staring after them.

"*Danke*," she added in a whisper that set his pulse on fire.

He couldn't help admiring Rachel's poise. The way she took control and didn't let Cathy's nastiness affect her reminded him of the self-confident little girl she'd been when they'd first met. She never let anyone get the best of her, but she did it with a sweetness that left people speechless.

That was one of the many reasons he'd fallen in love with her.

He cut off that train of thought. He'd been much younger then. What had Mrs. Vandenberg said about moving on? Rather than letting past emotions entangle the present, he needed to stay focused on Anna Mary. And his future.

CHAPTER 8

As soon as Josh arrived at the construction site, his brother Adam yelled down from the roof, "It's about time."

It figured Adam would call attention to Josh's lateness. All his brothers jabbed him, but Adam tormented Josh the most. They'd grown out of the punching and pummeling. Now they used their mouths as weapons.

Daed's tightlipped scowl revealed his displeasure. "I hope you and your girl said whatever you needed to say, because there's no time for a noon meal today. Maybe not even enough time for a supper break."

"Yeah," Adam spat out. "We had to do extra to make up for your courting."

"Sorry, Daed. I'm not going back to the market today." Maybe not ever. Once he figured out what to say to Anna Mary, he'd go to her house.

Josh strapped his tool belt around his waist and picked up a load of shingles.

"Stop standing around, Josh," Lloyd called down. "We're sweating up here and could use more help."

Daed shot a warning glance at Adam and Lloyd. "Leave

your brother alone. You all went courting when you were *youngies*."

Despite being a married man with two children, Adam shot Josh an envious glance. He opened his mouth to make another crack, but then pinched his lips into a line as Josh climbed the ladder.

Adam must know if he contradicted Daed's comment about courting, everyone would taunt him, because he'd been the worst abuser of Daed's patience back then. He'd stroll in late and leave early almost every day. Sometimes, he'd even slip away from sites after Daed had forbidden him to go.

Josh hustled to make up the time he'd lost. But he had to endure Adam's snide comments.

"Bet you had to beg for forgiveness. A rumor's flying around you fought with Anna Mary and then abandoned her at the volleyball field. Real nice, *bruder*."

Josh ground his teeth together and stayed silent. No point in arguing. Adam would only rub it in more.

"Even worse, she caught you with Rachel Glick twice." Lloyd shook his head. "Poor Anna Mary."

Did the whole community know? How embarrassing for Anna Mary! Josh had humiliated her. And he'd damaged Rachel's reputation, too, judging by Cathy Zehr's reaction.

He had to find a way to make it up to Anna Mary. He'd intended to do that today. Instead, she'd been absorbed in staring at Abe, and Josh had added to the gossip by helping Rachel.

And now, with Mrs. Vandenberg's purchase of shingles, she'd expect Josh to repair Rachel's roof, which meant spending even more time with Rachel. Why did that make his heart pump harder?

* * *

Suzanne's quizzical glance when Josh handed her the pillows discomfited Rachel. She'd explained the situation to Cathy, but repeating the excuse to Suzanne without being asked might make Rachel sound defensive. And guilty.

Keeping her expression neutral, Rachel complimented Suzanne's most recent crafts and asked, "Did anything sell?"

Suzanne didn't answer. She stared after Josh's retreating back. "Isn't he dating Anna Mary Zook?"

"*Jah*, he came to the market to see her."

"Then why was he carrying your pillows?"

Gut. That gave Rachel the opportunity to explain. "We ran into Mrs. Vandenberg at the side doors, and she told Josh to carry the quillows so they wouldn't fall off my stack."

"Mrs. Vandenberg? Hmm . . ." Suzanne gazed off into the distance, a smile playing around her lips. "She loves to matchmake. In fact, she's matched quite a few couples here."

Rachel nodded. "I've heard that." Maybe Mrs. Vandenberg would use her skills to help Josh and Anna Mary. They might need someone to intervene after the rumors about Josh and Rachel being seen together. And if Abe was also interested in Josh's girlfriend.

Suzanne laughed. "Anna Mary had better watch out if Mrs. Vandenberg plans to match you and Josh."

Me and Josh? Rachel tamped down the excitement that seized her. "Don't be silly. Josh wouldn't date me." *Would he?*

"That almost sounds like you'd be interested." Suzanne studied her.

Tipping the quilt from her arms onto a pile of embroidered dish towels, Rachel avoided Suzanne's eyes. "Josh is courting Anna Mary." Rachel made her words firm and final.

"Guess we'll see what Mrs. V has in mind," Suzanne teased.

Rachel pinned Suzanne with a serious look. "Please don't say that to anyone. Anna Mary's already upset with me. I don't want her to think I'm going after her boyfriend."

"I understand. You can't help being the prettiest girl in the *g'may*."

"What? That's not true." Why would Suzanne say such a thing?

"Don't tell me you've never looked in a mirror."

Not often. Rachel had no desire to focus on her appearance.

"I can see you haven't. Why do you think the boys follow you around?"

That was a question Rachel wished someone would answer. She'd love to have a solution for that problem.

A trio of *Englisch* women stepped up to Suzanne's table and fingered the quilt Rachel had just laid down.

"How much is this?" one asked.

Suzanne named a price that made Rachel gasp. None of the women did, though.

"I see you don't take credit cards. If I give you a down payment, would you hold the quilt until Saturday?"

"Gladly." Suzanne handed the lady a notebook. "If you put your name, address, and phone number in there, I'll prepare a receipt."

The woman reached into her wallet and counted out

five twenties. "Is this enough? I'd like to keep some for the rest of my shopping."

"Yes," her friend said, "some of the Amish stands here still don't take credit. They really should get with the times."

Suzanne acted as if she hadn't heard the comment. She jotted the price paid and amount owed on the receipt and in the notebook the woman handed back.

"Thank you so much." The *Englischer* fingered the quilt again. "You'll keep this in a safe place, won't you? I don't want anything to happen to it."

"I'll box it up. Would you like to meet the quilter? She's right over here." Suzanne waved in Rachel's direction.

Rachel wished she could escape as all three women surrounded her, exclaiming over her talent. Remembering Mrs. Vandenberg's advice, she managed a timid *thank you*.

As soon as the women left, Rachel collected her payment for the items Suzanne had sold last week and hurried from the market. But as she exited through the door Mrs. Vandenberg had blocked earlier, Suzanne's suggestion haunted Rachel.

Had the elderly woman intended to match Josh with someone? *Someone like me?* If she had, she must not realize Josh already had a girlfriend. Despite the impossibility, Rachel wished things were different. She'd so love to have that come true.

Josh planned to talk to Anna Mary after work this week, but his *daed* kept them on Mrs. Vandenberg's job until dark every day. Then it rained on Saturday afternoon, so volleyball got cancelled. He'd have to do it before the singing.

He walked past the kitchen after church a few times, hoping to get Anna Mary's attention. Instead, he homed in on Rachel huddled in the corner of the kitchen, cutting pie. She appeared so sad and burdened, his heart went out to her. Everyone seemed to be giving her a wide berth. Her isolation must be his fault. Were people upset with her because he'd been spending time with her? It had all been innocent. At least on her part.

"Searching for someone?" Caroline's loud, arch question drew everyone's attention to him studying Rachel.

He met a roomful of curious, hostile, and critical glances. "A—Anna Mary," he stuttered.

"You're looking in the wrong direction." Caroline's withering statement added to Josh's embarrassment. She waved to the counter nearest him.

Rather than matching everyone else's disapproval, Anna Mary's eyes held pain and sadness. That cut him more deeply than all the judgment others sent his way. He hadn't intended to put her in this position.

He only wanted to ask if he could stop by earlier this afternoon, but with so many gazes fixed on him, he couldn't make a date. "Could you step out in the hall?"

She focused on the platter she'd partway filled with meats and cheese. "I have to finish this."

Caroline elbowed Anna Mary out of the way. "Go on. He wants to make things right. Give him a chance."

Josh couldn't decide if he appreciated Caroline's suggestion or not. The way she'd said it, she came across as bossing him, insisting he'd better be planning to apologize. He took a deep breath and let go of his resentment at her interference. After all, he did want to ask forgiveness.

Anna Mary stepped outside the door and moved a few paces along the hall. "*Jah?*"

The short, sharp question held a world of hurt. So did the brief nod she gave him when he asked about stopping by her house at two thirty. Then she whirled around and scurried back into the kitchen.

As much as Josh wanted to check on Rachel again, he counted the floor tiles in front of him as he made his way back to the tables where the men were eating to avoid even glancing in her direction.

Rachel's stoic expression and Anna Mary's sorrow at church that morning weighed on Josh as he set out for her house later in the afternoon. He had to make her understand helping Rachel had not changed his relationship with his girlfriend. But had it?

Guilt gnawed at his insides. He had to admit he spent more time thinking about Rachel, worrying about her, dreaming about her. That didn't seem fair to Anna Mary. He needed to get those feelings under control. He hoped this talk would erase them.

But somehow, their discussion didn't make things better. Anna Mary hit him with a barrage of questions right after he walked through the door. She'd not only heard about him leaving Rachel's house on Monday with a big smile on his face, but Cathy also had given her a detailed account of seeing him and Rachel at the farmer's market.

He tried not to sound too defensive. "I went to Rachel's house to repair the barn roof. It had a huge hole that was letting in water."

"And that's why you were smiling afterwards?"

Josh tried hard to remember what had been on his mind

as he drove away from Rachel's. Making things right with Anna Mary had been one. "I'm pretty sure as I headed home, I thought about you. And maybe sugar cookies."

"Sugar cookies?"

He wasn't sure why that had slipped out. "Rachel gave me a bag of cookies to thank me for the repairs. They're my favorites."

Anna Mary pouted. "You never told me that. How did Rachel know?"

Why couldn't he keep his mouth shut? He didn't want to share his special childhood memories with Rachel, but he had to give Anna Mary an answer. He waved a casual hand. "We used to play together back when we were nine. That was before you moved here, I guess."

"I see." But she didn't sound as if she did. "So you were smiling about sugar cookies from Rachel?"

Jah, he was. But it wouldn't be diplomatic to admit it. "I'm happy for sugar cookies from anyone, especially delicious ones from you."

Hands on her hips, Anna Mary narrowed her eyes. "I never made you sugar cookies."

"I, um, only meant I'd be happy to have them if you did." He quickly tacked on, "But all your cookies are delicious. I like every kind."

Anna Mary blinked as if assessing his truthfulness. Then she moved on to her next line of questioning. "And spending time with Rachel at the market?"

Josh had been expecting this. Whatever Cathy saw, she spilled. But she didn't always get it right.

"I ran into Mrs. Vandenberg, and she told me to take those pillows. I couldn't refuse, could I?"

"Mrs. Vandenberg paired you with Rachel?" Anna Mary's voice slid up the register to nearly hysterical.

What had upset her so much? "Paired us? I only walked a short distance to the craft stand."

"You don't understand. Mrs. Vandenberg is a match-maker. Caroline told me every couple she's matched has gotten married."

Josh laughed, which only upset Anna Mary more. "Mrs. Vandenberg wouldn't pair up someone who already has a girlfriend. Besides, she'd have to do a lot more than that to get me together with Rachel."

Anna Mary frowned, and he wished he hadn't added the last sentence. He also pushed aside a niggling thought. Mrs. Vandenberg had asked him to repair Rachel's roof and fix other things around her house. Had that been a matchmaking plan?

"Did you come to the market with Rachel? Or did Mrs. Vandenberg ask you to come there to meet her?"

"*Neh* to both."

"Then why were you at the market?" Anna Mary, a petulant expression on her face, crossed her arms. "You didn't stop by and talk to me."

"I came to see you."

"Why didn't you come up to the counter?"

"You were busy."

"We could have talked for a few minutes between customers."

"You weren't waiting on customers."

She wrinkled her brow. "Huh?"

"Looked like you were pretty busy with that guy from volleyball—Abe."

"Josh, that's not true. And you know it. I didn't even say anything to him."

"Your eyes and smile seemed to be doing the talking."

"I can't believe you said that. I was only trying to thank him for rescuing me after the volleyball game."

"He obviously appreciated the thanks."

"*Ooo*, that's mean. You know I'd never—"

He held up a hand. "Of course not. And neither would I."

That brought her up short. "I guess not," she mumbled, but she didn't sound so sure.

Josh pointed to the clock on her living room wall. "We'd better get going, or we'll be late."

They went out to his buggy together, but their unity had been broken. And rather than mending the cracks, they'd only widened them. If neither of them trusted the other, how could this relationship work?

One other thing bothered Josh. He hadn't shared his plans for the next few weeks. How would Anna Mary react when she discovered he'd be spending all his spare time working at Rachel's house?

If the girls at church had been chilly to Rachel before, now they iced her out completely. Even the few who sometimes gave her polite smiles or nods in passing ignored her.

News had spread fast. Anyone who'd been at the volleyball game a week ago made sure to tell those who hadn't heard that Rachel had been caught in the woods with Josh. Others discussed Anna Mary seeing Josh on Rachel's porch. One girl reported seeing Josh, a huge grin on his face, driving his buggy out of Rachel's driveway on Monday. And Cathy added to the devastating stories with her account of running into Josh carrying Rachel's pillows at the Green Valley Farmer's Market.

Many of them made sure Rachel overheard their pointed

comments after church that morning. She retreated to an isolated corner of the kitchen after church, unwilling to read the condemnation in everyone's eyes. Blinking back tears, she kept her head down while she cut twenty apple snitz pies into even slices.

And Caroline embarrassed her further when Josh came searching for Anna Mary. Caroline's booming voice echoed around the kitchen and hallway, putting Josh on the spot and making it seem as if he'd been focusing on Rachel instead of Anna Mary.

Rachel hadn't lifted or turned her head when Josh appeared in the doorway, but she'd sensed his presence. And she'd sneaked a few peeks from the corner of her eye. Despite that, the whispers about her increased once Anna Mary left the room to talk to Josh. Each criticism stabbed Rachel in her already battered and bleeding heart.

She'd loved Josh from the first day she'd met him, and that love had never died. Over the years, she'd endured the agony of his abandonment after her brother's death and the misery of watching him date Anna Mary. But as much as she longed for him, she'd never interfere with his relationship or his happiness.

If only she could go back and redo all the events of the week, she'd stay away from him, not accept his ride, perhaps even skip the volleyball game. Even thinking about erasing all those experiences sucked the joy from her. She'd enjoyed every minute with Josh, but she shouldn't have. From now on, she'd keep her distance.

But Anna Mary and the others had no way of knowing Rachel had no designs on Josh, so the cruelty continued. By the time Rachel arrived at youth group, as close as possible to the starting time to avoid facing everyone, the girls' coldness had expanded like an arctic blizzard, freezing her out entirely. The boys who gathered around Rachel couldn't block the icy blasts directed her way.

And when Josh and Anna Mary showed up, her eyes sent daggers in Rachel's direction. Anna Mary's lips, pinched into a thin line, struggled to hold back a volcano about to explode. Anna Mary's resentment pained Rachel, but she had no idea how to reassure everyone she posed no threat.

Standing rigid and unsmiling beside Anna Mary, Josh avoided glancing anywhere near Rachel. She, too, averted her gaze, but she sympathized with the distress written in every line of his face.

It had always hurt to see the two of them together, but now that Rachel had spent time around Josh, the ache intensified and left an emptiness inside. A hollowness that no one else could ever fill. Even worse, it pained her to see him so unhappy—all because of her. If she had to sacrifice her own desires, she wanted him to be joyful and cheerful.

To compensate for her guilt and misery, she forced herself to be attentive to the admirers who'd gathered around her. She semi-smiled at the stories of their exploits and fake-laughed at their jokes. By the time she realized her mistake, more boys than usual appeared smitten and stared over their shoulders at her as they filed in for the singing.

After they finished the songs from the second book, chairs scraped back, and people fled for the refreshments, but Rachel remained seated. If she stayed here, she wouldn't have to endure the frosty glares from the girls or the adoring gazes of the hangers-on fluttering around her. Spending time with Josh had pointed up their shallowness. The younger ones showed off, trying to attract her attention with goofy antics. But Rachel ignored them, pretending to study words in the songbooks. She had interest in only one person. And she couldn't even glance his way for fear of stirring up trouble.

"Rachel, do you want me to get you something?" Martin called.

Her "*Neh, danke*," got stuck in her throat, and he didn't hear her.

After filling two plates, he hurried over and handed one to her, then hovered over her. She thanked him with a lackluster smile that triggered his answering beam, one that shone brighter than car headlights on a dark country road.

Someone else carried over a cup of punch. Her eyes, clouded with misty memories from the past, barely distinguished one from the other. Soon, she sat in the midst of an eager group, feeling even more awkward than usual with everyone looming over her.

"My *mamm*'s at your house tonight." Martin's scrawny chest puffed out with pride as the other boys eyed him enviously.

Rachel studied the cookies on her plate. After she chose one, she replied, "I appreciate her staying with Mamm so I could come."

"She's always happy to do that. She said to tell you she'd be glad to watch your *mamm* so you can go to volleyball."

"*Danke*. That's kind of her." Rachel had no intention of asking Martin's *mamm* for that favor. With Rachel's luck, Martin would insist on dropping his *mamm* off and driving Rachel to volleyball.

Sensing her interest waning, Martin announced, "You did a great job at volleyball last week, Rachel." His enthusiasm sounded over the top.

She needed to cool his excessive attention. "I didn't play

as well as Caroline and J—" Rachel snapped her mouth shut. She'd better not praise Josh. "Caroline had so many awesome saves."

"Until she fell in the mud," someone remarked, and everyone tittered.

Caroline must have heard, because she looked over at them. When she caught sight of Rachel in the center of the group, she looked surprised and hurt. Rachel wanted to protest she hadn't been mocking Caroline, but who would believe her?

All Rachel could do was endure the cold shoulders of the girls and the inane chatter of the boys until she could leave. The first minute she could politely escape, she carried some dishes to the kitchen and thanked her hostess. Then she slipped out the side door to avoid getting caught up in the crowds saying goodbye. Grateful to escape to the loneliness of her buggy, she drove the deserted roads home.

CHAPTER 9

Josh dreaded the conversation he had to have on the way home after the singing. If Anna Mary had been upset before, wait until she heard his plans for the coming week. He braced himself for an explosion.

"Anna Mary, we didn't get to finish talking before the singing. I'm sorry my actions upset you."

She sniffled. "It wasn't you so much as it was Rachel. She's such a flirt. Did you see how she kept all those boys waiting on her, bringing her food and everything? Disgusting."

Josh swallowed hard. He viewed things from a totally different perspective. Poor Rachel had appeared desperate to get away. He'd even considered rescuing her himself, but he didn't want to add to the gossip. He debated with himself before asking mildly, "Do you think she really likes all that attention?"

"Of course, she does. If she didn't, she'd tell them to go away."

Neh, she wouldn't. Rachel would never hurt anyone's feelings. But Josh held his tongue. No point in riling Anna Mary by defending Rachel, even if, in his heart, he believed Anna Mary had judged Rachel wrongly.

He took a deep breath and forced himself to plunge ahead with the subject he'd rather avoid. "Speaking of Rachel, I'm scheduled to do repair work on her roof this week. I wanted to let you know so you wouldn't be upset about rumors of me being at her house."

"What?" Anna Mary shifted in her seat to stare at him. "How can you do this to me so soon after all the other things that happened?"

"It's not like I have a choice."

"Ask your *daed* to let you work on a different job. I don't want you at *her* house."

Now came the part Josh worried about most. "Daed didn't book this job. I did." At the fire in her eyes, he hastened to explain. "Not with Rachel. Someone else asked me to do it and is paying for it."

Anna Mary narrowed her eyes. "Just you? Not your family business?"

Josh focused on turning his horse onto the narrow lane that led to her house before answering. "*Jah*, it'll only be me. It's not a big job. Shouldn't take more than a few days."

"You'll be at Rachel's for several *days*?"

The high-pitched ending on Anna Mary's question scraped along his spine. To ease her anxiety, he replied in a matter-of-fact tone, "I'll be on Rachel's *roof* for a few days."

"But you'll have to see her."

"I'll knock on her door the first day to get permission to store the shingles in their barn and find out what times will be best so I don't disturb her *mamm*. After that, I'll be coming and going without being around her."

"Can't you ask the person who's paying you to get someone else to do the job?"

He didn't want to give up this job. "If she gets upset with us, Daed might lose a lot of work. She hires us for many different jobs."

Anna Mary frowned. "She?"

Josh would rather not say who'd requested him for this job, not after Anna Mary's earlier worries. But when she tilted her head, expecting him to answer, he did.

"Mrs. Vandenberg?" Anna Mary screeched. "She had you carry Rachel's pillows? And now she wants you to work at her house?"

Anna Mary's panic almost convinced Josh to give up the job. Maybe one of his brothers could do it.

"What if Mrs. Vandenberg's doing this to match you up with Rachel?"

"She'd be making a big mistake. No matter what she does, I could never get together with Rachel."

"Why not?" Anna Mary eyed him with suspicion.

He couldn't meet her eyes. "Something happened between us years ago. Before you moved here."

"You . . . you . . . ?" she faltered.

Josh read the meaning in her expression. "*Neh.* Absolutely not. Nothing like that." It sickened him that Anna Mary would even think that about him. And even more so about Rachel.

"Oh." A satisfied smile crossed Anna Mary's face. "She flirted with you like she does with all the boys, and then she turned you down?"

He shook his head. "I never joined that group of admirers." Not that he didn't want to. But if Rachel knew the real reason he'd turned away from her, she'd do more than turn him down.

"What happened then?" Anna Mary demanded.

Josh had never told anyone, and to his surprise, he

didn't trust her to keep it private. She'd tell Caroline, and then the whole world would know. Caroline didn't mean to be a gossip, but she bounced around like an untrained puppy, sharing everything she knew just to be friendly.

"It's a long story, and I need to get home soon. Daed wants to start extra early tomorrow because we lost roofing time when it rained Friday and Saturday. We got interior work done on the Myers' house, but . . ."

Anna Mary's eyes glazed over. Sometimes that hurt his feelings, but tonight he was grateful. He'd started rambling to distract her from the truth he never wanted to admit to anyone.

As he turned into her driveway, she wasn't about to let him go so easily. "Just tell me a short version of the story."

"It occurred so long ago. Better just to forget it."

"But I can't forget it if I don't know what it is."

He forced a laugh. "That's true." He waved a hand to quell her protests. "It doesn't matter to *us*."

She studied him with worried eyes. "You won't go in her house?"

"I don't need to go inside for anything."

"You'd better not." Anna Mary hopped out of the buggy and hurried toward her house without even a goodbye wave, making it clear she'd issued her final word on the subject.

Josh sat there staring after her. Why had he accepted this job? He didn't want to hurt Anna Mary or tear apart their relationship. At the same time, he wanted to help Rachel.

Staying out of her house should be easy. He had no reason to spend time with her. Why did that thought leave him feeling adrift in a sea of sadness?

* * *

As Rachel pulled into her driveway after the singing, Martin's mother fluttered around the door, wringing her hands. "Oh, *gut*, you're back. Thank heavens."

Rachel could barely breathe. "Is everything all right?" *Did something happen to Mamm?*

"I don't know." Mabel wrung her hands. "I just don't know." She stood in the doorway, blocking Rachel from entering.

Rachel wanted to push her aside and run to check on Mamm. "Is anything wrong with Mamm?"

"What?" Mabel's owl-like eyes blinked several times, as if Rachel's question made no sense. "Your *mamm*'s just fine."

"She is?" Rachel wished Martin's mother would get to the point. Like Martin, she seemed given to dramatics.

"*Jah*, she slept the whole time I was here."

Rachel hid a smile. When Mamm preferred not to talk to someone, she feigned sleep. But what had gotten Mabel this agitated?

"Did something bad happen?"

Mabel sucked in a breath. "*Jah*, it did, for sure and certain. Your neighbor came over with a message."

While Mabel patted her chest as if staving off a heart attack, Rachel mused over whether it would be faster to run over to their *Englisch* neighbor's house to find out the news than to wait for Mabel to parse it out in tiny pieces.

"Your cousin Cindy is in the hospital for an emergency operation. Appen—something. I forget what it's called."

"Appendectomy?" Rachel suggested.

"That's it." Mabel beamed at Rachel. Then, her face fell

into grave lines again. "Anyway, she wants you to watch her two children."

Rachel would love to help her recently widowed cousin. "But I can't go to Ohio. I have to take care of Mamm." It made no sense for her cousin to ask Rachel to drive to Charm, not when her *g'may* would happily assist her.

"I wondered about that," Mabel said. "She arranged for a driver to bring the children to your house tomorrow. They should be here in the early evening."

"What?" Why didn't she keep them at home? Perhaps Mabel had gotten the message mixed up. Rachel would have to check with her neighbor after Martin's *mamm* left.

Mabel fanned herself. "I can't believe anyone would send their children with an *Englisch* driver all this way. Why not let her church take care of them?"

Rachel had wondered that too. None of this sounded like Cindy, who'd organized her life so well after her husband's death she'd barely needed any assistance from the church. She'd stepped into running the family business, had the baby she'd been expecting without her husband around to assist her, and kept the children with her when she went to work every day.

When Rachel didn't respond to her question, Mabel's hand-flapping increased. "*Ach*, I'm sorry. I'm standing here keeping you from your *mamm*. And you have plenty to do with two little ones arriving tomorrow."

"*Danke* for everything." Rachel reached for the screen door to open it wider, hoping to slip past Mabel.

"Let me just get my knitting." Mabel pivoted and headed to the living room.

The door to Rachel's sewing cupboard stood open, revealing stacks of fabric and unfinished projects.

Red-faced, Mabel closed it. "I couldn't help noticing your lovely quilts."

Evidently, she'd been inspecting more than just the almost-completed quilt in the frame and the partially finished quillow resting on the couch arm.

"*Danke*." Rachel hoped to hurry Mabel away. "I appreciate you staying with Mamm all this time."

"I'm happy to do it. I told Martin to let you know I can come anytime. Did he tell you?"

"*Jah*, he did. That's kind of you." Rachel had no intention of taking her up on the offer. Mabel's rotation once every few months taxed Mamm's patience.

"I'll tell Martin you said hello, shall I?" Her words came out in rapid, nervous bursts. "It'll make his night. He thinks so highly of you. You two would be—"

Mercifully, she stopped before she finished. Though Rachel caught the drift. Mabel thought Rachel and Martin would make a perfect couple. And how could Rachel stop his *mamm* from implying Rachel had sent a special greeting to Martin without being impolite?

Rachel sighed inside. She had too many other things to think about. Cindy's children coming tomorrow meant she couldn't make as many quilts and quillows as usual. Bills would pile up. How would she make enough to catch up?

But she'd love having the children around, even if only for a week or two. Especially since she'd have no chance for children of her own. It worried her that she'd never met Cindy's children, except through Cindy's descriptions in her letters. How would they adjust to being so far from their *mamm*?

Cindy sending the children here concerned Rachel. It seemed so odd and out of character. Ever since her husband died, Cindy's letters had praised the women in her *g'may*. She considered some of them closer than sisters. Why hadn't she asked her sisters or friends for help rather than sending her children to stay with a cousin who was a stranger to them?

CHAPTER 10

Rachel spent much of Monday moving her quilting supplies to higher spaces, baking snacks suitable for young children, grinding homemade baby food, carrying baby furniture down from the attic, and setting up a nursery. In her few minutes of free time, she finished as much of her work as possible. With two small children to care for, she might not have time to quilt during the day.

When a knock sounded on the door in the early evening, Rachel hurried to open it. The *Englisch* driver would be exhausted after long hours in the car with two young children.

"*Kumme in, kumme in,*" she greeted as she swung the door open. Instead, she came face to face with Josh.

His wide eyes showed she'd startled him as much as he'd surprised her.

"I'm sorry," she apologized. "I was expecting someone else."

His face tightened. "I see."

"Not that I'm not happy to see you." Had she given herself away with that lilting, overeager tone?

"I won't keep you," he said stiffly. "I just wanted to let you know I'm dropping off the shingles and other materials from Mrs. Vandenberg's job. Is it all right to store them in the barn?"

"Of course, but you don't have to do this job."

Hurt flashed in his eyes, but he recovered rapidly. "I *want* to do it. Remember what Mrs. Vandenberg said. All I want is a *danke*." The corners of his lips lifted in a teasing smile. "And maybe a few sugar cookies."

Rachel laughed. "Perhaps not tonight, but I will bake some more. I spent most of the day straining applesauce, mashing potatoes, and baking teething biscuits."

Josh quirked his eyebrows, but before he could ask her any questions, an *Englisch* van drew in behind his buggy.

A red-faced, exhausted woman maneuvered herself out of the driver's seat. In the back seat, a three-year-old yowled as he squirmed, trying to free himself from his car seat restraints. That must be Zak. Beside him, in an infant car seat facing backward, a baby squalled.

Rachel rushed to the car. "Let me get them out for you." She unbuckled Zak, gave him a quick hug, and set him on the ground.

As she raced around to the other side to get the baby, Zak wailed, "Want Mamm."

The poor boy. To travel all this way without his mother. Rachel longed to cuddle and comfort him, but first she had to calm the baby.

"Marianna," she cooed, unsnapping the hooks and lifting the baby from the car.

With a few hiccuping sobs, Marianna collapsed like a rag doll against Rachel's shoulder. Rachel rubbed a hand up and down the baby's back to soothe her. Then it dawned on her Zak had stopped crying.

On the other side of the car, Josh held Zak tight. The

small boy had wrapped his arms in a chokehold around Josh's neck, while he whimpered against Josh's chest.

"It's all right, buddy. You're safe," Josh repeated.

Rachel's pulse fluttered. With a child in his arms, Josh's attractiveness jumped sky high. Seeing the man she'd always loved with a baby in his arms was like a dream come true. What a wonderful father he'd be.

Her mind warned her he had other commitments, but Rachel pushed those thoughts away, preferring to immerse herself in the fantasy.

"Are you hungry?" Rachel asked the driver.

"We had a meal about an hour ago, but I'm sure the baby's ready for a diaper change. And Zak here loves to snack."

"Josh?" Rachel gave him a pleading glance. "Could you take him in and get him an oatmeal cookie?"

"Sure. Any chance of a hungry grown-up getting a bite?"

"Help yourself." The cookie jar remained on the high shelf where Mamm kept it when they were children, so Josh should be able to find it. Rachel turned to the driver. "*Danke* for bringing them all this way."

"Happy to help. Cindy and I have been neighbors for six years now, and she helped me out many a time with my ailing dad before he passed. I just hope she'll be all right."

Rachel's brows drew together. "I thought it was her appendix."

"It is, but Cindy's been ailing for a while now. She wasn't doing too well before her husband passed. That reminds me"—the driver reached into her pocket and pulled out a letter—"Cindy asked me to give you this."

"*Danke*." Shifting the baby so she could take the envelope reminded Rachel about paying the driver. "How much is the bill?" she asked as she slipped the message into her pocket.

"Don't worry about that. I've already been paid."

While Rachel unloaded suitcases and baby gear and set it by the front door, the woman unfastened and removed the car seats and set them on the porch. "I'd better get going."

With a grateful wave, Rachel hurried inside. She peeked in the kitchen to see Zak on Josh's lap, munching a cookie. Actually, Josh had broken the cookie into smaller pieces, and for each bite he gave Zak, Josh took one himself.

Rachel giggled. "I see you found the cookie jar all right."

"I have a good memory." His words started out joking, but then he swallowed hard and stared down at the table.

"Me too," she whispered. Embarrassed, she whirled around and took Marianna to the new nursery.

Mamm called out as Rachel mounted the stairs. "Who's here?"

"The children. I'm going to change the baby. Then I'll bring them both in to see you."

"*Neh*, not the children. The man. Is it the driver?"

Ever since Josh had brought her home from volleyball, Mamm had nagged at Rachel to invite him over. For some reason, her mother couldn't get it into her head that Josh had a girlfriend. Mamm still insisted on talking to him. Rachel debated about pretending she hadn't heard the question, but she couldn't be dishonest.

"It's Josh. He came to drop off the shingles for our roof and is giving Zak a cookie."

"Tell him to come in here and see me when he's done."

"I'm not sure he has time. He only came to put the

supplies in the barn. His *mamm* is probably expecting him for supper."

"Ask him, please." Although Mamm tacked a *please* onto the end of her request, it rang with a *you'll-do-what-I-say* authority.

"All right. Let me change Marianna."

"You can bring her in here too."

After Rachel bathed and changed Marianna, she slid her into a tiny nightgown and swaddled her in a light blanket. With a soft sigh, the baby closed her eyes. Rachel should put the sleepy little one in her crib for now, but Mamm had asked to see Marianna—and Josh.

Rachel wanted to sigh along with the baby. She hoped Mamm wouldn't say anything to Josh about restoring their childhood friendship. No matter how many times Rachel had explained things to Mamm, her mother still insisted Rachel should reach out and make things right between them.

The baby's adorable nuzzling noises brought Rachel into the present. It must be time for a bottle. She headed downstairs and entered Mamm's darkened room. Blackout curtains hung at the windows, blocking the sunshine outside. They allowed Mamm to nap during the day.

After propping her mother up, Rachel handed the baby to Mamm. Her face lit up. "*Ach*, Rachel, I can't wait to hold your little ones."

Rachel turned away so Mamm couldn't see how much her words hurt. With no hope of having a husband, Rachel tried not to long for children she'd never have. Unless she agreed to marry someone she didn't love. But would that be fair to her husband?

* * *

Josh regretted making the comment about the past to Rachel. Reminding her of what they'd shared brought up so many feelings he'd been trying to squash. But holding a small boy on his lap and watching Rachel cradling a baby had left Josh awash in nostalgia. All the feelings he'd tamped down over the years flooded over him.

Once, he'd expected Rachel to be his wife. Now, taking care of two young children together, sitting in this familiar kitchen, and eating Rachel's cookies made it hard to think about anything but her, his early teen crush, and their shared dreams of a future together. Once, they'd even talked about what they'd name their babies. They'd hoped to have at least eight children.

He shouldn't be here, but it all felt so right, so perfect. He'd only meant to drop off the shingles, but he couldn't leave Rachel alone to cope with two bawling children. Besides, the small boy had raced over to Josh and hugged his legs. What else could Josh do other than pick up the crying child? And Josh had to keep Zak company until Rachel got the baby ready for bed.

Josh had already become attached to the little one who missed his *mamm.* Maybe the bond between them had strengthened because they were in Rachel's kitchen, which had always been Josh's favorite place in the world, eating her cookies.

He'd never tasted treats as delicious as those she'd baked. One time, he'd told her that, and she'd smiled.

"I have a secret ingredient I put in all my cooking," she'd told him.

When he begged her to share the ingredient, she'd teased for a while, then finally admitted, "My secret ingredient is love. If you put love into everything you make, it always tastes better."

Josh had to agree. The chewy oatmeal cookie dotted with raisins melted in his mouth, and a sweet sense of serenity warmed him all the way through. Rachel must still be using that same recipe.

Zak popped the last bite of cookie in his mouth, murmured in contentment, and rested back against Josh's chest.

"You tired?" Josh asked, and the small boy nodded. "I'm sure Rachel will get you ready for bed soon. Maybe we could help her." Josh set Zak on the floor. "Want to help?"

He held out his hand, and Zak slid his fingers into Josh's palm, warming Josh's heart. He liked that he'd earned the small boy's trust.

From the kitchen, Josh had seen Rachel set suitcases and totes inside the front door. Holding the cookie jar in one hand and Zak in his other arm, Josh hadn't been able to help. Now he could.

They brought in the suitcases with Zak's tiny hand wrapped around the handle of his bag, and Josh assisting. It meant he had to lean to one side so Zak could hold on. They continued this awkward walk down the hall and up the stairs, but Josh wanted Zak to feel like he was handling most of the weight, even if he wasn't.

A low murmur of voices came from the bedroom at the bottom of the stairs as they passed. Rachel must be in there with her *mamm*. Had they just mentioned his name? Although he wanted to stop and listen, he forced himself to keep climbing the stairs.

Upstairs, he and Zak checked the bedrooms. The one

beside Rachel's held a crib, a dresser with a pad on top to serve as a changing table, and a single bed.

"I think this must be your room," he said to Zak. "There's the crib for your sister."

His lip quivering, Zak stared around him. "Where's Mamm's bed?"

"You be staying with Rachel for a little while." Josh had no idea why the children had come here without their mother and wished he could offer more comfort.

For now, all he could do was distract Zak. "Let's set the suitcase down and see if we can find your pajamas."

As if he'd borne a super heavy weight, Zak heaved a huge sigh as they set the bag on the floor beside the bed. Josh set the other suitcases and bags beside it, then rotated the stiffness from his back and shoulders. They'd cramped from hunching over to share the suitcase-holding with Zak.

To keep the little boy occupied, Josh suggested they unpack. He had Zak set his favorite pajamas on the bed and choose a drawer for his clothes. Josh hoped Rachel wouldn't mind. Zak picked the largest bottom drawer and carried the neat stacks of folded clothes to the dresser. Josh helped him arrange them.

They put the baby's clothes in the middle drawer. Rachel had set diapers, creams, wipes, and other baby items in the two top drawers. After they'd dumped the toy bags into a box and a chest on the far side of the room, Zak dragged his suitcase to the closet, and Josh stowed the other luggage with it.

"Now let's bring in the rest of the things on the porch," Josh suggested.

Zak trailed Josh as he placed the car seats on a bench

near the front door. Zak hefted a can of baby formula to carry while Josh carted the rest of the bottles and formula into the kitchen. After setting out a bottle and lifting Zak, so he could set the can of formula on the counter, Josh stored the rest of the baby items in the pantry. Rachel might want to rearrange everything, but at least he'd save her a bit of trouble tonight.

He should be getting home soon. He'd told Mamm he might miss supper because he wasn't sure how late they'd work at the site, and he'd be dropping off the shingles at Rachel's afterwards.

Her eyes had brightened at the news he'd be stopping by here. "Spend as much time as you'd like there. I'll heat up soup when you get home."

Most likely, she'd be delighted he'd stayed this long. Some of her excitement might dim, though, if she discovered Josh had spent most of his time with a three-year-old, while Rachel remained in a different room.

Just then, she entered the kitchen, her face flushed, her *kapp* slightly askew, and several strawberry curls escaping onto her forehead. She cradled the baby in her arms, and Josh couldn't turn away. She looked stunning.

Not only her physical beauty arrested his heartbeat. Her eyes shone and her lips parted in awe as she gazed down at the baby in her arms. The setting sun bathed her in rainbow colors, turning her into an angel.

A holy hush fell over Josh, and he sat as still as if he were in God's presence. He experienced the deep peace and contentment that washed over him when words from a sermon touched his soul. Or when he stood in the woods, the pines whispering in the breeze, their scent spicing the air, and his heart swelled with gratitude to the Creator.

He had no idea how long he sat there mesmerized before Zak broke the silence.

"I'm hungry."

"After all the cookies?" Josh couldn't believe it.

Rachel laughed. "Maybe if someone else hadn't eaten most of them . . ." Then she grew serious. "Marianna's getting fussy. I have to fix her a bottle. Can you wait until I feed her?"

Zak whined, and Josh reached down to scoop up the little boy and set him on a chair at the table. "I can fix him something or make the bottle. Which would help you most?"

He turned to face Rachel, who stood there with a be- mused expression.

"What?" he asked. "You don't trust me to do it? I've taken care of plenty of nieces and nephews." His three older brothers had nine children among them.

"If you could warm some soup? I have spaghetti soup in the pantry."

"I know." Josh had noticed shelves of soups when he'd put away the formula.

Rachel blinked. Then her gaze fell on the formula can. "How did that get in here?"

"Zak and I brought in the things from the living room. Hope that was all right."

"All right?" The appreciation vibrating in her voice as- sured him it was more than all right. "*Danke* so much."

"We also took the suitcases up, and Zak picked out his favorite pajamas."

"You're amazing. I don't know how I'd have done all this without you."

The gratefulness in Rachel's eyes lit Josh's whole body

on fire. For a moment, he couldn't answer. "You would have managed."

"I'm not so sure." She broke their connection and turned toward the counter by the sink, but when she tried to remove the lid of the formula canister, it slid away from her.

Marianna's lusty cry signaled she wouldn't wait patiently for Rachel to feed her.

"Let me get that." Josh hurried over.

Although Rachel scooted to one side, Josh still brushed her arm as he pried off the lid. He stopped for a moment to catch his breath before peeling back the foil. This time, he pulled it off in the opposite direction so he didn't bump her.

Visions of being in the kitchen helping his wife with their child rose, and his words caught in his throat. "Why don't I fix the bottle? You have your hands full." He turned the container so he could read the instructions while Rachel jiggled the baby to quiet her.

Zak's whining grew louder.

"I'll be right there, Zak." Josh rushed through preparing the bottle and handed it to Rachel. Then he opened the refrigerator, took out a slice of cheese, and handed it to Zak. "Why don't you eat that while I heat the soup?"

Zak chomped down on the cheese, and Marianna clamped down on the bottle. Blessed silence reigned—at least for a few minutes.

"I can't thank you enough, Josh." The tense lines around Rachel's eyes dissolved as her face relaxed into a smile. "You'll be a great *daed*."

Her words ignited a storm of emotions swirling inside him. Longings for everything he wished for, wishes that could never come true.

* * *

Rachel turned away to hide her flaming face. She couldn't believe she'd said that aloud. Her desires had gotten the better of her.

Josh hadn't answered, and she prayed he hadn't heard. He rustled through the pantry and came out with one of the jars she'd recently canned. She got out a saucepan and set it on the stove while Josh muscled open the lid. When it popped, he poured it into the pan and flicked on the propane burner.

"Did you have supper?" she asked.

"You don't have to feed me. Mamm promised to have something when I got home."

"May as well eat with Zak. I'm sure he'd be glad for your company." *And so would I.* Rachel stopped herself short. She shouldn't be encouraging Josh to stay.

She handed him a wooden spoon to stir the thick tomatoey sauce. "Oh, I almost forgot. Mamm asked if you'd go back and talk to her."

"Of course. I'll do it as soon as I finish eating unless she wants me right away."

"Knowing Mamm, she'd prefer you have a meal first."

Josh laughed. "She always did like to feed me."

A sharp pang pierced Rachel. *Jah*, Mamm enjoyed having Josh for meals. He gobbled everything on his plate and always asked for seconds. And he complimented everything she and Rachel made.

If only they could go back to those times and move forward from there, staying best friends. Although Rachel yearned for more than just friendship.

She wished she could understand why Josh veered away from her. She'd been too brokenhearted over Tom's death to pursue it. By the time she'd gained some normalcy over her emotions, the rift had widened too far to mend, and Josh was gone for good.

She wanted to ask him about it, but his ties to Anna Mary prevented Rachel from trying to renew her past closeness with Josh. Even just as friends.

CHAPTER 11

The soup nourished Josh's body and soul. Between the love Rachel put into the food and the small boy who needed help to spoon soup into his mouth, Josh's contentment at being in the kitchen grew until he wished he'd never have to leave. Rachel had taken the baby upstairs, and the soft strains of a lullaby drifted downstairs.

He cleaned Zak up as much as possible, considering his tomato-splattered shirt, and pulled a chair over to the sink. The two of them washed and dried the dishes, and Josh mopped up the water Zak sloshed out of the sink. Then they headed for the stairs, Zak in Josh's arms.

As he passed Betty's door, he stopped and tapped lightly.

"Come in, Josh," she called in a cheery voice.

How had she known it was him? He smiled at her. "Have you eaten? I could bring you some spaghetti soup, if you'd like."

"*Danke*, I've already had my supper." She studied him. "It's been a long time since you've come to visit. I've missed you."

A lump rose in Josh's throat. He'd missed her too. And

Rachel. And everything this family and this house meant to him. He wanted to get out those words, but he couldn't.

She smiled as if she understood. "No mistake is too large to fix if you truly want to."

Josh started. Did she know the truth? He wanted to ask her what she meant, but he wasn't sure he wanted to know. He longed to ask Betty if there are ever mistakes too gigantic to forgive, although he already knew the answer. But what if you were too ashamed to confess?

Zak rested his sleepy head on Josh's shoulder. "Rachel said you wanted to talk to me, but maybe I should take this little guy up to bed first."

Betty nodded. "You do that. I've waited for years. I can wait a little longer." As he turned to go, she added, "Holding a little boy suits you, Josh. I told Rachel I couldn't wait to see her with an infant in her arms."

His gut clenched. Seeing Rachel holding Marianna had filled him with a whirlwind of feelings and desires, but the thought of her married to someone else roiled his stomach. He was glad he'd turned his back to go upstairs, or Betty might read the truth in his expression. She'd always been good at that.

Once when he was young, he'd knocked over a vase, and when she asked who did it, he scuffed his toe on the floor and tried to come up with an excuse for the broken pieces on the wooden floorboards. Rachel stood there, silent. She'd never accuse him, but she wouldn't lie.

"Look at me, Josh," Betty said gently.

When he lifted his head, her eyes, soft and caring, but also expecting the truth, met his. He couldn't tell the fib he'd been planning. "I did it," he admitted.

She made him clean it up, then she hugged him. "We

all make mistakes," she'd said, "but it's always best to own up to them."

And he'd never forgotten that lesson. Except one time. And that time had cost him his relationship with Rachel.

Cuddling Marianna close, Rachel rocked back and forth in a rocker her *dawdi* had carved as a wedding gift for her *mammi*. As the baby neared the last of her bottle, her sucking motions slowed, and Rachel sang a soft hymn. Holding such a precious, sweet-smelling bundle in her arms created a deep longing to have children of her own. If only . . .

"Rachel?" Josh whispered. He peeked into the room with Zak in his arms. The small boy held one finger to his lips, and Josh nodded at him. "Good job. We need to be quiet so Marianna stays asleep."

"I didn't hear you coming up the stairs." The intimacy of being in the nursery with children swept over Rachel, hushing her words to match Josh's.

"We tiptoed"—he gave Zak a conspiratorial look— "didn't we?"

A small blond head nodded vigorously, and Rachel smiled at both of them.

"*Danke.* I think Marianna is asleep."

The baby's rosebud lips had parted, and her tiny chest rose and fell with each sigh of breath. Across the room, Zak leaned his head on Josh's shoulder, and his eyes drifted closed. The tenderness in Josh's face as he glanced down at the little boy tugged at Rachel's heartstrings.

She wished she could freeze this moment in time to warm her during the long, lonely days and nights. Nights when she dreamed of Josh's arms around her and jolted awake in a chilly, empty bed. Days while she quilted and daydreamed of a different future. A future encapsulated by this moment.

Josh broke the spell by setting Zak on the bed. Rachel, eager not to let Josh see where her thoughts had floated, stopped rocking and started to rise, but she'd settled too deeply into the worn seat.

"Wait." Josh hurried across the room. "Let me help you." He reached down for the baby.

As he slipped his arms under Marianna, he brushed Rachel's arms, sending shock waves through her. If her fantasy were true and they were married, she'd reach up, wrap her arms around his neck, and draw him toward her. Then their lips would touch . . .

Josh swallowed hard. Had he been as affected by that touch as she had?

Rachel lowered her lashes so he couldn't see the longing in her eyes and soul.

"I—I should go down and see your *mamm*." Cradling the baby, he headed to the crib and lowered her gently to the mattress. Then, without turning around, he rushed out the door as if he couldn't get away fast enough.

Had he sensed her reaction? Rachel had no right to view him like that, not when he had a girlfriend.

Lord, please keep my heart and mind pure and focused on Your love. And give me a generous heart and help me to rejoice over Josh's choice of a wife.

Josh took the stairs two at a time, fleeing from temptation. Helping Rachel with the children had warmed him all the way through, and he'd loved every minute of it. He enjoyed caring for his nieces and nephews, but somehow sharing those duties with Rachel made everything so special, so—

He broke off. Better not to dwell on the yearning she stirred in him to have a family. Because when he imagined it, Anna Mary didn't enter the picture, but Rachel did. A future he could never have.

His heart pounded rapidly—as much from being around Rachel as from his marathon down the stairs—and he stopped outside Betty's door to compose himself. He didn't want her to know how muddled his life had become since he'd spent so much time with Rachel over the past week.

Betty had eagle eyes for liars. And for pretense. She'd see right through his ploy of disinterest in her daughter. Josh couldn't fool Betty for a minute. Maybe it would be better not to try. But where would that leave him?

"Josh?" Betty's voice came through the door faintly. "If you'd rather not come in, it's all right."

Ach, he hadn't intended to hurt her feelings by standing out here. He pushed open the door. "*Neh*, I've been looking forward to talking to you." *Mostly. Except for the topic of Rachel.*

"For someone who's eager to see me, you spent an awful lot of time in the hallway deciding whether or not to come in."

"That's not what I was doing." Although he had been worried about her guessing his mixed-up emotions. "I was just trying to, um, get my thoughts straight."

"Hmm. That sounds like you were making up stories to tell me instead of confessing the truth."

He started to say *neh*, but one glance into her eyes, and he changed his mind. "I guess I was. I have some things I want to keep private. And I know you have a way of pulling information from people." He smiled to soften his words, but she'd know what he meant.

Betty chuckled. "I won't pry, if that's what you're worried about. And you don't have to tell me anything you don't want to."

Josh heaved an audible sigh. A great weight lifted. She'd given him permission to keep his feelings to himself.

"That's a huge amount of stuff you want to keep from me." She motioned to an armchair near her bed. "Have a seat."

He settled close to her and struggled with how to start a conversation when he had so much to hide.

"You don't have to be scared of me passing judgment or passing on your information. I don't have much chance to share gossip."

Josh wished he could pour out his troubles the way he used to. As a boy, he often spilled his secrets to Betty. He told her things he didn't want to admit to his parents. She always talked him through it and helped him figure out the best solutions. His concerns bubbled up and almost spilled over at the caring on her face.

She patted his arm. "You don't have to tell me now. It seems like you're not ready. But if you ever need some advice or just a listening ear, I'm happy to help."

"*Danke*." Would there ever come a day when he'd be open enough to tell her his problems? One huge confession stood in the way of being totally honest and transparent.

"Keep in mind I'm very forgiving. And so is Rachel."

Had she guessed the reason he'd stayed away from them all these years?

"Relax, Josh. I don't plan to question you or put you on the spot. I only wanted to ask you a favor."

"Of course. I'd be glad to do anything for you." After all she'd done for him, it was the least he could do.

"It's a big responsibility, but I don't know anyone I'd trust more than you."

"It doesn't matter how large it is. I'll do it." Maybe, in some small way, it would help to atone for what he'd done.

Exhaling a long, slow breath, Betty leaned back on the pillow and closed her eyes. Tears trickled down her cheeks as she said in a broken voice, "I've waited so long for this day. I kept hoping you'd come back."

Josh's insides twisted. Why hadn't he checked up on her? The answer came loud and clear: guilt. Plus, he hadn't wanted to cause her and Rachel any more grief. "I'm sorry." The words, heartfelt as they were, seemed inadequate. And though he didn't say it, he meant the apology for more than not being here when she'd needed him.

"I know." Betty struggled to a sitting position and fixed damp eyes on him. "Every day, I get weaker and weaker, and Rachel has to take on more and more. She quilts until the wee hours of the morning and then gets up early to take care of me and the house."

Everyone in the *g'may* knew Rachel supported her *mamm* by quilting, but he had no idea she stayed up late to do it. The church should have been helping her. *Neh*, not just the church. He should have done something.

"And now she has two little ones to care for. I don't know how she'll do it all. My daughter's strong, but it's a lot for her to handle. She needs help, Josh, but you know as well as I do, she'll never ask."

He nodded. Rachel would do everything herself.

Betty gave him a pleading look. "You take care of my girl. Please promise me, Josh. I know I can trust you."

More than anything, Josh wanted to assure Betty he'd take care of Rachel the way his heart was begging him to respond. But what could he do to help her? And what would it mean for his relationship with Anna Mary? If he agreed to this, he'd be tying himself to more than fixing Rachel's roof. And he'd be exposing himself to temptation. Not that he'd ever cross the line and do anything he shouldn't, but he already struggled to keep his mind on his girlfriend.

How could he say *neh*? He owed Betty and Rachel a debt he could never repay. After one look at Betty's haggard face, Josh found himself saying, "I'll do what I can," before he could stop himself.

The anxious lines around her eyes smoothed out, and she relaxed back against her pillow. "You've always kept your word, Josh. I know I can depend on you."

But could she?

And speaking of keeping his word, what about Anna Mary? Unfortunately, he'd forgotten all about her ultimatum. He hadn't actually promised her, but he'd left her with the impression he wouldn't go inside Rachel's house when he went to work on the roof.

Josh still couldn't believe what had just happened. He'd gone up to the door to tell Rachel about the shingles and ended up staying for hours. But how could he leave Rachel with two crying children?

No doubt someone from the *g'may* drove by while Josh's buggy was parked in Rachel's drive all this time, which would spark more rumors. He'd have to explain to Anna Mary and hope she'd understand.

But what about the promise he'd made to Betty? This

time he *had* given his word. And he couldn't go back on it. Anna Mary would never accept that.

A loud cry long before dawn startled Rachel from pleasant dreams of Josh. She didn't want to wake. She'd rather nestle down under the covers for a few more minutes. But when she reached for the quilt to cover her chilly arms, she touched a warm body.

Her eyes flew open. She lay on the single bed in a spare bedroom, a small boy curled next to her. The romantic moments with Josh vanished, and her fuzzy brain struggled to make sense of reality.

The shrill wails drew her out of bed. She sleepwalked to the crib and picked up Marianna. A soaking wet diaper greeted Rachel. The baby's bawling lessened by a few decibels as Rachel laid the small girl on the changing table and cleaned her up. Once she was dried and changed, the baby nuzzled to be fed.

Rachel shifted Marianna to one arm, picked up the quilt Zak had kicked to the floor, and tucked it around him. She prayed he'd sleep for a while longer. He'd been up three times during the night, crying for his *mamm*. The final time, Rachel had crawled into bed and held him until he fell into a deep sleep.

Thankfully, his sister's bawling didn't seem to disturb him. She'd woken twice in the night at different times than her brother. Rachel wasn't sure how mothers coped with interrupted sleep and still managed to function during the day.

She stumbled to the kitchen and prepared a bottle with half-open eyes. Then she sank onto the living room sofa and dozed while Marianna drank it. The pitter-patter of little feet woke her.

"Where's Mamm?" The quavering words threatened a new cloudburst of tears.

"Oh, Zak." Rachel held out an arm, welcoming him to cuddle beside her.

He did, but the plaintive note in his voice made her draw him even closer. "I want Mamm. And Josh."

Josh? Zak had gotten that attached in only a few hours? True, Josh had comforted Zak, fed him, helped him unpack, and put him to sleep in his tomato-stained clothes. And Zak was still wearing his dirty clothes. Right after breakfast, she'd see he had a bath and put on a clean outfit.

Inside, Rachel berated herself. What kind of a *mamm* would she make if she let a little one sleep in filthy clothes? And if she napped on the sofa in the morning instead of making breakfast?

She jolted upright. She'd even forgotten about Mamm. What should she do first?

A rumbling noise and stinky smell answered her question. She jumped up from the couch, almost upsetting Zak, who clutched at her skirt to steady himself.

"I'll change Marianna, then we'll have breakfast." She rushed for the stairs, stopping at Mamm's door on the way.

"Mamm," she apologized breathlessly, "breakfast isn't ready yet. I need to take care of the baby and then—"

Her mother held up a hand to stop the rapid-fire flow of words. "*Dochder*, calm down. I can wait."

Mamm's serene acceptance spread a soothing balm over Rachel's frazzled spirit.

"Taking care of children isn't easy. And dealing with two at once when you haven't birthed them and learned their needs and personalities can be overwhelming. Don't worry about me. Focus on them."

"But—"

Mamm raised a hand to interrupt Rachel's protests. "If there's one thing I've learned here in bed, it's patience. Do what needs doing. I'm not going anywhere. I'll still be here when you have time."

Rachel didn't want Mamm to wait, but she had no choice.

"Who's that young man hanging onto your apron?"

Zak peeked out from behind Rachel's skirt.

"*Ach*, I should have introduced him to you yesterday." Rachel couldn't believe she'd forgotten to do that.

"We met last night when he was in Josh's arms." Mamm beckoned to Zak. "Do you remember me?"

He nodded but made no move to approach her.

"Why don't you sit up here with me while Rachel changes your sister and makes breakfast? Have you ever had breakfast in bed?"

Zak's eyes widened. "*Neh*." When she patted the quilt beside her, he tiptoed over, looking both frightened and intrigued.

A lump rose in Rachel's throat as Zak climbed up beside Mamm and she wrapped an arm around him. Most mornings, she was so stiff, she could barely move until Rachel massaged her limbs. Had Zak's presence worked a little miracle?

The warm glow suffusing Rachel was doused when Mamm pointed to the splatters on Zak's shirt.

"Looks like you enjoyed your dinner last night." Mamm smiled.

Rachel's face flooded with heat. "He fell asleep on the

bed right after Josh brought him upstairs last night. I didn't want to wake him up to bathe and change him."

"*Dochder*, letting a child sleep in their clothes at times like this won't hurt them. Love makes up for a multitude of parenting mistakes."

Except Rachel wasn't a parent. Still, she did have love to give.

Leave it to Mamm to point out the most important thing Rachel needed to do. That still didn't lessen her overwhelm, but it did help her let go of some guilt at not getting everything done.

But both the guilt and overwhelm came back full force later that morning. She'd fed everyone, cleaned the kitchen, bathed and dressed Zak, changed Marianna for the third time, massaged Mamm with Zak's tiny hands assisting her, and sank onto the couch to read a picture book to Zak while Marianna finished her midmorning bottle. The quilt frame called to Rachel from across the room. When would she find time to finish that? And Mamm needed her medications and a snack.

Rachel tried to make a mental list so she wouldn't forget anything. One picture book. Next, she'd take care of Mamm. Then lunch. Then more dishes and diapers and bottles and . . . Rachel couldn't see anything but endless chores, with no time to make money.

Nothing could alleviate her worry over the undone quilting. Usually by this time of morning, she'd made good headway on her projects. She shifted on the couch, and Cindy's letter crinkled in her pocket, still unopened. Rachel couldn't believe she hadn't even looked at it yet. Cindy had probably explained her children's schedules and other important details, like how long they'd be staying.

"Can you look at the pictures for a moment, Zak? I

need to read this letter." She slid the thick envelope from her pocket while he paged through the book. As expected, the first two sheets of stationery had plenty of information about the children that Rachel skimmed. Three lines stood out to her:

> *Zak has trouble sleeping at night without his*
> *cuddly giraffe. Be sure it's tucked in next to him.*
> *And if Marianna has some baby food right before*
> *her bedtime bottle, she'll only wake up once.*

Too bad Rachel hadn't read this yesterday. If those tips did the trick, she might cut her night wakeups down to one or two, which would be wonderful.

She slid those pages to the back of the stack and started the letter:

Dearest Rachel,

I have prayed long and hard about what to do, and God keeps bringing my mind back to our wonderful childhood summers together. You were a bright, shining star, full of joy and fun, whenever I visited. You and your brother were so kind and let me tag along with you, even though I was two years younger than you.

I remember your friend Josh too. I always thought the two of you would end up married. You made the perfect couple. I've never seen two friends who were so in tune with each other. You'd do anything for each other. I hope you're still best friends—and much, much more—and planning for a future together.

Rachel's eyes stung as memories flooded back of their past closeness. Lifting her head, she stared off into the distance. If only that were still so. How had things gone so wrong between them?

She bowed her head and continued the letter:

I haven't told anyone this, but I've been ill for quite a while. With Uri's treatments and his death and then waiting for Marianna's arrival, I tried to push aside my own pain. But I'm certain this is more than my appendix. If I don't make it through this operation, I want my precious babies to be in a home where they're loved and cared for.

Rachel blinked back the moisture building behind her eyes. Perhaps Cindy was wrong. An operation could be scary. Maybe fear had gotten the better of her.

I selected you because I know I can trust you with my children's futures. Your mamm is such a wonderful and loving mother, so I'm positive you'll be one too. And if Josh has stayed the same person he was back then, he'll be an example of godly manhood for Zak. Poor Zak took his daed's passing hard and is looking for a man to bond with. I pray it'll be Josh. But even if your hearts have gone in a different direction, I know you'll choose a husband who will follow God's will to lead his family.

The tears Rachel had been holding back rolled down her cheeks. Her whole being overflowed with sorrow—for the children who'd lost their *daed* and might soon be losing their *mamm*, for the lost opportunities with Josh, who'd be a wonderful *daed* for a lonely little boy. Seeing Josh and Zak together last night showed how quickly they'd bonded.

Her vision blurry, Rachel finished the letter, her heart breaking for Cindy.

> *Please don't share this with the rest of the family. Perhaps I'll come through the surgery and recover. Then it'll be our secret. If I don't, I pray God's blessing on you and Josh and my two darling gifts from God. I've enclosed a letter for each of them. You can give these to them when they're old enough to understand. I hugged them tightly before they left and told them how much I love them. I want them to remember me and know I never wanted to leave them, but God has called me home. I hold you all in my heart.*
>
> > *With much love and God's peace,*
> > *Cindy*

"You crying?" Zak reached up and touched the wetness on Rachel's cheeks.

She hugged him tightly. She'd give him all the love she could for as long as she had him.

"Mamm hugs me when she cries," he said.

Rachel imagined Cindy did, especially if she never expected to hold him again.

Zak nestled up to Rachel. "Can we read now?"

"In a minute," she choked out. "Let me go wipe my eyes."

Marianna was sucking hard on the empty bottle. Rachel should have been paying more attention. She lifted the baby to her shoulder and patted her back, while heading into the bathroom for a tissue.

As she walked past the front door, someone knocked. Maybe the mail lady? Some of Mamm's herbal supplements came by mail. Jen wouldn't care if Rachel had been crying.

She opened the door, and Josh stood on the porch. Of all people to see her while she was having a meltdown. Especially one over him. Well, not only him, but of all they'd lost. And all she couldn't give these almost orphaned children.

CHAPTER 12

"Rachel, what's the matter?" Panic edged Josh's question. The only other times he'd seen her cry had been after the funerals. *Ach*, had something happened to her *mamm*? Was that why Betty had asked him to take care of Rachel last night?

"Josh, what are you doing here?" Rachel didn't sound upset about him showing up, only puzzled.

"Didn't you want me to come?" Now it was his turn to be perplexed.

She blinked. "Of course." She pulled open the door, gratitude—or was that joy?—dancing in her eyes.

Zak barreled over from the living room sofa and collided with Josh's legs.

"Whoa, buddy, you'll knock me over." Not that Josh minded. He tousled the little boy's hair and bent down to pick up his enthusiastic greeter.

Zak beamed. Then he pointed at Rachel. "She's crying."

"I see." Josh wanted to comfort her. "Is it your *mamm*?"

"*Ach*, Mamm!" Panic flared in her eyes, and she raced down the hall to her mother's bedroom and flung open the door.

Josh jogged after her. What was going on? He skidded

to a halt outside the room. Betty's startled look slid into one of happiness when she spotted him in the doorway.

"Mamm, I'm so sorry." Rachel hurried to the bedside table. "I forgot all about your medicine."

Betty waved a hand. "Ten minutes late is not a problem."

"But if Josh hadn't mentioned you, I never would have remembered." Rachel appeared guilt-stricken.

"I would have called you." Betty smiled. "I can read the clock as well as you. I could tell you were busy, so I waited."

Josh struggled to figure out what was going on. Betty seemed fine, but Rachel fidgeted, her body like a coiled spring about to snap. Not to mention she'd been crying. And she'd begged him to come to the house, but she hadn't explained why.

While Rachel readied her *mamm*'s medications, Betty examined the two little ones. "Shouldn't they be napping? You always took naps in the morning and afternoon until you were four."

"Naps?" Rachel glanced up, as if her *mamm* had thrown her a lifeline.

"See how sleepy Zak is? And if you didn't keep jostling her, I bet Marianna would already be sound asleep."

Rachel stilled. "I'm messing everything up." She sounded close to tears again.

"*Dochder*, be as patient with yourself as you are with the children. They only arrived yesterday. It's a big adjustment to make. Just remember, they'll only be here a short while, so we can all handle a few schedule changes."

At her mother's words, Rachel bit her lip, and her eyes misted. She mumbled something that sounded like *Maybe not*.

She seemed at her breaking point. Josh needed to do something. He had promised Betty he'd take care of Rachel.

"Why don't I take Zak up to bed?" he offered. "I could take Marianna too."

Rachel tried to balance the baby against her as she opened a pill bottle with both hands. "She hasn't been burped yet."

"I've done that before." Josh set Zak on the floor and clasped his hand. "Let's get your baby sister up to bed."

Before Rachel could protest, Josh slipped the cloth diaper from her shoulder and draped it over his own. He steeled himself to accept the baby from Rachel. Last night, taking Marianna from Rachel's arms had set off a firestorm. Today, under Betty's watchful gaze, he tamped down his fizzing nerves after the brief touch as they transferred the baby.

Lest he give anything away, he turned and propped Marianna against his shoulder. With one hand holding Zak's, he couldn't pat her back, but he'd do that upstairs. While he mounted the stairs, voices floated up to him.

"*Dochder*, he'd make the perfect husband and father. I don't understand why you two can't—"

"*Mamm!*" Rachel's tone, sharp and cutting, stabbed into Josh. "You know he has a girlfriend."

The bedroom door snapped shut. Perhaps Rachel had realized their conversation was carrying. The finality in her words indicated she wanted nothing to do with him. So why had she wanted him to come here?

When they entered the bedroom, Zak made a beeline for the toy chest.

"Not now," Josh said. "Time for a nap."

"I need Giraffey," Zak whined.

Josh hesitated. Did Zak have a toy he took to bed with him? Josh patted and rubbed Marianna's back while Zak dug around in the jumble for a minute or two. He emerged with a scruffy giraffe clutched to his chest.

After tucking Zak and Giraffey under a light blanket, Josh settled in the rocker Rachel had occupied last night. The warmth of her presence enveloped him. He closed his eyes and hummed under his breath as his mind replayed the scene. Soon, his breathing slowed like the baby's. He wished he could stay in this peaceful place.

"Josh?" Rachel's call startled him from his reverie. She stood in the doorway studying him, a teasing smile on her face. "Are you napping too?"

A hot flush rose from his neck to his forehead. "*Neh*, I, um, was just resting my eyes." *And thinking about you.* To cover his embarrassment, he rose and put Marianna in her crib.

"*Danke* for putting them to sleep." Rachel's gaze strayed to Zak, and she sucked in a breath. "How did you know?" she asked, wonder in her words.

"Know what?"

"That Zak needs the giraffe to sleep."

"I didn't. He pulled it out of the toy box himself."

"I wish he'd had it last night. He woke three times."

No wonder she had dark circles under her eyes. Even those didn't mar her beauty. They made her appear fragile and in need of care, raising Josh's protective instincts. "Maybe you should take a nap. I could watch the children while you rest."

"Don't you need to get back to work?"

"Not today. Mrs. Vandenberg made some deal with my *daed* so I can spend the rest of the week over here." He'd seen an exchange of money and hoped the elderly woman wasn't paying for Josh to do something he'd do for free.

"I need to find a way to pay her back."

Josh shook his head at Rachel's stubborn insistence. "Her charity is paying, and she already told you how to pay everyone back."

"That's not enough. And I'm sure Mrs. Vandenberg meant for you to be working on the roof, not babysitting."

"*Neh*, she said you needed me urgently today and that I had to hurry over here to help you."

"What?" Rachel stared at him, dumbfounded. "Why would she tell you that?"

"You didn't ask her to come and get me?" Josh tried to remember Mrs. Vandenberg's exact message. She'd been insistent he should stay all day. When he'd arrived, Rachel had needed a hand.

Her face colored, and she lowered her lashes. "I didn't ask her to send you, but I did need your help. I couldn't have done this"—she waved a hand to the sleeping children—"and cared for *mamm*."

Josh shifted awkwardly. Now he felt like a fool. He'd barged in here assuming she'd begged for his assistance. He should leave, but the tears he'd spotted in Rachel's eyes when he'd arrived made him hesitate.

"Divine intervention," Rachel mused softly. "God sent you right when I needed someone."

"Glad I could help."

"Me too. Would you like something to eat?"

He should refuse, but he understood Rachel wanted to pay him back, so he agreed. Or did he have other unexamined reasons for accepting?

* * *

Rachel couldn't believe it. The Lord had blessed her today. Mrs. Vandenberg claimed to have nudges from God. She'd spoken the truth.

Had He also heard Rachel's wishes that Josh would show up again? Having him here yesterday had been such a relief. She could never have done everything herself. Josh had calmed Zak, and she was grateful.

Fixing him a meal couldn't repay all he'd done, and a smile didn't seem like much reward.

Josh accompanied her downstairs, and Rachel steered him past the living room. In her haste to answer the door earlier, the pages of the letter had drifted to the floor and lay scattered like fallen leaves, some of them trapped under an upturned picture book. An empty baby bottle, a spilled box of crayons, and an unwashed snack plate littered the coffee table. What would Josh think of her slovenly housekeeping?

But no judgment shone in his eyes when he looked at her, only sympathy. "Your *mamm*'s right, it's not easy to have two children arrive for a visit when you're caring for her. And when will you have time to work?" His gaze rested on the quilting frame she'd shoved into the corner of the living room.

"I don't know." She tried not let her concern affect her answer, but he sensed it anyway.

"You need to make money, don't you?"

"*Jah*, but I haven't figured out how and when to do it." Plenty of *mamms* did, which added to her sense of inadequacy.

"Like your *mamm* said, it takes time. The children only arrived yesterday. You can get back to work soon. They won't be here long."

A choked cry escaped her lips.

"What?" His face registered alarm. "What's wrong?"

Her throat too tight to answer his question, she gestured to the pages on the floor. He knelt and gathered them without reading them.

"You got a letter with bad news?" he guessed, and she nodded. "Want to talk about it?"

Instead of answering, she went into the kitchen and pulled out the cast-iron skillet. Slowly, methodically, she layered the condiments for grilled ham and cheese. That used to be Josh's favorite sandwich. She hoped it still was.

Josh said nothing. He sank into a chair at the table and waited. Exactly what he'd done after Daed died. He sat in silence with her, patiently, day after day . . . until she'd been ready to talk. Then he listened with empathy.

Cindy was right. She and Josh had fitted together like hand and glove. They understood each other without speaking. What had caused that final split?

Now she was older and had weathered two deaths and major heartbreak. She didn't need as much time to recover. She fixed Mamm a plate with pickles, chips, and applesauce, then set the condiments on the table.

"I'll be right back." She carried Mamm's meal to her and returned to the kitchen, still debating what to tell Josh.

He'd turned the letter upside down on the table to show he hadn't pried. He didn't need to do that. She trusted him.

Once she'd served them both and they'd said a silent prayer, Josh bit into his sandwich. "Mmm. Delicious. My favorite."

"I know."

His hand stopped partway to his mouth, his eyes questioning if she'd prepared it especially for him. She lowered her gaze before he could discover the answer.

Josh ate without saying anything else until he'd finished

everything on his plate. Rachel had barely finished the first half of hers, because her stomach had tied up in knots. The letter only played a small part in her inability to eat. Being across from Josh brought up so many memories, including the last time they'd shared these sandwiches. Three days before Tom's death.

"Rachel, you don't have to answer if you don't want. You were crying when I came in. What's wrong?"

She debated, because she hadn't even shared it with Mamm. But this Josh, seated across from her, had the same open, caring expression as her childhood friend, her confidant. She nodded to the letter. "You can read it, if you want."

As she took tiny bites and chewed robotically, he slid the pages toward him and turned them over. The sheets with the children's schedules and preferences lay on top. Josh perused them, smiling at certain details.

He tapped a finger on the sentence about the giraffe. "Guess this would have helped you last night, huh?"

"*Jah.* I hope it will work well tonight."

"Me too." He laid those sheets aside and smoothed out Cindy's letter. "This is your cousin that came to visit in the summers. I remember her."

"She hasn't forgotten you either."

"I see that." He tensed, and his jaw tightened.

Had he gotten to the part about them getting married? A guilty look crossed his face. Reading that had probably reminded Josh he was courting Anna Mary. No matter how innocent his visit today, most likely it would be misinterpreted.

She shouldn't have given it to him to read. It would have been better to summarize the contents.

Josh lifted his head. Concern creasing his face, he

asked, "Is Cindy a worrier? She didn't seem like it when she was young, but people change."

"*Neh*, she lost her husband before Marianna was born. She stayed strong in her faith while she nursed her husband and afterwards."

"So there's a good chance you'll be caring for her children?"

"*Jah*." Rachel had been trying not to admit it to herself, but Josh had hit on the truth about Cindy. She wouldn't have asked this unless she'd been certain of her future.

"That's a wonderful gift, but also a heavy burden. I can't think of anyone who'd do a better job of raising Zak and Marianna."

Rachel ducked her head. That compliment coming from Josh meant so much more than he'd ever know. *Ach*, she shouldn't have let *hochmut* turn her head. She should have stopped Josh from reading the part about Cindy expecting him to be a godly example to Zak.

Before she could reach out and snatch it away, Josh swallowed hard and rubbed his forehead, shading his eyes from view. When he spoke, his words came out thick. "I'm honored Cindy wanted me to be an example to Zak, but I'm not worthy of her trust. Besides, I'm—I'm . . ."

He didn't have to say the rest. The fantasies Rachel had created of future possibilities came crashing down. Of course, he couldn't do it. She'd known it all along.

"I—I don't know what to say. I'm happy to help with Zak for now while he adjusts to being here, but—"

"I understand." Her answer came out dull and flat.

"Maybe Cindy will pull through." Josh injected hope into his suggestion. "God can work miracles."

"I've been praying for one." Actually, more than one.

* * *

"I'll pray too." Josh shoved his chair back from the table. "I should go. I, um . . ." No excuse came to mind readily. He couldn't say, *I need to escape before I make a fool of myself by saying things I shouldn't.* "*Danke* for the delicious lunch."

He'd almost made it to the front door when Zak's whimpers floated down the stairs. "Daed, Daed."

Was he talking in his sleep? The plaintive cry wrapped around Josh's heart and squeezed it so tightly, he couldn't breathe. How could he abandon a needy little boy? One who might soon be an orphan.

The next shuddery cry galvanized him.

Zak wailed, "Josh?"

He bounded up the stairs and into the room and swept Zak into his arms. "It's all right. I'm here."

Zak gave him a fierce hug and pressed his head against Josh's chest. "Mamm's all gone. Daed's all gone." He gazed up so trustingly. "You stay."

How could he resist that sweet plea? But what would happen if he didn't?

CHAPTER 13

With Zak nestled in his arms, Josh did what he should have been doing all along. He prayed.

Lord, I want to help this little boy. And Rachel too. But I've asked Anna Mary to court, and I can't go back on my promise. You know the long hours I work, and I have so little time for a relationship with her already. It's not fair to Anna Mary.

Josh broke off his prayer. He'd been unfair to her in other ways. Although he'd never act on his feelings, he'd been unfaithful to Anna Mary in his thoughts every time he found himself drawn to Rachel. He bowed his head and continued:

Forgive me for all my tangled thoughts, and show me how to get myself back on the right path. Please guide me in the right direction and show me how to take care of Zak and ease his sorrow.

"I'm hungry." Zak rubbed one hand over his belly.

Peace descended on Josh's spirit. He'd leave everything up to the Lord and follow wherever He led. Right now, he could do something practical.

He set Zak on the floor and took his hand. "Rachel

makes the best grilled ham and cheese sandwiches. How's
that sound?"

"Yummy." Zak skipped along beside Josh to the
kitchen, where Rachel already had started frying another
sandwich.

While it was browning, she had her hands in the soapy
dishwater, cleaning their dishes, but she dried her hands
on a towel and bent to hug Zak. In the sunlight, her hair
glinted gold, almost matching Zak's. Hers had more of a
reddish glow, but it was close enough that she could be his
mother. Maybe she'd have to be.

Josh's heart ached for both of them and for Cindy. He'd
already prayed earlier, but he sent up a fervent plea:

Please, Lord, show me what to do to help.

As if God had whispered in his ear, an idea popped into
his mind.

A slight charcoal odor wafted into the room. The sandwich was burning. He reached for the spatula as Rachel
rushed for the stove. She collided with his arm and sent the
spatula flying through the air. It splashed into the soapy
water, showering them all with bubbles.

Zak's belly laugh filled the room. Smoke curled from
the sandwich. Rachel sat on the floor, rubbing her head.
Josh snatched the frying pan from the burner and flipped
the charred sandwich onto the small plate waiting on the
counter. Zak clapped.

Josh reached down to help Rachel to her feet. "Sorry
about that."

Her eyes shone with tears, but judging by her chuckle,
they were tears of laughter. "We make quite a team. You
just saved the day. I was picturing the kitchen going up in
flames."

The word *flames* sent a curl of dread spiraling through

his stomach. A terrifying image of fire engulfed him, and he choked on the smoke—both real and imagined.

Rachel glanced at his face, and her giggles died. "You're thinking about Tom, aren't you?" With a small cry of pain, she threw herself at Josh and hugged him. "Sometimes it hurts so much."

Josh could barely nod. His arms curved around her, and he embraced her as fiercely as she'd hugged him. They clung to each other for a long time, locked in past pain. He rested his chin on the top of her head and willed the agony to abate.

Now was the time to confess. To tell her about the guilt that had severed their friendship. But no words came.

A tug on his pants leg brought Josh crashing back to the present. What was he doing? Standing in the kitchen holding Rachel when he had a girlfriend? And going against the *Ordnung*?

He dropped his arms and took a step back, ashamed. "I'm sorry." *For much more than the embrace.*

Rachel gave a shaky laugh and didn't meet his eyes. "I'm the one who's sorry. I shouldn't have done that."

"I'm hungry," Zak whined.

"*Ach*, Zak, I'm so sorry. I'll fix your sandwich." With a little grin, Rachel picked up the sandwich. "*Waste not, want not*, Mamm always says." She took a knife from the drawer and scraped the blackened parts off the bread. Then she cut the sandwich into quarters. "Here you go."

She set the plate on the table, added a dollop of applesauce, a handful of chips, and a pickle. Josh boosted Zak up as he climbed into the chair.

Josh had expected awkwardness after their encounter, but Rachel dispelled his worries by her matter-of-fact manner. He blew out a relieved breath.

His whole body still pulsed with the impression of her soft, warm body pressed against his. Tenderness flooded through him at the way she'd clung to him for comfort. He'd almost fled earlier. Now he definitely needed to get out of here.

Once again, a small voice stopped him.

"Sit next to me?" Zak begged, as if sensing Josh's plan to bolt. The small boy slid a hand into Josh's and tugged him toward the chair.

Josh hesitated, his conscience sounding an alarm. The whole weight of his future could rest on his choice. If he yielded to this plea, he might be entangling his life with this small boy's forever.

Rachel couldn't believe she'd put her arms around Josh. She was so ashamed, she couldn't look at him.

It took every ounce of her strength to act normal, to scrape burned bits off the sandwich, to plop applesauce on Zak's plate, to spear a pickle from the jar. Her hands shook as she maneuvered chips from the bag. But when Josh sat beside Zak and wound an arm around his shoulders, Rachel's feelings for both of them expanded inside her chest until her ribs hurt.

She pivoted on her heel and headed for the refrigerator to get Zak milk. Struggling to hold her hand steady, she managed to fill the cup without spilling. She set it in front of Zak, avoiding Josh. If their eyes connected, would his hold condemnation?

Why had she let her emotions sweep her away? Even if they'd been dating, which they definitely weren't, it would be wrong to hug like that. But she'd been so wrapped up in the past and the sorrow of her brother's passing, she'd reacted as she might when they were young. Except they weren't ten or twelve.

Her actions not only broke *Ordnung* rules, she'd also interfered in Josh's relationship and caused him to stumble. He'd backed away quickly, but not before he'd given her that spontaneous hug. A hug that meant the world to her, even when it shouldn't. Being in his arms was a forbidden dream come true that ended in self-loathing.

Upstairs, Marianna wailed. Grateful for a reason to escape Josh's presence, Rachel hurried upstairs to get the baby. After a quick diaper change, Marianna whimpered to be fed, and Rachel had to reenter the kitchen. She dreaded facing Josh, but he was too busy concentrating on Zak to notice her.

Cindy had written instructions about the baby's noon meal, but Rachel didn't recall them. Giving Josh a wide berth, she circled the table, picked up the letter, and shuffled through the pages. She found the list of Marianna's favorite foods and selected a jar of pears from the pantry. Sitting with her back to Josh, Rachel fed Marianna.

The baby's meal ended with pears smeared in her hair and on her hands and face. Because Rachel had forgotten a bib, Marianna had dribbled pears down the front of her dress. Rachel wiped her own hands and arms before sponging off the baby.

"That's always a messy process," Josh said sympathetically. "The only thing worse is changing diapers."

He seemed to be studying Marianna rather than Rachel, and she relaxed a little. He was acting unfazed about their earlier encounter. Maybe he'd forgotten it already. She wished she could, but she'd never forget her cheek resting against his broad chest and the rapid thumping of his heart. And the moment he encircled her with his arms . . .

* * *

"Rachel, I've been thinking." Josh could barely get the words out. His blood still pounded through his veins from touching her. Even the memory of it heated the back of his neck, and he rubbed it. "At least for this week, I could take Zak outside with me while I work. If you have a playpen or something to put Marianna in, you'd be able to quilt, even when they're not napping."

"I couldn't ask you to do that. It would interfere with your work."

"I'm used to it. My brothers often bring their sons to the site. I enjoy teaching the little ones. It's good for them to learn skills."

Rachel hesitated. "I guess we could try it. It would be *wunderbar* to get some work done."

"What do you say, Zak? Ready to help me fix Rachel's house?"

The small boy exploded with an enthusiastic *jah*.

"Let's wash your dishes and go outside." Josh ignored Rachel's protests that she could do it, and Zak scrubbed his plate and cup. Josh dried and put them away. Then, hand in hand, they went outside.

Might be best not to do the roof today. They could repair the paddock fence. Some of the rails and posts had fallen. Zak padded around after Josh, straining to hold up heavy rails even though Josh bore most of the weight and digging tiny bits of dirt for the new post holes. Josh had to admit he enjoyed working with Zak, even though it slowed him down.

By midafternoon, Zak began yawning, and Josh carried the sleepy boy inside and put him to bed. When he came back down, Rachel was working on the quilt with Marianna tucked in the car seat nearby, holding a rattle and teething ring. Rachel was talking and singing to the baby. Her sweet voice brought back memories of her singing as she did her chores. He'd always loved that about her.

Marianna screwed up her face, as if readying to cry.

"I can take care of her," he offered. "I'll get her bottle and put her in the crib."

A short while later, he jogged down the stairs. "Two sleeping angels."

"Oh, Josh, I don't know how to thank you."

"You don't have to, remember? Besides, you made me a great meal." He waved toward the yard. "Now might be a good time to get some of the roofing done, but will the noise wake them or disturb your *mamm*?"

"We can see about the children, but Mamm said to tell you, she can sleep through any noise."

"If you're sure you don't mind . . ."

"I mind you doing it when I can't pay."

"I meant having me out there pounding on the roof."

Her eyes twinkled. "I know. It won't bother me." She ducked her head. "I'm happy it's getting done, even if I don't like accepting charity."

"Jobs like this are what Mrs. Vandenberg's foundation does. She helps lots of people."

Rachel bent over her sewing. "So I've heard."

"Let me know if it disturbs anyone."

She nodded, but Josh wasn't sure she'd heard. Her needle flashed in and out of the fabric. He marveled at her speed and the beauty of her work. He tried hard not to think of her other kind of beauty—both inner and outer—and how much he enjoyed being around her.

* * *

The banging on the roof didn't wake Zak or Marianna, and Rachel enjoyed the rhythmic hammering. She closed her eyes a moment and, without meaning to, she fell asleep.

Two hours later, she awoke to Marianna's *gretzing*. Rachel jumped up from the couch and hurried to get the baby before she woke Zak. But Zak was already sitting up, rubbing his eyes.

"Josh?" His face screwed up, as if he were ready to cry.

"He's outside fixing the roof. Do you hear that noise? That's Josh."

Zak brightened. "I can help."

Rachel was pretty sure Josh's offer to let Zak assist didn't extend to climbing onto the roof. "We can go out and watch him as soon as I change Marianna."

But Zak didn't wait. While Rachel changed the baby, he charged downstairs and out the back door. At the slam of the screen door, the pounding on the roof stopped.

"Hey, Zak," Josh called.

"I help you." Determination rang in Zak's voice.

"Great. Wait down there until I finish this section right here. Then I have a job you can help with."

The banging on the roof resumed. Rachel changed Marianna into dry clothes and replaced the damp sheet in the crib. She had a lot more laundry to do, and the children had only been here two days. Well, she'd always dreamed of being a *mamm*. This was giving her good practice. And if anything happened to Cindy . . .

Rachel tried not to think about that possibility.

She headed downstairs and peeked in on Mamm, who was still napping despite all the noise. Then she headed for the back door. She'd almost made it when a loud *neh* exploded from the roof.

"*Neh*, Zak. Stay off the ladder. Go back down."

Rachel raced to the door and yanked it open. Marianna, who'd been whining for a bottle, stopped mid-cry. Zak had reached the fourth rung of the ladder. Before Rachel could dash over to grab him, Zak tilted his head to look at Josh.

The little boy lost his grip and tumbled backwards, landing with a thud. He lay on the ground, silent and unmoving.

Shifting the baby to one side, Rachel knelt beside him. His eyes fluttered open, and he wailed.

Josh rushed down the ladder and crouched beside Rachel. "Is he all right? I should have come down to watch him."

"What hurts, Zak?" Rachel couldn't stop her anxiety from spilling into her question.

"My head . . . my back . . . my every . . . thing." His cries increased in volume.

Rachel panicked. She should have been watching him more closely. What if Zak was badly hurt?

Josh longed to pick up the little boy, but if he'd injured his neck or spine, it would be dangerous. He set a hand on Zak's chest to keep him from moving. Before Josh could suggest calling 9-1-1, Zak struggled to a sitting position and rubbed the back of his head.

He was still crying, but Josh breathed a sigh of relief. Zak wouldn't be sitting up if he'd been badly injured.

"I . . . wanted . . . to . . . help," Zak gasped out between sobs.

Josh put an arm around him. "I know, buddy, but I need you to help with jobs on the ground. The roof is too dangerous."

"I'm not scared."

"Of course you aren't. You're very brave, but you need to listen when I say *neh*." As soon as he said that, it hit Josh that he sounded exactly like his *daed*. He seemed to be taking on a father role here, but Zak wasn't his child and never would be. The thought saddened Josh. How had he gotten so attached to this small boy in only two days?

"What else hurts besides your head and back?" Rachel asked.

"Here and here." Zak patted his bottom and his legs.

Rachel's brows drew together. "Can you stand?"

Zak jumped to his feet. "*Jah*."

Josh wanted to calm Rachel. She sounded so worried. "It wasn't a far fall. Zak probably just had the wind knocked out of him."

He turned to Zak. "Come here a minute. Let me check your head." Josh ran his hands over the back of Zak's scalp. "No bumps or bruises. That's a good sign."

The tension in Rachel's face eased. "You think he'll be all right."

"What do you think, Zak? You going to be okay?" When Zak nodded, Josh asked Rachel, "Any more of those oatmeal cookies left?"

She smiled. "I think so. Unless you two ate them all last night."

"Cookies?" Zak swiped away his tears with the back of his hand and dashed to the kitchen door.

"Looks like cookies did the trick."

"I should have been watching him. Suppose he'd gotten higher on the ladder? What if something terrible had happened?"

"Rachel, you can't be everywhere at once, and he seems to be fine. You have nothing to feel guilty about." *Unlike me.*

The screen door banged behind Zak.

"*Ach*, what if he gets in trouble in the kitchen?"

"I'll keep an eye on him." Josh sprinted to the house but called over his shoulder, "Remember, whatever happens is God's will. Mamm always says worrying means you aren't trusting God."

"She's right," Rachel called back.

But she wasn't the only one who had to let go of fears and trust God. Ever since Josh had talked to Rachel in the woods after the volleyball game, his life had taken so many twists and turns, he wasn't sure what direction to head. He needed to find his way. *Neh*, not his way, but God's way.

CHAPTER 14

Rachel had settled Josh and Zak at the kitchen table with cookies and milk, taken a snack to Mamm, given Marianna her bottle, and put together a hamburger and macaroni casserole when someone knocked at the door. She went to answer it.

"Did you want me to put the casserole in the oven?" Josh called as Rachel opened the front door.

Her *jah* withered in her throat as she came face to face with Anna Mary. What was Josh's girlfriend doing here?

Anna Mary blinked rapidly. "Was—was that Josh?"

Rachel's tongue stayed glued to the floor of her mouth. She couldn't lie, but she didn't want to cause trouble.

Josh, holding Zak, stepped out of the kitchen. "Rachel, I put the casserole in. Hope that was—" He stopped dead when he saw who was in the doorway. "A-Anna Mary? What are you doing here?"

"I should be asking you that, don't you think?" she snapped. Thrusting an envelope at Rachel, she said, "Mrs. Vandenberg asked me to drop this off, because she knows I drive past your house to get home. I thought it was an odd request, but now I know why."

Rachel took the letter, clutching it so hard it crumpled.

Anna Mary's eyes brimmed with moisture, adding to Rachel's guilt. No matter what reason Rachel gave for Josh being here, it still looked bad.

"Anna Mary," Josh pleaded as he headed for the door holding Zak. Would telling her about the two children outweigh being discovered at Rachel's house and about to have a meal with her? Josh had no idea, but he had to try.

As he neared the doorway, Anna Mary whirled around and fled.

"Wait," Josh called after her. "I can explain."

Her voice thick with tears, Anna Mary yelled, "You have no excuse." She yanked her horse's reins from around the post and jumped into her buggy. She turned the horse and galloped off.

Josh set Zak down. "I have to go after her, buddy. You be good for Rachel."

"Don't go," Zak wailed.

But Josh had to make things right with Anna Mary—if that was even possible. He jogged around the house to hitch up his horse. He'd pulled his buggy behind here to make it easier to unload his tools, but that only made things worse. Anna Mary would probably accuse him of parking his buggy where it couldn't be seen.

He fumbled with the traps and tracings, his hands clumsy and nervous. Did he have any excuse for spending all this time with Rachel? Even worse, he had no defense for his unfaithful thoughts. Would Anna Mary believe him? Forgive him?

Rachel's *Englisch* neighbor rushed across the lawn,

calling to her, "You have a phone call, Rachel. It's an emergency."

Josh's hands stilled. Rachel might need someone to stay with the children while she took the call. It wouldn't hurt him to stay here a few extra minutes. Maybe it would give Anna Mary time to calm down.

He tied his horse to a fence post and sprinted up the driveway. "I'll take Zak and the baby."

With a grateful smile, Rachel passed him the baby. Zak, who'd been clinging to her skirt, bawling for Josh, dashed toward him.

"I can't pick you up right now," Josh told Zak, but he shifted Marianna to one side and took Zak's hand. "Let's get you something to play with."

If the call turned out to be bad news about Cindy, it might be good to have something to distract Zak. Josh headed for the toy chest in the bedroom. On the way, he peeked into Betty's room. Her face was twisted in pain as she tried to sit up.

"Wait. Let me help you." Josh set Marianna on the bed beside Betty, then gently lifted her and propped pillows behind her back.

"Could you set the baby on my lap?" she begged.

He did as she asked. "Rachel went to answer a phone call," he explained. "I'm going to get some toys for the children to play with. Would you like them to play in here?"

Betty radiated joy. "That would be *wunderbar*. *Danke*, Josh."

"Want to help me pick out toys?" he asked Zak.

"*Jah*." Zak slid his hand in Josh's.

They brought down a rattle and a busy box with things for Marianna to turn and touch. Zak had chosen a wooden

Noah's ark with a bevy of animals. He sat on the rag rug beside Betty's bed, lining up pairs of zebras, elephants, and kangaroos.

"Play with me, Josh?"

Josh should be headed to Anna Mary's, but he'd only be here a short while. He sank to the floor and picked out animal pairs with Zak. They marched the animals up the ramp and into the boat.

Zak sorted the "biting" ones onto the lower deck. "That way they won't hurt the nice ones."

"Makes sense," Josh agreed.

In the living room, the screen door slammed. Rachel must be back.

"We're in your *mamm*'s room," Josh called, starting to get to his feet. He hoped he hadn't dawdled too long and added to Anna Mary's anger.

But when Rachel walked through the bedroom doorway, tears streaming down her cheeks, he couldn't move.

Cindy? he mouthed, and she nodded. Josh wanted to gather her in his arms and comfort her. When she gazed down sadly at the children, Josh wished he had a way to protect them from pain. Marianna was too young to understand, but Zak—

A sharp pain pierced Josh's heart. How would the small boy deal with the loss of his *mamm* so soon after his *daed*'s passing? Josh couldn't leave right now. Zak might need a shoulder to cry on and arms to hold him. Perhaps Rachel would too.

An overwhelming sense of sorrow weighed down Rachel's shoulders as she entered her mother's room. She barely registered the poignant scene of Josh on the floor, playing with Zak, and Marianna cooing in Mamm's lap as she batted at a whirling bird.

Josh took one look at her and guessed the truth right away. The mistiness of her eyes blurred his reaction.

Mamm glanced up from the baby. "Rachel, what's the matter?"

Her voice seemed to come from far away. "Cindy passed during the operation. Earlier this afternoon."

Her *mamm*'s eyes filled with tears. "*Ach*, how sad." She took in the playing children, who didn't seem to comprehend the news. "Who will take care of them now? I'm going to miss them when they go."

Rachel swallowed hard. She hadn't shared Cindy's letter with Mamm. Now she'd have to. Josh's sympathetic expression gave her the strength to get the words out.

"They won't be going anywhere. Cindy sent a letter saying she wanted us to take them in if anything happened to her."

When she said the word *us*, Rachel's gut twisted. Cindy had included Josh in that request. How was she going to do this without his help? And how would she support two more mouths to feed if she couldn't work on her quilts? And she knew nothing about mothering. All she could offer these little ones was lots of love.

Josh seemed to sense her thoughts. "Cindy made a good choice for her children. You'll be a great mother. And your *mamm* will be the perfect *mammi*."

Echoing Rachel's fears, Mamm burst out, "How will you make quilts with children to look after?"

"I don't know. I just don't know."

Josh had offered to help this week, but he couldn't stick around indefinitely until she got the hang of being a mother.

The children napped and played, giving her some time, but they needed attention too. How did mothers do it?

If all her cousins didn't live in Charm, she might have had some practice with their children. And Tom hadn't lived long enough to give Rachel nieces and nephews. She had no experience balancing chores, quilting, and caring for children.

Rachel sniffed the air. Onions? *Ach*, she'd forgotten about the casserole. How long had it been in the oven? She didn't need another meal going up in smoke.

"It's time for supper. Let's go into the kitchen," Josh said to Zak. "I'll bring the meal back for you, Betty."

Rachel might be too overwhelmed to handle everything right now. The least he could do was pitch in for a few minutes.

Zak clung to Josh's hand. "You come too."

"I'll walk you to the kitchen, but then I have to go."

"Nooo." Zak's grip tightened on Josh's hand.

Onions and tomatoes scented the air. Rachel pulled the dish from the oven, and the sauce bubbled up, whetting Josh's appetite. The homey smells drew him into memories of sitting at this table with Rachel, her parents, and Tom. For a while, Josh enjoyed the reverie, but then the painful truth knifed through him, and guilt blotted out the happiness of the past. And with it came the sharp pain of reality.

He'd also spent time with Cindy back then. She'd followed Rachel everywhere, so he'd helped keep an eye on her. Josh still couldn't believe Cindy was gone. Two years younger than them, she was much too young to pass.

Zak's small hand kept Josh grounded and pulled him back to the present. Zak was the one who needed attention. He'd just lost his *mamm*.

Josh hadn't paid attention, and Rachel had filled a plate for him.

"I hadn't planned to stay." But he couldn't bring himself to push away the food.

"I understand."

Rachel's voice, heavy with grief, kept him in place. She needed someone to be with her, to listen if she needed to talk. And she might want support when she told Zak. The little boy hadn't seemed to connect their talk about Cindy to his *mamm*.

Josh had to stay for that talk. Surely, Anna Mary would understand his reason for taking so long to make things right.

"I'll stay," he said.

Rachel looked so relieved Josh was glad he'd decided not to go yet.

"I promised your *mamm* I'd bring her supper," he told Rachel.

She filled a plate, and he carried it back to Betty.

Rachel's *mamm*, her face contorted with grief, thanked him. "You'll try to be here for Rachel while she adjusts to all this, won't you? She and Cindy grew close over the summer weeks when her cousin stayed here."

I did too, Josh wanted to say, but he held his tongue.

"You were such a great comfort to Rachel after my husband died. She's told me many times over the years your friendship and prayers pulled her through."

Josh noticed Betty didn't mention him being there for Rachel after Tom passed. Because Josh hadn't been. He'd disappeared and left her to cope alone. Perhaps God was giving him a chance to make up for the past.

When he returned to the kitchen, he sat across from her. Her damp eyes glimmered with tears, and he wanted to reach out and take her hand, to be there for her the way he hadn't been after her brother's death.

Please, God, give me the words to say to ease her sadness. And Zak's.

As if God had whispered in Josh's ear, the answer came to him. *You don't need to say anything. Just listen.*

That's what Josh had done after her *daed*'s passing. He'd just kept her company and sat patiently waiting, letting her talk whenever she wanted. And he never pushed when she didn't speak. In time, she spilled her feelings and cried often. He'd try to give her the same support now.

He also needed to be here for Zak. After the silent prayer, he mouthed to Rachel, *When will you tell Zak?*

"After dinner," she replied aloud.

"What's after dinner?" Zak wanted to know.

Rachel winced. Then, making her voice cheery, she answered, "Dessert. But it's a surprise." She nibbled her meal between feeding Marianna.

Zak ate every bite and asked for seconds. Then he eagerly awaited his surprise.

Josh had a lump in this throat. He couldn't enjoy Zak's excitement even when Rachel announced they'd be making ice cream.

Zak squealed and jumped up and down.

"We should have given you the cream," Rachel said. "You could have churned it into ice cream already." Her light, teasing words didn't match the sorrow in her eyes, but Zak didn't notice.

He begged to be first to crank the handle. In the end, Josh ended up doing most of the work. They made strawberry, and the delicious icy sweetness melted on Josh's tongue and slid down his tight throat. He closed his eyes and focused on the sensations of the coldness freezing the roof of his mouth before turning soupy. The flecks of strawberry added to his pleasure.

"You look like you're enjoying that."

At Rachel's comment, Josh opened his eyes. "I am. Best ice cream I've ever tasted."

"You said that every time we made ice cream."

"And I meant it. Still do."

That made her smile a little. Not her sunshiny smile that radiated joy. Not her soft, tender smile when she drifted back to the past. But an attempt to lift her lips as she bore her loss.

He loved all her smiles, but this one held a poignancy that made him want to take her in his arms and never let go.

The tender, caring look in Josh's eyes set Rachel on fire. If only . . .

She jerked her gaze away. Soon, she'd have to break the news to Zak. But she wanted to avoid it as long as possible.

"I'll make Marianna a bottle and take her upstairs to bed. Will you stay with Zak until I get back?" Rachel hated to ask him to delay his leaving again, but she hoped Josh would be willing to stay while Zak heard about his *mamm*'s passing.

When she came back down, Josh and Zak had just

finished the dishes. Rachel couldn't get over how kind and thoughtful Josh was. He always had been.

"Giraffey!" Zak yelled when he spied the stuffed animal in Rachel's hand.

She held it out to him, and he raced over to claim it. He hugged it against his heart.

"I thought it might make it easier for him," she whispered to Josh.

"*Gut* idea. Should we go into the living room so we don't wake your *mamm* or Marianna?"

"That makes sense." She led the way and waited until Josh and Zak were seated. She paced the length of the room while they settled into place.

Josh sat on the couch, one arm around Zak. Rachel knelt in front of her soon-to-be son and took his hands. She drew in a shaky breath.

"Zak, I had some bad news on the phone call. Your *mamm* didn't get better after her operation. She went home to Jesus."

His lips quivered. "Like Daed?"

She nodded.

"But I want her. I want Daed." Instead of bawling, like she'd expected, he sniffled and lifted large, frightened eyes to her. "Who's going to take care of me? Who's going to hug me?" He clutched his giraffe to his chest.

"I will. You'll stay here." Rachel struggled to keep it together.

Zak turned to Josh. "Will you take care of me too?"

Although Zak asked it as a question, confidence oozed from it, as if Zak were absolutely certain Josh would agree.

The request took Josh by surprise. He'd only met the small boy yesterday, yet they'd bonded right away.

Could he make this commitment? If he did, he'd need to spend a lot of time here. Josh wavered. He'd already put his relationship with Anna Mary in jeopardy. He couldn't chance adding any more damage to an already shaky situation. But how could he deny Zak's request? Could he say *neh* to a child who'd just lost both parents?

CHAPTER 15

Josh had never forgiven himself for walking away from Rachel when she needed him after her brother's death. He'd suffer the same regrets if he didn't help now.

Taking a deep breath, he made a promise he'd be bound to keep. "I'll take care of you, Zak."

Rachel's eyes brimmed with gratitude. Josh forced himself to glance away before he found himself trapped in their beautiful sea-green depths.

Zak snuggled closer, and Josh enveloped the little boy in a hug. But how would he manage it once the jobs at Rachel's had been completed? He worked long hours, and Anna Mary surely would object to him spending his spare time at Rachel's. Maybe he could take Zak to work sometimes if his nephews would agree to keep an eye on a three-year-old. Josh didn't need any more ladder incidents.

"Time for bed, Zak."

Rachel's soft voice strummed Josh's heart. She'd make such a good mother.

Giraffey dragged on the floor behind Zak as he followed her to the stairs, his shoulders drooping. Josh longed to pick up the little boy and carry him upstairs, but if Zak went willingly with Rachel, Josh could leave.

Before Zak headed up the stairs, he turned. "Josh," Zak said in a panicked voice, "come wif me."

So Josh accompanied them upstairs and helped Zak get ready for bed. Once he'd had his bath, put on pajamas, and said his prayers, he had the breakdown Josh had been expecting earlier. Maybe the news had just sunk in, or perhaps going to bed made him miss the safety and security of his home and parents.

When Zak burst into tears, Josh gathered the little boy into his arms and let him sob. Rachel sank into the rocker and buried her head in her hands, her shoulders shaking.

Zak's great, gulping sobs slowed to grizzling, and then he conked out in the middle of a whine. Josh tucked Zak under the covers with Giraffey and bent to kiss his forehead. When he straightened, Rachel had lifted her head. Her eyes wet, she stared at him with admiration and—

Josh wasn't sure what she meant to convey, but he couldn't, wouldn't let himself get drawn into the message he suspected—or fantasized—she was sending. He needed to get to Anna Mary's.

Avoiding her eyes, he eased himself off Zak's bed. "I need to go."

Anna Mary had left at least two hours ago. Was she steaming as she imagined him staying with Rachel instead of coming after her? Would he be upset if the situation were reversed? Josh couldn't answer that question.

"Josh," Rachel said softly, "you don't have to do this. I don't want to cause trouble for you. I'll figure out a way to calm Zak."

"I don't mind."

"But you have to work. Zak will need to get used to spending time away from you."

"I'm sure he will, but right now, he's been through a

lot. It's only been two days. He's in a brand-new home, and he's lost both his parents. If I can help him through some of that pain, I'll do what I can."

"*Danke.*"

"What about you? You've been through a lot too. Having two children dropped off yesterday who you have to mother, plus losing Cindy."

Rachel drew in a breath and squeezed her eyes shut. "I'll manage. I just wish I could take away Zak's sorrow. Grieving for a parent is hard for children."

"You would know all about that," Josh said gently. "These children are lucky to have you as their *mamm* because you understand their sorrow."

"God uses our pain to help others. I'll never forget the gaping hole Daed's death left inside me. I just worry I can't give Zak the support he needs, the support you gave me."

Josh choked up. *Only the first time. Then I failed you.* He forced words past the huge lump blocking his throat. "You'll do fine."

Rachel appeared doubtful.

"You will," Josh reassured her again. "God will guide your steps. Trust him to lead you."

He should be applying that advice to his own life.

Rachel followed Josh to the door. "I'm so sorry about Anna Mary. I hope she isn't too upset." Rachel regretted causing even more trouble for him.

"Once Anna Mary hears what happened, I'm sure she'll understand." At least he hoped she would.

"I appreciate what you did for Zak. I couldn't have done it without you."

Josh grimaced, as if her praise made him uncomfortable. "I'd better go. See you tomorrow." He hurried out the door.

She leaned her forehead against the door until the clatter of his buggy wheels left her driveway. Then she let tears slip down her face to release the tangled ball of sorrow. She cried for Cindy, for Zak and Marianna, and for herself. For all her losses—Daed, Tom, Cindy. And Josh.

Spending time with Josh caused exquisite pain. When she forgot about his commitment to Anna Mary, she slipped so easily into their past comradery. And most of the time, for her, that bond went much, much deeper than friendship.

Trying to keep her feelings hidden often proved impossible. Had he sensed her yearnings, her desire for closeness and connection?

As Rachel headed to prepare Mamm for bed, she remembered Anna Mary holding out an envelope. Rachel has no idea what she'd done with it. Her neighbor had yelled about the phone call, and Rachel had dropped the letter somewhere to run out the door. She retraced her steps and discovered the thick yellow envelope on the small table in the entryway.

She opened it and pulled out the stationery, sending several hundred-dollar bills fluttering to the floor. As much as she needed money for expenses, her temper rose. She didn't want to be treated as a charity case.

It was all very well for Mrs. Vandenberg to lecture Rachel about accepting gifts graciously with only a simple *danke*. It was another thing to be the recipient of that generosity. It stung her pride. Maybe it was *hochmut*, but it angered Rachel to be thought of as needy. Even if she was.

She gathered the bills and stuffed them back in the envelope. Ten in all. One thousand dollars? Rachel intended

to march into the market on Thursday and return every last
dollar. She almost didn't read the letter. She had no desire
to see how Mrs. Vandenberg tried to rationalize this gift.

But Rachel couldn't return it without at least giving an
excuse for why she was rejecting the money. She pulled
out the letter without dislodging any of the hundreds. It
was tempting to use them to pay bills, but she couldn't
do that.

Mrs. Vandenberg's note was short:

*Rachel, I've long admired your lovely quilts. I'd
like you to make one for a charity auction in six
months. Bidding goes quite high as people are
generous. Quilts usually go for several thousand
dollars. I always give the quilter a percentage of
the sale price. This isn't your full payment yet, but
I wanted you to have it so you can buy supplies.
I'll trust your judgment on the design.*

Thanks ever so much,
Liesl Vandenberg

A quilt? Rachel held her breath. She'd be earning this
money. And she'd make sure to create the most beautiful
quilt Mrs. Vandenberg had ever seen.

Rachel pulled the bills from the envelope, fanned them
out, and counted them one more time. With the money
she'd received from Suzanne, Rachel could pay everything
they owed for this month.

Her mother groaned. Rachel had forgotten Mamm.
Maybe seeing the money would cheer her up.

"I'm sorry I took so long, Mamm." Rachel couldn't
keep her lips from stretching into a broad smile. She still

ached inside over Cindy, but having money for their expenses lightened one of her concerns.

As Rachel helped Mamm get ready for the night, she related the contents of Mrs. Vandenberg's note. "And I have six months to make it. That will give me time to take care of the children."

"That's wonderful." Mamm's wan smile showed she was in more pain than usual, and Cindy's passing had added deeper lines to her face. But her eyes reflected Rachel's relief.

Rachel thanked God for the support He'd given her by bringing Josh into her life right when she and Zak needed him. Now Mrs. Vandenberg had provided an added blessing. But she had one more request:

Dear Lord, thank you for sending Josh and Mrs. Vandenberg to help me, but I have no idea how to be a parent. Please direct my steps and show me how to be a godly mother.

Josh arrived at Anna Mary's house but had to wait until another buggy pulled out of the narrow driveway. He lifted a hand in friendly wave as it passed by him on the road, startling the other driver, who waved but averted his face. Josh did a double take. He checked his rearview mirror after the man passed.

The buggy belonged to Tim. Josh was certain of that. But the driver was much too tall to be Tim. Tall, with dark hair. Had to be Abe. But what would Abe be doing at Anna Mary's house? None of her sisters were old enough to court.

Had Anna Mary hoped to make him jealous? If so, his late arrival may have foiled her plans. He chided himself.

Anna Mary wasn't the type to scheme like that. His own embarrassment at being caught with Rachel made him latch onto farfetched theories.

When Josh knocked, one of Anna Mary's younger sisters answered the door. "Your boyfriend's here, Anna Mary," she shouted.

"I told you he's not—" She stopped abruptly when she caught sight of Josh. Her eyes widened. "I didn't think you were coming."

Instead of apologizing and explaining as he'd intended, a question—more like an accusation—rushed from his mouth. "Is that why Abe came over? You didn't expect me?"

Anna Mary blushed and crossed her arms. Her tone sarcastic, she dug at him. "When you didn't come right away, I figured you'd rather be with Rachel." Her attempted defiance wobbled when she said *rather be with Rachel.* Her wavering voice and her reproachful gaze pierced Josh more than words ever could.

"I'm sorry for being at Rachel's."

"You promised me you'd stay outside."

Josh didn't want to quibble, but he hadn't agreed when Anna Mary issued her ultimatum. "I said I didn't need to go inside for anything."

"Looked like you found plenty of reasons."

"I was inside for one reason, and only one." *Is that the whole truth?*

"*Jah*, to spend time with Rachel, eat with her, and—"

He held up a hand. "I went inside because of the little boy I had in my arms."

"She asked you to help her babysit? I could use your help here if you want to care for children."

"I know." Not that Josh had never lent a hand with Anna Mary's younger sisters. He'd done that quite often, especially during the winter, when construction work slowed down. And several times, he'd come over here to keep an eye on them when Anna Mary worked late. He'd also stepped in several times when her *mamm* . . .

He brought himself up short. No point in making excuses to make himself feel better about hurting Anna Mary.

Josh launched into his explanation. "The little boy, Zak, is Rachel's cousin's son. His *mamm* died today, and his *daed* passed a few months ago. He must miss his *daed*, because he latched onto me and wouldn't let go. I had to bring him into the house—" Josh started to add *yesterday*, but didn't finish, because Anna Mary interrupted.

"And then you just happened to help her fix dinner too? I assume you also stayed to eat it, instead of coming here to spend time with me."

"I didn't plan to."

"Seems like you don't *plan* to do lots of things, but end up doing them anyway."

"Look, Anna Mary, I know it looked bad, but if you'd been there the whole time, you'd have seen nothing to upset you." *Except if you could peek into my mind.*

She looked skeptical, so he added, "Zak stayed outside with me while I worked, and I played with him in Betty's room."

"And you didn't spend any time with Rachel?" she asked sarcastically.

"When Rachel and I were in the same room together, I was holding Zak, and she had the baby." Maybe this wasn't the best time for him to bring up Abe, but he did it anyway. "There was nothing to it, like you seeing Abe, right?"

To his surprise, Anna Mary's cheeks reddened again, and she evaded his eyes. After hesitating a few moments, she said defensively, "He only came to say goodbye. He's headed back to New York State tomorrow."

"And he thought you'd want to know?"

She nibbled at her lip. "*Jah*, I did want to know."

"You did?" Abe had ridden in the buggy to bring her home from the volleyball game and stopped by the market once that Josh knew of. Had she seen Abe more than that?

"He was very nice to me. After the volleyball game, when you drove off without me, Abe understood how upset I was and comforted me. It was his idea to drive me home. I thought that was kind of him."

"And you've seen him other times?"

At first, Josh thought Anna Mary wasn't going to answer. She ducked her head and dropped her voice so low he could barely hear her. "Maybe three times, four if you count tonight."

"How long was he here tonight?"

"About as long as you stayed with Rachel. I was crying when he arrived, and he stayed to listen and offer advice."

Josh couldn't say anything about Abe's visit while he'd been at Rachel's. But Josh had to admit, it made him wonder. Just like Anna Mary wondered about him and Rachel.

"And he helped out twice with Mamm and my sisters."

Josh should have been here for that. "I'm sorry I wasn't around to do it."

Even if he hadn't been at Rachel's, Daed wasn't likely to let him off work during the day. Josh had tried Daed's patience by asking to go to the market that one morning before work. Heaven help him, if he'd asked off for more time than that.

"I know you have to work long hours, Josh. I've tried to be understanding about not having a lot of time with you. But to find out you were spending your free time with Rachel . . ."

"I didn't go to Rachel's to visit. I went to work. Helping the little boy kept me there for longer than I intended, but it couldn't be helped."

"I know. I'm sorry for being so grumpy. It's just that I miss you. And it's hard to give up time with you. It's so sad the little boy lost his parents, and I know you're only trying to help."

"*Danke* for being so understanding. I'm sorry for causing you worry."

Anna Mary nodded. "How long do you plan to work on Rachel's house and spend time with Zak?"

"I'm not sure. A week or two at most." Josh didn't plan to abandon Zak after that, but he'd make plans to take the boy other places instead of spending time at Rachel's house.

Rather than looking at Josh, Anna Mary stared off into the distance. "Maybe we should spend the next few weeks apart, praying about our relationship. Not spending time with each other might help us decide if God means for us to be together."

Josh opened his mouth to protest, but he discovered her idea brought a sense of relief. Not that he intended to change his mind about marrying Anna Mary, but he wouldn't have to feel guilty about how much time he spent at Rachel's. And he had to admit, he hadn't really prayed about their future together. Now would be a good time to do that.

CHAPTER 16

Rachel woke early the next morning and tiptoed downstairs so she wouldn't wake the children. Marianna had gotten up only once during the night. Zak had whimpered often in his sleep, but he never woke or cried out.

Rachel needed to finish the quilt on her frame so she could start Mrs. Vandenberg's. The elderly lady had covered the cost of the household repairs, and she'd sent Josh here when Rachel needed a helping hand. By doing this project, Rachel could repay Mrs. Vandenberg in a small way.

Josh had been a godsend. Rachel had no idea how she would have coped with Zak on her own. She owed Josh and Mrs. Vandenberg both a great debt. Rachel longed to give them both more than a smile and a *danke*. She vowed to donate one quilt a year for the charity auction without taking any money. That way, she could repay Mrs. Vandenberg. Repaying Josh would be harder. Besides baking cookies, what could Rachel do for him?

As she made tiny stitches in the fabric, she prayed God would show her a way to bless Josh as he'd blessed her. She had two quiet hours of prayer and communion with the Lord before the first tiny whine signaled Marianna had awakened. Rachel slid her sewing box onto a high shelf and inserted the needle into the quilt. She hurried upstairs to reach Marianna before she cried and woke her brother.

Rachel changed and fed the baby, cuddled her for a while, and tucked her into the car seat with a rattle. Then, singing and talking to Marianna, she quilted until Zak padded down the steps, rubbing his eyes.

He peered into the kitchen and checked the living room, even looking behind the sofa. "Where's Josh?"

"He's not here yet. I'm sure he'll come soon." At least Rachel hoped he would.

Zak's face crumpled, as if getting ready to bawl, when someone knocked on the front door. His expression transformed into a sunny smile. He raced to the door and tugged at the knob. Rachel arrived before he melted down with frustration.

"Josh," Zak yelled as she opened the door.

But rather than Josh, Mrs. Vandenberg stood on the doorstep. "Good morning, Rachel. I take it Josh hasn't arrived yet?"

"*Neh*, he hasn't."

"I need to ask a favor of him, but I'd like to ask one of you as well."

Rachel realized she'd left Mrs. Vandenberg standing on the porch. "Please come in."

"Thank you, dear. I'll try not to take up too much of your time." She smiled down at Zak. "And who's this fine young man?"

Zak had scrunched up his face to cry, but at her compliment, he stood a little straighter. He tapped a thumb on his puffed-out chest. "I'm Zak."

"I'm Mrs. Vandenberg." She held out a hand to shake. Zak looked enraptured at being treated like an adult.

"Pleased to meet you," she said.

"I am too." Then his face fell. "My *mamm* is gone."

Mrs. Vandenberg's wrinkled face softened into sympathy. "I'm sorry to hear that. It's hard to lose a parent."

His face solemn, Zak nodded. "My *daed* is gone too."

"Oh, my. Who will be taking care of you?"

Zak pointed to Rachel. "And Josh. I miss him." Zak burst into tears. "I miss Mamm and Daed and Josh."

"I'm sure Josh will be here soon. Why don't you have some breakfast while you wait?" Rachel suggested, with an apologetic glance at Mrs. Vandenberg.

"Go ahead and feed him. My questions can wait." She headed for the living room. "Is it all right if I hold this darling baby?"

"Of course." Rachel hurried into the kitchen and measured out oatmeal, Zak clinging to her leg, whining for Josh.

Mrs. Vandenberg soon followed, with Marianna cradled in her arms. Fearful for the baby's safety, Rachel took the elderly woman's arm and steered her to the table and exhaled a relieved sigh when Mrs. Vandenberg settled into the chair.

Rachel helped Zak into his place at the table and turned to Mrs. Vandenberg. "Would you like some oatmeal?"

"That sounds delicious. I had an early breakfast, but after all my errands this morning, I am a tad hungry."

While Rachel stirred the oatmeal, Mrs. Vandenberg plied Rachel with questions. By the time she'd filled the bowls, Mrs. Vandenberg had extracted all the details about Cindy, from the time Josh and Rachel played with her as children to her husband's passing.

Zak's chin wobbled. "My *daed* went to heaven."

"Then he's very happy, isn't he?" Mrs. Vandenberg said. "But it's hard for you because you miss him."

Tears welled in Zak's eyes, and he nodded.

Rachel set a bowl of oatmeal in front of him and added applesauce. She gave Mrs. Vandenberg a bowl. "Would you like applesauce on it? Or would you prefer honey or brown sugar?"

"I've never had applesauce on oatmeal before. I like to try new things. Do you always eat it this way?"

"Most of the time. We put applesauce on a lot of things."

Rachel fixed a small bowl to share with Marianna. "Why don't I take the baby so you can eat?" As soon as Rachel had Marianna on her lap, she bowed her head.

Zak followed suit. And so did Mrs. Vandenberg. It warmed Rachel's heart to see the elderly lady pray.

As she ate, Mrs. Vandenberg kept up her inquisition. "Will you be going out to Charm for the funeral?"

"I don't think so."

"Don't you think the little ones should say goodbye?"

"*Jah*, they should." Rachel ducked her head so Mrs. Vandenberg couldn't see how that pained her. She could use some of the money she'd gotten yesterday to pay for a driver, but then she wouldn't have enough to pay bills and buy quilting supplies. Was she being selfish? Or making sure the little ones would have a roof over their heads?

Mrs. Vandenberg slid some oatmeal in her mouth and savored it. "Mmm, this is tasty." She spooned up another bite but halted with her hand partway to her mouth. "Maybe this will work out perfectly." Without explaining, she ate the spoonful.

Rachel cleaned applesauce dribbles from Marianna's mouth and waited for Mrs. Vandenberg to continue.

"I felt the Lord nudging me to come here today, and I think you'll be the perfect solution. Last December, I went out to Ohio for the Amish Christmas Cookie Tours and met a young couple."

Her eyes twinkled. "Well, they weren't a couple when I met them, but . . ."

But she used her matchmaking skills to bring them together?

"Now they're planning to get married, but they can't afford a house. I intend to take care of that problem."

Mrs. Vandenberg's generosity stunned Rachel. "You're buying them a house?"

"They won't let me do that, but I have a plan for them to earn it." Her lips curved into a self-satisfied smile. "So many of my projects and plans dovetail when I leave them to God. He's amazing, isn't He?"

"*Jah*, He is."

With a vigorous nod, Mrs. Vandenberg waved her spoon in Rachel's direction. "Take you, for example. I'm hoping you'll be an answer to my prayers."

What? How can I be an answer to prayer?

Mrs. Vandenberg tapped her lip with a finger, as if trying to decide something. "What day is the funeral?"

"Friday."

"I planned to leave here on Thursday for Charm and stay until Monday, and I prayed for company during the long trip. Would you and the children be willing to go with me?"

"I couldn't do that."

"Not even to help a lonely old lady?"

Rachel almost laughed out loud. Somehow, she had a feeling Mrs. Vandenberg never lacked for company. Had she made up a trip to Ohio so she could take Rachel to the funeral?

If so, she'd put Rachel in a tough spot. Saying *neh* meant hurting Mrs. Vandenberg's feelings and feeling guilty about making her travel alone. But saying *jah* made Rachel feel obligated to pay Mrs. Vandenberg back.

"You don't have to answer right away." The knowing expression on Mrs. Vandenberg's face made it clear she understood Rachel's dilemma.

Then Rachel realized she had an excuse that wouldn't hurt Mrs. Vandenberg's feelings. "It's so kind of you to offer, but I can't leave Mamm."

Mrs. Vandenberg brightened. "Oh, wonderful! I know an Amish woman who's been looking for work as a home health aide. This would give her a chance to get started and make some money. She's been struggling financially, but she won't accept any help."

"I don't know," Rachel said cautiously. She had no idea how much it cost for services like that.

"My charity will pay her wages. This would be a great solution to my worries about Barbara. Do you think your mother would be willing to have a caregiver for a few days while we're gone?"

Evidently, Mrs. Vandenberg already assumed Rachel would be going. "I can ask her." Knowing Mamm, she'd love having a new person for company. "I'll be taking her some breakfast shortly."

"Why don't I take that precious baby while you fix it? And maybe Zak would like to see the little surprise I have for him in my handbag?"

He looked up eagerly. "*Jah.*"

While Rachel fixed Mamm's breakfast tray and did her mother's morning massage, Mrs. Vandenberg entertained Zak with a small truck that twisted into different shapes.

The whole while Rachel cared for Mamm, she wondered about Mrs. Vandenberg. Did she always carry small toys in her purse, or had she known about Zak and Marianna being here? Mrs. Vandenberg said God gave her nudges. Had He convinced her to bring that little truck?

Mamm studied Rachel. "You're distracted this morning, *dochder*."

Rachel nodded. She pulled her attention from the questions tumbling through her mind long enough to tell Mamm about Mrs. Vandenberg's offer of a trip to Charm.

Then Rachel explained Mrs. Vandenberg also planned to have a woman stay with Mamm. Her mother's eyes filled with tears. "I'm so glad you have a chance to go. I felt so guilty about you having to stay here with me. And it would be lovely to have company. This Mrs. Vandenberg sounds like quite a blessing."

"*Jah*, she most definitely is."

An impish light danced in Mamm's eyes. "Now that I think of it, I have heard some of the church women mention her. Isn't she a matchmaker?"

"*Jah*, that's what Suzanne at the market said."

"Maybe Mrs. Vandenberg has plans to match you up." Mamm dropped her voice to a mumble, but Rachel still made out the words. "I hope she chooses Josh."

The thought made Rachel's spirit sing. Only one problem: his heart was already taken.

Josh had to help Daed with a job in the morning, so he didn't get to Rachel's as early as he'd planned. But in the end, his arrival time worked out well because it coincided with morning naptime. After a brief hug and story, Josh tucked Zak into bed and waited while he fell asleep.

Exhaling a sigh, he dragged his gaze from Rachel, who was humming and rocking Marianna. "I'll get to work now."

If all went well, Josh intended to finish the rest of the shingles before Zak woke. He didn't need the small boy falling from the ladder. Once Zak awoke, he and Josh could do some less hazardous work together.

Rachel chuckled. "We don't need any accidents today."

"That's for sure." But he might have one if he didn't watch where he was going instead of basking in the sunshine of her smile.

"I forgot to tell you," she said, as he started out the door, "Mrs. Vandenberg came by earlier. She left to do a few errands, but she'll be back to talk to you."

Josh inclined his head. "*Danke* for the message." Knowing Mrs. Vandenberg would return made him even more eager to get the roofing completed. He wanted her to know he took his responsibility seriously.

An hour later, Mrs. Vandenberg approached Josh as he climbed down from the roof for another bundle of shingles. "I need to ask a favor."

He brushed off his hands. "Anything."

The lines of concern on her face smoothed out. "I knew I could count on you."

Those words echoed Betty's from yesterday. If people knew what he'd done to Rachel, they might doubt his reliability.

"I need someone to do some repairs to a house I bought recently. I'd like them done this weekend. Friday and Saturday, to be exact."

It would mean missing volleyball, but he could skip the game to help Mrs. Vandenberg. "I'll see if Daed can spare me."

"Oh, I already checked with your father yesterday, and he agreed. The only problem is I'd need you to leave for the site tomorrow and return on Monday."

"It's not around here?" Why hadn't Daed mentioned this to him?

"*Neh*, it will mean some traveling. I've arranged a place for you to stay and a driver to take you."

"If it's all right with Daed, it's fine with me." Maybe that's why Daed had him come over to finish that job this morning.

"Wonderful, wonderful." She inspected the roof. "Looks like you'll soon be done up there. I do hope you're planning to secure that paddock fence." She waved toward the nearby pasture.

"*Jah*, I am, and I'll repair that old well cover and—"

"*Hmm*." She pursed her lips and surveyed the property and buildings. "Do whatever you need to do to get this place in top shape. I want those little children to have a safe and beautiful home. Rachel too. She deserves it."

Josh nodded. "She does." The way she was coping with becoming an instant mother impressed him. And she'd selflessly cared for her own mother over the years. She needed someone to care for her. A part of him longed to take on that duty, but he had no right to even think about it.

He shifted his feet, and heat crept into his face. He hoped Mrs. Vandenberg hadn't read his mind.

But she was gazing off into the distance, a satisfied smile playing on her lips. "*Danke* for agreeing to do this work." She let out a long, contented sigh. "You don't know how happy it makes me. And I appreciate you agreeing to come with me tomorrow. Can we pick you up early? Perhaps around five thirty in the morning?"

"I'll be ready." Movement behind the kitchen window

distracted him. Rachel was bustling around the room, lining up ingredients on the counter. He couldn't help hoping for more cookies. If Mrs. Vandenberg hadn't turned to watch him, he might have spent more time enjoying that view.

"I won't keep you," she said. "You don't have much time before the children wake. I'll see you tomorrow morning."

Josh bid her goodbye and returned to the roof. If he hurried, he might get to spend some time with Rachel before Zak and Marianna got up from their naps.

The pounding on the roof had ceased. Outside, Mrs. Vandenberg gestured and talked to Josh. Although Rachel was curious about what they were discussing, she moved away from the window. She should be quilting, but she wanted to make some cookies to thank Josh, and she planned to bake extra for the trip with Mrs. Vandenberg tomorrow.

Before Rachel put the first batch of cookies in the oven, Mrs. Vandenberg tottered off, and Josh reclimbed the ladder. Thank goodness Zak wasn't out there to follow Josh up those rungs again and take another tumble.

By the time the last batch of cookies went into the oven, Josh had come down from the roof. Rachel angled herself so he was in view as he put his supplies away. She couldn't help admiring his strong, rippling muscles as he hefted the extension ladder and carried it to the barn. When he emerged, whistling, she ducked back from the window so he didn't catch her staring.

Was he coming into the house? Her heart lightened at the thought.

He knocked and stuck his head in the back door. "Zak up?" he whispered.

Rachel's spirits plummeted. So much for him coming to see her. She should have known better. "Not yet. Would you like some cookies?"

He sniffed the air appreciatively. "That's one invitation I'll never turn down."

From anyone? Or only from me? Rachel shook off the question. She shouldn't be wondering such things.

"All right if I wash up here?" He nodded toward the kitchen faucet.

"Of course." She stepped aside so he could reach the sink. The timer dinged, startling her from admiring his broad back and strong hands. Reluctantly, she picked up pot holders and opened the oven door.

"*Mmm*, those smell *gut*."

At Josh's voice so close to her, Rachel almost dropped the tray she was sliding from the oven. *Steady, Rachel.* She sucked in a breath to calm her excited nerves. He'd only moved closer to peer over her shoulder at the cookies.

In this small kitchen, if she stood abruptly, she might bump into him. The idea was tempting, but she forced herself to straighten slowly, and Josh backed up. She hid her disappointment.

"Are those sugar cookies?"

He hadn't moved very far away, and his breath tickled her neck. But he'd fixed his gaze on the cookies rather than her. That was for the best, but a tiny sigh escaped her lips. And she hadn't answered his question.

"*Jah*." She gestured toward the counter, where other batches were cooling or had been tucked into containers. "I also made chocolate chip and peanut butter." His other two favorites. She'd made the sugar cookies last because he loved hot, melty ones best.

"You can help yourself to any of them."

"I'll have one of each, but can I have one of those?" He pointed to the tray in her hand.

She held back a smile, happy she'd been right. "Of course. Why don't you grab a plate, and I'll slide a few on it?"

Rachel loved how at home he appeared in her kitchen. He went right to the cupboard and then held out the plate with the same eagerness he'd had as a young boy. The painful years between them melted away as she transferred three hot, gooey cookies onto his plate. His smile, appreciative and genuine rather than guarded, bathed her in warmth and closeness.

A lump rose in her throat as she returned his smile, and their gazes and hearts connected. The tenderness and caring in his eyes and on his face left her breathless and dizzy.

"Rachel?" Her name flowed from his lips like a plea.

A plea her heart, her whole being, answered eagerly.

And then his eyes shuttered, and he dropped his focus to the plate in his hands.

Bereft, she forced out, "You'd better eat those before they get cold." As cold as his expression had become.

He nodded and sank into the nearest chair. After taking a bite, he chewed with his eyes closed. "Delicious," he pronounced when he finished. But he didn't look up from the table.

She spun around so he couldn't see the moisture stinging her eyes. To hide her disappointment, she packed one more batch of cooled cookies into the tin she'd take tomorrow. Going to the funeral meant she'd avoid him for the next few days. That should give him enough time to complete the repairs, and when she returned, she wouldn't endure the torture of fighting her feelings every time she was near him.

Once he stopped working here, she'd concentrate on the children and hope her loving them would compensate for not having a husband. At least, she'd have children like she'd always dreamed. And perhaps the little ones might ease the sorrow of loving someone who'd never love her.

CHAPTER 17

Josh picked at the cookie on his plate. He couldn't believe he'd responded to Rachel like a schoolboy with a crush. All his old feelings for her had flooded to the surface before he could block them. What was wrong with him? Why couldn't he control these long-ago emotions?

When he sat in this familiar kitchen, past longings swirled through him as he breathed in air scented with vanilla, peanut butter, and melted chocolate. Special memories pushed to the surface, leaving him yearning for the relationship he and Rachel once shared.

He needed to swim to the surface of reality before he drowned. Picking up another bite of still-warm cookie, he forced himself to close his eyes, blot out the image of Rachel boxing up cookies, and savor the taste of the buttery, sugary goodness melting on his tongue. He almost groaned with pleasure.

But when he opened his eyes, Rachel still drew his attention. He needed to get out of this kitchen. He stood abruptly. "Um, why don't I take some cookies to your *mamm*?"

Rachel pivoted to stare at him, surprised and pleased, which only added to his guilt.

"Mamm would love that." Her grateful smile didn't quite erase the sadness in her eyes.

Josh broke their gaze. "You look busy. I can fix it."

Her soft *danke* touched him. He'd obviously hurt her, but she forgave quickly and easily. Why hadn't he trusted her forgiveness years ago?

The answer came in a swift, sharp rebuke. Because he didn't believe he deserved forgiveness.

Tamping down that thought, he rounded the table and removed a plate from the cupboard, careful not to brush against Rachel as he selected two of each flavor. He poured a glass of milk and picked up his plate as well as Betty's.

Juggling everything, he made his way down the hall. He tapped at Betty's door with his foot, then struggled to turn the knob when she called out for him to come in.

"Josh!" Her delighted expression reminded him of Rachel's.

He'd come here to escape his jumbled emotions about Rachel, but he'd come face to face with an older replica. No matter what he did, he couldn't seem to outrun his attraction to her daughter. Not even by dating another woman.

He lifted his lips in a semblance of a smile. "Thought you might like some cookies and company."

Betty set a book on her bedside table. "I'd love both, but especially the company."

"The cookies are better," Josh teased, and she laughed.

After she'd taken a few bites, they talked about the weather, the children, the work he planned to do. Like Rachel, Betty seemed concerned about paying Mrs. Vandenberg back, so Josh didn't mention the extra work she'd asked him to do.

Betty's concerned frown lifted as she confided, "Mrs. Vandenberg asked Rachel to make a quilt for the charity auction and paid a large amount."

Josh admired Mrs. Vandenberg's sneaky ways of getting others to accept her charity. "I'm sure the quilt will be worth much more than she paid. Rachel's quilts are beautiful."

Her *mamm* beamed. "I'm glad you think so."

"I'm not the only one," Josh protested. He didn't want Betty to read anything into his praise of Rachel's handiwork. "Plenty of other people believe that too."

Betty's knowing smile revealed she cared more about Josh's reaction.

Trying to distract her from that thought, Josh added, "Mrs. Vandenberg always chooses the best quilter for the auction." He didn't know that for sure, but with her eye for quality, he assumed she'd select only top-notch crafters. The auction had a reputation for bringing in massive amounts of money for charity.

"*Jah*, many women who stay with me while Rachel's at church have complimented her designs and lovely stitching." Betty tried to appear modest, but pride for her daughter shone through.

Josh didn't blame her. She did have an exceptional daughter. One he'd come back here to escape. Instead, he'd ended up talking about her.

"I should get back to work," he said, standing and reaching for Betty's dishes.

"*Danke* for the cookies and for taking time out of your busy day to cheer up an old woman."

"You're not old," he protested. "And I always enjoy spending time with you." As long as she didn't expose feelings and deeds he wanted to keep hidden. She had ways to make him squirm.

"You have a good heart, Josh," she said as he exited. "Let it lead you in the right direction."

What did she mean by that? Did she think he was doing something wrong?

As always, after he talked to Betty, his conscience bothered him. He had the same reaction to Mrs. Vandenberg's cryptic comments. Was God trying to send him a message through them?

When he reached the kitchen, Rachel was fitting the lid on a cookie tin. Beside her on the counter, several more trays sat cooling. She glanced around the kitchen at the dirty dishes and groaned.

Josh went straight to the sink, turned on the water, squirted in detergent, and put his and Betty's dishes in the suds. "I'll clean up. It's the least I can do after eating those delicious cookies."

"*Neh*, Josh." Rachel appeared distressed. "I made cookies to thank you for your work."

"And I'll wash the dishes to thank you for yours. That seems fair."

Rachel stared at him, confused. "Wait, this isn't right."

He waved her away when she marched toward the sink to take over. "Go do some quilting before the children wake. You don't have much time."

"But—but . . ." She stood near him, blinking. "I wanted to do something for you." She sounded close to tears.

"You are doing something for me." He shot her a cheeky grin. "You're going into the living room to work so you won't see me stealing cookies."

She laughed, and the sound pierced Josh's heart. What he wouldn't give to make her laugh like that every day.

* * *

Rachel shook her head and left the kitchen. Josh had gotten the best of her, the way he often had during their childhood arguments. While she appreciated the chance to do more quilting, somehow, she'd ended up owing him even more.

His voice floated out from the kitchen. "Yum. How can I ever pay you back for all these delicious cookies?"

His tone jabbed her, just the way he'd intended. Rachel had no doubt of that. And he'd made her face a truth. She didn't expect him to repay her for the cookies. She'd done it to make him happy. Trying to pay her back would take away from the gift she'd given him. It almost cheapened it by turning it into a transaction.

Rachel pondered that as her needle wove in and out through the layers of fabric and batting. Would she expect Zak and Marianna to pay her back for taking care of them? Of course not.

And gifts that could never be repaid brought to mind the Savior. He'd given His life as a gift. A gift nobody could ever repay. A gift she had to open her heart and accept. She'd accepted that gift, grateful for His sacrifice. Why was it so hard for her to accept gifts from the people He brought into her life? And maybe doing things for her gave them as much pleasure as she felt when Josh closed his eyes and enjoyed her cookies.

Dear Heavenly Father, danke *for the gift of Your Son. Please show me how to open my heart and graciously accept the gifts and help You send my way.*

Small feet padded downstairs. Zak peeked into the living room, searching for Josh, and Rachel rejoiced he was in the house rather than outside on the ladder.

"Josh is in the kitchen," she told Zak, and he lit up and bounded off.

A short while later, Marianna woke, and Rachel set aside her quilting. Time to be a *mamm*. At that, her spirit bubbled over with happiness, despite her pain at Cindy's passing.

With the baby balanced on one hip, Rachel entered the kitchen to fix a bottle. Zak had dragged a chair to the sink and stood, elbow deep in soap suds, while Josh instructed him. Each time they worked together like that, it floated Rachel off into impossible daydreams.

By the time she had the bottle ready, the last of the dishes had been dried and put away. Josh and Zak put the chair back at the table and shared a cookie.

"Okay if we take a few outside to snack on while we work?" Josh mimicked his boyish begging voice, making Rachel laugh.

Zak mirrored Josh's pleading glance, and Rachel gave in. "Don't eat too many. I'm making macaroni and cheese in an hour or so."

"We'll save room for that, won't we?" Josh raised an eyebrow at Zak, who nodded. "But we'd better hurry and get some work done."

Rachel's eyes misted as Josh headed for the door, one hand on Zak's shoulder. She stood at the window while she fed Marianna her bottle. Outside, Josh lugged several posts and fence rails out to the paddock. Zak's face scrunched up as if he bore most of the weight, even though he only supported the tail end of each board.

The cuteness made her heart ache to give Zak a *daed*. He gazed up at Josh with such hero worship Rachel wished Josh could stay around forever. Not just for Zak.

* * *

Zak helped move wood even though it slowed Josh down, but he'd brought a hammer and some nails to keep the small boy busy while he repaired the fence.

"Here, Zak." Josh demonstrated how to pound nails into scrap wood. He'd started six nails, so all Zak had to do was drive them the rest of the way in. "Keep your fingers away from the nails. Hold the board here and hit the top of each nail like this." Josh demonstrated with the small hammer he'd used when his *daed* taught him.

Excitedly, Zak set to work, giving Josh time to reset a fallen fence post. "Look," Zak called a few minutes later, proudly pointing to bent and twisted nails he'd smashed onto the wood.

"Good first try," Josh encouraged.

He hadn't expected that small project to be finished so quickly. As a boy, he'd been meticulous, tapping each nail straight down. It had taken a while to get them all flush with the surface. Zak hadn't pounded them down into the wood. He'd just crushed them messily.

Sucking back a sigh, Josh set up a dozen nails and showed Zak how to hit them carefully to drive them straight down. Again, Zak made short work of all twelve.

"I'll be right there," Josh promised as he secured a rail in place. He'd planned to let Zak pound a few nails into the fence after he'd gotten the hang of it. But Josh couldn't chance it. Not until Zak understood he had to hit them straight.

A bloodcurdling shriek startled Josh. He dropped his hammer and sprinted over to Zak, who was dancing in a circle, shaking his fingers.

"Let me see." Josh reached for Zak's hand, but the little boy jerked it away and continued screaming and hopping around.

The back door banged open, and Rachel raced out. "What happened?"

"I think Zak hit his fingers, but he won't stand still for me to check."

"Can I help?"

"I'll grab him. Can you look at the wound?"

A determined look settled over Rachel's face. "I'll do my best."

Josh grabbed Zak around the waist and plopped to the ground, holding Zak on his lap.

Rachel bent down and examined Zak's small fingers. "*Ach*, that looks like it hurts." She held up his thumb and forefinger for Josh to see. The tips of both fingers were red and swollen. She straightened. "Let me get some ice."

She returned with ice in a towel and a chocolate chip cookie. After distracting Zak with the cookie, she wrapped the icy towel around his fingers. He squealed but soon returned to chewing.

"I don't like leaving Marianna alone too long." Rachel turned the ice over to Josh and hurried into the house, returning with Marianna in the car seat and two more cookies. She passed one to Josh and ate the other herself.

He didn't tell her he still had the other cookies he'd taken out earlier. He'd save them for later. His lips curved into a smile at the way she'd comforted him with a cookie. She must have realized how guilty he felt about Zak getting hurt.

"I should have paid closer attention." Josh wished he'd done more to ensure Zak's safety. Hugging Zak closer, Josh whispered, "I'm sorry, Zak."

Zak's crying had dissolved into sniffles. He lifted his head to look at Josh. "I did what you did," he said in a bewildered voice.

"You kept your fingers away from the hammer?" Josh regretted saying that. They already had proof Zak hadn't.

To his surprise, Zak's brow furrowed. "But you don't."

Ach, Zak must have been trying to start a new nail. Josh shouldn't have done that where Zak could see him.

"Don't blame yourself," Rachel said softly. "It's not your fault."

She must have read his face. If only he could hear her say that about the pain he'd caused her in the past.

CHAPTER 18

Mrs. Vandenberg's van pulled in before dawn. Josh hurried outside with his duffel bag. He'd already set his tool box and a bucket of supplies on the porch. The tailgate of the van flew up as Josh approached, and he placed his things inside.

Mrs. Vandenberg greeted him with a cheery smile when he got into one of the back seats. She sat up front beside her driver. "All ready to go?"

"*Jah*, I am." This trip came at the perfect time. Getting away from Lancaster might help him sort out his muddled feelings.

The more time he spent away from Anna Mary, the more his spirit lightened. That shouldn't be the case. He still hadn't prayed about the future. Maybe because he suspected deep down that God wanted him to marry Anna Mary. Yet, despite his commitment to her, he kept being drawn to Rachel. Perhaps being away from her for these five days might help him break the pull she had over him.

Josh relaxed back into the seat and closed his eyes. *Lord, please help me to sort out my future. Lead me in the*

*right direction, and take away all thoughts and feelings
that draw me away from Your will.*

"Feel free to sleep a bit. I'm going to rest," Mrs. Vandenberg told him.

Josh closed his eyes and dozed off. He jolted awake when the van bounced down a driveway. What were they doing at Rachel's house?

She stood on the front porch, and his heart leaped at the sight of her, holding Marianna. What a beautiful face to wake up to every morning! Josh reined in his thoughts. He had no right to think of her that way. And even if he and Anna Mary broke up, he'd never be able to date Rachel. Not with the past standing in the way.

Mrs. Vandenberg broke into his thoughts. "God gives us the desires of our hearts."

Josh's face flamed. Surely, she hadn't read his mind, had she? He'd been so preoccupied, he hadn't noticed Rachel struggling to carry the baby seat to the porch while balancing Marianna. He hopped out of the van and hurried over.

"Let me get that." He reached for the seat.

Rachel stared at him. "What are you doing here?"

"I came with Mrs. Vandenberg."

"Oh, she dropped you off."

Huh? Josh's brain, still foggy from sleep, fought to make sense of her remark. But he had to help her with the seat. "Where do you want this?"

"I guess the seat farthest back. Zak would probably prefer the middle seat so he can see out the window."

Josh almost dropped the seat on his toes. "You're going along?"

"With Mrs. Vandenberg? *Jah*, she said she wanted

company. I just hope the children won't disturb her too much. Remember how they cried for the *Englisch* driver?"

He did. But he was trying to figure out this situation. Mrs. Vandenberg had invited both of them on this trip? What in the world was she thinking? And what would everyone in the *g'may* say when they found out? It might totally end things with Anna Mary.

"Josh?" Rachel studied him. "Are you all right? I can take the car seat. I don't want to keep Mrs. Vandenberg waiting."

"Did you know she asked me to come along?"

Rachel looked as stunned as he felt. "What? You're going to Charm too?"

"Is that where we're going?"

"You didn't know?"

"She just said a long trip. And . . ." His voice trailed off. Suddenly, everything became crystal clear. *Matchmaking.*

Mrs. Vandenberg had asked him to carry Rachel's quillows, knowing people would see him and gossip. She'd paid for him to work on Rachel's house and sent him there on Tuesday. Then she'd asked Anna Mary to drop off a letter at Rachel's, knowing he'd be there. Now she'd planned an out-of-state trip. But she'd made one major mistake. She didn't know Josh's guilty secret, and neither did Rachel. Once she did . . .

Rachel's breath caught in her throat when she realized Josh really was coming along to Ohio. After he loaded her luggage, he sat in the middle seat with Zak, so she had a perfect view of his profile when she buckled in the back beside Marianna's car seat. How lucky could she get?

The miles flew by rapidly as Mrs. Vandenberg encouraged Rachel and Josh to tell her about their childhood friendship. Even Zak laughed over the many times they'd gotten in trouble. And he loved hearing about catching tadpoles and crayfish.

"I can take you to do that," Josh promised Zak.

Zak bounced with excitement, straining at the restraints that held him. "When?"

"As soon as we get back. We won't see tadpoles this time of year, but we can find frogs." With a teasing grin, he glanced back at Rachel. "Maybe Rachel would want to come too. Maybe she might even fall in so we can rescue her."

Rachel flushed, picturing Josh wrapping his arms around her and lifting her from the water now, the way he'd done when they were young. She lowered her lashes to cover the feelings flooding through her.

Mrs. Vandenberg turned her head to study them both. "It sounds as if the two of you are perfectly suited as a couple."

Rachel's eyes stung. She'd always thought so. And at one time, Josh had too. But things had changed. And all her romantic daydreams wouldn't rewind time back to their unbreakable childhood bond.

For a few miles, silence reigned as they all considered Mrs. Vandenberg's comment. Then she interrupted their contemplation.

"So, what happened to break you two apart?"

In front of Rachel, Josh's shoulders stiffened, and he busied himself with adjusting Zak's seat belt and pulling toys from the bag Rachel had packed to keep Zak occupied.

Rachel shrugged. She didn't have a real answer to the question. "I guess it happened when my brother passed. I didn't feel like being around people." Though she would have made an exception for Josh. "We just drifted apart after that."

With a pointed look at Josh, Mrs. Vandenberg said, "That's such a shame."

Josh didn't respond. He seemed absorbed in Zak's demonstration of all the ways his tiny truck could turn. Had he missed Mrs. Vandenberg's question, or was he avoiding it?

Rachel wished he'd answer. If she knew what had gone wrong, maybe she could find a way to mend things. Then she shook her head. It was much too late for that.

Mrs. Vandenberg's question pierced the deep, dark place in Josh's soul. A sharp arrow sliced through to the poison he kept pent up, hidden, buried. Corrosive guilt and shame gushed out, gnawing at his insides. He should answer, but his mouth dried out, and his throat pinched shut.

Zak pointed to the bag of toys at Josh's feet. Grateful for the distraction, Josh lifted the tote again and dug through the bag, holding up one toy after another so Zak could choose. In the end, Zak selected another small truck and chattered about how it moved. Josh pretended to be absorbed in that conversation, but he heard nothing except his conscience berating him, warning that he needed to confess.

Except he couldn't do that here and now. Not in front of everyone. But Rachel deserved an explanation. And unless Josh told her the truth, his relationship with Anna Mary couldn't move ahead either.

"It can be hard to face what happened." Mrs. Vandenberg echoed the message of Josh's conscience. "But admitting it can lead to healing."

How did she always know what he was thinking? Only this time, she'd be wrong about the healing. Even if Rachel forgave him, what he needed to tell her would drive a wedge between them.

Mrs. Vandenberg was right. Rachel blamed herself for the gulf that had formed between her and Josh. He'd put up with her moodiness after her father's death. It had taken her more than a year to emerge from her sudden silences, her preference for sitting and staring into the distance rather than playing. He'd stayed beside her all that time, despite longing to join his friends in games or chase after the older boys. Josh had given her constant companionship along with time and space to heal.

After her brother died, she didn't blame Josh for not wanting to repeat another year of sacrifice. They were older, and their early teen activities held so much more excitement and promise. Plus, like her, he was grieving.

When they were ten or eleven, Josh had confided that Tom felt more like his older brother than his own three brothers. Rachel could understand that. When Josh's brothers teased and bullied him, Tom stood up for Josh and included him in all the plans. Josh looked up to Tom and spent more time at her house than he did at his own.

Until the funeral.

And now she'd be attending another funeral. Memories of her brother, her previous closeness with Josh, and the sadness of Cindy's passing swamped Rachel's spirit. If only Mamm had been able to attend, they could have shared their heartache for all three of their losses. Josh, too, shared in the sadness of all three deaths, but he'd only been there for her after the first one. He'd avoided her after

Tom's funeral, and he wouldn't be comforting her this time either.

With multiple stops for meals, stretches, and diaper changes, they pulled into Charm in the evening. A trip that usually took seven or eight hours had taken more than twelve. The frequent breaks had allowed Zak to run and play, but two hours ago, he'd gone to sleep with his head drooping against Josh's arm. Josh eased his arm away so he could carry the bags and sleeping children into the house.

He yawned and stretched his arms high overhead, while trying to peek at Rachel behind him without being noticeable. She'd been silent for the last hour. Now, he understood why. Like Mrs. Vandenberg, she'd fallen asleep. With nobody but the driver to notice, Josh allowed himself to admire her beauty. With her long lashes fanning shadows across her high cheekbones and a sweet smile on her rosebud lips, she resembled an angel. She was one of those rare beauties who were as lovely inside as outside.

A burning tightness seared his chest. Why had he ever walked away from her? Left her when she needed him most? If only he could go back and undo the past.

"Josh?" Mrs. Vandenberg's words came to him in a whisper. "It's never too late."

He whirled around, embarrassed to be caught staring. "You don't know what happened." He almost spilled the whole story, but if he told anyone, it should be Rachel.

"I don't need to, but someone else does." Her caring expression softened her stern tone. She added to the heavy press of guilt weighing him down.

He bowed his head. "I know."

"Know what?" Rachel's words floated to him on an airy breath.

He couldn't face her. Nor could he tell her the truth here and now. They needed to be sitting down, facing each other, so he could gauge her reaction. And he wanted them to be alone.

Also, she'd come to Charm for a funeral. He couldn't open an old wound when she was already grieving. He'd wait until they returned to Lancaster and some time had passed. But he made up his mind to be honest, even if it meant Rachel would never speak to him again.

Rachel sucked in a breath. "Are we staying here?" The van had pulled into the parking lot of a huge Victorian bed-and-breakfast. She'd brought along some of the money Mrs. Vandenberg had paid her, but she couldn't afford to spend it on this. So far, Mrs. Vandenberg had paid for meals, insisting it was the least she could do after Rachel agreed to accompany her, but Rachel was determined to take care of her own hotel bill.

Inside, her spirits shriveled as the pot of money she'd hoped to use toward household expenses shrank. She tried to hide her distress. It was too late to find somewhere else to stay tonight, but tomorrow, she'd check with Cindy's cousins. Surely, one of them had room for Rachel and the children. She'd gladly sleep on a couch.

"Rachel, Rachel," Mrs. Vandenberg chided, "do you remember the Scripture verse about the lilies of the field? God provides for them. Trust Him to provide for you."

Of course, Rachel trusted God in all things, but didn't He also expect her to make sensible decisions? Maybe if she were honest, Mrs. Vandenberg might understand.

Although how could a rich woman know how it felt to watch every penny?

"You might be surprised." Mrs. Vandenberg pinned Rachel with a searching gaze. "I see the worry in your eyes, and I'm guessing at the fast calculations going on in your brain. You're trying to figure out how to pay for the room and still afford to cover your expenses at home."

Rachel lowered her eyes. "*Jah*, I am."

"I'm happy to help," Josh broke in.

Mrs. Vandenberg beamed at him. "Wonderful, but unnecessary. I stayed here last year when I attended the Amish Christmas Cookie Tour of Inns." Her eyes twinkled. "It so happens, I introduced their daughter to a wonderful Amish man I met on the tour."

Uh-oh. From Mrs. Vandenberg's sly smile, she planned to bring another couple together. Worry churned in Rachel's stomach. Suppose Mrs. Vandenberg had brought Josh along to meet an Ohio girl?

With a laugh, Mrs. Vandenberg continued her story. "The girl's parents were about to sell their bed-and-breakfast at a loss. I made a few suggestions, and now their business is turning a profit. As a thank you, our rooms are free."

A miracle worker. God had given this elderly woman many talents, and she'd multiplied them many times over. Not only for herself, but for everyone she encountered. Rachel wished she could be a blessing like that to others.

Only one part of the story didn't make sense. "If her parents are doing well, why does the couple need help buying a house?"

"They're still reinvesting their profit in restoring the last few rooms. I hope to help with that. I know someone who's auctioning off an estate. They could furnish the rooms with genuine antiques for a low price."

Rachel shook her head. How did Mrs. Vandenberg keep track of all these details? Everywhere she went, she brought people together, helping both the connections she matched. Rachel's face heated. She'd been thinking of partnerships, but the word *match* brought to mind Mamm's comment about Josh. Rachel hoped Josh didn't think she'd set this up. But she couldn't help hoping Mamm was right. Better than him falling for an Ohio girl and staying here.

To get her mind off that dire outcome, Rachel switched to a different topic. "I forgot to tell you. Mamm really likes Barbara. She stayed last night, and they got along well."

If Mrs. Vandenberg seemed surprised at the change of subject, she didn't show it. "I'm so glad. The two of them will have a wonderful lifelong friendship. Something you'll be grateful for soon enough."

Mrs. Vandenberg sounded as if she could see into the future. But that was impossible. She said God gave her nudges. Did He also let her know the outcomes of events?

CHAPTER 19

Rachel had never stayed anywhere so luxurious. The living room had a floor-to-ceiling stone fireplace surrounded by couches and chairs, giving it a homey look, and the bedrooms had been decorated with rustic Amish furniture accented with colorful quilts on the beds and walls.

Upstairs, her room had a queen-sized bed for her, a small twin bed for Zak, and a crib for Marianna. After Josh had carted all the suitcases and supplies to the various rooms, he got Zak ready for bed, gave him Giraffey, prayed with the little boy, and told him a Bible story while Rachel fed, changed, and settled Marianna into the crib.

Rachel tried to keep her attention on the baby, but she found her eyes drawn to the father-son bedtime routine. Every time she glanced that way, her desire for a husband and a large family gripped her, making her chest ache with longing. If only Josh were free. But even if he were, he had no interest in her. She had to stop torturing herself with impossibilities.

Behind her, the bed creaked as Josh rose. "Zak's asleep already."

"That's *gut. Danke.*"

"You're welcome. I enjoy it."

Rachel pretended to brush wrinkles from her black dress for tomorrow so Josh couldn't see the yearning in her expression.

"Sleep well," he said softly before he shut the door.

She ran a hand over her face, hoping to wipe away the emotions swamping her. Although it was early, Rachel's eyelids were drooping. Tomorrow would be draining. She'd go to sleep early. After a quick shower, she brushed her long hair, plaited it, and slid into bed.

She wasn't sure if the long trip, the softness of the beds, or being near their hometown had soothed the children, but they'd both fallen asleep as soon as they'd been tucked in bed. Within minutes, she, too, had drifted off. And she didn't stir until the delicious aroma of coffee and cinnamon tickled her nose the next morning.

The homey scents mingled with the spiciness of the pine trees surrounded her in the foggy morning mist of the woods. She cocooned deeper into the pillowiness cradling her. Holding hands with Josh, she sat on a creekbank, water trickling lazily around them. She reveled in their closeness as they dangled their feet in cool water while the sun's rays warmed their cheeks.

The sun? Rachel jolted upright. She should have been up before dawn. Mamm and the children needed her. *The children?* Rachel's heart banged hard against her chest. Were they still breathing?

Snuffles came from the crib on her right, and to her left, crisp sheets rustled. Both children had slept through the night. *Danke*, Lord! For the first time since she'd been caring for Zak and Marianna, Rachel had had a full night's sleep.

Never in her life had she slept this late. Agitated, she almost leaped out of bed until it sank in that she had no chores to do. From the delicious smells, someone else had made breakfast. And the flowing creek of her dream turned out to be a shower in the room next door. Still, Rachel remained in bed, clinging to her delicious, dream-like state.

Since age eleven, she'd made breakfast every morning. She'd never had anyone else prepare a meal for her, except for church meals. People had dropped off casseroles after Daed passed, but Rachel still had to heat them. She'd always been up and dressed by sunrise, and never had a day off from household work. Her responsibilities lessened on Sunday, but she still needed to fix meals for Mamm and give her massages.

That reminded Rachel of her mother. They'd never been apart a day since Tom passed. Rachel hoped Barbara was seeing to Mamm's meals, medicines, and routines.

Lord, please help Barbara take good care of Mamm until I get back.

Rachel wished Mamm could be here for the funeral. Mamm would understand Rachel's feelings, and they could reminisce together. Josh would have some child-hood memories, but he hadn't been sharing the letters that flew back and forth between Cindy and Rachel.

Mrs. Vandenberg tapped at the door. "Breakfast will be served in twenty minutes. Need any help with the children?"

Rachel gasped. She hadn't dressed or done her hair, let alone readied the children.

Before she could answer, the door opened, and Mrs. Vandenberg peeked in. "Hmm, you do need some assistance." Over her shoulder, she said, "Just wait, Josh."

Ach! Josh was outside the door? Rachel could have died from embarrassment. What would he think of her laziness?

Mrs. Vandenberg laughed at Rachel's nervousness.

"Why don't you gather your things and lock yourself in the bathroom? Josh and I will dress the children."

Rachel hastened to gather her garments, *kapp*, and pins. Then she shut herself into the large, tiled room where the mirror reflected her shame-filled face. She rushed so fast to get into her clothing, she stuck herself with her half-apron's straight pins. Sucking on her twice-stabbed forefinger, she splashed water on her face and undid her braid one-handed.

Outside the door, Zak wailed when he woke. Josh's quiet words soothed the cries. Marianna whined. Rachel should be out there taking care of them instead of in here, clumsily trying to twist the sides of her hair back. She had to restart twice before getting her hair smooth and tight enough to complete her bob. As soon as she pinned on her *kapp*, she opened the bathroom door to find Zak dressed and clinging to Josh's pant leg.

Josh was assisting Mrs. Vandenberg by keeping Marianna from rolling off the changing pad Rachel had spread on the dresser.

She dashed over. "I'm so sorry. Let me do that." In her haste, she bumped into Josh, who steadied her with one hand. His touch seared every nerve ending in her body, and the shock immobilized her.

He stared into her eyes, and she couldn't break the connection. Marianna rolled sideways on the table. Mrs. Vandenberg squawked, and Josh jerked his gaze away to stop the baby from falling.

"Please let me do it," Rachel begged, but Mrs. Vandenberg ignored her. Rachel couldn't meet their eyes. "I'm sorry I didn't have the children ready by now."

"You're entitled to a day off." Mrs. Vandenberg struggled to wrap the diaper around Marianna's chubby leg.

212 *Rachel J. Good*

Josh reached in to assist her, still keeping one hand on Marianna's chest to prevent her from rolling again.

"She's quite a wriggler." Mrs. Vandenberg secured the diaper with a proud smile and slid Marianna's little dress down. "Now let's go down for breakfast."

Rachel scooped up Marianna, trying to ignore the thrill of brushing past Josh, and concentrated on the baby. She kept her head lowered so no one could see her reaction or glimpse her shame. What must they both think of her?

Josh swept Zak into his arms before they descended the grand, curving staircase. The last thing they needed was for the little boy to take a tumble before breakfast. Or after, for that matter. *I've been responsible for enough accidents.*

Proof of it showed in the two bright strips with strange cartoon characters decorating Zak's fingers. Mrs. Vandenberg had insisted on buying a box of garish, neon-colored bandages. She claimed they helped children heal more quickly. Zak agreed they made his sore hand better, so Josh had reapplied new ones after Zak's bath last night.

When they reached the inn's living room, Rachel appeared so distressed Josh longed to comfort her. He leaned over and whispered, "I'm glad you got some much-needed sleep last night."

Crimson streaked her cheekbones. He'd only embarrassed her more.

"I'm sorry I didn't have the children dressed. I, um, overslept." More color suffused her face.

"It's no problem. Did they keep you awake last night?"

"*Neh.* Both of them slept the whole way through."

"That's great. You needed to catch up on your rest."

Rachel sounded close to tears. "I should have been up by dawn."

"Why? You don't have any chores to do here."

"That makes me even guiltier."

Josh nodded. "I know what you mean. It does feel odd to wake up and have nothing to do."

Although Mrs. Vandenberg had said he'd be doing repairs today, she had yet to mention it, and he didn't want to disturb her breakfast with talk of work. Maybe she'd wait until they dropped Rachel off at the funeral. For now, he'd do what he could to comfort Rachel.

"I'm glad I could help with Zak. That made me feel a little useful." He rejoiced inwardly when her lips curved up a little.

A sudden rush of feeling splashed over him, making him want to wrap her in his arms and touch his mouth to hers. Now it was his turn for a heated face. He cleared his throat. "I, um, think the dining room is that way." He waved toward their left.

After he did, he felt like a fool. Of course it was. The huge farm table was visible through the archway, along with a buffet laden with platters of food and stainless-steel serving dishes. Delicious smells wafted on the air.

When he noticed the buffet, Zak bounced in Josh's arms. "Is all that for us?"

Josh laughed. "You think you could eat all of it?"

"*Jah!*"

"Maybe we should share with others."

"All right. But I want some of everything."

Josh raised his eyebrows at Rachel, and she smiled. "A tiny bite of everything maybe," she told Zak.

"Awww."

But when Josh helped Zak fill his plate, the small boy

seemed satisfied with a child-sized helping of a few items. They sat across from Rachel, and once again, Josh struggled to keep his gaze from straying to her lips.

What was wrong with him?

Rachel sat at the table with a plate of pancakes, sausage, a cinnamon biscuit, and a cup of yogurt for Marianna. When she bowed her head for the silent prayer, her heart overflowed with gratitude for her many blessings. Two children to love. Josh across from her, smiling directly at her. Mrs. Vandenberg's generosity and wisdom. And, although guilt niggled at Rachel for enjoying it, she did like being pampered at this lovely bed-and-breakfast.

But the dreaminess of the morning soon faded, and reality crowded in. She had a funeral to attend today.

The front door to the inn banged open, and an Amish girl rushed into the dining room, breathless, dragging a friend with her. She glanced around at the diners, including several *Englischers*, and headed straight for Rachel. The girl halted a short distance away to give Mrs. Vandenberg an enthusiastic hug.

"You'll be coming for my wedding this fall, won't you?" Her eyes brimmed with joy.

"I wouldn't miss it, Annika. I always attend the weddings of couples I match. That's my greatest joy in life."

"I'm so glad." Annika whirled from Mrs. Vandenberg to Rachel. "And you must be Rachel."

"I am. It's nice to meet you, Annika."

"Same here." She tugged at her friend's hand and sobered a little. "This is Gloria. She's one of Cindy's husband's cousins."

Gloria, her eyes filled with tears, held out a thick manila

envelope. "Cindy wanted Daed to give you this. He's busy getting ready for the funeral, but he asked me to drop it off."

Rachel took the packet with a quiet *danke*. At Cindy's familiar handwriting scrawled across the envelope front, Rachel sucked in a shaky breath. Never again would she receive a letter from her cousin. Her eyes stung.

"Let me take Marianna." Josh stood and came around the table. "And I'll keep an eye on Zak if you want to read that upstairs."

Josh's thoughtfulness almost made Rachel break down. She handed the baby to him.

Mrs. Vandenberg laid a hand on Rachel's arm. "You can take your plate to your room. Many people do. Just leave the dishes, and someone will collect them later when they clean the room."

When Rachel stood, Gloria and Annika each gave her a quick hug. "We have to get back to the house, but we'll see you later today." They dashed off.

Clutching the envelope to her chest, Rachel fumbled her way upstairs with tear-blinded eyes, balancing her half-eaten plate of breakfast. After she closed the door, she sank into a cushiony chair beside the fireplace with its carved mantle and set her plate on the small table beside her. She couldn't let the delicious meal go to waste, but she had to see what Cindy had sent.

Rachel removed a thick sheaf of papers with a letter on top. Through blurry eyes, she struggled to make out the message. Then she read through it a second time, and a third.

She couldn't believe it. Cindy had left her house and all its contents to Rachel. The deed behind the letter had a note attached with instructions. Cindy's letter said Rachel

could live in the house or sell it to provide money to care
for the children.

With shaky hands, Rachel dropped the papers into her
lap. Move to Ohio? Could she uproot Mamm? What about
the children? Would they be more comfortable in their
own home? Should she stay here for their sakes?

The thought of moving overwhelmed her. How would
Mamm travel all this way? What would they do with their
house? Rachel knew nothing about selling houses. And
would they have to sell their furnishings? Leave behind all
the furniture Dawdi had made? Or should they sell Cindy's
home? What if that upset Zak?

Worry after worry swarmed through Rachel's head.
Whatever she chose, she'd have to sell a home and furniture either in Lancaster or Charm. Being hit with all these
decisions so soon after she'd taken over as a mother overwhelmed her. And she still had a funeral to attend to today.
She had to turn all this over to God.

*Dear Lord, please show me what to do. I don't want to
leave Lancaster, and I'm not sure I should move Mamm.
But if that's the best for the children, I'll do it. Please give
me a sign to direct me toward Your will.*

The clock on the bedside table flickered on another
number. They'd need to leave for Cindy's funeral soon.
Rachel hurried through the other papers. Cindy had poured
out her heart and left many suggestions on raising the
children. Rachel would come back to these again later and
keep them for future reference. Cindy had also written
letters for Zak and Marianna. One for each birthday until
they turned eighteen. How had she done all this when she
was ill?

Stuffing the papers into the envelope, Rachel jumped
up from the chair. She didn't want to make everyone late.

Her tardiness had already embarrassed her enough for one day.

Rachel's childhood training wouldn't let her leave food on her plate, so she finished the last bites and picked up the cinnamon roll to eat on her way downstairs. Despite Mrs. Vandenberg's advice to leave her dishes, Rachel couldn't bring herself to do that. She juggled the plate, the envelope, and her cinnamon roll as she headed back to the dining room.

Josh stopped feeding Marianna some yogurt to study Rachel's tear-glazed eyes. "Are you all right?"

"I—I'm not sure." She sank into the chair beside Mrs. Vandenberg, who patted Rachel's arm.

"Sometimes God's blessings can feel overwhelming, dear. But trust Him. He has the perfect plan."

"I hope so." Rachel set down her empty plate but clutched the envelope to her. Was this a blessing? At the moment, it seemed more of a burden.

CHAPTER 20

Mrs. Vandenberg waved to the driver, who was deep in discussion with the man beside him at the table. "We should leave in ten minutes."

Rachel's stomach roiled. Rushing to get dressed and reading Cindy's messages had pushed the funeral from mind, but now they had to face the day. A day filled with anxiety. And deep sadness.

How did she end the fears, concerns, and questions swirling through her mind? Not to mention the sorrow of losing her cousin. And how could she deal with Zak's grief when he saw his *mamm* at the funeral?

The *tap, tap, tap* of Mrs. Vandenberg's cane approached behind Rachel. The elderly woman reached out and squeezed Rachel's arm. "You'll get through it, my dear. You've done it before, and you can do it again."

That was the whole problem. Rachel dreaded this because she had done it before, and at times, the pain had been unbearable. Sometimes, it still engulfed her. And having Josh here only made it worse. Back when she'd needed him most, he'd left her. And now, though they were only feet from each other, they were oceans apart.

Her attraction to him—her love for him—only deepened that hurt.

How could she deal with all the old pain of losing her *daed*, losing her brother, losing Cindy, and losing Josh? She'd never gotten over his abandonment.

"Be open to forgiving," Mrs. Vandenberg counseled. The words seemed more like a message from God than from the elderly woman.

And the message hit Rachel in her soul. The clatter of dishes and silverware, the low murmur of conversations faded into the background as she drew within herself. She'd spent years nursing old pain. She'd never considered holding onto hurt to be unforgiveness. But it was, wasn't it?

Had she ever truly forgiven Josh?

Neh. Deep down, she still ached over his not being there for her after Tom died. And her wounds often reopened when she spent time around him.

She couldn't look at Josh as she struggled with yet another emotional dilemma that morning. Until Mrs. Vandenberg had jabbed her conscience, Rachel had never considered her own spirit of unforgiveness. She couldn't fully forgive Josh if she judged his actions or held a grudge. All along, she thought she had let it go, but in truth, she'd hardened her heart against releasing the resentment even as she longed for a closer connection with him.

Lord, I'm still clinging to my old pain and hurt. I've never truly forgiven Josh. Please make me willing to let go of everything I'm holding against him.

"Sometimes we have unrealistic expectations of

others . . ." Mrs. Vandenberg zeroed in on Rachel. Then turning to Josh, she added, ". . . and of ourselves."

He squirmed, and Rachel wondered what unrealistic expectations he held. She shook off her curiosity. Often, applying sermons and admonitions to others served as a way to avoid facing them yourself. Right now, she needed to shine the light on her own mistakes.

"The Lord forgives you for everything if you ask." It seemed Mrs. Vandenberg hadn't finished her preaching. "A point both of you would do well to remember."

Rachel sent up a quick prayer for God's forgiveness, strength to get through today, and wisdom for dealing with the future.

Mrs. Vandenberg's lecture hit Josh hard. He'd never asked God's forgiveness for the guilt twisting his soul in knots. He'd carried this heavy load for years, and it seemed too great to let go. Before he asked for God's mercy, though, he wanted to confess to Rachel.

While he wrestled with his inner torment, he stared down at baby Marianna in his arms. Her sweet innocence made him yearn to go back to that state again. He had to clear his conscience and make things right with Rachel and with God.

Zak clamored to be picked up, jarring Josh from his contemplation. Josh's strained smile grew into a genuine one as Zak tugged on his pant leg.

"Hang on, buddy. Let me give your sister to Rachel."

As Josh handed over the baby, his gaze met Rachel's. He couldn't bear the agony on her face. Mrs. Vandenberg's message seemed to have affected her as deeply as it had him. Or had the envelope she clutched or the upcoming funeral caused her distress?

He wanted to ease her troubles if he could. He only hoped he hadn't been the cause. Was she remembering her brother's death? He whispered, "Can I do anything to help?"

"Not now. Not today." She bit her lip and glanced away. "Maybe we could talk tomorrow or when we get home?"

"*Jah*, that would be *gut*." When they got back would be best. He needed to unburden himself, and for that, they'd need time and privacy.

But right now, he made an inner promise to be here for her the way he hadn't been after her brother's death. Perhaps in some small way, he could assuage his guilt over failing her before.

She lifted her head again to reveal eyes drowning in misery. He ached to throw her a lifeline. The memory of pulling her from the creek flooded back, filling him with the same urgent need to wrap his arms around her, save her, comfort her. But he couldn't embrace her. What could he do?

Mrs. Vandenberg answered his question in an unexpected way. "The best thing you can do, Josh, is come with us to the funeral. Zak will be dealing with another major loss in his young life, and he looks to you for comfort."

"I can't." Josh tried not to let his shock show. "I wasn't invited, and I only brought work clothes."

She went on as if he hadn't spoken. "Rachel can also use some support." When Rachel started to protest, Mrs. Vandenberg cut her off. "Believe me, you'll be grateful for Josh over the next few days."

He wasn't sure how much help he'd be if he was working on a construction job, but he'd do his best.

"*Hmm . . .*" Mrs. Vandenberg assessed Josh's clothes. "I'm sure one of Annika's brothers can lend you a proper outfit. I'll ask." Leaning heavily on her cane, she hobbled away and returned a few minutes later with a tall, broad-shouldered young man, who took Josh to the family's rooms on the ground floor.

"I'll be right back," Josh assured Zak, who thrust out his lower lip in a pout. Josh didn't want a crying spell now. Being at the funeral would be hard enough.

Josh thanked Annika's brother profusely and hurried into the garments he provided. Josh was still sliding his arms into the black jacket sleeves as he returned to the dining room. Zak dashed toward him and practically tackled him.

"Careful, buddy." Josh laughed to show he was teasing, swung Zak into his arms, and rejoined the group.

His face heated when Rachel cast appreciative eyes over him. She glanced away quickly, but she'd already set his pulse throbbing. He drew in a shallow breath that did little to calm the sensations racing through him.

Get control of yourself. We're heading to a funeral.

But even that inner scolding didn't lessen the chaos in his body. A chaos that lasted the whole way to Cindy's house and lingered long after they arrived. Until Zak saw his *mamm* and had a meltdown.

Josh picked up the small boy and strode outside to calm him. They walked up and down the road, past green plants springing up from the ground. Signs of new life bloomed everywhere, while they were facing death.

Hugging Zak close, Josh rubbed his back and whispered soothing Scripture verses about God's comfort.

The twenty-third Psalm reduced the sobbing, and in a tear-clogged voice, Zak asked Josh to repeat it. He did until Zak's head collapsed onto Josh's shoulder. After several shuddery sighs, Zak's deep breathing signaled he'd fallen asleep.

When Josh returned to the house, Rachel was cuddling a drowsy Marianna. Both children needed their morning naps. Maybe their sleeping was for the best, because soon after that, everyone headed to the cemetery for the burial.

Josh debated waking Zak, but Rachel shook her head. "Let him sleep."

Her tear-stained face tore at him, and he moved as close to her as he could. Once, she stumbled on the rough ground, and he reached for her elbow to steady her. The thankful look she gave him jump-started his heart, and he didn't let go, even though he should have.

After they headed back to the house, Rachel choked out, "I miss Cindy so much. But this is also hard because it reminds me of Daed . . . and . . . and Tom."

She couldn't have said anything that could stab Josh so deeply.

"I'm sorry I wasn't there for you." The words were torn from his soul. He owed her more than apology; he owed her an explanation.

Eyes shining with tears, she tilted her head to look up at him. "I wish you had been. I needed you."

At the depth of pain swimming in her eyes, Josh squeezed his eyes shut for a moment to block the waves of shame and regret. He forced himself to meet her gaze. He deserved every reproach she gave him. "If I could go back and do it again, I'd . . . I'd do things differently."

If he'd done things differently, though, maybe Tom

would still be here, and Rachel never would have suffered through that death.

"It's all right," she said softly.

But it wasn't all right. If she knew the truth, she'd never have said that. And Josh could do nothing to right his wrong.

Rachel longed to lean her head on Josh's shoulder the way Zak was doing. She yearned for the comfort of his arms around her. If it hadn't been for his hand on her elbow, she might have fallen apart at the cemetery. All the old memories had washed over her, drowning her in past sorrows and heartaches.

Her eyes burning with unshed tears, Rachel had been praying for peace when she'd tripped on a tuft of grass. If Josh hadn't grabbed her elbow then, she'd have pitched forward on her face and dropped Marianna. But his hand hadn't only prevented an accident. It had sent strength and courage through her, enabling her to face not only this loss, but her new future.

If only she could continue to lean on him as she mothered these two precious children. She stumbled back to the house with him beside her, trying not to puncture her hazy daydream that his touch had been real and meant for her alone.

Although he'd have done the same if someone else had nearly fallen, would he have held on after the person had gotten their footing? Perhaps he worried she was still unsteady, and he wanted to ensure she didn't drop the baby. Rachel shook herself. She was making too much of his kindness.

* * *

Zak didn't wake until they returned to the house. As Josh headed inside, Zak lifted his head, his eyes blurry with sleep.

"I'm hungry," he mumbled.

"Plenty to eat here." Josh headed for a table filled with food. "Want to get down?"

When Zak nodded, Josh placed the small boy on the floor. After they filled their plates, Josh steered Zak toward the living room. Before they entered, Zak squinched his eyes shut and turned around to face Josh's legs, almost spilling his plate. Josh set his plate on the mantel and grabbed for Zak's.

His voice muffled, Zak protested, "Don't want to go in there."

Setting Zak's plate beside his own, Josh squatted to wrap his arms around Zak. "Your *mamm*'s not in there anymore."

Zak tilted his head to look straight into Josh's face, as if checking to see if he was telling the truth. "Where is she?"

"We buried her while you were sleeping, but she's in heaven with God now."

Instead of bawling like he'd done earlier, Zak's face grew somber. "Like Daed."

"*Jah*." Josh's husky whisper sympathized with Zak's world of pain. Poor little guy.

Blinking, Zak stared down at the floor. "I got no *mamm*. I got no *daed*."

What could Josh say to such a heartbreaking announcement? The *I'm sorry* he offered to adults would have no meaning to a child. While he searched for the best response, Zak glanced up at Josh with trusting eyes. Eyes filled with loss and hope.

Zak wound his arms around Josh's neck and squeezed hard. "You be my *daed*."

Too choked up to respond, Josh only held Zak tightly, trying to give him the sense of security he needed. But how could Josh commit to Zak's heartfelt plea?

CHAPTER 21

After they finished their meals, Zak, still sleepy and yawning, stumbled beside Josh through the crowd of people to dispose of their plates. Some called Zak by name. He gave a wan smile to those he recognized. With others, he hung back and shrank behind Josh.

One older woman peered through her thick glasses at both of them. "I know this is Zak." She patted him on the head, and he twisted away. "But you are?" She studied Josh closely. "You don't resemble the Glicks or the Schrocks. Which side of the family are you from?"

Josh had answered this and similar questions at least two dozen times. He pasted on a polite smile. "I'm Josh Yoder, Rachel Glick's friend." He gestured toward Rachel, deep in discussion with Gloria. "I'm here helping with Zak."

"You came all the way from Lancaster with her?" The woman looked shocked.

"We came in the same van, but I'm here to do some construction work." To allay her fears, he added, "We have an *Englisch* driver and an older lady for a chaperone."

Even though that didn't ease her frown, at least he'd

tried. "Zak asked me to come to the funeral with him, so I did."

"He has family here. Plenty of us would be happy to care for him."

"*Neh.*" Zak stiffened and wrapped his arms around Josh's legs. "I want Josh."

"Well, he seems quite attached to you."

"Mammi?" Gloria joined them. "I see you've met Josh. He and Rachel are getting married."

Josh bit back a gasp. Is that what Rachel had been talking to Gloria about? He didn't want to contradict Gloria, but . . .

Before he could decide whether or not to correct her mistake, Gloria turned to him. "Rachel says Zak has been clinging to you since the day he arrived at her house. It's *wunderbar* that he's taken to you."

"Well, I—"

Gloria's enthusiasm bubbled over like a fountain, cutting off Josh's attempt to explain the truth. "Don't you think so, Mammi?"

Her grandmother didn't share Gloria's upbeat, cheerful nature. "Well, now, I don't know. Is it *gut* having a stranger show up in Rachel's life? Or in Zak's?"

"*Ach*, he's not a stranger. He and Rachel have been friends since they were how old?" She turned to Josh.

"Nine," he answered.

"See?" Gloria said triumphantly. "They've known each other for years."

"That depends on your point of view," her grandmother responded drily. "I wouldn't consider a decade or two long."

"Cindy knew Josh too, Mammi. And she wanted Josh to adopt her children."

This time, he couldn't stay silent. "You mean Rachel. She's the one Cindy asked to care for Zak and Marianna."

Gloria wagged a finger at him. "Cindy wanted both of you." Gloria's generous smile spilled across her face. "I know you don't want to be prideful, but I saw you with Zak at breakfast and here earlier. He's already taken to you as a *daed*."

"I—I . . ." Josh couldn't get words out past the lump in his throat. Part of him longed to fulfill that role, especially with Rachel as the children's mother. But a huge obstacle stood between them. In addition to that, was he ready to take on two children when he married?

Gloria snagged two young mothers who were headed to the buffet table with their small children. "Didn't Cindy always tell us how well Josh and Rachel got along and that they'd marry someday?" She nodded in his direction. "This is Josh."

Both women enthusiastically agreed. "*Jah*, she said the two of you had an unbreakable bond," one said.

Josh swallowed hard. He'd once believed that, but now . . .

"*Jah*," the other chimed in. "It eased Cindy's mind to know you'd be the children's father."

Behind him, Rachel sucked in a sharp breath.

From her gasp and shocked expression, she hadn't been behind this talk. Josh shifted uncomfortably. Had she heard the rest of the conversation?

Rachel couldn't believe what she was hearing. Josh looked as if he wanted to bolt. She'd already endured Gloria's nonstop chatter about what Cindy had planned. Rachel ached inside because she had no way to fulfill all

of her cousin's wishes. Still, Josh didn't deserve this
pressure. She needed to rescue him.

"Cindy thought you were the perfect couple." Gloria
smiled and turned to welcome Rachel to the circle, nudging her over until she and Josh were cozied up next to each
other.

Rachel's heart bumped in her chest, and she struggled
to breathe. Even when Josh had held her elbow, they
hadn't been this close. And with everyone pressing in, neither she nor Josh could move.

He probably longed to escape this group of nattering fe-
males, but because they were talking about him and her,
along with their future wedding, it would be awkward to
back away.

Zak saved them both by whining. The young mother
who stood beside Josh had accidentally trapped Zak outside the circle because he'd been hiding behind Josh's leg.
Now he'd been left out and let Josh know it. Josh turned
and stepped back to pick up Zak.

"He could play with the other children," the young
mother suggested. "My two just took off with several
friends."

Zak buried his face against Josh's borrowed jacket and
whimpered.

Josh gave the woman an apologetic smile. "*Danke*, but
I don't think he's quite ready for that yet."

Her face melted in sympathy. "I understand."

Rachel now had breathing room, but rather than being
relieved, she felt bereft.

Josh regretted stepping away from Rachel, but it was for
the best. Being close to her brought up so many emotions

he had no right to feel. He was doubly grateful when Mrs. Vandenberg's van pulled into the driveway.

"Rachel, are you ready to go?" Josh whispered and gestured to the van waiting outside the window.

The tension in her face relaxed. "*Jah.*"

Gloria grabbed Rachel's arm. "*Ach*, no, you can't leave now. I wanted you to spend the night here so we can get to know you. Several cousins live nearby."

"But the children . . ." Rachel glanced at Josh as if begging for help.

Before Josh could find a way to rescue her, Gloria jumped in. "They can stay in their rooms upstairs. This house has plenty of bedrooms."

Rachel said hesitantly, "But Zak needs Josh . . ."

"Young lady," Gloria's *mammi* thundered, "you will *not* spend the night under this roof with a man."

A beet red flush rose on Rachel's cheeks. "I didn't mean . . ."

"I should hope not."

Zak twined his arms around Josh's neck. "I stay wif you."

Josh's heart was about to burst, and he could barely speak. "Rachel, I can take Zak back to the B and B with me if you want to stay here with Marianna."

"I don't have enough of her things with me. I already used up all but one of the diapers. Maybe we should all go back." Rachel sounded relieved.

As they turned to leave, Josh had a sudden thought. "Is there anything you want to take with you, Zak?"

A tear trickled down Zak's cheek. "*Jah.*"

"Show me." Josh set Zak down and let him take the lead.

Zak started in his parents' bedroom. He picked up a children's devotional book. "Mamm reads this to me afore bed." Eyes filled with tears, he handed the book to Josh. "Will you read to me?"

Josh managed a husky *jah*.

From there, they went into his bedroom, where Zak selected an armload of toys.

Josh took a plastic storage crate from one of the shelves and emptied the contents into other crates. "Why don't we put some of the things in here?" He set the devotional book carefully in the bottom.

Zak dumped his toys into the box, took Josh's hand, and pulled him into the nursery. While he collected several baby toys from a low shelf, Josh lifted a cloth baby carrier from its hook. His sisters used them all the time while they worked. Maybe Rachel could use it to keep Marianna close while she quilted.

When they finished, Zak took one last look around in the hallway and bawled. "Mamm . . . gone. Daed . . . gone."

Josh set down the crate and swept the crying boy into his arms. "I'm so sorry, Zak. But I'll be here for you. I promise."

CHAPTER 22

On the way back to the B and B, Marianna and Zak both fell asleep almost instantly. Zak still clutched Josh's hand tightly and pressed Giraffey to his tear-stained cheek.

Rachel's heart ached for her sweet children having to go through such sadness at such a young age. Marianna might not realize she'd lost her birth parents, but she seemed to sense the heavy press of sorrow around her. Instead of her usual smiles and gurgles, she'd gone silent and somber as the day wore on. Maybe once she returned to Lancaster, she'd revert to her cheerful disposition.

Rachel resolved to act as positive as she could around the children and only give in to her own grief in private. She'd also try to turn all her concerns over to the Lord— her worries about what to do with the two houses, her fears about mothering two small children, and her unrequited love for Josh. From time to time today, he'd gazed at her as if he might share her attraction, and she almost forgot he'd made a commitment to another woman.

Mrs. Vandenberg broke into Rachel's musing. "My dear, you appear to be carrying some heavy burdens. Sometimes sharing them lessens their weight."

"I'm trying to leave everything to the Lord."

"A wonderful plan, but God also has placed others here on earth to lighten your load."

Talking about it might help. Mrs. Vandenberg was so wise. She could offer some advice, so Rachel confided about Cindy's letter and being unsure what to do with two houses.

A chuckle from the front seat interrupted her complaints. "Many people in this world would be happy to have such a dilemma."

Mrs. Vandenberg's tart comment brought Rachel up short. She should have been thanking God for this opportunity rather than seeing it as problem.

"You're right," she said humbly. "I am grateful." The sale would alleviate her financial worries for a long time. "It's only that I can't decide if staying in Ohio would be better for Zak and Marianna's sakes. And the thought of figuring out how to sell a house feels overwhelming."

"About your first concern . . ." Mrs. Vandenberg semi-turned in her seat so she could look directly into Rachel's eyes. "Where would you feel happiest?"

"Lancaster, of course. But I should do what's best for the children."

"Don't you think it would be in their best interests to have a happy mother?"

Rachel hadn't thought about that. "I suppose it would, but. . ."

Mrs. Vandenberg smiled. "I've learned that it's often best to cut whatever comes after *but*. Generally, that word is only an excuse to avoid making a decision." She glanced at Josh, who *rutsched* in his seat, before fixing her gaze on Rachel.

Fleetingly, Rachel wondered what Josh needed to decide

that made him so nervous. Maybe they should be talking about his concerns rather than hers.

"And where would you have the most support in caring for the children?"

"Lancaster . . ." Rachel swallowed the *but* she'd almost added. Still, she wanted to consider both sides of the question. "We could make friends here. And I'm sure the community here would be just as supportive. Plus, Zak might feel more comfortable with people he knows."

"Did you notice Zak clinging to anyone at the funeral?" Mrs. Vandenberg looked thoughtful.

That question had only one answer. *Josh.*

Before Rachel could answer, Mrs. Vandenberg's face broke into a self-satisfied smile. "Exactly. Would you want to keep Zak from the person he's most attached to?"

"*Neh,*" Rachel said in a small voice. *And I wouldn't want to move so far from the person I'm most attached to either.*

Mrs. Vandenberg seemed to pick up on Rachel's unspoken thought, and her grin broadened. "Also, it would be hard on your mother to move so far away, wouldn't it?"

All of Rachel's arguments for moving to Ohio collapsed under the questioning.

"*Jah,* I do worry about Mamm making the move." She also hadn't thought about Mamm's friends in the *g'may* who came on Sunday to care for her. Mamm would be lonely in Ohio until she made new friends.

"And if you chose to sell the Ohio house, it would save me a long, hard search for a suitable place for Annika and Mark. Buying an Amish house would be much better than renovating an *Englisch* one. Taking out electricity and making other accommodations can be costly."

Mrs. Vandenberg had demolished Rachel's final argument. She gave in. "Then I'll give it to you."

"No, I couldn't let you do that. You'll need money to care for those two precious children. It's their inheritance, and I won't deprive them of that. If you don't need the money, you can put it away for their futures."

Rachel couldn't believe how God had worked everything out so easily and quickly.

"Now, about price. My financial advisor can research the fair market value and deposit that amount in your account today. I'll have him back out taxes so you don't need to worry about those. We can sign the paperwork after my lawyer finishes the title search and gets everything in order."

After a quick phone call to give her assistant all the information, the deal was done.

"*Danke.*" Rachel's voice trembled. The Bible said God could do exceedingly abundantly more than she could ask or think, and He certainly had. Despite her grief, her gratitude for her many blessings overflowed.

"My dear, could I ask one last favor?" Mrs. Vandenberg acted as if she hadn't just done Rachel a huge favor.

"Anything at all."

"I'm really concerned about Barbara being homeless. Could you find it in your heart to let her stay and care for your mother until I can find her a permanent position? That way, I can keep paying her salary."

Rachel would be happy to help. "You don't need to pay. I'll have more than enough to do that."

"Save the money for the children. My charity is covering Barbara's paycheck. And maybe she'd be willing to help out some with the children so you have more time to quilt."

Mrs. Vandenberg raised a hand when Rachel tried to protest. "It benefits me. I can't wait to see my finished quilt."

How did Mrs. Vandenberg do it? Somehow, she managed to make every one of her gifts seem as if the receiver were doing her a favor.

Rachel's heart overflowed with gratitude. God had supplied everything she needed and much, much more. Except for the one thing her heart desired more than any other. The man sitting in the seat in front of her.

"All good things come to those who wait," Mrs. Vandenberg said as the van turned into the B and B driveway.

Was that directed at me? Rachel couldn't be sure, but the good thing she wanted seemed out of her reach forever.

When the van pulled into a parking space, Josh unbuckled Zak and lifted him gently so he wouldn't wake. Throughout the short ride here, Josh had struggled with so many emotions.

His stomach had clenched when Rachel mentioned moving to Ohio. The thought of never seeing her again upset him greatly. He couldn't imagine not having her around after being with her so much recently. Their time together had strengthened the childhood bonds between them. If she left, she'd leave a gaping hole in his life.

"Josh?" Mrs. Vandenberg approached him as he headed toward the door of the inn. "Once you have Zak settled, would you be able to go back to the house with me to see what repairs might be needed before Annika's fiancé moves in?"

"Of course." That's what he'd come here to do.

He headed up to Rachel's room, set Zak on the bed, and took an afghan from the chair to cover the little boy.

Then he turned to find Rachel staring at him with tears in her eyes.

He longed to take her in his arms and comfort her, but he shoved his hands into his pockets and forced himself to stay where he was.

"You're so good with him." She waved toward Zak. "You'll be a good *daed*." Then she flushed and pressed a hand over her mouth. She'd done it again. "I, um, shouldn't have said that." She whirled around and patted the sleeping baby.

Something had flashed in her eyes as she said he'd be a good *daed*. Something that appeared to be longing. Did she mean she wanted him to share the parenting duties with her? Or to be Zak's *daed*?

Josh's heart swelled with a desire to fulfill that wish. He brought himself up short. What was he thinking? He had a girlfriend. And a shameful secret. One that would keep him from ever holding that place in Rachel's life.

"I—I'd better go." He hurried toward the door before he acted on the impulse to ask her what she'd meant, before he got himself in so deep, he'd never be able to get out. "Mrs. Vandenberg wants me to fix the house."

He rushed through the door without looking back and almost ran into Mrs. Vandenberg, waiting in the hallway.

"My goodness, you look as if you're fleeing the hounds of hell."

Josh skidded to a stop. Had she just sworn?

"I'm sorry. I didn't mean to shock you. It's just a reference to old myths, but I expect you've never read those or seen any TV shows or movies based on those evil black dogs with flaming red eyes."

"*Neh*, I haven't." And he'd never want to. There was

enough evil in the world—and in his heart—without adding more. But his past did resemble vicious dogs, chasing him and nipping at his heels.

"You know, Josh, sometimes tragic things that happen in childhood seem monstrous and unforgivable. In a child's mind, these events get blown way out of proportion."

He wished that were the case here, but what he'd done had been unforgivable.

Mrs. Vandenberg's eyes filled with compassion. "God can forgive anything, no matter how terrible. Until you accept His forgiveness and forgive yourself, you'll never be free of that burden."

She had missed one other important part. He had to confess to Rachel and ask for her forgiveness. "Sometimes other people are involved, and you need to make things right with them too," he explained.

"That's true." Mrs. Vandenberg headed for the staircase. "You'll have an opportunity to do that soon enough."

Jah, he'd already decided he had to tell Rachel the truth after they returned to Pennsylvania. Although maybe he should give her some time first. He didn't want to intrude on her grief over Cindy. Rachel didn't need him stirring up old memories that brought her even more pain.

"The sooner, the better," Mrs. Vandenberg advised as she gripped the railing, tapped her cane on the first stair, and took her first unsteady step.

Josh took her elbow. The last thing he wanted was to see her tumble down this elegant staircase. And as they descended, he marveled yet again at how this elderly *Englischer* not only read his heart and mind, but also preached better sermons than the ministers and bishops.

"That's not my doing," she said, as if in response to his thought. "God's the one who gives me the ideas."

And Josh couldn't help wondering: If the hounds following him were bringing evil, were angels following to bring him good? He wouldn't be at all surprised to learn he'd been spending time with one of those angels.

Rachel couldn't believe she'd blurted out her innermost thoughts to Josh about being a *gut daed* again. What must he think of her? From the way he'd rushed out of the room, he'd been eager to put as much distance between them as possible. She sank into the nearest chair and covered her face with her hands.

Her cheeks still stung from embarrassment. She'd been so overwhelmed at the sight of Josh gently covering Zak, gratitude and admiration flowed from her lips. No doubt her eyes had revealed her heartfelt desire. After all the gossip at church about her being a flirt and stealing other girls' boyfriends, she'd just proved that to Josh.

Lord, please show me how to make this right. And please keep my heart from straying from the path you have for my future.

Perhaps she should keep the house here after all. Rachel had no idea how she could go back to Pennsylvania and watch Josh marry Anna Mary. It would be so wrong to pine after another woman's husband. Maybe when they returned home, Rachel would admit she'd changed her mind. Hopefully, Mrs. Vandenberg would understand.

Neh, she shouldn't wait until then. What if Mrs. Vandenberg deposited money in her account? What if Josh did some work on the house tonight? She'd need to pay him. And . . .

Rachel jumped up from the chair and raced to the door, letting it bang shut behind her. *Dear Lord, please keep the little ones safe until I get back.* She wouldn't be going far. She just had to catch them before they left.

Luckily, they had only made it halfway down the stairs. "Wait!" she yelled from the upstairs landing.

Mrs. Vandenberg teetered on the step and would have fallen if Josh hadn't been so quick. He'd been holding her arm, but he rotated and threw out his other arm to protect her.

"I'm so sorry. I didn't mean to startle you." Breathless, Rachel blurted out, "I've changed my mind. I want to move to Ohio after all."

Mrs. Vandenberg raised an eyebrow. "You do?"

How could Rachel answer that? *Neh* would be the truth, but she couldn't say that. Nor could she say she needed to get away from Josh.

Loud wailing from the bedroom behind her gave her a blessed opportunity to avoid the question. She whirled around and yanked open the door.

Zak sat on the bed, bawling. Rachel ran to the small boy and gathered him into her arms. He wrapped his arms around her neck and squeezed hard, but he kept crying. If only she had some way to comfort him.

With a shuddery sob, he pushed out one teary word. "Josh?"

"He's . . ." Rachel couldn't say where he was. They wouldn't have gone to the house now, would they? Would they come back upstairs to talk to her?

The door burst open, and Josh stood framed in the doorway.

Rachel's heart stuttered to a stop. "He's right here, Zak."

Zak stopped mid-cry, let go of her neck, and wriggled around in her arms. "Josh," he breathed.

Rachel pinched her lips together so she didn't do the same. But she worried her face mirrored Zak's thrilled expression.

When Josh hurried over and gathered Zak in his arms, every longing Rachel had ever harbored to be in Josh's arms rose full force and almost knocked her off her feet. She wanted him to hold her, to comfort her, to be there for her forever and ever. And even more, she wanted to unblock all the love for him she'd hidden all these years and let it flow into the open.

She clenched her fists around the folds of her apron to prevent herself from acting on her true feelings and pressed her lips together more tightly to keep from revealing her innermost desires.

Josh focused on the small boy he was holding and comforting, but part of his mind still reeled from Rachel's announcement. She planned to move to Ohio.

Hearing those words had shattered his world. And all the broken parts made one point crystal clear—he'd fallen in love with Rachel. Totally and completely.

In childhood, they'd had a special bond, a deep connection. He'd cared for her, wanted to spend time with her, cherished her friendship. Those feelings had never gone away, but now they'd been replaced by tenderness and the love of a man for a woman. He'd never loved anyone else and never would.

If the barrier from the past and his commitment to Anna Mary didn't stand in the way, Josh would rush across the room, sweep Rachel into his arms, and ask her to marry him. But that couldn't be.

Bending to kiss Zak's soft blond hair, Josh kept his head bowed so no one could see his face or read the desire racing through him. Deep shame filled him. With every fiber of his being, he knew he could never court or marry Anna Mary after this. It wouldn't be fair to her. Not when he was deeply in love with another woman.

Even worse, he always had been. Because he'd betrayed Rachel, he'd refused to admit it. What was he going to do with all these newly recognized feelings? He could never express them to Rachel, even after he asked for forgiveness. Because he couldn't bear to have her turn him down.

Mrs. Vandenberg broke the silence in the room. "Pride often keeps us from revealing what's in our hearts. Don't let it keep you from speaking the truth."

Across the room, Rachel shifted uneasily. Josh sensed every one of her movements, felt them in his soul. The old connection remained unbroken. Could she sense him, as well? If she could, she'd know his heart was full to overflowing with love for her.

But he couldn't speak those words. Too many other things stood in the way. He needed Rachel's forgiveness—if she'd give it once she'd heard what he'd done. And he had no right to even think about a relationship with anyone until he'd ended his courtship with Anna Mary.

A pang of guilt shot through him at the thought of Anna Mary. He'd chosen to date her because she was the opposite of Rachel in every way. Now he realized he'd been using her to escape from his true feelings. Poor Anna Mary. She deserved to have a boyfriend and future husband who cherished her for herself, not as a substitute for another woman. He'd jumped into that relationship blindly, hiding from the truth that Rachel was the only woman he could ever love.

But despite Mrs. Vandenberg's wise advice, Josh could never tell Rachel.

CHAPTER 23

Mrs. Vandenberg's words lingered in Rachel's heart and mind. They made perfect sense, but the elderly woman didn't know the blocks that stood between Rachel and Josh. You didn't declare your love for a man who was dating another woman.

And that brought her back to her reason for moving to Ohio. Her only honorable choice. Perhaps once she'd settled far from Josh, her feelings would fade over time. Her heart railed at that false hope. She'd love him forever.

"So, Rachel . . ." Mrs. Vandenberg broke into her thoughts. "You want to stay in Ohio?"

Neh, neh, neh, her spirit raged, but Rachel tamped down her true desires and answered hesitantly, "*Jah.*"

"May I ask what changed your mind?"

Rachel couldn't say *because I've fallen totally, hopelessly in love with Josh.* But what could she say? She needed a reason. "Um, maybe the children would be happier here?"

"You don't sound very certain."

"I'm sure they would be." She tried to make the words sound firm and sure, but her voice wobbled.

Mrs. Vandenberg gestured toward Josh, who cradled a

softly weeping Zak in his arms. "You think it would be
better for those two to be separated forever?"

The words *separated forever* sliced through Rachel's
soul with a sharp blade. She bled not only for Zak, but for
herself. Would her selfish decision deprive Zak of a comforting father figure as he grieved his parents' death? What
was she thinking?

She bit her lip. "*Neh.*"

"So, what other reasons do you have?" Mrs. Vandenberg's question was gentle, but it twisted the knife in
deeper.

Rachel had no answer. At least not one that she could
share. She offered hesitantly, "I just think it would be
best."

"For whom?" Mrs. Vandenberg tottered toward the
door. "I'll leave you for a bit to sort out your feelings and
make a firm decision."

Rachel had already sorted out her feelings, but how
could she share them? She had no right to Josh's affection.
She'd also made a final decision, but was it fair to Zak?

Pausing with a hand on the doorknob, Mrs. Vandenberg
delivered one final piece of advice. "Until you admit the
truth in your heart, you'll never find happiness."

But how could Rachel admit the truth she'd hidden in
her heart?

"Rachel, you don't really want to move to Ohio, do
you?" Josh's voice sounded anguished.

Would he miss her? Or maybe he didn't want to be
separated from Zak. They'd formed such a close bond.

"I just think it would be best," she repeated tonelessly.

"But wouldn't you miss Lancaster? And what about

your *mamm*?" The questions rushed from Josh's mouth. He had to find a way to change her mind. But how?

"And what about your quilting business?" Too late, he realized she'd have money from the house sale. She might not need to work.

"I could do that here. Besides, I probably won't do as much quilting until the children are older."

He almost took Mrs. Vandenberg's advice to heart and blurted out his true reason for not wanting her to move: *I'll miss you! I can't live without you!* But he swallowed back the words.

After taking a deep breath to calm his racing emotions, Josh forced out a calm and measured argument. "What about Mrs. Vandenberg? She's counting on the house for Annika. And I'm sure her financial adviser has done a lot of work to prepare for the sale and paid for a title search and . . ."

"I hadn't thought about that," she said miserably. "If Mrs. Vandenberg told Annika, she'll be disappointed. And I didn't mean to make extra work and trouble for Mrs. Vandenberg. Not after she's been so kind."

Had she already transferred the money? She'd said they'd do it today. Rachel had made such a mess of this.

Josh pressed his point. "And we—I mean the *g'may*— would miss you."

Rachel's hollow laugh cut into him. "I think most people there, especially in our buddy bunch, would be glad if I never came back."

The sadness pooling in her eyes made Josh wish he'd never brought that up. Perhaps that's why she'd decided to stay in Ohio. The girls at the singings would sigh in relief to be rid of the girl they called the Amish flirt.

Rachel sighed heavily. "But you're right about Mrs.

Vandenberg and Annika. I shouldn't back out of a deal I agreed to. I should let my *yea* be a *yea*."

Josh rejoiced. "Maybe you should tell Mrs. Vandenberg before she stops the process."

"You're right." Rachel headed for the door, but before she reached it, Marianna flailed her arms and whined. "*Ach*. She needs to be changed and fed."

"I'll take care of her while you tell Mrs. Vandenberg." Josh didn't want to take a chance of Rachel changing her mind. And he didn't want Mrs. Vandenberg to undo any of the processes she'd already set in motion. And most of all, he didn't want to lose the opportunity to keep the woman he loved in Lancaster.

Rachel didn't see much of Josh on Saturday, because he and Zak stayed busy at the house. Mrs. Vandenberg and Rachel toured the area, and spent time with Annika, who squealed with delight over the house and furnishings.

They all went to church with Annika on Sunday, which took up most of the day. When Josh wasn't carrying Zak, the little boy followed Josh as closely as a shadow. Rachel appreciated Josh putting Zak to bed both nights. And Josh sat beside a sleepy Zak to read from the Bible storybook after Zak said his prayers.

Every day, the bond between the two of them grew stronger. Rachel dreaded returning home and losing Josh's help. He'd be around for a few more days working on the house, but after that, she'd be on her own. Alone with the children. Maybe not completely alone. Barbara would be there to help. But Rachel didn't want to impose on the health aide for assistance with the children.

And Rachel would have to learn to live with this aching

yearning. That would be the greatest trial she'd ever faced. Even her grief over Cindy's death couldn't match the pain of losing Josh to another woman.

Early Monday morning, Josh whistled while he loaded the van, grateful to be going back home. His joy came from spending a long trip with Rachel, but even more, from knowing she'd be staying in Lancaster.

He had another reason for his eagerness to return. He needed to untangle himself from his relationship with Anna Mary. That would erase at least one blot from his conscience. He couldn't believe how lighthearted that made him. Ever since he'd asked Anna Mary to date, he'd been depressed. He hadn't realized it at the time, but his heart had sent him warning signals.

Maybe Anna Mary also had been questioning their courtship. She seemed much happier to see Tim's cousin, Abe, than she'd ever been to see Josh. And she'd been the one who'd suggested taking time apart to reevaluate their relationship. He'd done that and come to an unexpected conclusion. A conclusion he hoped wouldn't hurt her.

When they arrived at Rachel's house after their final meal break, Zak clung to Josh and refused to get out of the van. No amount of cajoling convinced the small boy Josh would return later.

"We can wait here until you put him to bed," Mrs. Vandenberg said.

She looked exhausted after the long trip, and Josh hated to impose on her more than they already had. But after she pointed out that the little boy had just lost two parents, Josh acquiesced.

While Rachel took Marianna inside, readied her for

bed, and looked in on her *mamm*, Josh, with an exhausted Zak dragging at his pant leg, made every trip from the van and back with the luggage and plastic crate of toys. Once they'd delivered everything to its proper place, Josh lifted Zak and carried him up to bed, where Zak begged for a bedtime story.

Mindful of Mrs. Vandenberg waiting, Josh selected a short one. Before he even finished, Zak had fallen asleep. On his way out, Josh said a quick hello to Betty and Barbara as well as a brief goodbye to Rachel, who'd been regaling both ladies with tales from Ohio.

"I'll be over tomorrow morning to finish the paddock fence and whatever else needs to get done, if that works for you." After getting everyone's approval, he waved and jogged out to the van.

As the driver headed for Josh's house, Mrs. Vandenberg swiveled her head to look him in the eye. "You might not remember my advice from back when you helped Rachel deliver her quilts at the market, but I believe it's time to remind you. Perhaps this time, you'll see it in a different light."

Josh sifted through his memories of that day, but he'd mostly stored impressions of Rachel's softness, gentleness, and her beautiful smile.

"Remember, Josh, sometimes we hang onto the old when God wants us to move ahead to the new. Does that ring a bell?"

It certainly did. He'd puzzled over it for quite a while afterward. And Mrs. Vandenberg was right. The meaning had completely flipped. She'd tried to warn him not to misinterpret it. He'd thought she meant give up dreams of Rachel to focus on Anna Mary. Now, all he wanted to do was to let Anna Mary go, but he didn't see a path forward with Rachel, even though his heart burned with that desire.

"One other thing to keep in mind: don't limit what God can do if you're honest about your feelings."

Josh intended to do just that—tell Anna Mary the truth. He no longer wanted to live with this on his conscience.

As soon as the van dropped him off, Josh hitched up the horse and headed off. Anna Mary would still be up in the early evening. Best to do it while he had courage and determination. As he knocked on the door, he prayed for God's wisdom and guidance.

"Josh?" Anna Mary looked surprised and not too pleased to see him. "What are you doing here?"

"There's something we need to talk about. May I come in?"

She opened the door reluctantly. "I thought we agreed to spend the next few weeks apart."

After Anna Mary led him into the living room, she didn't offer him a seat. "Please keep your voice down. Mamm's finally fallen asleep. She had a rough day."

"I'm sorry." Guilt welled up in Josh for adding to Anna Mary's burdens. Maybe now wasn't the best time to tell her he wanted to break up.

"I have to say I didn't expect you to show up here again." Anna Mary's words held a tinge of bitterness. "Not after Cathy Zehr saw you and Rachel driving out of town together at five in the morning on Thursday. She had to go in to the bakery early that morning. Did you just get back?"

Josh stared down at his shoes. "*Jah.*" He wished Cathy hadn't gossiped. That might make this even harder.

"So right after I say we should spend a few weeks apart to think about our relationship, you take off with Rachel for a long weekend. You told me you were traveling to do a job for Mrs. Vandenberg, but never mentioned anything about Rachel."

"I didn't know Rachel was going until that morning. And I was supposed to do construction work. Rachel was attending a funeral."

"I thought it was odd that you'd be going out of town when you have plenty of jobs around here. And you didn't protest when I suggested taking time apart. Now it all makes sense."

"It wasn't like that." Josh didn't want to argue over this. He had something more important on his mind. Before he could sort out the gentlest way to say it, Anna Mary beat him to it.

"Maybe it's for the best. I asked for time because I wasn't sure about my feelings for you. I don't think we're well suited."

Although Josh agreed with her, he couldn't help wondering if she was saying it to save face or if meeting Abe had prodded her to break things off. Either way, he was relieved.

When he didn't respond right away, Anna Mary hung her head. "I didn't mean to hurt you."

"It's all right. I came to the same conclusion while I was gone."

"That's good, but I hope she doesn't break your heart like she's done to so many others. You know what a flirt she is."

Josh wanted to blast Anna Mary for saying that about Rachel, so he pressed his lips together until he could cool his temper. "I don't think it's flirting to turn down rides after the singings."

"It is if she makes people think she's interested."

"I don't think she does that." If anything, Rachel always reminded him of a cornered animal searching for an escape route.

Anna Mary snorted. "Guess you'll find out."

Everyone would think Rachel turned him down when they didn't get together. Josh didn't mind. Let people think he had a broken heart. That might keep away predatory *mamms* hoping he'd marry their daughters.

When Josh didn't answer, Anna Mary yawned. "I'm tired. It's been a long day." She walked him to the door. "For your sake, I hope she gives up her flirting and settles down."

As he crossed the lawn to his buggy, his spirits sank as he pictured Rachel settling down. If she did, it wouldn't be with him.

CHAPTER 24

Josh arrived early the next morning as Rachel was starting her quilting. The children were still asleep.

"I didn't want Zak to wake up and find me missing," Josh explained. "I'll try to keep his life as stable as possible for the next few weeks."

Her mood soared. Did that mean he'd come here every morning? She schooled her face not to show her joy. "He's not awake yet, but come in."

"It's too early to start pounding outside, so could I talk to you while you work?"

"Of course."

His forehead creased. "It won't distract you, will it?"

Jah, it totally would! But Rachel didn't care. Quilting didn't compare to spending time with Josh.

He sat down across from her, a serious expression on his face. "I don't want to keep you from that quillow. It's really pretty."

"*Danke.*" Rachel ducked her head and pretended to concentrate on her stitches, but she could move her fingers almost by rote.

"Last night, after we got back from Ohio, I went to see Anna Mary."

Ach! Rachel almost pricked her finger. She set down the needle and shifted the fabric in the frame to give herself time to hide her reaction.

"Anna Mary broke up with me."

Rachel's head jerked up. "Oh, Josh, I'm so sorry."

"It was for the best. We hadn't been getting along well, and I have some things in my life I need to get straightened out."

"I see." She returned to her stitching with a joyous heart.

"Mrs. Vandenberg made me realize I needed to confess to things I've hidden out of shame. I need to make things right."

Rachel nodded. She'd come to the same conclusion. And the person she needed to talk to was Josh.

He rubbed a hand across the back of his neck and *rutsched* in the chair. "Rachel, I, um, need to apologize."

Apologize was too mild a word for what he had to confess, but he could think of no other way to phrase it. He started again. "I mean, I—"

A loud wail from upstairs disrupted his stammering. Josh jumped up, both relieved and disappointed not to tell Rachel his dark secret. "I'll go up and get Zak." Josh raced from the room and up the steps.

By the time he'd helped Zak dress, Marianna had begun crying. He changed and dressed her, then carried both little ones downstairs, where Rachel had already fixed a bottle and started breakfast.

If only this could be their daily routine together . . .

With both children awake, Josh would have no time to

unburden his heart. He'd need to wait for another time. Maybe at naptime.

"I'll take Zak outside with me," Josh said after they'd finished breakfast and washed the dishes.

Rachel must have found the baby carrier in the plastic crate, because she tucked Marianna into it and wrapped the straps around her. A sharp ache of longing filled him at Rachel's tenderness toward the baby. She looked so appealing as a mother. That brought back her comments about him as a *daed*.

He turned away quickly so he didn't give his feelings away. "Come on, Zak. Time to get to work."

The little boy trotted over and took Josh's hand. And once again, the desire to be a *daed*, to parent with Rachel, made his chest expand with yearning. His dream of every day beginning like this, of him having the right to hold her in his arms and kiss her when his heart overflowed with love. His deepest feeling for her begged to be expressed.

But now was not the time. This was not the place. And a huge barrier stood between them—his confession. Once he told Rachel the truth, that time might never come. The thought plunged him into gloom.

Daed always said hard work was the best antidote for heartache. Josh had plenty of that waiting for him in the backyard. After one last glimpse of Rachel cuddling Marianna in the carrier, he forced himself to turn away.

Hand in hand, he and Zak headed for the pasture to mend the fence. The way Zak stared up at Josh adoringly and held his hand so trustingly eased some of the emptiness in Josh's life. God had given him the privilege of caring for this small boy who'd lost both his parents. He needed to concentrate on being a fitting substitute for Zak's *daed*.

Josh let Zak assist with the lower rails, holding his hands as he pounded new slats onto the fence. Once Zak had done his part, he waited while Josh hammered the upper ones into place.

After a while, though, Zak grew bored and restless. He wandered around, picking up pretty stones.

"Look, Josh." Zak held up a pebble striped in tan and brown.

"Very nice." Josh agreed and went back to work.

He wanted to finish as much as he could so he could take a break at naptime and talk to Rachel while the little ones slept. With Barbara taking care of Betty now, he and Rachel could be alone. Maybe he could even convince her to take a walk. They could stroll to some of their favorite childhood spots.

While he hammered, Zak lined up a row of small stones. As Josh moved down to the next section of fencing, he lost track of Zak. Before they'd started, Josh had stored all the tools and sharp objects, so he wasn't too worried about Zak getting hurt. But Josh didn't want the little boy wandering off. After Josh had nailed the final board into that segment, he glanced around.

The row of pebbles had grown, but Zak was nowhere to be seen. Josh panicked. "Zak! Zak!"

A happy voice came from his left. "I'm here. Look at me!"

Josh spun around to see Zak bouncing on the rotted wood covering the old well. "Nooo!"

Josh's scream startled Zak. He tumbled backward. Landed with a thump that cracked the wood. Crashed through the opening and disappeared. His shriek of terror ended in a loud splash.

Racing toward the spot, Josh prayed one prayer after

the other. *Please, Lord, let him survive. Let me get to him in time. Show me what to do.*

When he reached the edge, he peered down into the depths. The hand-dug, old stone well appeared to be twelve feet deep. Thank goodness, it was shallow. Only a foot of water covered the bottom. Zak had landed on his rear, with his head above water. Josh prayed the water had cushioned his fall.

"Are you all right?" he called down.

Large, frightened eyes stared back up at him.

Thank the Lord, Zak was conscious. But he appeared stunned. Had he hit his head?

The shock on Zak's face squinched into pain, and he wailed, "It hurts."

"What hurts, buddy?"

"Ev . . . we . . . think," he gasped out between sobs. He held his arms up to be lifted out.

Everything? Zak's arms were covered in scrapes, but he seemed to be moving them with no trouble. But what about his leg, his spine, his back? And how could Josh get him out.

"I can't reach that far, Zak, but I'll get you out as fast as I can."

Rachel ran out the back door. "What happened? Why's Zak screaming?" She must have put Marianna to bed because she no longer had on the baby carrier.

"Zak's in the well. Can you talk to him? Keep him calm?" As soon as she reached the well, Josh sprinted to the barn and grabbed the ladder he'd used for roofing.

As he neared the well, Rachel's gentle voice floated to him. "Josh will save you. He'll get you out. He'll be right back."

Josh sucked in a breath as a sharp pang stabbed him.

Josh will save you played over and over again in his head. *Neh*, nobody should count on him. Sometimes, no matter how hard you try, you can't save someone. And then you pay for that the rest of your life . . .

So many things he could have done differently . . .

He couldn't let past failures paralyze him. Not now, when Zak needed him. Pushing the tormenting thoughts into the dark recesses of his memory bank, Josh staggered toward the well as fast as he could while balancing the heavy ladder.

"Josh is here, Zak. He'll help you." Rachel's relief colored her encouraging words.

But Josh didn't know if he could get Zak out or even if he should. What if Zak had spinal injuries or something and moving him made them worse?

"I'm so sorry, Rachel." All the burdens Josh carried spilled out into that heartfelt apology.

She glanced up at him surprised. "For what?"

"For not paying enough attention to Zak. For being irresponsible." *For hurting people you love now and in the past.*

"Accidents happen." Her gentle acceptance added to his guilt.

Some accidents were preventable. Those were the unforgivable ones.

Josh peered down into the well. "Doing all right, buddy?"

Zak shook his head. "I'm scared. And it's cooold."

"I'm going to get you out." At least Josh hoped he could.

Was he making a mistake in trying to do it himself? That's what he'd done wrong before. His chest constricted. Maybe he should call the fire department. An ambulance.

"Josh?" Zak's panicked cry pushed those all thoughts from Josh's mind. He had to get Zak out now.

This old well was wider than modern deeper ones, but it would be a tight squeeze once he got the ladder down there and had Zak in his arms. What if the two of them got stuck partway up?

Please, Lord, help me.

He called to Zak, "Don't move. I'm going to put this ladder down there. I don't want to hurt you. Then I'll come to get you."

Praying the whole time, Josh lowered the ladder. He had to angle it over Zak's head to brace it against the far wall. "This is going over you. I won't hit you."

Zak whimpered and covered his head as the ladder descended. Josh's arm muscles quivered from holding the heavy ladder out in the air and aiming it precisely. If he dropped it . . .

Beside him, Rachel sucked in a breath. Could she see his straining?

"It's all right. You're okay," she crooned over and over in a sweet, melodious voice.

Was she saying that to him or to Zak? Either way, it soothed Josh's nerves.

Behind them, the screen door banged open. Josh jumped and almost lost his grip. His breath, fast and choppy, echoed the blood pounding in his temples.

If the ladder slid from his hands, it could crush Zak.

Josh's palms grew sweaty at the picture. He needed to wipe them so the ladder didn't slip, but he couldn't let go.

Oh, God, please don't let me hurt another innocent person. Help me.

After the prayer, calm flowed through Josh, and he

barely heard Barbara's anxious questions or Rachel's steady answers.

He focused on clinging to the metal in his hands, hoping he wouldn't lose his grip as he maneuvered it into the tight spot by the wall. He had only a few additional inches to keep the sides clear of Zak's outstretched feet. The rungs almost touched Zak's head, but the small boy couldn't duck because he was almost up to his neck in water.

"I'll call 9-1-1," Barbara yelled.

She dashed off toward the neighbor's house as Josh settled the ladder feet onto the stone floor. The slippery, uneven surface would make the ladder wobbly and prone to slide when they climbed. He wiggled it a little to test it.

"I can hold it while you go down," Rachel offered.

Although he doubted she'd be strong enough to stabilize him, let alone handle the added weight of Zak, it couldn't hurt to have her try. "*Danke.*"

"I'm coming down, Zak," Josh yelled.

A tiny cry was Zak's only answer.

Wiping his hands on his pants to dry them, Josh gulped in several deep breaths and prayed the ladder wouldn't tip and send him crashing into the stones. Or slip and smash into Zak. Then Josh slung one leg around to straddle the ladder.

Rachel grasped both sides of the ladder as it shifted under his weight. She provided a good counterbalance as he lifted his other leg and set it in place.

"I'll be praying," she said as he took his first step down. Her reassuring voice inspired greater confidence.

For a few seconds, the two of them were face to face with only ladder rungs between them. Josh tamped down the thrill that ran through him as their eyes met. He needed his full attention on his task, so he broke their gaze to focus on Zak below.

"I'm coming, buddy. I'll be there soon."

A few feet above Zak's head, Josh's back scraped the stones. He couldn't go much farther down. And he hadn't thought about how he'd get Zak around to the climbing side of the ladder. If he bent down and reached around, he might be able to haul Zak up by the arms—if the ladder didn't tilt from the heavy weight and if Zak didn't have injuries Josh would aggravate by lifting him that way.

"Can you stand?" Josh asked.

Zak's eyes filled with tears. "My leg hurts."

"Maybe we should wait for the ambulance."

"Noooo!" Zak screeched. "I want you."

"I'll stay here until they come."

Zak swished his head back and forth in a vigorous *neh*. He scooted sideways and slid toward the ladder.

"Just wait," Josh cautioned. "We don't want your leg to get worse." If he'd broken a bone . . .

But Zak ignored him, grabbed a ladder rung, and pulled himself upright on one leg.

Josh squeezed his eyes shut for a moment. Would he be responsible for another injury?

Zak's teeth were chattering. From fear? Freezing water? Or both? Josh couldn't let Zak get sick too. By stretching, Josh managed to reach down between the rungs and just touch Zak's extended hands. Despite the stones ripping his shirt and back, Josh squatted lower and tried the next opening down. Their hands connected.

Danke, Lord!

When Josh had a firm grasp, he supported Zak's hopping steps to the side of the ladder. Now came the hard part. Lifting the small boy without dislocating his arms, without dropping him, without tipping the ladder, and without falling off.

He glanced up at Rachel. "Think you can keep us both steady when I bend over to pick him up?"

"I'll pull this way with all my strength. And I'll pray."

"I'm going to lift you up," Josh told Zak. "It might hurt for a little while, but soon you'll be in my arms."

Filling his lungs with air, Josh hefted the boy up. The ladder tipped. Rachel couldn't right it, but she hung on and kept it from falling over.

Zak's shrill cries as he dangled in the air worried Josh. Was he hurting the little boy? Doing permanent damage?

With another whispered prayer, he strained his burning muscles to boost Zak high enough to set his foot on a ladder rung.

"Try to put your good foot on the ladder. The one that doesn't hurt."

"They both hurt." Zak moaned, but he complied.

The weight on Josh's arms lessened, and he let out a long, painful breath as the ladder tilted back into position. Then, wrapping one arm around the soaked and slime-coated boy, Josh used the other to haul himself up to the next rung, ignoring the ripping sound as the rough stones caught his shirt and tore into his flesh.

One step, two steps higher, he broke free of the wall. Searing pain shot through his tired muscles, but he pressed on. Twelve feet wasn't far, but it felt more like twelve miles as Zak's shivering body soaked Josh's shirtfront with ice water. And Josh struggled to hold the waterlogged little boy and fight his way to the next rung with arms that threatened to give out. He couldn't let go.

When they reached the surface, Zak needed one more boost off the ladder and into Rachel's outstretched arms.

She leaned so far over, Josh worried she'd tumble headfirst into the well.

"Be careful," he warned.

But she ignored him and wrapped her arms around Zak, drawing him close to her. He huddled into her arms, one leg sticking out in the air. "You're freezing." She lifted the hem of her apron and pulled the fabric around him.

Josh stood where he was, dripping with slimy well water and sweat, mesmerized by the sight of them.

Barbara came running toward them. "Anything I can do to help? The ambulance is on the way."

"Some blankets from the upstairs hall closet," Rachel pleaded, and Barbara took off.

Josh hesitated to step off the ladder. Without steadying hands, it could pitch him sideways into the well.

He readied himself to jump.

"*Neh!*" Rachel shouted. "Don't move."

Her fearful expression froze him in place.

"Wait for Barbara to hold the ladder. We don't need another accident." Rachel squeezed her eyes shut, as if to block out terrible memories.

Memories he'd caused?

He didn't want to hurt or frighten her more, so he tamped down his impatience to be on solid ground and waited.

Barbara came flying back, panting and breathless. She dropped a stack of blankets on the ground and then tucked two heavy ones around Zak.

"Can you help Josh?" Rachel's tear-filled voice tugged at Josh's heart. "He needs someone to hold the ladder."

"Of course." Barbara's brisk, no-nonsense tone matched her stride. She reached Josh and grasped the ladder.

Her sturdy frame and set jaw assured Josh she'd hold on no matter what. He had no doubt she could hold his weight, unlike petite Rachel.

Josh stretched his leg as far as he could to step onto the rim, praying his slippery shoes would hold. Then he twisted his hold on the ladder to swing his other foot into place. Releasing his death grip on the ladder, he jumped onto solid ground.

With the way Josh's heart was pounding, he might need the EMTs Barbara had called. He collapsed onto the grass for a moment to catch his breath. They'd gotten Zak out!

All Josh wanted to do was stay here and rest for a while, but he staggered to his feet and headed toward Rachel.

"You going to be okay?" Barbara examined him closely.

He nodded. His muscles might ache for days, but he'd recover. What about Zak?

CHAPTER 25

Josh reached Rachel as Barbara bent over and ruffled Zak's hair. His straw hat must be floating in the well.

"You'll be fine," Barbara assured Zak. Then she lifted her head. "I'd better get in to tell Betty what happened. She sent me out here to check on the screaming." She hustled off.

Zak hadn't answered Barbara's question, and he was still trembling. His head drooped on Rachel's shoulder, and his eyes were closed. His pallor worried Josh.

"Is he all right?" he whispered.

I'm not sure, she mouthed.

Zak whimpered, and Josh studied the leg that stuck straight out from under the covers. Zak's pants had ripped from hem to thigh, exposing a gash.

His leg, Josh mouthed, and gestured toward it. *He may need stitches.* Josh was reluctant to touch it for fear of infecting the cut with slime from Zak's pants.

Sirens whirred in the distance. The ear-piercing wails grew louder as a police car and an ambulance pulled into the driveway. A fire truck followed.

Josh sucked in a breath. The sight and sound of the red

engine jolted him back to the last time a fire truck had raced into Rachel's driveway. He swayed on his feet.

Rachel screamed his name. "Josh! What's wrong?"

He lowered himself to the ground and closed his eyes, hoping to block out the images swirling past his eyes.

"I think he's going to faint," Rachel called as footsteps pounded up to them. "And this little boy fell in the well."

Josh wanted to tell them he wasn't fainting, but he couldn't croak out words, couldn't fight his way out of the nightmare clawing at him. "It was all my fault," he mumbled.

"Don't blame yourself." Rachel's soft voice floated to him from a great distance. "It was an accident. I'm sure Zak will be fine."

Not Zak. Josh wanted to correct her, but guilt and shame dragged him into the quicksand of the past and closed over his head, suffocating him.

A heavy hand on his shoulder drew him back to the present. "You okay, man? What hurts?"

Josh looked up into a craggy, concerned face, but he couldn't answer the question. Not with the words that ached to tumble from his mouth. *My conscience hurts. My heart hearts. My soul hurts.*

"Hmm, looks like you got some cuts and abrasions on your back here. Are you hurt anywhere else?"

"*Neh*, don't worry about me. I'll be fine. Just take care of the little boy."

"Dottie's already doing that."

Josh blinked away the mists of the past still clouding his eyes. Dottie and a young man barely out of his teens were lifting Zak onto a litter. He clung to Rachel's hand, but tears streamed down his face.

"Josh! Want Josh!"

The agonizing cry penetrated the lethargy surrounding Josh. He stumbled to his feet. "I have to go to him."

"Wait," the EMT called after him.

But Josh made a beeline for Zak. When Josh reached Zak's side, Rachel glanced up at him with adoration and relief.

"He wants you." Her soft, breathy words seemed to carry another message: *I want you too.*

But Josh had no time to be sure he hadn't dreamed her response. He grabbed the hand Zak held out as the litter moved rapidly toward the back of the ambulance. After it had been loaded, Josh, Dottie, and the teen squeezed inside. Josh had to move away as they took Zak's vitals, shined a penlight into his eyes, cut away the pant leg, cleaned the cut, and did their best to staunch the bleeding. Josh kept his eyes trained on Zak, trying to send him courage and strength.

Focusing on the small boy kept the memories fighting for Josh's attention at bay. But it couldn't lessen the waves of guilt racing through him over his failure to keep Zak safe. And another tragic mistake he'd made that hurt Rachel. Maybe she'd be better off if he stayed away from her forever. He only caused her grief.

Rachel stood frozen while they loaded Zak into the ambulance. She should go along, but what about Marianna, who'd just fallen asleep? Rachel had never had the responsibility for two children before. What did parents do when they needed to be in two places at once?

Barbara stuck her head out the back door. "You go on

with the little boy. I'll see to the baby. And don't you worry none, I raised six of my own. The little one will be fine."

Several neighbors had emerged from their houses at the sound of the sirens and clustered around Barbara, probably clamoring for news.

Even her Amish neighbor from across the road had left his fields. "Me and my boy'll cover up that well so's nobody else falls in."

"*Danke*," Rachel called to him and Barbara. And *danke*, Lord!

The ambulance driver motioned for her to sit in the passenger seat. After he closed the back doors, he climbed in and took off for the hospital. When he didn't drive at breakneck speed or turn on the siren, Rachel expressed her surprise.

"That's only for emergencies. Both patients are stable, and Dottie can handle cleaning and prepping the cut before we get there. Didn't look like your husband was hurt too bad."

Husband? Rachel's heart leaped at the thought. Oh, how she wished that were true. "He's not my husband. He's, um . . ." What was he? A friend didn't do justice to their bond, but she had no claim to anything more.

Still, he had broken up with Anna Mary. *Neh*, she'd broken up with him. Maybe he was still pining after her. Would he try to get back together? He hadn't looked heart-broken when he'd said they hadn't been getting along lately. Rachel could only hope.

Beside her, the older man chuckled. "Sounds like you're hoping he might be."

Jah, she was, but she couldn't admit that. What if he mentioned it to Josh? "He's just a friend."

"I don't know about that. Appeared like he was staring at you and wishing for the same thing."

Had he really been looking at her like that? Rachel beamed at the thought.

"Well, now, that brightened your day. He's a lucky man."

Maybe the driver just used this kind of patter to calm nervous passengers, but a small sprout of possibility poked up from the parched ground of Rachel's heart, and she watered it with hope.

If this *Englisch* stranger had read it in Josh's eyes, then maybe her own eyes weren't playing tricks on her when she thought he'd gazed at her with longing.

"So, is that your little brother back there?"

"*Neh*, he's my *sohn*." That was the first time Rachel had ever said that aloud, and the word felt odd and exciting at the same time. *Her sohn. And her dochder.*

"Your son?" The man's words came out stiffly. "I apologize. I shouldn't have said what I did earlier. I didn't realize you were married."

"I'm not." At the man's shocked expression, she hastened to explain. "My cousin just died and wanted me to adopt her children."

His face softened. "I'm so sorry about your cousin. My condolences. That's a big responsibility you're taking on."

"I know." Rachel's voice came out small and scared. Had she taken on too much?

She wasn't skilled at parenting. Having no nieces or nephews, no cousins close by, and no friends at church to visit, plus taking care of Mamm, meant Rachel hadn't spent much time around children. If today was any indication, she wasn't cut out for the job. Who let their little *sohn* fall into a well?

Jah, Josh was watching Zak, but it was still her duty to

keep track of her children. She'd failed miserably. If
Barbara hadn't come to the rescue, Rachel wouldn't have
known the best way to solve her dilemma over waking
Marianna and carrying a screaming baby into the hospital
or letting Josh go to the hospital alone.

"Don't worry," the driver assured her as he pulled
under the emergency entrance. "You'll do fine. The thing
kids need most is love. And you have plenty enough for
them and that handsome dude back there." He winked at
her. "Also, don't forget God. Prayer's the best resource
when you don't know what to do."

"*Danke.*" Rachel's soul overflowed with gratitude.
She'd been too focused on what she needed to do. It was
time to let God take over. He had the answers to everything, including her dreams of a relationship with Josh.

Josh followed the litter into the hospital. His back
burned where he'd scraped it raw, and the breeze as he
jogged beside Zak stung it more. Until now, with being so
fixated on Zak, Josh hadn't even noticed his wounds. And
he'd forgotten he'd torn the back of his shirt to shreds.

Coming up behind him, Rachel gasped. "Josh, your
back. They'll need to look at that."

"Maybe after they take care of Zak."

Rachel's face creased in distress as she took in Zak
lying on the stretcher. "I'm such a terrible mother."

"You? I'm the one who should have been keeping an
eye on him."

"But it's not your responsibility. It's mine."

And with those words, Rachel edged Josh out of the
picture. The picture of her life that included two children,
but not him. He swallowed hard as his dreams crumbled to

dust. He had no right to expect anything else. Especially after what he'd done.

When a nurse motioned the ambulance crew to follow him down a hallway, Dottie glanced over at Rachel and Josh. "Someone needs to fill in paperwork at the desk."

Rachel cast a troubled look at Zak. "I guess I need to do that, but . . ."

"Don't worry. I'll see if I can stay with him until you're done."

The frown lines on her face melted away. "*Danke.*"

As the crew pushed Zak forward, he extended a hand toward Josh. "I want my *daedddd.*"

The poor boy. Josh ached for him. He rushed to catch up with the stretcher.

"Are his parents here?" the nurse asked.

Josh reached them and waved to Rachel standing in line by the check-in counter. "His *mamm* is over there."

Zak thrashed on the stretcher. "I want my *daed.*" He pointed straight at Josh.

"Stay still, buddy," Josh warned as he moved closer and reached for Zak's hand.

"You his dad?" the nurse asked.

Josh opened his mouth to say *neh*, but Zak shouted out, "*Jah!*"

How could Josh deny that with Zak, his eyes wide in fright, so small and tiny on the stretcher, clinging to Josh's hand? He didn't answer the question. "I can go with him."

"Stay with me," Zak pleaded.

At the nurse's nod, Josh headed back with Zak and stayed beside him while they numbed him to stitch up his leg, sent him for x-rays, and cleaned and disinfected all his cuts and scrapes. Rachel joined them as soon as she finished filling out all the paperwork. Because Zak's clothes had been cut off, they let him keep the hospital gown on and wrapped him in a blanket.

Then she held Zak while Josh got checked in. Zak didn't want to let Josh out of his sight, so he and Rachel both accompanied Josh into the room to get his back treated.

Rachel looked away when the nurse asked him to take off his shirt. "Maybe we should go get a packet of cookies from the machine, Zak." She stood and headed to the door.

"*Neh*, stay with Daed!" He wriggled in her arms.

"Be careful of that leg," Josh warned, and Zak's *rutsching* ceased. "Go with Rachel for a snack. I'll meet you out there."

Embarrassed, he surrendered his shirt to the nurse who cleaned his wounds. It stunk of pond scum and was torn into strips. She probably wouldn't let him put it back on once his back had been treated. What was he going to do? He couldn't walk out there without a shirt.

Rachel carried her fussy *sohn* into the lobby. They must have a vending machine somewhere in the building. The line at the desk stretched even farther than when Rachel had stood in it.

As she glanced around for someone she could ask for directions, she spotted an elderly white-haired woman sitting patiently in the far corner of the waiting room. Rachel hurried over.

"Mrs. Vandenberg? Is something wrong?"

The elderly lady smiled up at Rachel. "Ah, just the person I was waiting to see. I stopped by your house to sign some papers, but Barbara explained you'd gone to the hospital."

"Papers?" After all that had happened today, Rachel blanked on the reason for signing—*Ach*, the house. "I'm sorry I wasn't there."

"I can see you've been busy. We can take care of that later." Mrs. Vandenberg handed Rachel a tote bag.

"What's this?" Rachel pulled out a man's shirt and broadfall pants.

"I thought Josh and Zak might need some clothing. Barbara found me some for Zak. And Josh's mother gave me those."

"You're an angel."

Mrs. Vandenberg chuckled. "I'm not sure God would think so, but I'm glad I could help." She reached into her purse and pulled out several snack packs of peanut-butter crackers and handed one to Zak.

Rachel opened them and settled on a chair next to Mrs. Vandenberg to dress Zak. "I should take these back to Josh." Her cheeks burned as she remembered him shrugging out of his filthy, tattered shirt. The sight of his broad, bare back had discomfited her.

"You can leave Zak here." Mrs. Vandenberg held up the other packets. "I'm sure he'll be fine until you return."

Zak, his mouth stuffed with cracker, barely uttered a sound of protest when Rachel set him on the chair beside Mrs. Vandenberg.

"I'll be right back." Rachel got permission to go back and tapped at Josh's exam room door.

The nurse opened the door a crack.

"These are for Josh." The door opened wider so Rachel could hand over the clothes. She hadn't meant to glance up and—*Ach!* She fled down the hall, her face flaming.

She stopped before she reached the lobby to compose

herself, but she couldn't erase the image of . . . Taking a deep breath, and hoping her face wasn't still stained the color of tomatoes, she strode across to the back corner. Zak was curled up in Mrs. Vandenberg's lap, sound asleep. He'd missed his morning nap and his lunch.

"I predict he'll sleep until dinnertime. He's had quite an adventurous morning." She glanced up with a smile. "Ah, here comes Josh."

Rachel turned, but couldn't meet his eyes. Had he seen her reaction?

"*Danke* for the clothes. How did you know?"

"In ninety-plus years, I've had plenty of emergency room visits. When Betty told me about your injuries—and Zak's—I figured you might need fresh clothes."

"You thought right. I'm grateful."

Mrs. Vandenberg handed them each a pack of crackers. "You're probably hungry."

"I am. *Danke*."

Josh's deep bass voice expressing gratitude strummed chords inside Rachel and reminded her of the very masculine muscles rippling on his chest when—

She had to get control of her runaway thoughts. She spun toward the desk. "I, um, need to go pay the bill."

"It's already been done, dear. For both of you. My charity has an account here to help people in need."

"But I'm not in need." Not anymore. She now had the money Mrs. Vandenberg had transferred to her account.

"You didn't need to do that." Josh looked distressed.

"I didn't want you waiting in that long line when my driver and I have other errands to do. Come along now."

When Josh again tried to protest, she waved it away.

"If it bothers you, donate whatever you'd like to the charity. Now, can you lift this little man so I can stand?"

That stopped Josh. He bent and scooped Zak into his arms. Rachel vowed to send a large donation.

After they pulled into Rachel's driveway, Mrs. Vandenberg smiled at both of them. "I think it might be wise if the two of you put that little boy in bed, asked Barbara to keep an eye on the children, and took a walk. It's about time you both were honest with each other."

Rachel gulped hard. How did Mrs. Vandenberg always manage to put her on the spot?

His face and conscience burning, Josh carried Zak up to bed. No getting around it this time. Josh had to be completely honest with Rachel.

He tucked a cover around Zak and ran a finger over the tiny teddy bears Rachel must have quilted. Her handwork was as beautiful as her soul. He'd wounded her once, and now he'd do it again.

Josh bent and kissed Zak's forehead. This might be the last time he'd ever get to do that. He crossed the room to pat Marianna. Once Rachel heard what he had to say, she'd never want him to come back here again. Josh would miss this little guy. And his sister. Even more, he'd miss Rachel.

He descended the steps with slow, measured steps, as if he could stop the passage of time. Laughter came from Betty's room, so he tapped at the door. He'd say goodbye to her too.

Betty's smile widened when she saw him. "Josh, come in and join us."

"I can't stay. I just came to let you know Rachel and I will be going for a walk." How did you say goodbye without actually saying it?

While he stood shuffling his feet, Betty chuckled. "I know you're eager to go." She shooed him toward the door. "Stop back here after your walk. I want to hear all about it."

Josh was certain she'd hear all about it from Rachel. And she'd understand why he hadn't come back here with her daughter.

"Don't worry about the children," Barbara said. "I'm happy to listen for them. Take whatever time you need. Liesel Vandenberg said you had some important matters to discuss."

Josh choked back the lump that rose in his throat. *Jah*, they did. He couldn't speak, and even if he could manage words, he couldn't say he'd see them later. He settled on waving before he shut the door. Another door he'd be shutting forever.

Rachel waited by the front door for Josh, wringing her hands. Although Mrs. Vandenberg was right about them needing to confess things, why did it have to be on a day already so fraught with tension?

She wished for calm to sort out her thoughts, organize her words. But with two little ones, she might never have that luxury again. She needed to snatch this opportunity to make things right.

Josh emerged from her *mamm*'s bedroom with a serious expression. "Barbara's going to take care of both children so we can have some time to talk." From the grim set of his lips, he didn't appear to be looking forward to it.

Neither was she. But it would be good to get this off her conscience.

"Why don't we go for that walk?" he suggested.

He led the way out the back door and to the patch of woods where they played years ago. As they entered the trees, his face softened. "We had some good times here, didn't we?"

"*Jah*." Her eyes stung at the memories. If only they could go back to those days and that special friendship. Sometimes, when Josh let down his guard, they connected the way they used to, but then his eyes grew shuttered and distant. She wished she knew the key to unlocking those barriers between them.

When Josh reached the large, flat rock he'd been sitting on the day she'd first met him, he motioned for her to sit on the rock. Instead of joining her, though, he paced in front of her as if agitated.

Rachel wanted to pat the space beside her and beg him to join her. His jerky movements made her tense. She needed to unburden herself, but it was too hard to start a conversation while he strode back and forth like a caged animal. Maybe she could convince him to sit next to her.

"Josh?"

He waved a hand to cut her off. "Wait. Rachel, there's something I need to tell you. Something I should have said a long time ago."

Josh cleared his throat several times, but he didn't speak. His movements stilled, and his shoulders slumped.

She wanted to let him know she'd hear him out, no matter what, but she didn't get the chance.

He blurted out, "If you never want to see me or talk to me again, I'll understand. I deserve it."

"Nothing you say would make me do that."

A choked sound of disbelief came from his mouth. Then, he told the truth he'd held inside for eight years. "I killed your brother."

CHAPTER 26

Josh couldn't look at Rachel. He couldn't bear to see her face, but he'd finally said it. Admitted to his guilt.

"That doesn't make sense. Tom died trying to put out the barn fire." She waved in the direction of the old barn that had once stood in the field behind her house. "You weren't there." She hesitated. "Were you?"

"*Jah*, I was. And I was responsible for the fire."

Rachel drew in a shocked breath. "You set the fire?"

"I didn't set it, but I could have prevented it, and I didn't," he said miserably.

"I don't understand. You saw who set the fire?"

"They didn't set it deliberately, but . . ."

"Stop," she begged.

Her response startled him to a standstill. Was this too much for her? He should have approached it gradually instead of spitting it out without considering her feelings.

"Please," she pleaded, "stop pacing and sit down. And start at the beginning of what happened."

Josh settled on the rock a safe distance from Rachel, but he *rutsched*, his whole body antsy. "I'm not sure where to start. I guess it began on a Saturday soon after we turned thirteen. You had to stay home because your *mamm* was having a bad day. Your brother had off work, and you told me to go ahead and go fishing with Tom and his friends."

Rachel clenched her hands in her lap. She'd had many such days. By that time, her *mamm* frequently struggled to get out of bed. Rachel wasn't sure she wanted to hear this story so soon after Cindy's funeral.

When she'd told Josh to *stop*, it hadn't only been because his pacing made her dizzy. She didn't really want to relive that horrible experience again. Yet, she could sense his need to tell the truth. Mrs. Vandenberg's lecture must also have made an impact on him.

Josh's Adam's apple bobbed up and down. "I was closer to you and your brother than I was to my own family." Sorrow hung on every word.

She couldn't look at him, or she'd cry. Tom had treated Josh more like a brother than his own brothers did. And her brother always made sure no one bullied Josh or any of the friends he brought along. When Tom wasn't around, Josh's brothers picked on him unmercifully. Rachel ground her teeth at the memory of their cruelty when they hadn't known she was around.

Josh took a breath. "After we'd fished for several hours, Tom picked up his catch, said he'd caught enough for dinner, and he needed to check on you."

Rachel's eyes welled with tears. That was Tom. Always looking out for her. She couldn't have asked for a nicer big brother. She stole a glance at Josh, but his eyes had focused off into the distance, as if watching scenes from the past scroll in front his eyes. From his anguished expression, this fishing trip had gone badly after her brother left.

* * *

Some sounds—the rushing of the creek over stones, the birds chirping in the trees, frogs splashing in the pond—surrounded Josh in the here and now, but they'd been present that day, as well. And just like that, the world around him disappeared, and he sat on the creek bank with the mossy scent of grass mingling with the tang of over-turned earth where they'd dug up worms and the pungent odor of caught fish.

Josh ran his hand over the smoothness of the fishing rod Tom had handed over before he left.

"Here, Josh, you can use this."

Josh set aside his homemade stick and string to take Tom's glossy pole. His brothers' eyes glowed with envy. They'd each bought themselves a rod, but none could compare to this one. Usually, Josh had to make do with left-overs, hand-me-downs, or whatever he could cobble together.

He took Tom's loan reverently and gratefully. "I'll take good care of it," he promised.

"I know you will." Tom smiled. "I can trust you."

But that trust had been misplaced. Josh had taken special care of the fishing pole, but he'd never been able to return it. It still sat in his bedroom closet.

Beside him, Rachel stirred.

Josh tried to pick up where he'd left off. "You should have seen how jealous my brothers were when Tom lent me his fishing pole."

Rachel laughed, but it sounded hollow and sad. "I can imagine. Tom always liked doing things for you. He said you were the younger brother he never had."

Her words twisted a blade in Josh's gut. He'd always

imagined Tom as his brother, but he'd never realized the feeling had been mutual. Knowing that made Josh's story even more unbearable.

He sifted through his memories to find the next important thing to tell Rachel.

A few other youngie *drifted off, and soon only Josh and his three brothers remained on the bank. His oldest brother set down his pole and nudged the other two. Marv held something in his hand, but Josh couldn't see. All three of them laughed.*

"What do you have?" Josh demanded. He edged closer, trying to peek.

Marv closed his hand and tucked it in his pocket. "None of your business. You're too young to know."

"Tom doesn't think I'm too young."

"Well, we do."

Adam, his second oldest brother, chimed in. "You'd better take the fish home before it goes bad." He thrust his fishing pole at Josh. "And take our poles back to the house. We have something important to do."

"I want to come with you."

"Neh. You have jobs to do." Marv handed Josh the other two poles. "See you later."

Josh dropped their poles, but he set Tom's down carefully. Then he jumped to his feet and planted his hands on his hips. "I'm going along."

Marv's eyes narrowed. "If you do, I'll tell Mamm you broke Mrs. Smith's window."

"I did not." Josh pointed at Adam. "You did. I saw you."

Adam smirked. "But if all three of us say you did it, who will Mamm believe?"

Would his brothers really lie? Josh's hands balled into

fists as his brothers took off into the nearby trees. This was so unfair.

The more he thought about it, the angrier he grew. His brothers often forced him do some of their chores, but today he wouldn't do what they said.

Leaving their poles where they'd fallen, Josh picked up Tom's and started off after them. He had no trouble following them because they joked and laughed as they tramped through the woods. Josh just had to stay quiet and not crunch branches underfoot.

When his brothers left the woods, they headed across a fallow field toward an old rundown barn on the back of Rachel's property. The roof had fallen in years ago, and Tom had warned everyone to stay away from it. He claimed the rotten floorboards might collapse if anyone stepped on them. Closer to their house, the Glicks had another, newer barn they used for their horse and buggy.

If Josh followed his brothers out of the trees, they'd see him. He stayed behind a large maple.

His brothers trooped over to the entrance, and Marv pulled on the saggy door. As it creaked partway open, the building shook.

Lloyd laughed. "Be careful. We don't want the whole thing to collapse on us."

"Jah, that'd spoil our fun." Marv eased the door just enough so they could squeeze through.

What were they doing in there?

At the time, he had no idea, but now he knew. And if he'd been braver, he could have at least tried to stop them.

"Josh?" Rachel's soft voice indicated she was waiting for more of the story.

He didn't want to admit his cowardice, but she needed to know the truth. "When my brothers took off from the fishing hole, they didn't go home. I followed them, even though they warned me not to. They headed for that old barn."

She sucked in a breath. "But everyone knew it was dangerous. Tom always warned everyone. I hope they didn't go inside."

"*Jah*, they did. And I sneaked over to see what they were doing."

Once again, he plunged into the past.

He crept closer, circling to the back of the barn. The walls had chunks of wood and even parts of boards missing. If he scrunched down, he might be able to crawl inside. But Tom's warning rang in his head.

Moving along the back wall, he peered through all the openings until he found one that gave him a good view of his brothers. They each held a small piece of paper. Then Marv pulled a plastic bag from his pocket and sprinkled what looked like dead leaves on each paper. Lloyd rolled his up.

Cigarettes? Josh stared at them, shocked. Mamm had a rule about that.

His brothers weren't going to smoke in there, were they? They all knew better. Daed had lectured them many times about fire hazards in the barn.

Josh held his breath. Maybe they wouldn't light them. For a few moments, they put one end in their mouths and pretend-smoked them, making faces while they laughed at each other. He relaxed. They were only playing.

Hanging around his brothers wasn't as much fun as he imagined. He was about to take off when Marv pulled out a pack of matches. Josh froze. Marv wasn't going to use those, was he?

Although Josh assured himself they'd pretend with the

matches, too, his stomach hurt. Marv's serious expression warned Josh before his brother struck the first match.

A tiny flame flared. Josh's throat was so dry and tight, he couldn't say a word as Marv lit each cigarette.

As he had then, Josh tensed and clenched his fists. He struggled to breathe. But he had to explain this to Rachel.

"When my brothers went into your barn, they lit home-made cigarettes."

Rachel stared at him, horrified. "Is that when the fire started?"

"I don't think so." The blaze hadn't begun until later that evening. "I didn't get to watch what happened next because my brothers caught me spying on them."

"*Ooo,* Josh." Rachel sounded worried for him.

He'd tried to stay hidden, but when smoke drifted his way, he coughed. And as usual, his brothers had ganged up on him.

Marv whirled around, ash drifting from his cigarette as he tucked his arm behind him. If his brother thought he was hiding what he was doing, he was mistaken. Smoke drifted from behind his back.

"Josh!" Marv's face twisted. "You little sneak." He charged out of the barn and dashed around the building, but Josh had taken off.

"You'd better not tattle," Adam yelled after him. "Re-member the window."

Josh had no intention of tattling, even though he should. Besides blaming him for the smashed window, his brothers would make his life miserable. He didn't stop running until he reached the clearing by the creek.

Panting hard, he snatched up the fishing poles and bucket of fish. Then he raced home. When Mamm asked where his brothers were, he waved in the direction of the

Glicks'. His hand-sweep encompassed the woods and the creek. He hadn't meant to mislead Mamm.

She sighed. "They're where they usually are when there's work to be done."

He should set her straight, but Marv's furious face danced before Josh's eyes.

Mamm set a hand on his shoulder. "Did they leave you alone again?"

Josh shrugged. "This time, I left them."

A foolish mistake he'd regretted ever since.

"Rachel, I'm sorry. I should have stayed, stood up to my brothers, forced them to put out the cigarettes. I should have gone inside the barn and stomped out every spark."

"Josh, that's a lot to expect of yourself, especially when you were outnumbered three to one. Just remember, I saw some of the mean things your brothers did to you."

"David beat Goliath. Maybe if I'd been stronger. Trusted God more." Josh hung his head. "But when they threatened me, I ran away."

"I don't blame you."

Her words were a healing balm to his soul, but she hadn't heard the whole story. When Josh got home, he'd longed to spill his brothers' secret. Fear of their revenge kept him silent. A silence he'd come to regret.

"I should have told Mamm and Daed, but I didn't."

He'd wriggled through dinner, the words on the tip of his tongue. But every time he opened his mouth to speak, one of his brothers shot him a menacing glare.

Two hours later, tendrils of smoke curled above the trees. Josh bolted from his chair and ran to the window. In the distance, flames shot into the air. Although the woods blocked his view of the building on fire, a heavy ball of dread settled in his stomach. He had no doubt which one it was. The Glicks' old barn was burning.

That's when he made another fatal mistake.

"Later, when I saw the fire, I should have run to the phone shanty and called the fire department. I should have called Daed and my brothers to help. Instead, I ran through the woods by myself to check."

When he emerged from the trees, he froze in horror as flames licked up the sides of the barn and across the top roof beam. Sparks shot into the air and showered down from burning wood. Terrifying and fascinating, the flickering flames captivated him.

Several minutes passed before he realized he needed to do something. Rather than racing for a phone, Josh dashed to Rachel's house and called for Tom to come and see.

As soon as they got close enough for Tom to see the source of the fire, he shouted for Josh to run to the nearest phone. But Josh ignored him and helped pour buckets of water from the well onto the grass around the fire.

"I'm not worried about that old thing." Tom waved toward the barn. "But we need to keep the woods from catching fire. If this fire spreads to the trees, all the houses on the other side of the woods could burn down. Including yours."

Josh tried to keep up with Tom, but Josh poured one bucket to every three of Tom's.

"I don't think we're going to make this. Go call the fire department while I do this. Bring your daed *and brothers with you."*

Although Josh didn't want to leave, he did what Tom said. And soon, he and his family were sprinting toward the fire.

As sirens wailed in the distance, Josh spotted two kittens inside the barn. He pointed them out to Tom.

"I'm going to get them out," Josh yelled.

"Neh, I'll do it." Tom elbowed Josh out of the way.

Ignoring Daed's shouts to stay away from the building, Tom ran past Josh and leaped over two burning floor beams to reach the trapped kittens. They wriggled and scratched, but Tom wrapped them in his shirt and raced for the doorway.

Rachel reached out and touched his arm, startling Josh back to the present. "You came to get Tom then, didn't you?"

Josh nodded. "I wish I hadn't. Why didn't I call 9-1-1 like your brother told me to? I wanted to help him, but if I'd done that, maybe Tom would be here now."

"Oh, Josh, don't blame yourself."

He groaned and buried his face in his hands. "I was the one who pointed out the kittens."

"Kittens?"

"They were caught in the barn behind two fallen beams. I was going to rescue them, but Tom pushed me out of the way."

Rachel sucked in a sharp gasp of air. "That's so like him."

"*Jah*. It should have been me, not Tom." *I'll never forgive myself for that.* "He saved the kittens, but . . . ."

Josh shut his eyes, trying to block the picture of Tom in the doorway.

Tom reached over the burning beams on the floor to tip the kittens from his shirt onto the grass. As the kittens scampered to safety, he stepped over the beams. He almost made it . . .

As fire engines, police cars, and an ambulance screamed

to a halt in the grass nearby, Tom hesitated and turned to look. That's when the fiery lintel overhead crashed down.

Rachel squeezed his arm. "One of the neighbors told us what happened. I'm so sorry you had to go through all that."

"Me?" *How can Rachel possibly sympathize with me? Tom's the one who's gone. And it's all because of me.* Josh blurted out, "But I'm the reason your brother is dead."

"It's not your fault."

"But if I'd confronted my brothers about smoking . . . If I'd told Daed, he would have marched them over to the barn and made sure every last spark had been put out. If I'd called the fire department first, instead of running to look and then getting Tom . . . If I'd gotten the kittens out myself . . ."

"Then you'd be the one I'd be missing." Tears sparkled on Rachel's long eyelashes.

She'd miss him?

"Even though I've struggled to understand it, we have to accept it as God's will." Her throaty whisper touched his soul.

But Josh still struggled to see it as God's will. He'd never considered it as anything but his own failure. One he needed to confess and be forgiven for. "I know it's too much to ask for your forgiveness—"

"For what? Your brothers' foolishness? You wanting to save the kittens? My brother beating you to the barn? Tom being his usual heroic self? A burning beam falling?"

"*Neh.* All the things I didn't do."

"We all make mistakes."

"But mine killed someone."

"Are you saying God isn't powerful enough that He couldn't have undone your mistakes and prevented that beam from falling? Are you more powerful than God? You caused all this to happen?" Rachel challenged.

Josh's head spun. Rachel's logic left him twirling in circles, like he'd done as a child on that tire swing, until he collapsed, dizzy and spent, unsure which end was up.

"We don't know why God chose to take Tom when he did. And we both wish it had never happened, but I'm grateful you weren't taken."

She'd said something similar earlier. What did she mean? Josh filed it away to consider later. Right now, he still hadn't finished his confession.

Tom had died in the hospital two days after the fire. Josh had gone to the funeral, but he'd never been able to look Rachel in the eye again. He'd abandoned her when she needed him the most.

CHAPTER 27

Rachel had squirmed inwardly throughout Josh's confession. Although she understood why he blamed himself, she didn't look at it that way. She wished she could get him to see the events through her eyes. But he only appeared confused when she tried to reassure him, and the guilt on his face hadn't lessened.

And hers had increased. If only she'd known he thought Tom's death had been his fault, they could have talked about it earlier, gotten all this straightened out. But she'd chosen to hide in her shell and nurse her bruised feelings.

Josh broke into her self-reproach. "That's not the only thing I need to ask forgiveness for. I—" He shifted uncomfortably and stared at the ground. "I wasn't there for you after the funeral. I couldn't face you. I didn't stop to think about how you were hurting, how you needed comfort. I'm so sorry."

"It's all right." Now that Rachel knew what he'd been going through, she berated herself for holding onto her wounded feelings rather than reaching out. But they'd both been thirteen, young, and self-centered.

"*Neh*, it's not all right. I should have been there for you."

Before he could ask, she said, "I forgive you. And I hope you can forgive me."

"Forgive you? For what?"

"For holding a grudge." Hot waves of color washed over her face. It pained her to admit her pettiness. "I judged you without asking why you stayed away. Mrs. Vandenberg pointed out my unforgiveness."

"I don't blame you. If someone had treated me like that, I'd have been angry and hurt."

"*Jah*, I was. But if I'd gotten over myself and tried to heal the break, we could have spent the last eight years as friends." Rachel lowered her lashes. "I'm sorry."

"I am too. Can you ever forgive me for not owning up to my part in Tom's death and for abandoning you after the funeral?"

Her answer came out soft and breathy. "*Jah*, I forgive you for everything." Speaking those words released the resentment that had chained her spirit. Her soul rose light and free. She should have done this years ago.

Rachel glanced shyly over at Josh. Without the barrier of her grudge, she had nothing to hide behind. Nothing to conceal her true feelings for Josh. Nothing to protect her from hurt if he rejected her.

He seemed to be studying her intently. "Rachel?" The tentative way he said her name revealed he, too, felt exposed and uncertain.

Too overwhelmed to respond, she only tilted her head to let him know to continue.

"As long as we're confessing things, can I tell you something about Anna Mary?"

Rachel tensed. She wasn't sure her newly opened heart could bear to listen to him talk about another woman.

Before she could stop him, Josh launched into his explanation. "Do you know why I chose to date her?"

Wrapping her arms around herself, Rachel steeled herself against the pain. If only she could block her ears so she didn't have to hear the details about the woman he'd chosen to court.

"I picked her because she had straight black hair instead of strawberry-blond curls, brown eyes instead of sea-green ones, and because she was practical and didn't wander off into her imagination."

Rachel hunched in on herself. In other words, Josh wanted someone the exact opposite of her. A complete and total rejection of her.

"But that's why it didn't work out. I'd picked someone who would never remind me of you because I couldn't bear to remember the past. It hurt too much."

"I'm sorry."

"Sorry?" Josh's brows drew together in a puzzled frown. "About what?"

"That you couldn't bear to think about me."

"*Ach,* Rachel, I didn't mean it that way. I only meant I didn't want to think about you because I couldn't bear to remember all I'd lost. But it didn't work. I kept dreaming of you, not Anna Mary."

Rachel sucked in a breath. Did he mean what she thought he meant?

"Although I didn't realize it at the time, I'd chosen her to forget you. But the whole time I was with her, I wished I could be with you instead."

Rachel clasped her hands together. Had Josh really wanted to be dating her? It seemed too good to be true.

"Poor Anna Mary. I believe she always sensed it. I'm pretty sure that's why she got so upset when she saw us under the tree. She could tell who my heart really preferred."

"Me? You wanted to be with me?" Rachel floated the question like a fragile soap bubble that the slightest pinprick could puncture.

"*Jah.* The truth is, my feelings for you never changed, but I didn't feel worthy of you after what I'd done."

"Josh Yoder, how could you?" Rachel straightened her spine. "You didn't trust me to forgive you? Do you think I'm that cold and hard-hearted?"

He shook his head. "Never. I just didn't think I deserved forgiveness after what I'd done."

"All those wasted years," Rachel murmured under her breath. But hope dawned in her heart. Had Josh been trying to say he still felt the same way about her? That he still loved her?

"I never stopped loving you," she admitted.

Now it was Josh's turn to suck in a breath. "Do you mean that?"

Rachel put on a haughty expression. "You should know I never say things I don't mean." Then just as quickly, she bowed her head. "That isn't true, is it? I spent the past eight years pretending I didn't care, acting like I didn't notice you going out with Anna Mary."

"That bothered you?"

"*Jah.* Seeing the two of you together shattered my heart."

A pained expression crossed Josh's face. "*Ach*, Rachel, I never meant to hurt you. Is there any chance you can forgive me for that and we can start over?"

For a moment, Rachel couldn't breathe. She only stared at him, filled with wonder. "You mean go back to being friends?"

* * *

Josh wanted so much more than that, but if that's all Rachel was ready for, he'd take it. "*Jah*, I'd like to be friends."

If he wasn't mistaken, she looked disappointed. Did she want something more? He hesitated to ask.

Mrs. Vandenberg's words echoed in his mind. *Don't limit what God can do if you're honest about your feelings.*

He'd spent the past eight years afraid to speak the truth. One conversation had cleared away so much of that residue. What if he followed Mrs. Vandenberg's advice?

"Rachel, if all you'd like is to be friends, then that's what we'll be." The tightening of her lips gave him the courage to continue. "But what I'd really like is to return to our childhood plans—all of them."

"You mean"—she examined his face with a hopeful expression—"our future together?"

"*Jah*, courting." He hesitated, hoping he wasn't going too far. "And marriage and a family."

She laughed. "We already have a family."

"We certainly do. Is that a *jah*?" On edge, he waited for her response, hoping it would be the answer to his prayers.

Rachel's heart ricocheted in her chest. She couldn't say *jah* fast enough. "It certainly is." She'd never dreamed she'd marry, let alone to the only man she'd ever loved. God had not only given her children, but He'd also provided her *sohn* and *dochder* with the most *wunderbar daed*.

Tears spilled down her cheeks. "Tom always claimed

I'd marry you someday because we made the perfect couple. I wish he could be here to know he was right."

"Me too." Josh reached over and brushed away the teardrops. "I wouldn't be surprised if he already knows."

Rachel laughed. "You might be right. I hope he does."

"I know two other people who'll be overjoyed."

"Zak and Marianna?" Rachel couldn't wait to tell Zak. He'd be thrilled to have Josh for a *daed*, and Marianna would soon become attached to her new daddy.

"Them, too, but that's not who I'm thinking of. Our *mamms* always hoped we'd marry. Remember how my *mamm* kept trying to throw us together the day of the volleyball game?"

Rachel smiled at the memory of Josh's mother's obvious matchmaking.

"And your *mamm* asked me to take care of you."

"She did?" Rachel couldn't believe Mamm would be so bold. "Sounds like we'll be making a lot of people happy."

"Not as happy as you've made me. I'm sure I'm the happiest man in the world."

Tears welled in Rachel's eyes. "And I'm the happiest woman."

"I'm glad." Josh gave her a special smile that set her spirit singing. Then his grin broadened. "Oh, and we can't forget Mrs. Vandenberg."

"*Jah*, she was the one who set this whole thing in motion. Well, her and her direct line to God."

When they headed back to the house, they weren't the least bit surprised to see Mrs. Vandenberg's Bentley pull into the driveway. Her nudges from God always seemed to put in her in the right place at the perfect time. She should be the first to hear their news.

She emerged from the car and tottered toward them,

tapping her cane in a jaunty rhythm. "Looks like this was good timing. I wondered how long it would take before you worked things out. Maybe you'll be ready to hear an idea I had."

Josh hurried toward her and took her elbow. "If it's anything like your plan to get Rachel and me together, I'm all for it."

"Awesome." She tapped her huge handbag. "And I have those papers in here for you to sign, Rachel. The notary should be here shortly."

As they headed through the front door, a loud cry echoed from upstairs. Josh made sure Mrs. Vandenberg was steady on her feet before he dashed upstairs to Zak.

Mrs. Vandenberg stared after Josh with a fond smile on her face. "He'll be a good father."

"The best," Rachel agreed. "Zak has bonded with Josh already."

"That's wonderful. Now, dear, I wonder if I could speak with your mother."

"Mamm?" What did Mrs. Vandenberg need to talk to Mamm about? "I'll just check to see if she's awake."

"Oh, she will be." Mrs. Vandenberg followed Rachel down the hall.

Before they reached the room, laughter drifted from behind the closed door. Rachel rarely heard her mother laugh. Having Barbara here had been good for Mamm.

Rachel tapped at the door and then stuck her head in. "I've brought you some company." She stepped aside to reveal Mrs. Vandenberg.

"Liesl, so good to see you," Barbara said. "Come in, come in. Leave the door open, Rachel, so Josh can bring the little ones in to see Betty."

"I have something I'd like to discuss with all of you,"

Mrs. Vandenberg announced, "but we should wait for Josh because my idea concerns him too."

Upstairs, Zak's cries had quieted, but Marianna yowled. Rachel started to dart out the door, but Mrs. Vandenberg stopped her.

"It's good practice for him, dear. Relax. He'll do fine."

"But—"

"Oh, goodness gracious, that word again." Mrs. Vandenberg pinned Rachel in place with a searching look. "Do you think Josh can cope with two children at once?"

"Of course." Rachel had no doubts about that. It was only that she should be helping.

"There'll come a time when he needs to handle many more than two little ones, and you won't be able to help him. Give him a chance to prove he can do it."

Rachel's face burned at Mrs. Vandenberg's implication that she and Josh would have many children. It wasn't the Amish way to discuss pregnancies.

Mamm and Barbara glanced at her curiously. Rachel didn't want to share her news without Josh present. Because it had been so sudden and recent, it still seemed fragile and uncertain, like a dream she might wake from to discover it hadn't been real. She needed to be sure she hadn't misunderstood what had happened between them. Maybe he'd regret what he said. Or maybe taking care of two children might change his mind.

She clutched fistfuls of her dress skirt as footfalls sounded on the stairs. What if Josh decided he'd made a mistake?

He appeared in the doorway with Zak in one arm and Marianna in the other. When Josh spied Rachel, his whole face lit up, reassuring her she wasn't about to wake from a dream. This man—the one she'd loved and longed for—truly did care for her.

She went to him to take Marianna from him, because Josh had to hold Zak at an awkward angle to protect his stitched leg.

"Do you want to make our announcement," Josh whispered, "or do you want me to do it?"

"I'll do it." Rachel turned around, and standing beside Josh, told everyone, "We have something to tell you."

"I can guess." Mamm beamed. "Oh, Josh, I'm so happy to welcome you to our family."

Josh flashed her a fond smile. "I can't think of anyone I'd rather have as a mother-in-law than you, Betty. You'll keep me on my toes."

"You always did take my lectures to heart." Her fondness for him radiated from her words. Then her face fell. "*Ach*, but I'm in the main bedroom. This should be yours and Rachel's."

"Well," Mrs. Vandenberg said, "that's the perfect segue to my idea." She reached into her huge handbag and pulled out a set of blueprints. "I thought this day would be coming soon, so I had one of my architects work out a plan for a *dawdi haus* that can accommodate a proper hospital bed and also be wheelchair accessible."

Mamm stared at Mrs. Vandenberg. "But I don't use a wheelchair."

"Not yet." Mrs. Vandenberg's brisk voice left no room for doubt. "But you soon will."

Although Mamm's expression revealed her disbelief, Rachel had seen her own miracle come true. She believed

God, working through Mrs. Vandenberg, could certainly provide another.

"Betty, I've made an appointment for you with a specialist. I think you might be surprised at the results."

A tiny spark of hope lit Mamm's eyes. "I appreciate it."

And thanks to Mrs. Vandenberg paying for the Ohio house, Rachel could afford any special treatment Mamm needed. *Danke*, Lord.

"I also included an en suite with a sitting room and separate entrance for Barbara, if she wants to stay and care for you."

"I'd love that," Mamm said. "You will stay, won't you, Barbara?"

"*Ach*, Liesl and Betty." Barbara broke into tears. "I've been so worried what I'd do once Rachel returned."

"And asked them to design an open area for a playroom and nursery, just in case the newlyweds need someone to babysit."

Rachel's heart skipped a beat at the word *newlyweds*. She still could barely believe she'd be getting married.

Her eyes wet with tears, Mamm said, "I'd love to have my precious grandbabies around me anytime."

"That's all settled, then." Mrs. Vandenberg handed the plans to Josh. "I'm sure you know how to execute these. You'd better get to work."

"I'll get right on it." He shot a loving glance at Rachel and then leaned close to whisper, "I think we should talk to the bishop about getting married as soon as possible so the children have a *daed* around full time."

"For sure." The children weren't the only ones who needed and wanted Josh around full time.

CHAPTER 28

Rachel's days flowed like a dream. Josh arrived early each morning, and he stayed until after the children's bedtime, so they could plan their future together. He helped her with the children as much as he could, but he and his *daed* and his brothers spent most of the time working on the *dawdi haus*.

She couldn't spend those hours with him. But whenever she missed him, she went to the window to watch him sweating under the broiling sun, flexing his muscles and demonstrating his skills with a hammer.

Whenever Josh was on the ground, Zak followed him around like a baby duck. And Josh patiently demonstrated skills, waiting while Zak tried and tried again. The first time Zak hammered a nail in straight, they both whooped with joy, and Josh sent Zak to the house to show her. She'd already been watching, and her eyes met Josh's through the glass, sending signals of love and caring.

Both of them were reluctant to break the connection, until Josh's brother Adam passed and clipped Josh on the shoulder. "Stop mooning and get to work."

Josh ignored him and waited until Rachel came to the door to admire Zak's handiwork and to smile at Zak's soon-to-be *daed*. He returned the admiring glances until his father called for him to mix more mortar. Josh waited until Zak had toddled back, then scooped him up, winked at Rachel, and taught Zak how to mix mortar.

When Josh did tasks Zak couldn't share, his future cousins kept him occupied. Three of Josh's nephews came with their *daeds*. At four and five, they'd been around construction sites for several years, so they played with Zak when Josh was on the ladder or working with dangerous tools. And later in the afternoon, the school-age cousins swarmed around the little ones, teaching them skills and organizing games when they weren't busy helping with building.

Every day at noon, Rachel brought out a hot dinner and set it on a large folding table under the spreading branches of an old oak. Everyone grabbed plates and filled them, then sat around on the ground to devour the meal and desserts hungrily. But Josh came into the kitchen to eat with Rachel and the two children. It became their oasis in the midst of busy days. And they took turns feeding a different child at each meal to strengthen their bonds.

With the baby carrier strapped around her, Rachel quilted . . . when she wasn't staring longingly out the window at Josh or fixing meals or talking with Mamm and Barbara. Keeping Marianna cuddled close, Rachel cooed and talked to her tiny *dochder* as she finished her quilt for Suzanne and began Mrs. Vandenberg's.

Rachel put her heart and soul into an original design and hoped it would turn out as beautifully as she'd imagined. She wanted to thank Mrs. Vandenberg for all she'd done in their lives.

Not that Rachel had to quilt anymore. She'd signed over the deed to the Ohio house the day Mrs. Vandenberg

had given them the plans for the *dawdi haus*. Now Rachel
felt free to spend the money that had been deposited in the
bank. She'd already decided this quilt would be the last
one for a while. Her next task—one that would be pure
joy—sewing her wedding dress. She'd already picked
out the pretty blue fabric. And she'd selected a soft green
material for Mamm's dress.

While Rachel cut out quilt pieces on the kitchen table,
she kept an eye out for her beloved. Each time he passed
by the window, she thanked God for blessing her with
such a *wunderbar* man.

But she couldn't help noticing something else with
the kitchen window open to bring in the breeze. Josh's
brother Adam needled constantly, criticizing Josh and
making cutting comments. Rachel's ire rose, and by the
time she set out the noon meal, she could barely contain
her annoyance.

Everyone flocked around the table but Josh, who picked
up Zak and headed for the kitchen.

"Too good to eat with the rest of us?" Adam challenged.

Rachel stiffened and started to turn, but Josh touched
her arm. "Don't say anything. He likes making people
angry."

"*Ooo*, Josh," Adam called, "good thing the bishop isn't
here. You're not supposed to be touching her."

Josh flushed to the roots of his hair. "I'm so sorry,
Rachel."

"You're not the one who should be sorry." She whirled
around to face Adam. "That's enough of your bullying."

"Rachel?" Josh's low, urgent whisper begged her to
stop.

But Rachel had had enough. She marched over to
Adam, one hand cradling Marianna close in the baby

carrier, wagging a finger at Adam with the other. "Josh doesn't deserve to be treated that way. I don't know what he ever did to you, but whatever it was, you should forgive and forget."

Adam stood there sputtering while Rachel spun around and flounced toward the back door.

"*Ach*, Rachel," Josh said, once they'd closed the kitchen door behind them. "You're a wonder." He laughed. "I've never seen Adam at a loss for words."

Josh didn't say she shouldn't have done it, but when the hearty laughter floated through the window, and his two older brothers taunted Adam, Rachel rued losing her temper.

Marv spat out words between chortles. "She really put you in your place, Adam."

"*Jah*, that's for sure," Lloyd agreed. "And you just stood there with your mouth hanging open like this." He put on a stupid expression, his jaws wide.

Knowing Adam, all this teasing would only add fuel to the fire.

Rachel pinched her lips together. "I'm so sorry, Josh. I've only made things worse for you, haven't I?"

He gave her shoulder a gentle squeeze. "Don't worry about me. I've endured plenty of teasing. I can take a bit more." He turned her around to face her. "And it's much easier to bear when I know I have a beautiful woman who'll soon be my wife." A teasing glint entered his eyes. "A woman who loves me enough to stand up to bullies to defend me."

"Oh, you." Rachel gave him a playful shove, the way she had when they were younger. But her heart pitter-pattered the way it always did when she was near him. "I hope Bishop Troyer agrees we should get married soon."

Tomorrow night, they had a meeting with the bishop to talk about their wedding. They planned to use the children's welfare as their excuse for a hasty marriage.

"I do too. I can't wait for you to be my wife."

Those words stayed with Rachel as Josh and Zak went back outside after dinner. She floated on a cloud as she washed the dishes, a little more slowly than usual, so she could appreciate her view of Josh.

But as she feared, Adam lit into Josh. "Too cowardly to confront me yourself, so you send your girlfriend after me?" Adam's mocking laughter had a cruel edge.

Josh ignored the taunt, but Rachel ground her teeth. Rather than making the situation better for him, she'd increased Adam's anger and meanness.

Lord, I'm sorry for losing my temper. Please help Josh not to have to pay for my runaway tongue.

After both children had gone down for their afternoon naps, Rachel prepared plates of cookies and pitchers of strawberry lemonade. She set everything out on the table under the oak and waited. Not for Josh this time, but for Adam.

He was the first to break for the snack. He jogged toward the table but halted several feet away when he noticed her standing there. A wary expression crossed his face.

"Adam, can I talk to you a minute? Alone."

His face scrunched up, as if expecting a trick. "What for?"

"I have something I want to say to you."

"I don't want to hear it." He swooped over to the table, grabbed a handful of cookies, and turned his back.

Josh's two older brothers and their children headed for the table but stopped at the sight of Rachel and Adam.

Rachel wouldn't let Adam's attitude or the staring audience keep her from what she intended to say. "Adam, I let my temper get the better of me at dinnertime. I shouldn't have said those things. Will you forgive me?"

She couldn't see Adam's face, but his stiff shoulders melted a little.

Across the yard, Josh spied her and rushed in her direction. Rachel held up a hand to stop him. She tilted her head slightly toward Adam. Understanding dawned in Josh's eyes, and he stayed still.

After a long pause, Adam croaked out a *jah* that sounded reluctant and forced. Then he stalked off to eat by himself as everyone else crowded around the table.

Josh pulled her aside. "What did you say to Adam?"

"I apologized for losing my temper earlier and asked him to forgive me."

Love and admiration blazed in Josh's eyes. "You are the most amazing woman. Beautiful inside and out." He cast a quick glance at Adam, alone under a distant maple. "What did he say?"

"Just *jah*." But that was enough.

The rest of the afternoon, Adam worked in sullen silence. Each time Rachel glanced out the window, he was keeping to himself. She prayed she hadn't caused a rift in the family.

The next morning, as Rachel slipped downstairs to get some quilting done before the children woke, a knock on the front door startled her. Josh had arrived earlier than usual. She rushed to the door and flung it open to greet him. Then, her smile faded.

Adam stood on the doorstep, shuffling from one foot to

the other. "I'm sorry," he mumbled, without looking her in the eye.

"It's all right, Adam. I forgive you," she said gently, so he wouldn't have to ask.

She could barely hear his *danke* as he turned to leave, his steps tense and awkward.

"My brother's a lucky man," he muttered, before high-tailing it around back to work on the *dawdi haus*.

Josh pulled in half an hour later and eyed the other buggy in the driveway. "What's Adam doing here already?"

"He came to apologize."

"What?" Josh stared at her, disbelieving. "Adam's never said he's sorry for anything in his life. At least, not that I know of."

"He did today."

With a stunned look, Josh followed Rachel into the kitchen. They had only a few minutes alone before Zak and Marianna stirred, but they made the most of them, staring into each other's eyes while fixing breakfast.

When Rachel pulled a pan of cinnamon rolls from the oven, Josh sniffed appreciatively. "My favorite."

"I know. I made them for you."

His face alight with appreciation, Josh gripped his suspenders tightly. "I wish I could show you how much that means to me. But . . ."

But they shouldn't. He traced her lips with his eyes.

Rachel shivered and forced herself to stay on the opposite side of the table. "I wish you could too." She breathed in, hoping to calm her jittery pulse.

"Josh? Daed?" the plaintive call broke into the tension-filled moment.

Heaving a huge sigh, Josh headed from the kitchen,

murmuring, "*Danke* You, Lord, for keeping me from temptation."

Rachel echoed his prayer. Every day, it grew harder to stay apart. Most couples didn't share parenting duties and spend most of their days and evenings together. It was a blessing, but had its tough moments. So often Rachel longed to throw her arms around Josh or press a kiss to his lips. Their wedding day couldn't come soon enough for her.

By the time Josh returned to the kitchen with Zak and Marianna, Rachel had prepared the baby's bottle and cooked scrambled eggs. Josh took the bottle and fed Marianna.

After covering the eggs to keep them warm, Rachel headed for the back door.

He stared at her, puzzled. "Where are you going?"

"To invite your brother for breakfast."

Josh groaned. "Go ahead." Although his words sounded sarcastic, he grinned.

When Rachel approached Adam and extended the invitation, he stared at her, bug-eyed. Then he swallowed and looked away. "I'm too busy," he choked out.

So Rachel returned to the house, fixed a plate with eggs and two cinnamon rolls, and filled a mug with coffee. "How does your brother like his coffee?" she asked Josh.

"Black." Josh shook his head. "You're too nice," he said, but his words held only admiration.

Adam didn't even glance in her direction when she set the breakfast plate on a nearby stack of lumber. But after she went inside, she peeked out the window, and he was wolfing down the food.

The rest of the day, Adam didn't tease Josh. At least not in Rachel's presence.

* * *

"Will wonders never cease?" Josh asked as he entered the kitchen for supper, holding Zak. "That has to be a record. Not one nasty remark from Adam all day. Thanks to you."

Josh resisted the urge to take Rachel in his arms and cradle her close to his heart. Every day, it grew more difficult to be around her and keep his hands to himself. All the hard work outside and the childcare inside didn't do enough to distract him. His every waking thought began and ended with Rachel.

And when she looked at him with the same longing . . .

Josh headed for the sink and scrubbed his and Zak's hands, as if it could rub away wayward thoughts. It didn't work.

After setting Zak on the bench, Josh slid in beside his *sohn*—Josh's soul thrilled at the thought—to help Zak cut his food. Josh had fed Marianna that morning, and for the first time, she'd smiled up at him.

I'm their daed. Soon, he'd be a *daed* and a husband.

He'd brought along a change of clothes for their meeting with the bishop, so he switched into them while Rachel readied both children for bed. Then he prayed with Zak, read to him from the Bible-story book, and bent to kiss him goodnight.

"You need to go right to sleep because Rachel and I are talking to the bishop tonight."

"You be back when I wake up?" Zak asked sleepily.

"I promise." *And someday soon, I'll be here all through the night too.*

But later, when they sat across from Bishop Troyer, Josh wondered if he'd been too optimistic.

"I understand you wanting to marry quickly, and the children's welfare is certainly a consideration"—Laban frowned and tugged on his beard—"but . . ."

But what? Josh longed to interrupt. He forced his hands to stillness in his lap and prayed for patience.

"I know you were childhood friends."

"*Jah*, we were. And we know each other very well." He hoped that reassurance would speed things along.

"I'm not so sure about that." This time, rather than staring off into the distance, the bishop fixed Josh with a pointed look. "You two haven't talked in years, and you've been courting Anna Mary."

"Not anymore." Josh debated about giving a reason, but maybe it would help their case. "We broke up because I realized I was in love with Rachel, and I always have been."

"That's my concern. Who's to say you won't change your mind about Rachel a few months from now?"

"I won't."

Laban tapped a finger against his lip. "Suppose two or three months ago, I'd asked you if you were planning to marry Anna Mary. What would you have said?"

Josh couldn't look the bishop in the eye. "I would have said I was," he admitted miserably. Then he turned a pleading look to Laban. "But only because I didn't think I had any chance with Rachel."

She intervened to explain. "Josh blamed himself for my brother's death. He thought I wouldn't forgive him."

This time, Laban turned his searching look on Rachel. "And was he right about that?"

She shook her head. "*Neh*, I didn't blame him."

Josh groaned inwardly. He guessed the bishop's next question.

"And you're willing to marry a man who so misjudged you that way?"

"Of course. I forgave him for the misunderstanding."

"It's more than a simple mistake. He completely misread your character. That's a grave error."

"He didn't misjudge me. He just believed he couldn't be forgiven . . . by anyone."

"I see." Laban rounded on Josh. "Not even God?"

Josh squirmed.

"And did you even try asking for forgiveness? Seems to me if you'd caused such great harm, your first act would be to ask forgiveness from the people you'd wronged."

Hanging his head, Josh admitted, "I didn't think they'd . . ."

"*Neh, sohn*, perhaps you were too cowardly to admit what you'd done."

"He was only thirteen," Rachel burst out.

"Eight years ago, he was thirteen. He's had plenty of years since then to face up to this."

Josh lowered his head into his hands "You're right. Maybe I'm not mature enough to get married."

Rachel's sharp intake of breath cut through him.

"That's the first step to maturity, *sohn*, admitting the truth." Laban cleared his throat. "I'm going to ask you to do one more thing. Did you ask Anna Mary for forgiveness?"

Had he? Josh couldn't remember. "But she broke up with me."

"Perhaps," Laban said drily, "to save face after hearing rumors about you traveling out of state with another girl?"

"I think she's interested in someone else."

"You don't sound too sure. And once again, you're

making excuses for not asking forgiveness. Seems to me *hochmut* might have something to do with that."

Josh couldn't argue. Pride had kept him from confessing to Rachel. He could show the bishop he'd learned to face his mistakes by talking to Anna Mary. Josh stood, and Rachel followed his lead. "I'll ask Anna Mary for forgiveness."

Bishop Troyer clapped him on the shoulder. "That's a good start."

"What about our marriage?" Josh didn't want to be the reason for putting off their wedding.

Bishop Troyer walked them to the door. "You know what they say, 'Marry in haste, repent in leisure.' Seems to me waiting at least six months would be wise to be sure you have no more sudden changes of heart."

"I won't," he insisted. "I've always loved Rachel. And I always will."

"Then you'll still love her several months from now."

"But . . ." Josh started to protest. Yet what more could he say?

The bishop's eyes narrowed. "Unless you have another reason for a hasty marriage?"

Josh couldn't believe the bishop had even suggested it. How humiliating! His face burned, and he couldn't meet Rachel's eyes. Not only because of that, but because postponing the marriage was all his fault.

CHAPTER 29

Josh and Rachel didn't speak as they headed to his buggy. They'd arrived here excited and bubbling, sure they could marry quickly. Now their hopes had been dashed. For most couples, who waited a year or more, six months wouldn't seem long. For him and Rachel, it stretched like an eternity.

He waited until he'd pulled the buggy out of Laban's driveway and stopped at the first stop sign before turning to Rachel. "I'm sorry. If I'd done things differently . . ."

She laid a hand on his arm, and sparks zinged through him.

"Don't blame yourself," she said gently. "Over the years, we both could have reached out to each other."

"And Anna Mary?" Asking for her forgiveness would be awkward. Once you broke up with someone, you didn't go calling on them. "Since when does a bishop interfere with relationships?"

"Adults usually don't. But Anna Mary is Laban's niece. Maybe he's concerned about her."

"Could be. And I do owe Anna Mary an apology. Although I definitely can't tell her the only woman I thought about while dating her was you."

"*Ach*, Josh!" Rachel pressed her hands to her cheeks. "Poor Anna Mary. You don't know how jealous I was when I saw you together."

"I'm so sorry. I never wanted to hurt you."

"I know."

"If Laban could have peeked into my mind and heart over the years, he'd know I'm not fickle. I've only ever loved one person. You."

Rachel sucked in a breath. "And I never stopped loving you. I'm so glad we discovered our feelings for each other before it was too late."

"So am I. We have Mrs. Vandenberg to thank for that."

"She's something, isn't she? Suzanne warned me that Mrs. Vandenberg was trying to set us up that day at the market."

"Warned you?" Josh growled playfully.

Rachel's musical laughter set chimes pealing in his soul.

A few seconds later, those bells were tolling a dirge. Six long months? That seemed like an eternity.

He could get one step closer, though, by asking for Anna Mary's forgiveness. "The market stays open until eight on Thursdays. Then they have to clean up. Anna Mary will be home soon. I can go over there now to talk to her."

Rachel's sigh revealed she was as disappointed as he was at not spending more time together tonight. "The sooner, the better," she said as he pulled into her driveway. "I'll see you tomorrow. And I'll be praying."

"*Danke.* I'll need prayers." Josh had no idea what he'd say. He couldn't tell Anna Mary he needed forgiveness because he'd longed for someone else while he dated her. He didn't want to hurt her.

Dear Lord, forgive me for how I treated her. And give me the right words to say.

When he approached the house, light shone from the dining room. *Gut.* She was still up. He looped the reins around the hitching post and headed for her front door filled with dread.

Anna Mary's younger sister Sarah opened the door. "Josh, come on in. Anna Mary's in the dining room." She leaned close and whispered, "She's writing letters like she does every night before bed."

Sarah didn't seem to realize he and Anna Mary had broken up. Hadn't Anna Mary told her family?

Josh followed Sarah into the dining room, where Anna Mary sat near the propane lamp, busily scribbling on pink stationery.

"Josh is here, Anna Mary," Sarah announced.

Anna Mary jumped, sending pink papers fluttering to the floor. Josh bent to pick them up.

"*Neh, neh.* Leave them," she ordered, flustered. Then she bent and retrieved all the pages, gathering them gently, and pressing them against her heart.

When she stood, she faced him with an annoyed expression. "What are you doing here? Don't tell me the flirt moved on to someone else already, and now you want to get back together."

Her cutting, sarcastic tone only made Josh sad. Underneath, she sounded hurt. The bishop had been right. Josh did owe her an apology.

"*Neh*, I came to ask your forgiveness."

"If you're trying for a second chance with me, it won't work."

"I'm not here to get back together. I'm still with Rachel and—"

"She doesn't mind you calling on your old girlfriend?"

"I'm only here to apologize. I wasn't the boyfriend I should have been to you, and I'm sorry for all the ways I hurt you. Will you forgive me?"

Anna Mary studied his face to be sure his request was genuine. Then, to his surprise, she burst into tears. "I forgive . . . you, Josh," she said between sobs. "Will you . . . forgive me?"

"For what?"

"For . . . for being . . . so grouchy . . . and mean . . . and for starting fights . . ." She hung her head. "I . . . wasn't upset . . . with you. I was . . . upset with . . . me."

"I forgive you, Anna Mary."

She lifted her head. Her eyes damp with tears, she pressed her lips together, as if to hold back her sobs. When she spoke again, her words were choked and thick. "That's not all."

"Whatever it is, I forgive you."

"You haven't heard it yet."

"It doesn't matter."

"*Jah*, it does. I said unkind things about you to others. And you didn't deserve it." Anna Mary held up a hand to stop him from responding. "There's more. I did it because I felt guilty, so I took it out on you." She lowered her eyes. "I, um, fell for Abe."

Josh's gaze fell to the pink pages in her hand. His suspicions had been right. Rather than bothering him, knowing she was interested in Abe lessened his guilt for wanting to be with Rachel. Anna Mary wouldn't be pining away for him.

When he didn't say anything, she glanced up and saw him looking at her letter. Her cheeks reddened. "*Jah*, it's a letter to Abe. I write one every night."

They must have a lot to say to each other, because she held at least four sheets of paper. "That's good," he assured her.

"The thing is," she continued, "I was attracted to him the first day I met him. The day you and I had the fight at the volleyball field. I didn't want to do anything about it, because we were dating."

"I'm sorry." If Josh had admitted his attraction to Rachel sooner, they both would have been happier and lived with a lot less guilt.

"*Neh*, I'm the one who should be saying that. Fighting those feelings made me argue and snap at you. I felt ashamed about wanting to be with someone else."

"I know how you feel. I felt guilty too."

"Will you forgive me?"

"*Jah*, and I wish you well with Abe."

Anna Mary's face crinkled, and her eyes filled with tears. "He's so far away and . . ."

"Pray about it," Josh advised. "God can work things out, even when we think it's impossible." After all, the Lord had gotten him and Rachel together. Something Josh had never believed would happen.

"We've both been praying. Mrs. Vandenberg keeps saying to wait for God's perfect timing."

"Mrs. Vandenberg thinks you and Abe will get together?" Josh laughed to himself. He had no doubt God was already on the job, with Mrs. Vandenberg assisting Him here on earth.

"*Jah*, she's so encouraging."

"If it helps, Mrs. Vandenberg is an excellent matchmaker, and she comes up with some amazing ideas to get people together. If she's on your side, it's because God gave her a nudge."

"I hope you're right, Josh."

He hoped he was too. It would relieve his conscience if Anna Mary had a relationship as happy as his.

Although Rachel's spirits lightened after Josh recounted his conversation with Anna Mary, waiting six months had added a heavy burden to their lives. Still, she focused on her blessings.

Josh worked at her house every day. She could see him as often as she wanted. He arrived early in the morning and stayed until evening. He helped get the children dressed in the morning. He put them to bed at night and ate all his meals with the three of them. Sometimes they ate in the bedroom with Mamm and Barbara. And whenever Rachel missed him, she only had to glance out the window.

Despite her happy weekdays, Sundays at church and singings remained trials to endure. The first Sunday after she and Josh started dating, he drove her and the children to church. Shock rippled through the crowd of women gathered in the kitchen when she walked in carrying a baby.

"Are you babysitting?" an elderly woman asked.

"*Neh*, this is my *dochder*. My cousin just passed, so I'm adopting her two children. I was at her funeral last weekend." Rachel spoke loudly, not only so the hard-of-hearing woman would catch her response, but also so the others gossiping about her would get the facts.

It didn't seem to matter. Small groups chatting together

after the service ceased abruptly when Rachel came into earshot. That didn't stop her from overhearing unkind and untrue comments.

"She and Josh Yoder went out of state together last weekend. I heard they went to the bishop this week to arrange a hasty marriage. You know what that means."

Rachel blinked back tears and tried to ignore the cruelties. Time would prove them wrong, but until the truth came out, the rumors hurt.

Others discussed her stealing Anna Mary's boyfriend. "She flits from boy to boy."

"She's never happy unless she's breaking up someone's relationship. She never talks to the girls."

"It's terrible how she flirts. All the boys circle around her at singings. They don't see her fakeness."

"Someone should warn Josh about marrying that flirt. He's too nice to be stuck with her."

Rachel bit her lip and cuddled Marianna closer. She prayed all this contempt toward her would die down once she married, and that it would never poison her children.

Curiosity erupted when Josh entered the barn to talk to other young men from the youth group. Zak's stitches sometimes hurt and pulled as they healed, so he whined to be held. Josh picked him up and had to answer a barrage of questions thrown his way.

When he announced, "This is Rachel Glick's son," he fielded jests and jealousy.

Questions came from all sides: "Where's she been hiding her son all this time? Why are *you* caring for him?"

"Trying to get in Rachel's good graces?"

"Thought you were dating Anna Mary."

Rumors hadn't spread to the males of the community quite yet, but they would soon. None of his friends in the church youth group seemed to know about him and Rachel or about his breakup with Anna Mary yet.

Some of that might be because the girls at church avoided Rachel. And now that Barbara had become Betty's caretaker, no women from the *g'may* went to Rachel's house to sit with Betty. Although Rachel's *Englisch* neighbor had mentioned a cousin's children visiting, and Josh had told Anna Mary, nobody else knew about the death, funeral, or adoption. Josh tried to tell his friends all those details in order.

He didn't mention marrying Rachel. Not yet. And he wouldn't until they had a date.

"What happened between you and Anna Mary? You're courting Rachel?"

After he explained he and Anna Mary were dating other people and confirmed he was going out with Rachel, the digs started.

"She's just a flirt."

"She won't stick with you. Sure you want a girl who's always surrounded by other boys?"

The negative comments about Rachel made Josh sick. He wanted to whisk her away from here and start over fresh. Maybe she shouldn't have sold the Ohio house.

Josh couldn't explain how he and Rachel had always loved each other or that Rachel never had any interest in the boys who swarmed around her. No one would believe him. Besides, he didn't want to hurt her admirers' feelings any more than they already had been by discovering she'd be courting someone else. He could only imagine the pain he'd feel if he were in their shoes. Every night at singings, he always held his breath, hoping and praying Rachel wouldn't ride home in anyone's buggy.

Josh did what he could to repair the damage to Rachel's reputation and answer questions about his breakup with Anna Mary honestly. But in the buzz around him, mistruths were being passed around, and he could do little to stop them.

He was grateful when the service started and they could file inside. He only hoped Rachel hadn't been treated the same way.

By the time she climbed into Josh's buggy after church, Rachel's eyes stung. She would not let one tear fall. She vowed not to let gossips destroy her happiness with Josh.

When he arrived, her spirits rose. He lifted Zak into the back, taking care to stretch Zak's sore leg out across the seat. Then, Josh beamed at her, and some of her sadness seeped away.

"Sorry I took so long," he said. "Daed wanted to introduce me to a newcomer he's planning to hire for our construction crew, but of course, we can't talk business on Sunday."

Josh's upbeat patter stopped when he caught sight of Rachel's face. "What's wrong?"

She waved a hand airily. "The usual. Everyone's upset about me stealing Anna Mary's boyfriend."

He winced. "I wish I'd made different decisions, so you don't get blamed for my mistakes." If she'd endured even half of the barbs he'd endured, it would be too much.

"It's not your fault." She choked back a sob. "You know my reputation. I'm sure you got an earful about me."

"They don't know the truth. But I'm sorry you have to go through this."

"I'm used to it." Or as used to being jabbed by cutting comments as anyone could be. They never stopped hurting.

"But it's worse now, isn't it?"

Rachel bit her lip and hung her head. "They said mean things about you."

That had been even harder to bear. She'd wanted to interrupt and correct them, but that would only make things worse. Sooner or later, she hoped the gossip about Josh would die down if she didn't stir it up. Although the comments might grow even more pointed, at least until they married. If only that could be much, much sooner.

"I wish I could protect you from all this." The caring in Josh's eyes lessened some of the gossip's sting.

"Being with you helps." She twisted her lips into a rueful expression. "Too bad we can't just spend all our time alone together."

Josh's eyes lit up. "I'd love that."

The burning desire in his eyes as he glanced her way sparked a flame inside that heated her from head to toe. *Gut* thing he was driving.

His hand clenched the reins tightly, and they rode in silence for several minutes. At a stop sign, Josh turned to her, his eyes brimming with compassion.

"You don't have to go to the singing tonight. I don't want you to hear more unkind remarks."

Rachel shook her head. "I don't want to get reprimanded for not attending."

"You could use the children as an excuse."

Maybe that might work, but Rachel couldn't lie. If she stayed home, it wouldn't be because of Zak and Marianna. It would be because she wanted to avoid hearing cruel words. Jesus had endured so much more, and He'd been innocent. Some of the comments about her were true.

She forced herself to say, "I'll go. Maybe we can pray for strength to face it."

"You're amazing."

Josh's admiring look made all the critical comments and judgmental gazes fade to nothingness. The only opinions she cared about were God's, Mamm's, and Josh's. Oh, and Mrs. Vandenberg's. And they all knew the truth.

"Besides"—Rachel flashed him a teasing grin—"I don't want to miss my first chance to ride to a singing with you."

"And I can't wait to take you."

That joy stayed with Rachel as they put the children down for naps, recounted the main points of the sermon for Mamm and Barbara, and went for a leisurely walk in the woods to many of their favorite childhood places. They shared their memories and laughed over various mishaps.

What wonderful bonds they already had, and what greater ones they'd be forging.

After the little ones woke from their nap, Rachel and Josh reminded Zak that Barbara would be putting him to bed that night. He fussed until Josh explained being a man sometimes meant doing hard things.

Zak, his face filled with trust and adoration, looked up into Josh's eyes. "I want to be a man like you."

Rachel's eyes welled with tears. "Josh is the best example of a man and a *daed* for you to follow."

Zak nodded sagely. "I know."

She could tell Josh was too choked up to answer, but the love blazing in his eyes revealed his appreciation.

He rasped, "With God's help, I'll try to be the best husband and father I can be."

Rachel left the two men in her life together while she went to fix a quick meal for Mamm and the children. Then she slipped into her room to redo her hair, fix her *kapp*, pinch a little color into her cheeks to match her sparkling eyes, and smooth out her dress and apron. Tonight, she'd be going on her first real date alone with Josh. She floated downstairs and out to the buggy, wanting to savor every minute.

For the first time ever, she rode to a singing with a man. Not just any man, but the man she loved with all her heart and soul. A man who loved her. A man who wanted to marry her. Rachel's spirit overflowed with so much happiness, her heart sang before she arrived and opened a hymnbook.

Even the chilly reception they received didn't dampen her joy. Anyone who'd missed the gossip that morning at church discovered it now. The girls who'd slandered Rachel's character in the morning, now turned their attacks toward Josh. And the guys who'd gone after Josh at church shot Rachel looks of reproach, sadness, or anger. She kept her attention fixed on her songbook or on Josh.

During the snack break, the whispers they'd faced earlier grew louder. Josh angled his body to block the chattering knots of *youngie*, shielding Rachel from the rest of the room. *I'm so sorry*, he mouthed. *It's my fault.*

She shook her head. His breakup might have caused some anger on Anna Mary's behalf, but Rachel's reputation had done equal damage. The word *flirt* floated on the air around them.

All of a sudden, Anna Mary charged over to them. "I caused some of this. Will you forgive me?" She even included Rachel in her apology.

"Of course," Rachel assured her, and Josh nodded.

Anna Mary's best friend, Caroline, joined them. With her willingness to blurt out whatever needed to be announced, she took it upon herself to set the record straight. She made sure everyone understood Anna Mary had broken up with Josh for someone else.

Rachel appreciated Caroline's efforts, but it didn't help with the miffed boys. At least a little of the girls' hostility lessened, but she and Josh would have to endure six long months of snubs and glares. Rachel sighed at the thought. If only the bishop would reconsider.

CHAPTER 30

The next morning, soon after Josh arrived, Mrs. Vandenberg paid them a visit. Josh let her in, and Rachel invited her to join them for breakfast.

"Have you set your wedding date?"

Josh didn't want to think about, let alone talk about, that subject.

"*Neh.*" Rachel fought back tears as she explained the bishop's directive and reasoning.

"He's a very wise man, and normally, I'd agree with him. But I don't think he understands the deeper bond you two have."

"We tried to explain it," Josh said, "but we weren't successful."

"I can see why." Mrs. Vandenberg stared off into the distance. "Well, now I know why I was sent here today. Trouble in paradise. Hmm . . . I guess we'll need to figure out how to change Bishop Troyer's mind."

Josh shook his head. "I wish we could think of something."

"Let's pray about it."

They all added that petition to their silent prayer before the meal. They had almost finished eating when Mrs. Vandenberg leaned on her cane and pulled herself to her feet.

"I need to speak to someone." She headed for the back door.

Josh and Rachel both stared at her. They exchanged glances, wondering if she'd lost it. The backyard was empty. Josh stood and started after her, but as she stepped off the porch, Adam rounded the house.

"Young man," she called.

He turned and stared at her, his forehead creased in a frown. "*Jah?*"

"I have a message for you." Her ringing tones carried into the open window.

"Who from?" Adam sounded annoyed.

"Let's just say I've gotten a little direction from above." She pointed skyward. "First of all, grumpiness is often a sign you need to ask for forgiveness."

Adam stared at her in shock. "You don't even know me." His eyes narrowed. "Unless my brother was complaining about me?"

"Not at all. He never mentioned you."

He squinted at her, disbelief evident on his face. "Then who told you I'm grumpy."

"You did." When he shot her a skeptical look, she smiled. "Not in words. The deepest lines on your face express discontent. So does the set of your mouth. Unless you just ate a lemon?"

"Do you always go around telling people what's wrong with them and their expressions?"

"Not unless God nudges me."

"And you're telling me God wants you to criticize me about being grumpy?"

Mrs. Vandenberg laughed. "No, I'm only supposed to give you some spiritual advice. People are often bad-tempered when they're trying to hide their guilt."

"What are you accusing me of?"

"That's between you and God." She wobbled in a half-circle to start back to the house. "I will say one more thing," she added over her shoulder. "From your manner, I'd say you have more than one person you need to apologize to. And don't forget your wife."

"Did she put you up to this?" Adam demanded.

"I've never met your wife. But grouchy people often take their tempers out on their spouses."

"I don't—" he blustered, but Mrs. Vandenberg was tapping her way back to the house.

Adam *harrumph*ed, shook his head, and set to work.

"Wow, she really hit the nail on the head there." Josh couldn't help laughing. "I know I shouldn't be enjoying this, but it was good to see Adam on the receiving end of the criticism for a change."

Mrs. Vandenberg stepped through the doorway in time to hear the end of Josh's statement. "Be careful not to judge, lest you be judged," she said. "And be ready to open your heart to forgive."

As usual, Mrs. Vandenberg managed to sting Josh with a pointed truth. He'd never truly forgiven Adam for his taunting and meanness. It was hard to do when the irritants happened almost every time Josh and his brother spent time together.

"I need to work on that," Josh admitted. He dreaded going out there to face more taunts, so he started clearing the table.

Rachel took the dishes from him. "I can take care of

this. It looks like Adam needs help." She pointed out the window.

Outside, his brother was struggling to do a two-person job. Josh bit back a sigh. Adam would snap if Josh tried to help, even though Adam couldn't do the task alone.

Josh bid Mrs. Vandenberg goodbye, and she tapped a hurried path to the front door. "I have people to see and romances to arrange. In fact, my first stop is at Anna Mary's."

Josh's head shot up. "I hope you can work something out for her and Abe."

Mrs. Vandenberg smiled. "All in good time. I have something else to talk about today."

Whatever it was, Josh had no doubt it would benefit Anna Mary. His lips curved up as he lifted Zak. Look at what Mrs. Vandenberg had done for him and Rachel.

By the time Josh settled Zak with some nails and a small hammer, Adam had dragged the beam to the right area and was trying to wrestle it up to where it belonged, but he couldn't get it high enough. Josh reached for the sagging end of the beam to lift it. Adam didn't bark that he could do it himself. He didn't even seem to notice Josh had picked up the opposite side and hefted it into place.

Adam seemed more focused on what Mrs. Vandenberg had said. "Did you put that old woman up to that?"

"Up to what?"

"Telling me I need to apologize to people, even Mara."

"Nobody tells Mrs. Vandenberg anything. She's dinged me many times. Her words are wise, so she's worth listening to."

"Of course you'd think that. You liked seeing her take me down a peg or two."

No way could Josh deny that. When he was younger,

he'd sometimes prayed his brother would get into trouble. So often, Adam did something wrong, but Josh took the blame.

"You probably think I should apologize to you." Adam's words held a touch of bitterness.

That would be nice, but Josh chose not to answer.

Adam mumbled something that sounded like *Fat chance*.

As the morning wore on, Adam's irritation increased. He yelled at everyone. The last straw came while he was on the ladder. He went to pound in a nail and dropped his hammer. It almost hit Zak, who'd been playing nearby.

Josh let out a worried cry and hurried down to comfort his frightened *sohn*.

"You probably think I did that on purpose," Adam snarled.

Again, Josh said nothing. He just cuddled Zak. "It's time for your morning nap." Josh stood and carried his little boy to the house as Rachel headed out with the morning snack. Cinnamon and yeast wafted from the two baking pans she held.

"Yum, that smells delicious." He gave her an appreciative smile. "Want me to take Marianna up too?"

Her face glowed when she looked at him. "That would be great."

After she set the coffee cakes down on the table, she unloosened the straps holding Marianna in the carrier and helped Josh nestle the baby against his chest. "I'll bring her bottle up as soon as I put out a pitcher of milk for your brothers and *daed*."

Josh flashed her a meaningful look, hoping to convey all the love in his heart. And the smile she returned set his heart dancing. He was still grinning as he headed through the kitchen.

Before he reached the hallway, a knock sounded on the front door. Rachel had just gone out the back door with the milk. He'd better get it.

Trying to open the door with a child in each arm proved a bit difficult. He bent over and juggled the children so he could turn the knob, then he nudged the door the rest of the way open with his foot. Zak still sniffled into Josh's shoulder because of his earlier scare.

Josh took a step back. "Bishop Troyer?"

"You seem to have your hands full." Laban studied the two children in Josh's arms.

"I was just getting ready to put these two down for their naps. Did you want to come in?"

"If you don't mind, I'd like to speak to Betty. Then to you and Rachel."

"Let me see if she's awake." Josh headed down the hall and tapped lightly at the door with his foot.

Betty laughed. "Do you have your arms full again, Josh?" she called.

"*Jah.* Laban Troyer is here, and he wants to talk to you."

Barbara opened the bedroom door. "I'll go get him so you can put the little ones in bed."

"Let me see them for a second before they go up," Betty begged.

Josh went into her room and leaned over so Betty could take Marianna.

Zak's whines increased. "My leg hurts, Daed."

Josh's chest expanded. Zak alternated between calling him Josh and Daed. He and Rachel had been encouraging Zak to say Daed. "Are those stitches pulling and itching again?" When Zak nodded, Josh rubbed his back. "I'll put something on them when we get upstairs, but the hurting means they're getting better."

Josh's own scrapes and bruises from the well accident sometimes bothered him, too, but he didn't have stitches like Zak. Still, Josh had had enough stitches as a child to know the stinging and burning they caused when they healed. He wished he could take away Zak's pain.

"I'll put Zak to bed first if you want a little more time with Marianna," Josh told Betty.

When she smiled and nodded, Josh turned to find the bishop standing in the bedroom doorway, observing him. Self-conscious, he edged past with a quick *pardon me* and headed for the stairs.

What did Laban want? If yesterday's rumors in church had reached his ears, he might think Josh and Rachel needed to wait longer to marry.

Josh feathered some salve over Zak's wound and tucked the teddy bear quilt around him. Then, Josh sat on the bed and stroked Zak's head until he fell asleep.

Rachel tiptoed in with the bottle. She peeked into the empty crib. "Where's Marianna?"

"Downstairs with your *mamm* and the bishop."

Rachel's head jerked up. "The bishop? What does he want?"

"I don't know."

The worry that flashed in her eyes mirrored his own concerns. "I guess we'd better go down and find out."

"I'm not quite finished speaking with your *mamm*," Laban said when they entered the room.

"Maybe we can get Marianna fed and down for her nap then," Josh suggested, crossing the room to take the baby from Betty. "I'll carry her up." He gave Rachel a tender glance. "I can feed her if you want to get more done on the quilt."

But after they left the room, Rachel followed him up the stairs. "I'd like to have a few quiet moments with you."

Josh was all for that. He cradled Marianna until she finished her bottle. Then, gently, he lowered her into the crib, and Rachel covered the baby with a cotton blanket. He shoved his hands into his pockets to keep from reaching out and drawing Rachel close.

Six months seemed an unbearably long time. That thought jerked his attention to the bishop waiting downstairs. They needed to get out of here.

He motioned for Rachel to precede him out the door and took several deep breaths to gain control of himself before he followed her.

When they reached the doorway of Betty's room, Laban rose from the chair beside the bed. Blood still pounded through Josh's veins, and he hoped the bishop couldn't hear his heart pounding.

Rachel ushered Laban into the living room. She gestured toward the quilt frame that took up a good portion of the room. "I'm sorry there isn't much space for sitting."

The bishop took the chair she indicated, and she sat on the couch, hemmed in by the quilt. Josh forced his gaze from Rachel's tense face and took a straight-backed chair nearby.

"I won't keep you long," Laban said. "I can see you have plenty of work."

Josh steeled himself for more bad news.

"I had two visitors today." Laban leaned forward.

"Both of them came to tell me something about the two of you."

Rachel caught Josh's eye. Like him, she seemed to be wondering which gossips from church had carried tales to the bishop.

Would he put off the marriage even longer? He wouldn't forbid them to marry, would he?

Josh sat on the edge of his seat, waiting for the blow.

"My niece stopped by to confess that she'd exaggerated her story of your breakup. She said you'd apologized, but she explained she had been at fault too." Laban paused. "That put things in a little different light.

"Then my next visitor gave me quite an earful."

Cathy Zehr? One of the boys who had a crush on Rachel? A girl who hadn't heard Caroline's announcement last night?

"I must admit, I didn't expect to hear so many carefully thought-out reasons for an Amish marriage coming from an *Englischer*."

Mrs. Vandenberg? Josh mouthed, and Rachel nodded.

The bishop must have caught Josh's message. "So, you know who I'm talking about?"

"We're guessing," Josh said, "but we do know a wise *Englischer* who often knows more about us than we know about ourselves. And this sounds exactly like something Mrs. Vandenberg would do." He grinned at Rachel.

The mention of Mrs. Vandenberg's name gave them both hope.

"She straightened me out on a lot of matters."

Josh bit back a grin. He could imagine she had. He wished he'd been there to eavesdrop on that conversation.

"I also spoke to your mother, Rachel. And she agreed

with Mrs. Vandenberg." Laban stroked his beard. "And when I saw you with the children, I realized I had not taken their welfare into consideration, which Mrs. Vandenberg kindly pointed out."

A tiny frisson of hope blossomed in Josh's chest. Mrs. Vandenberg sometimes worked miracles.

The bishop went on. "I noticed how the little boy clung to you at church on Sunday, Josh, and today, he called you Daed. I'm sure it's not good for him to be separated from his father all night, not after losing both his parents recently."

Rachel drew in a breath, and Josh waited eagerly to hear the bishop's decision.

"I've changed my mind about the waiting period. You may get married as soon as you'd like."

Rachel couldn't believe it. Her dream was coming true.

"Tomorrow?" Josh asked.

She nodded, although she suspected the bishop would object.

And he did.

The bishop held up a hand. "I expect you to use some discretion."

"Next week?"

Rachel's heart fluttered at Josh's eagerness. He wanted this as much as she did.

Josh laughed before the bishop could shoot down his suggestion. "I'm only teasing."

"I should hope so." The bishop's clipped tone belied the smile he tried to hide.

"The *dawdi haus* isn't finished yet. Perhaps we should

plan for a week or so after that's ready, so Betty can get settled."

The bishop rose. "That sounds like a more realistic timeline."

With marriage as an incentive, Josh would fly through the construction work, but Laban didn't need to know that.

CHAPTER 31

As soon as Laban was safely out the door, Rachel squealed.

Deep chuckles came from Betty's bedroom. "I thought that would make you happy, *dochder*. What date did you decide on?"

Josh was thrilled to know Rachel was as excited as he was to push the wedding date forward. He leaned close and whispered, "I'm going to do everything in my power to get the *dawdi haus* built as fast as I can."

"I planned to finish Mrs. Vandenberg's quilt before I sewed my wedding dress," Rachel said as they headed down the hall to her *mamm*'s bedroom, "but I'll change my plans around and do my dress first. I'm sure Mrs. Vandenberg won't mind."

"She'll be delighted." And so would he.

"And I'll need to find out when the wedding wagon is free."

"Well?" Mamm demanded, her face wreathed in smiles, when they reached her doorway.

Josh took the lead. "I told the bishop we'd wait until the *dawdi haus* is finished. And we'll give you a week to move in and get settled. Unless you'd like more time, of course."

He was relieved when Betty laughed. "A week is plenty of time."

Heaving a sigh of relief, he turned. "I'd better get out there and get busy." After a special glance for Rachel, he hustled from the room just as Barbara volunteered to help with wedding plans.

Barbara had been a godsend. Once again, Mrs. Vandenberg had made a perfect match. Not only was she an excellent caretaker, but she and Betty had become good friends. And Barbara loved to babysit. Both children had taken to her sweet, grandmotherly nature. Best of all, they were helping Barbara, who needed a place to live.

Josh jogged outside, whistling. He couldn't wait to complete this building. Every board, every beam, every shingle they put in place would bring him closer to his wedding day.

"About time," Adam groused. "We're working on your mother-in-law's house while you spend your time courting Rachel."

Too thrilled to argue with Adam, Josh only said mildly, "Sorry. We had to meet with the bishop, but I'll try to make up for it now." And he would.

But Adam seemed determined to needle Josh. "What'd the bishop want? People report you for touching?"

"He started out by talking about forgiveness." Which was partly true. Laban had mentioned Josh following the directive to ask Anna Mary's forgiveness. But Josh had said that on purpose to remind Adam of Mrs. Vandenberg's message.

To Josh's surprise, his brother squirmed and turned away. And for the next two hours, Adam said nothing.

When Rachel brought out the meal at noon, Adam hung back. She waved him over. "I don't know if potpie is still your favorite meal, but I made it today."

Adam didn't meet her eyes, but he did manage a gruff *danke*.

She and Josh went inside to wake the children for dinner. Before they went upstairs, she peeked out the window. "Your brother took a big helping, and he's gobbling it down."

"Heaping coals of fire on his head?" Josh teased, referring to the Scripture verse in Romans. "The Bible does say to feed your enemy."

Rachel laughed. "I wasn't thinking about that when I did it. I just want to have a good relationship with everyone in your family."

"I don't want to discourage you, but I don't think Adam will ever come around."

"That doesn't mean I won't keep trying."

"You're a wonder, Rachel Glick. I'm so lucky you're going to be my wife."

"*Ach*, Josh! Can you believe we can get married soon? I'm so excited. Mrs. Vandenberg is amazing."

"*Jah*, she is. And I think we can finish in three weeks if all the supplies come in on time. So, in a month or so . . ."

Her eyes burned with a passion that matched his.

A knock at the back door interrupted them. Rachel was fixing Marianna's bottle, so Josh went to answer it.

Adam stood there, twisting his straw hat in his hands. "I have something I want to say to Rachel."

"Come in." Josh tried to be as gracious as his future bride had been toward his brother. "I'm sure she'll be happy to know you liked her potpie."

But Adam frowned at Josh's teasing tone. "It's not that. It's private."

Private? What could his brother possibly have to say to Rachel that was private? Josh tamped down his jealousy. "I'll just go outside until you're done talking."

"I suppose you can stay," Adam said grudgingly, "since this kind of concerns you."

Rachel set down the plate she'd been filling and headed for the door. "Would you like to sit down and eat with us? We have plenty more potpie."

"*Neh*, but *danke*. It was good."

"I'm glad you liked it."

As Rachel headed toward that side of the kitchen, Josh tried to melt into the wall on the far side, out of his brother's line of sight.

"I, um, have something I need to say to you." Adam crushed the brim of his hat.

If he kept squeezing his hat that way, it might soon be unwearable. Josh wanted to reach out and take it from his brother's hands, but Josh didn't want to call attention to himself.

Rachel stood waiting, her eyes curious, but her expression open and welcoming.

"Guess it's best to just spit it out." Adam sucked in a ragged breath. "That old lady was right. I do have some apologies to make." He stared at the floor under his feet. "It's my fault your brother died."

Josh's chest constricted so much he couldn't draw in air, and black spots appeared before his eyes. Rachel looked stricken. Josh wanted to reach out to her, to comfort her, but all his muscles had frozen. Never, ever had he heard Adam admit he'd done something wrong. But to confess something this huge?

Adam's words came out pinched and tight. "Me and Marv and Lloyd was smoking in the old barn. Marv told us to be double sure we stamped out every bit of ash. They did. I didn't. So, I'm the one what killed your brother."

"It was an accident." Rachel's voice shook.

Adam plowed on as if he hadn't heard her. "I never wanted anyone to know. But I shoulda owned up. Will you forgive me?"

"*Jah*," Rachel said softly. "I forgive you."

Her eyes brimmed with tears, and Josh broke the stranglehold that had kept him in place during his brother's confession. He needed to get to her.

"I'm sorry." Adam turned to go as Josh reached Rachel's side. He wanted to wrap his arms around her, breaking the rules of the *Ordnung*, but he restrained himself. He didn't want to damage Rachel's reputation. Especially not in front of his brother.

Adam glanced sideways at Josh. "Guess you needed to hear that too, huh?" Then he rushed out the door, jammed his squished hat on his head, and went back to work.

Still in a daze, Josh laid a hand on Rachel's arm. Her damp eyes tore at him. "I'm so sorry Adam brought that up."

"I'm not," she said. "Don't you think it's *wunderbar* that he confessed and asked for forgiveness?"

Josh could only nod.

"I hope telling us is the start of a new attitude for him. Maybe it'll improve all his relationships."

"I'm sure his wife will appreciate it if he apologizes. I don't think he ever does."

"Well, we can pray about that, but we'd better get Marianna."

She'd started squalling.

"I'll go get both of them," Josh volunteered, "if you want to finish getting her bottle ready and set out lunch. I like when we both do it together, but I'm eager to get back out there and get to work."

"And I can't wait until it's done." Rachel sent him a joyous smile.

After he started up the stairs, she hugged herself. She could hardly believe everything that had happened so far today. They'd moved up their wedding date with the bishop's approval, and Adam had apologized. That had been a huge step for him, and she hoped it would be a start on a mended relationship between him and Josh. And best of all, she only had to wait a month to be Josh's wife.

By the time he came downstairs with their freshly changed *dochder* and still-sleepy *sohn*, Rachel had set out the food. She handed Josh Marianna's bottle and helped Zak into his place at the table. When they were all seated around the table, heads bowed for silent prayer, Rachel's heart was so full of thanksgiving, she couldn't even put it in words. All she could do was tack a string of *dankes* to the end of her prayer.

And that gratefulness bubbled up in her as each day grew closer to their wedding day. Barbara and Mamm helped with the planning while Rachel sewed. Only one small detail marred her happiness.

Josh had many friends at church, and once they realized Anna Mary loved someone else and Josh intended to wed Rachel, they rallied around him. He'd already picked his two sidesitters for the wedding. But Rachel had none. After the girls in her buddy bunch realized she wasn't after their boyfriends, their iciness thawed to a semi-friendly coolness. But none of them had become her friends. Perhaps some were still worried the "flirt" might break up with Josh before they married.

Rachel was lamenting this with less than two weeks to go before the wedding. Mrs. Vandenberg stopped by to see how the *dawdi haus* was progressing. She exclaimed over the lovely exterior as well as the interior layout. Josh had almost finished laying the hardwood floors, while Adam had started priming the walls his brothers had completed.

Rachel pointed out all the special details to make Mamm more comfortable. "And they added all the wheelchair accommodations you suggested," she told Mrs. Vandenberg, still unsure why those were needed.

"Good, good. Perfect timing," Mrs. Vandenberg said as they crossed the lawn back to the house. "I moved the appointment for your *mamm* to see the specialist until after the wedding. I think he can get your mother mobile enough for a wheelchair. He's done some marvelous things."

"That would be wonderful if he could help. And don't worry about the cost." With the money Rachel had from the house sale, she intended to pay for Mamm's treatments herself.

"Sounds like everything is going perfectly." Mrs. Vandenberg stopped walking and turned a searching gaze on Rachel. "So, what's bothering you?"

"How could you tell?" Rachel had kept her bubbliness, gratitude, and happiness front and center every day. She'd prayed about the one tiny thorn in her side, but so far, no sidesitters had appeared.

Mrs. Vandenberg tilted her head to one side. "You almost bounce when you walk, and your words overflow with joy, but there's a little quaver at the end of your sentences.

A tiny pinprick of sadness. It's not grief from missing those who've passed."

Rachel did wish Daed, Tom, and Cindy could be here for her special day. But the cause for her quaver seemed so petty in comparison.

"Sometimes we blow up little things until they take a huge amount of mental and emotional space. And we fail to see there's an easy solution." Mrs. Vandenberg's raised eyebrow encouraged Rachel to confess.

"Josh has asked his two sidesitters, but I don't have anyone I can ask."

"Well, that's not hard. They have to be single, right?" At Rachel's nod, Mrs. Vandenberg's face glowed with sunshine. "What about Gloria? Isn't she your second cousin?"

"*Jah*, but she lives so far away."

"It just so happens I invited her and Annika here for a visit. I'm sure they'd love to attend your wedding. Annika can't wait to thank you for the house. You'll have to see the pictures I've taken."

"They'll be here the week of the wedding?"

"That's the plan."

Rachel couldn't help wondering if this plan had also been a nudge from God. "Do you think they'd do it?"

"Let's find out." Mrs. Vandenberg rummaged through her purse for her phone. "I'll call the B and B. They both should be working there now."

Within ten minutes, it was all arranged. Both girls were delighted to be asked, and Annika insisted on speaking to Rachel. Annika's multiple *danke*s reminded Rachel of her own prayer full of thanksgiving a few weeks ago.

When the call ended, Rachel was so excited she hugged Mrs. Vandenberg, almost knocking her off her feet. "I can't thank you enough for all you've done for us."

"It's my pleasure. You'll never know the joy I get from bringing together the couples God has selected."

"You'll be at our wedding, too, won't you?"

"I wouldn't miss it for the world."

And Mrs. Vandenberg was as good as her word. She arrived early on the Tuesday morning of the wedding with Gloria and Annika. The two girls went upstairs with Rachel to get ready, and Mrs. Vandenberg headed into the kitchen to help the church women prepare the meal.

Annika gushed about the Ohio house and her own wedding plans in November, both of which made her doubly thrilled about Rachel and Josh's wedding.

Gloria's eyes filled with tears, and she leaned over to kiss Rachel's cheek. "I'm so happy to be here on this special day. Cindy talked about you and Josh so much, I feel like I've always known both of you. She'd be so happy you two will be parenting her children."

Rachel's eyes stung. She wished Cindy could have joined them. But having Gloria and Annika, Cindy's two closest confidantes, brought Cindy's presence to the gathering.

As Rachel descended the stairs, she trembled with nerves and excitement. Today, she'd marry the man she'd loved since she was nine years old. She'd dreamed about this day so often, but now it truly had arrived. And it was more beautiful than anything she'd ever imagined.

Upstairs in the nursery, Josh struggled to pull on his vest and jacket. Zak, overwhelmed by the crowds swarming into the house, begged to be held, so Josh switched his *sohn* from one arm to the other as he tried to maneuver his arms through the sleeves.

One more time, Josh explained that Zak and Marianna would sit with Barbara during the service.

"*Nehhh!*" Zak shrieked. "I stay with you."

"You can't," Josh said patiently for the tenth time that morning. Setting Zak on the bed, Josh tugged his vest into place while Zak sobbed uncontrollably.

Lord, please help me to find a way to comfort him.

Josh picked up Giraffey. "Do you want to keep Giraffey with you?"

Zak nodded, clutching the stuffed animal to his chest. "But, but," he blubbered, "I don't want you dead."

Josh stood stock-still. The last time they'd dressed in these clothes and had a crowd in their house had been for Cindy's funeral. Even Annika and Gloria had come.

"*Ach!*" Josh dropped to his knees beside the bed to be at Zak's eye level. "Are you afraid this is a funeral? That someone died?"

"*Jahhh,*" Zak wailed. He flung his arms around Josh's neck and squeezed so hard, Josh could barely breathe. "Don't be dead."

Gently, Josh untangled Zak's arms so he could look into his *sohn*'s eyes. "Nobody's dying. Your *mamm* and I are getting married. Remember what we told you?"

They'd explained they'd be marrying, but neither of them had thought to describe the crowds and activities of the day. They'd just mentioned about him sitting with Barbara during the service. Most likely, Zak had never been to a wedding before. Not with his *daed* ill.

"This is a happy day. I'm going to be your *daed* and

live in this house all the time. I'll sleep here tonight and every night, so I can take care of you and Marianna." *And any other babies he and Rachel had.*

Zak tilted his head to one side and studied Josh suspiciously. "You sure?"

"I'm positive. And after all these people go home, I'll be staying here. I won't ever have to leave at night again."

"That's *gut*." Zak's face relaxed into a rapturous expression, and he wiped his tears on Giraffey. Then he hopped off the bed and grabbed Josh's hand. "Let's go get married, Daed."

A fond smile playing on his lips, Josh descended the staircase to find Rachel at the bottom. At her answering smile, his grin broadened until his cheeks ached.

"We have to get married, Mamm," Zak announced.

Rachel laughed. "*Jah*, we do." She leaned over to kiss him, then said to Josh, "Barbara's in the back beside Mamm."

Rachel waved toward the women's section and the portable hospital bed Mrs. Vandenberg had rented so Betty could be in the room to watch her daughter's wedding. Josh left Zak in Barbara's care and patted Marianna as she lay in Betty's arms.

"*Danke* for raising such a wonderful *dochder*, Betty. Rachel's made me the happiest man ever."

Betty's eyes welled with tears. "And you've made her the happiest woman."

Josh forced himself to take slow, dignified steps back to where Rachel waited. He'd have sprinted if no one had been watching.

When he reached her, her beauty inside and out left him speechless. Echoing his *sohn*'s words, Josh whispered, "Let's get married, Rachel."

Her eyes lit up. "I can't wait."

And neither could he. God had blessed him with his deepest heartfelt desire—the only woman he'd ever loved. And now she'd be his forever. And he'd be hers. Their childhood promise to each other had come true.

Epilogue

Two years later . . .

As daylight slipped into nightfall, Rachel's mind drifted back to the first night Marianna and Zak had arrived. Little did she know then, her lovely daydream of Josh being a father to those two small children would become a reality. Only this time, instead of Zak in Josh's arms, he cuddled two-year-old Marianna, her head resting drowsily on his shoulder, while five-year-old Zak clutched at his *daed*'s pant leg.

"Rachel?" Josh whispered as they peeked into the room.

Zak held one finger to his lips.

Josh nodded at him. "Good job, *sohn*. We need to be quiet, so Marianna and Caleb stay asleep."

In the heirloom chair, Rachel rocked four-month-old Caleb in her arms, softly singing a hymn. "I didn't hear you coming up the stairs." She hushed her words to match Zak's and Josh's. "*Danke* for being quiet. I think they're both asleep."

Caleb's slow, sighing breaths spoke of contentment and deep slumber. As Rachel tucked him into the crib, Josh lowered Marianna onto the bed that used to be Zak's and covered her with the teddy bear quilt.

Across the room, Zak leaned sleepily against Josh's leg. Her husband—oh, how her heart leaped each time she said that word—bent and lifted their tired *sohn*, who rested his head on his *daed*'s shoulder until his eyes drifted closed. The tenderness in Josh's face as he glanced down at their pajama-clad little boy tugged at Rachel's heartstrings.

She wished she could freeze this moment in time. But they'd have many such moments. And she could enjoy each one of them.

"I'll take Zak to his room. Then . . ."

Rachel shook her head. "I'm coming with you." She didn't want to let her husband out of her sight. She wanted to spend every precious minute with him.

"You know," she said as Josh pulled the blankets over Zak, "back before we married, Mrs. Vandenberg stopped me from going upstairs to help you with Zak and Marianna. She said someday you'd have to take care of both of them while I was busy. I had trouble imagining it."

"Mrs. Vandenberg was right, as always." Fire blazed in Josh's eyes when he turned to face Rachel. "And as much as I love our children, my favorite part of the day is when we can be alone together."

"It's mine, too." And Rachel's heart overflowed with love for her husband.

The next morning, Rachel finished feeding Caleb and set him in his crib. Then she adjusted her Sunday dress and *kapp*, and headed to the kitchen to finish the breakfast dishes. After helping Zak get ready and caring for the horses before breakfast, Josh was now dressing for church.

Rachel had dressed Marianna earlier, and her *dochder* and *sohn* had run across the ramp to the *dawdi haus* to visit with their beloved grandmother.

"Mamm," Marianna squealed.

Rachel rushed to the back door and flung it open. Her daughter sat on her grandmother's lap in the wheelchair. Five-year-old Zak, holding onto the side, jogged beside them.

"Look," Marianna shouted, pointing to the two tiny braids sticking out in the air on either side of her head. "Mammi fixed my bwaids."

Swallowing back a giggle, Rachel praised the hairstyle. Her *dochder*'s hair was still too short to pull back into a bob. Rachel would pull the pigtails down a bit before they headed for church, but it thrilled her Mamm had attempted the intricate motions of braiding.

"Mamm," Rachel called as the wheelchair gained speed on the ramp Josh had built to connect the houses. "I can't believe you managed that."

"I've been doing a lot of things that will surprise you, *dochder*."

"Speeding seems to be one of them." Rachel leaped back as the wheelchair hurtled toward her.

"Whee!" Marianna chortled with glee. "Go faster, Mammi!"

"*Neh*, don't," Zak begged, panting. "I can't . . . keep . . . up."

To Rachel's relief, her mother pulled on the brake and slowed.

Rachel put on a pretend frown. "I'm afraid you're going to tip out of that chair and crush Marianna, Mamm." Secretly, she admired her *mamm*'s fearlessness, but didn't want to encourage it, especially not with the children onboard.

"Don't be such a worrier, *dochder*." Her mamm entered the kitchen, which Josh had enlarged and made wheelchair accessible.

Rachel backed up so Mamm could pass her. Then she reached for Marianna.

Before going to her mother, Marianna wound her arms around her *mammi*'s neck and kissed her. "Dat was fun!"

With a repentant look at Rachel, Mamm explained, "Do you know how hard it was to be confined to bed for years? Being able to move around and go where I'd like is so freeing that sometimes I just want to speed."

"I understand. I just don't want any accidents."

"I'll be more careful."

"Give me a ride please, Mammi," Zak pleaded.

"Let's wait until after church," she suggested. "I don't want to upset your *mamm* any more than I already have."

Zak's lower lip thrust out into a pout, but Josh walked into the kitchen just then. With a joyous shout, Zak raced across the room and flung himself at his *daed*'s legs. Now that he was older, though, his power had increased, and Josh took a step back to steady himself.

"Careful," Josh warned, "I have your baby brother here." He cradled five-month-old Caleb in his arms and met Rachel's gaze with lovelight shining in his eyes.

As always, whenever she caught sight of her husband, her pulse skipped a beat. The past two years had only brought them closer and increased their love for each other. Josh shifted Caleb to one arm and reached for Zak's hand.

Zak stared up at his *daed* with admiration. "Can we give the baby to Mamm so you can hold me?"

"That was my plan." Josh beamed down at his little boy, and Rachel's heart flipped over.

Josh had proved to be the best *daed*—and husband—ever. Rachel thanked the Lord every day for blessing her with the man of her dreams.

"Here you go, *liebe*." Josh leaned over to give Rachel a quick peck on the cheek.

Rachel set Marianna down and reached for the baby. Marianna tugged at Josh's pant leg the way her brother used to when he was small.

"Mammi gave me a ride. We go fast," Marianna told her *daed*.

"Uh-oh, Betty." Josh laughed. "I hope you aren't turning into a speed demon."

She chuckled. "Rachel here thinks I am."

Josh raised his eyebrows. "I trust my wife's judgment."

Rachel shot him a thankful smile. "We'd better hurry, so we're not late for church."

"I'll hitch up the horses." He set Zak on the ground. "You going to help me?"

"*Jah*." Zak took his father's hand, and they headed for the back door.

"Me too," Marianna insisted, following them.

Josh reached back for her hand, and the three of them headed for the barn.

"Betty?" Barbara stood on the porch of the *dawdi haus*, looking around.

"She's in the kitchen." Josh tilted his head toward the house. "Sounds like she might need some safe driving lessons."

Barbara laughed. "She runs circles around me."

"I'll hitch up your buggy too." Josh took his two helpers into the barn while Rachel packed the diaper bag and Barbara rounded up Betty.

A short while later, both buggies waited in the driveway. Josh lifted Betty from her wheelchair and into the passenger seat of Barbara's buggy. They kept her portable wheelchair stowed in the back.

Then, he helped Marianna and Zak into the back seat of their buggy. Once they were settled, he stowed the diaper bag, took the baby, assisted Rachel in, and handed Caleb back to her.

Rachel's spirits lifted as they headed toward Adam and Mara's house. Quite a change from when she dreaded going to church in the past. Back then, she'd always loved learning about God's Word from the sermons, but before and after church had been a nightmare of cold shoulders, judgment, and gossip. So much had changed after she and Josh married. Now, she loved Sundays.

After they pulled into Adam's driveway, Josh stopped and climbed out to lift Betty into her wheelchair. Rachel sighed in relief that the portable wheelchair had to be pushed, so Mamm couldn't get up to any of her antics at church. Barbara took Mamm to a flatter side entrance leading to the kitchen rather than up the front steps.

Josh's parents were waiting for them on the porch. They were always eager to see their grandchildren. Zak took Dawdi's hand while Josh took care of both horses with the help of Adam's two oldest boys. Josh's *mamm* hugged Rachel and begged to hold Caleb.

Marianna tugged at her other *mammi*'s dress. "Me too."

Miriam bent down to give Marianna a one-armed hug. "You can sit on my lap in church."

Marianna smiled. Rachel knelt down and held out her

arms to her *dochder*. "I can hold you for a while. We should go into the kitchen to help *Aenti* Mara."

Rachel had been over here earlier in the week and most of the day yesterday, along with Lloyd's and Marv's wives, helping Mara clean and bake snitz pies. Mara had pulled Rachel aside to thank her, as well as Mrs. Vandenberg, for the changes in Adam and in their marriage. Mara and Adam had never been happier, and it showed in Mara's contented expression.

Mrs. Vandenberg had matched several couples in the past two years, and many of them attended church in this *g'may*. Those couples had become good friends with Rachel and Josh. Girls who used to make snide remarks about Rachel had long since apologized and now invited her to their quilting bees and Christmas cookie exchanges and young mothers' get-togethers.

With her mother-in-law beside her carrying Caleb, Rachel entered the kitchen with Marianna in her arms. Older women, who had once looked at Rachel askance, now offered her the holy kiss they gave to the other married women and made her feel a part of the community.

"Are you making a quilt for the auction?" Caroline, who'd soon be marrying the love of her life, bubbled over with enthusiasm.

"*Jah.* I'm working on one." Every year, Rachel tried to outdo the design she'd made the previous year. She'd kept the promise to herself to donate a quilt to any of the auctions Mrs. Vandenberg helped organize.

"We should make one from all the couples she's matched."

Rachel loved the idea. "What about a double-wedding-ring quilt?"

Caroline laughed. "It would have to be more than a double one." She started listing all the couples.

Several of the older ladies laughed. "You're just naming the most recent ones. She matched many of us."

"What if we each make a square with our names and our husbands' names and our wedding dates?" Rachel suggested. "I'll piece it together, and we can work on it during quilting circle."

"Great idea." Caroline volunteered to contact all the couples Mrs. Vandenberg had matched. "It's going to be a huge quilt—big enough for a king-sized bed—or maybe even larger."

Within two weeks, the entire project came together. Rachel had never enjoyed a quilt as much as this one. Over the next few months, people stopped by the house to drop off squares. Each woman stayed to chat for a short while, telling the details of her courtship and how Mrs. Vandenberg had played matchmaker.

Even couples from Ohio—Gloria and Annika—and New York—Hannah and Anna Mary—participated. They sent their squares by mail, but asked to be invited when they gave Mrs. Vandenberg the final quilt.

"Let's have a party on Valentine's Day and present her with the quilt," Rachel suggested as the girls from her buddy bunch gathered at her house to stitch the designs into the quilt.

As Rachel invited people, more than seventy couples accepted. Although she was thrilled about the turnout, she wasn't sure she could fit all those people in their house if they brought their large families.

That night at dinner, she told Josh her concerns. He stroked his beard, a beard that made him even more handsome than he'd been the day they'd married.

"Why not talk to Nettie and Stephen? Maybe they could plan a party at Mrs. Vandenberg's center in the city."

"*Ach*, Josh, that's a great idea. Mrs. Vandenberg doesn't have to know about the quilt or the couples attending. She'll just think it's a center event."

The women at the quilting circle loved the idea, and Caroline volunteered to contact everyone who'd submitted a square to let them know about the new location.

The Saturday before the party, Rachel had a sisters' day in her kitchen with her three sisters-in-law to bake cookies. Several other friends did the same in their kitchens. Dozens and dozens of heart-shaped cookies cooled on every counter and table in Rachel's kitchen, as well as in the *dawdi haus* kitchen.

"I'm so excited," Caroline practically squealed when she stopped by with her family's contribution to the cookie count. "I can hardly wait."

Rachel couldn't either. By the time Josh returned home from his construction job with Zak in tow, she'd packed most of the cookies into containers.

Josh sniffed the air. "My favorite sugar cookies?"

"*Jah*, but you'll have to wait until Valentine's Day to eat them." She rushed over to kiss him and reveled in being in his arms.

"Well, that kiss made up for missing out on the cookies." But despite his glowing smile, his eyes showed a hint of disappointment.

"Don't worry," she said. "I saved a few just for you." She pointed to the last rack of cooling cookies. "If you hurry, those are still soft and warm."

Most of the cookies they'd made that day had been heart-shaped cut-out cookies, but Rachel had baked a few batches of the soft sugar cookies Josh loved and filled the cookie jar. And she'd timed the last batch to come out of the oven after he'd pulled in the driveway and cared for the horse.

"You're the best." Josh gave her an appreciative kiss before helping himself to several cookies. "Is everything ready for the party?"

"I think so. I wrapped the quilt today, all the cookies are baked, and Stephen hung brackets on the floor-to-ceiling wall in the building's entryway for the rod you made to hang the quilt. Oh, and Hartzler's Chicken Barbecue is donating chicken, drinks, and paper goods. And other stands at the market are donating different foods."

"Wow, you've been busy."

"All I organized were the cookies and the quilt. Caroline's taking care of all the market donations."

"I'd say you've done quite a bit. And good for Caroline." Josh kissed the tip of Rachel's nose. "You've come a long way from the girl everybody accused of being a flirt."

"I'm not?" Rachel pouted and fluttered her eyelashes.

"You can flirt with me anytime you want, *liebe*. I still can't resist you, but you did leave a lot of broken hearts behind."

"They must not have been broken too badly. Mrs. Vandenberg has matched quite a few of them—even Martin."

"True. But the best match she made was you and me." Josh wrapped his arms around her and drew her close.

Rachel melted against him. "I agree."

Two days later, all the couples assembled in the inner-city building Mrs. Vandenberg had converted to the STAR center, a facility with activities intended to keep children and teens off the streets and out of gangs. Stephen and

Nettie, another couple Mrs. Vandenberg had matched and offered jobs running the center, were keeping her in their office until they got word everyone had arrived and gathered. Even the children who normally used the gyms, art rooms, library, and other activity areas joined the Amish families in the lobby or hung over the second-story railing that overlooked the entrance.

"Anyone have a cell phone?" Rachel asked when the food tables were in place in one of the gyms. "It's time to call Stephen." Then she and Josh hurried to the lobby.

A few minutes later, an office door opened overhead, and Mrs. Vandenberg's voice floated down. "It's so quiet. Why aren't the children playing basketball? No ping-pong or air hockey?" She truly sounded puzzled.

Rachel wondered if God had kept this secret from her. She whispered that to Josh, and he laughed quietly.

"Careful," Stephen said. "Let me take your arm."

"Someone must have forgotten to unlock the doors downstairs."

In the lobby, muffled laughter followed that comment.

When Mrs. Vandenberg reached the place where the third story overlooked the lobby, she stumbled to a stop. "What in the world?"

"Happy Valentine's Day! And *danke* for matching us," the couples said in unison.

Mrs. Vandenberg pressed a hand to her heart. With tears in her eyes, she announced, "I know who organized this." She pointed directly to Rachel and Caroline, who stood beside each other. They held hands with their special men.

"Do you have any idea how many couples you've matched?" one older man asked.

"Well, last time I looked, I think it was one hundred."

"We've gathered seventy of them, even some from out

of state," Caroline announced. "And Rachel has a gift from all of us."

Rachel and Josh lifted the large box, wrapped in pink heart paper with a huge pink bow and heart streamers, so Mrs. Vandenberg could see it.

She looked shaken as she descended both flights of stairs with Stephen holding her elbow. "Oh, my. I can't believe this."

Rachel helped Mrs. Vandenberg into a chair, and Josh held the box as she unwrapped the gift with trembling hands.

Several people held it and spread it out so Mrs. Vandenberg could see all the squares. Rachel had pieced a large heart in the center and embroidered the words: *Matches made in Heaven. Thank you, Lord, for Liesel Vandenberg.* Each corner had a heart design, and she'd added heart blocks between some of the one hundred squares with couples' names.

Tears trickled down Mrs. Vandenberg's cheeks as she fingered each square. After she'd examined every one, Josh threaded the pole through the loops Rachel had sewn to the top, and Stephen and a maintenance worker climbed ladders to hang it on the brackets they'd installed.

Everyone stepped back to *ooo* and *ahh.* Then Rachel invited everyone upstairs to the gym for refreshments.

"You can stay here," she told Mrs. Vandenberg. "We'll bring some refreshments to you."

Fourteen-year-old Joline, Nettie and Stephen's daughter, hurried over. "I can get you a plate, Mrs. V."

"Thank you, dear. That would be wonderful. You're really growing up to be quite a helpful young lady. It won't be long before I'll have to match you up." Mrs. Vandenberg chuckled.

"I'm not baptized yet," Joline reminded Mrs. V.

"I know, but when you're my age, the years go by in a blink of the eye. It'll happen sooner than you think."

Joline leaned closer. "Just in case you want to be ready ahead of time, there is this boy I'm interested in." She whispered a name.

"Hmm . . . I'll pray about that and see what heavenly guidance I get."

With a skip to her step, Joline rushed to the gym and returned with a plate of cookies and a bottled water. "I can get some for you too," she said to Rachel and Josh.

As couples swarmed around Mrs. Vandenberg, Rachel smiled at Joline. "*Danke* for offering, but we're heading to the gym."

"I'll see if anyone else needs help." Joline headed off.

It was hard to believe that Stephen and Nettie had despaired about their daughter two and half years ago. Joline had turned out to be a loving older sister and a wonderful help to her parents, although some of her old rebellious spirit still twinkled in her eyes.

Josh lowered his voice. "I'd like some of your cookies. Any chance we can figure out which ones they are?"

"You're in luck. Gideon and Fern are supervising the tables. I put a small container back and asked them to save those for you. Let's go get them."

"I love having you all to myself." Josh's husky whisper tickled the hairs on the back of Rachel's neck.

Her pulse galloped. Mamm and Barbara were watching the three children, so Rachel and Josh could have time alone together. Josh had promised they'd take the long way home. She couldn't wait.

Josh paused at the second-floor railing to take in the quilt. "It looked beautiful while you worked on it, but seeing the whole thing at once is breathtaking." Then he pointed to one square. "I love all of it, but that's my favorite."

"Mine too." She'd put their square right under the central heart.

Rachel retrieved the small container she'd put aside behind the table, and filled a paper plate with pink-iced hearts, and hid a special one behind her back.

"Mmm . . . sugar cookies always remind me of your loving heart." He handed her a pink heart. "And this reminds me how much I love you and that I married the most *wunderbar* woman in the world."

"You still think so?"

"I do, and I always will."

"*Ach*, Josh, you say the sweetest things."

"That's because I have the sweetest wife." He lifted a teasing brow. "One who bakes the best sugar cookies I've ever eaten."

Rachel pulled the large, soft sugar cookie heart from behind her back. "I know you like these the best." She put on her flirtiest look. "For the sweetest husband. Will you be my Valentine?"

"Forever and always."

And Rachel thanked God He had blessed her with the sweetest, most *wunderbar* husband ever. And she repeated her gratitude as they stopped in a secluded spot on their way home to gaze at the moon and spend precious time alone together. She prayed for many more of these starspangled nights together along with love-filled days spent with their growing family.

Visit our website at
KensingtonBooks.com
to sign up for our newsletters, read
more from your favorite authors, see
books by series, view reading group
guides, and more!

BOOK CLUB
BETWEEN THE CHAPTERS

Become a Part of Our
Between the Chapters Book Club
Community and Join the Conversation

Betweenthechapters.net